Wolf's Red

SAMANTHA L. ENO

For Jerry Lee, my noble pup and beloved companion-
I still miss you, I haven't ever forgotten you, and I still will always love
you.

Contents

Prologue {Chloe} — 1

Chapter 1 {Rosella} — 10

Chapter 2 {Rosella} — 22

Chapter 3 {Sophia} — 40

Chapter 4 {Chloe} — 55

Chapter 5 {Rosella/Sophia} — 66

Chapter 6 {Rosella} — 88

Chapter 7 {Fenris} — 102

Chapter 8 {Rosella} — 111

Chapter 9 {Rosella} — 128

Chapter 10 {Frank&Creg} — 150

Chapter 11 {Rosella} — 163

Chapter 12 {Sophia/Rosella} — 177

Chapter 13 {Rosella/Chloe/Sophia} — 195

Chapter 14 {Rosella/Sophia} — 210

Chapter 15 {Chloe} — 226

Chapter 16 {Frank&Creg} — 241

Chapter 17 {Sophia} — 256

Chapter 18 {Rosella/Fenris/Felan} — 268

Chapter 19 {Rosella} 284

Chapter 20 {Rosella} 297

Chapter 21 {Frank&Creg/Chloe} 315

Chapter 22 {Felan/Frank&Creg} 338

Chapter 23 {Felan/Chloe/Frank/Creg} 352

Chapter 24 {Rosella/Fenris} 371

Chapter 25 {Rosella} 391

Chapter 26 {Fenris} 405

Chapter 27 {Rosella} 418

Chapter 28 {Sophia/Caroline} 432

Chapter 29 {Sophia/Felan/Chloe} 446

Chapter 30 {Fenris/Rosella} 456

Chapter 31 {Frank/Rosella/Fenris} 472

Chapter 32 {Rosella/Felan} 493

Chapter 33 {Rosella/Fenris} 501

Epilogue {Rosella/Hollow} 513

Bonus Artwork 521

Rosella Bloom (School Wear) 522

Rosella Bloom (Cloak & Dress) 523

Rosella Bloom (Forest Expedition Wear) 524

Rosella Bloom (Epilogue Wear) 525

Chloe Bloom 526

Felan Bloom 527

Fenris 528

Sophia Mitchell 529

Frank&Creg   530

Caroline Morse   531

AUTHOR'S NOTE

I'll keep this short, since this book is already incredibly long (I'm sorry, I couldn't help myself).

So... Here I am again. My second time in the publishing ring, only this time I had a team of people to help me put it all together. This book... Honestly, I think it's even more special than "Hikari's Wish", my first attempt, because this was my first real book. This was the project that I set aside to work on that. For six years, this was locked away, and I didn't pull it out until about mid to late of last year.

To be honest, like before, I'm petrified. I have no idea how well or terrible this is going to do, but the fact that someone out there picked this up means something. It means that someone is giving me a chance, or second chance if they've read "Hikari's Wish". This time, I know what I'm doing, and I have more experience.

Thank you, reader, for picking up this story. It went with a hell of a lot of revisions (and from an original draft that will never see the light of day because it is THAT BAD). I hope you enjoy this book, and that you'll look forward to Book 2 (yes, there will be more).

Good luck on your trip through the woods, the evil creatures out there mean business. :)

CONTENT NOTE:

This book contains dark themes that some individuals may find upsetting or disturbing. These themes include but are not limited to depictions of bullying, body shaming, slut shaming, heavy swearing, gore, torture, eye trauma, graphic violence, and self-mutilation, as well as mentions of overdose, religious trauma, sexual assault, and rape.

If any of this content is triggering for you, please take care of your mental health and skip this book.

PROLOGUE

Chloe

A GENTLE BREEZE BRUSHED the grass beneath my heeled boots, a shadow cast over my face. It did nothing to soothe the tension clamped to my shoulders as it combed back my hair. Hiding my expression beneath my ebony hat would only draw the flashing cameras closer, so I did my best to ignore the flickering strobe lights as the event went on.

Like starving children with their spoons at the ready, hungry for my words, the reporters awaited the next scoop of the mystery they craved, that which only I could provide. They savored every bite of information they took out of me, each more painful than the last. And no matter how many, their appetite would not be satiated...

Beside me, a nervous hand clutched mine, and for her sake I bit back a threat to the reporters. *Why can't they leave us alone? Just for one day. That's all I'm asking.*

"Ms. Bloom?"

I shuddered not at the voice, but at the status of my name. "Y-Yes... I'm ready. Rosella... Are you ready?"

My thirteen year old daughter nodded sadly, her blue eyes on the verge of spilling tears. "Y-Yeah, I'm ready," she whispered.

"It'll be okay," I whispered. "It's just a little longer."

"I know. I wanted to be here..."

My baby's fragile words shattered my heart like a hammer to glass. On the outside, she stood strong. But on the inside, she was curled taut in a weeping ball. Rosella always was frail, more so in mind than body, though she somehow made it through each day. But that was before everything fell apart, and now she and I were even lonelier. At least with Ben around, it wasn't so bad.

The man in front of us motioned to the stone beside him. "Be careful, watch your step."

Together, Rosella and I stepped cautiously toward the abysmal hole in the ground, where a beloved husband and father would forever sleep in a coffin. A kind soul, he was the light of our lives, the drive of my writing career and our daughter's encouragement. Now, like the gaping hole in front of us, another had formed in our mourning hearts.

It's going to be tough, I thought, as I let the red rose I held slip through my fingers. *I can easily cover the final expenses, thanks to the emergency funds I've saved. I'll just have to make sure my next release is a banger, or we might have to turn to Mom for assistance.* I shuddered. *She'll be furious if she finds out we're struggling.*

I gave a sigh, as my eyes fell upon the rose laying atop my husband's coffin. Of all the flowers Rosella had to pick, it had to be that one. I understood why, because it was Ben's favorite, though I wished it wasn't that particular one. I couldn't stand seeing a rose in depressing settings, since she was named after it. It always made me think terrible thoughts of her, ones that frightened me... But I couldn't scold her. What kind of mother would that make me? Not a good one.

"Mom," she asked, "can we go now?"

I shook my head with a hurried blink of my eyes. "Oh, uh, yes. I think it's okay now."

"Chloe." The man beside my late husband's tombstone nodded to the awaiting reporters several feet away. "Would you like me to escort you to the car?"

"No, but thank you." I smiled at him. "Mr. Lawrence, you have been such a huge help with everything. My husband couldn't have chosen a better lawyer for his legal affairs. And the fact you drove all the way out here from another state..."

He nodded meekly. "Well, I've known Ben for years, good man and friend he was." Mr. Lawrence gave a sigh. "It's a shame that he's now gone."

"I know, but we'll get through it," I assured him. "I'll be sure to call you if I have any other questions."

"Alright."

I rolled my shoulders. "Well, is there anything else we need to do here?"

"No..." Mr. Lawrence nervously glanced at my daughter, who then looked to me.

"Well..." I peered over my shoulder, to the awaiting crowd of flashes, and timidly bit my lip.

"I really don't mind escorting you," Mr. Lawrence urged.

"I-It's okay," I said. "Rosella, let's go."

Rosella clung to my back, as we proceeded through the field of gravestones around us. It wasn't far to the car, but it sure seemed that way with the sea of flashing cameras drowning us. As microphones were shoved in my face, these people demanding I give them a sappy grief story, I suffered in silence. For the sake of my baby girl, the only part of Benjamin I had left, I'd be strong.

"Chloe! Chloe, over here! Anything you want to say about your husband's abrupt passing?"

I groaned in annoyance, as I pulled open the passenger door for Rosella, then shut it once she was safely inside.

"Chloe Bloom! What are you going to do now that Benjamin Walsh is gone?"

That is none of your business. And his married name was Bloom. Now go away.

"Is it possible he fell sick after his three-week disappearance in the forest?"

He's been sick far longer than that. It just didn't show until then.

"You've said that the inspiration behind your books is the forest! Can you take a minute to explain that? Maybe it has something to do with your husband? He worked closely with you on the project."

He spent countless hours with me, whether in my office or his, and pulled many all-nighters, helping me piece together the perfect story...

"Did Benjamin know anything about the forest?"

He knew enough.

"Did Mr. Walsh know anything about the cult within the forest?"

Didn't you hear him support my denial of those claims? And again, it's Benjamin BLOOM.

"Did he ever find out you reopened the library?"

I didn't get the chance to tell him...

"What was your relationship with him like?"

"Please!" Unable to stand the madness any longer, I whirled around on the swarming crowd, my nostrils flared, and my lips curled into a snarl. "Please! Stop this!"

All around me, the flashing stopped, and a hush fell over the crowd. The silence blessed my ears, and I embraced the moment with open arms. The only other time I'd felt this comfortable was in my home, away from these snooping heathens.

"My daughter and I are having a rough time right now." I spoke quietly and calmly, so as not to give them what they want, a grieving woman whom they could easily portray as mindless and violent. "Please... Leave us alone. I understand that your job is to get answers to this damn town's questions, but please." I put my hands out in front of me. "Leave us alone. We need this time to heal."

I stormed around the front of the van, and threw open the driver's side door with quivering hands, then fumbled for the car keys in my pocket. Meanwhile, the reporters started up again, as if they hadn't heard me, but I didn't care. I just wanted to take my daughter home, and grieve with her. Ben's death was like a pair of knives through our chests, and these damn people were twisting them further into our hearts.

"Mom... Can we go see Great Granny Felan?" Rosella whimpered.

"Whatever you want, sweetie," I murmured. My eyes on the breaking crowd in front of me, I reached a hand to my right, and found Rosella's head. "Maybe Fenris will be there, too."

Rosella whimpered. "Mom... Why won't these people go away?"

I sighed. "It's because they know something's up, honey. Don't worry, it'll be fine. Just remember what your father told you. Stand tall, and be the strongest Bloom you can be."

"Mom, I..." A sob interrupted her, and it took a few moments for me to realize that it was mine.

"Oh Rosella, I'm sorry," I whispered, and blinked at the tears blurring my vision. "Oh god, I'm sorry."

"It's okay... really."

Though the comfort of my daughter's hand relaxed me a little as it settled upon my shoulder, I couldn't help but think that Benjamin was what made our family complete. Three blooms together in a field of dandelions, one of them had wilted, and now only two remained.

"Rosella..." I forced a sad smile. "I promise, things will be alright, and if anything is bothering you please come to me."

"You mean, like how Dad went to you?" she asked.

I shuddered. "Y-Yes, exactly like that."

"I see..."

Her pained response struck me with a hit of guilt, and as the van rolled to a stop before the exit, I shot a hesitant glance in her direction. "Sweetheart, I know you feel like your father was hiding things from you... He just didn't want you to see him so... so..."

"So what?"

I kneaded my lips together. I didn't want to respond.

Rosella nodded slowly. "Sick."

I sighed. "Yeah."

I got the van moving again after a quick look for others, and drove at a steady pace, my frantic thoughts running countless laps in my brain like a participant peeling the track in the Olympics. I had to stay focused on the road, I was worried about legal documents, and the well-being of Rosella, and the loss of my husband, and—

"I always got excited when he wanted to show me something," Rosella piped up again. "He was just like you, so passionate about his writing. I remember when I walked in on him one day, when I was really little. I thought he was mad, because he had a stern look on his face, but he told me he was actually thinking about an article detailing one of his trips outside America. He asked if I wanted to see what he was working on, and he showed me all this cool stuff he wrote." She sighed. "It was like traveling the world without ever leaving the house, and it got my brain stirring up some fun ideas."

"Yeah, you said you wanted to write stories about exploring different places," I said with a chuckle.

"I did... But I gave it up." Rosella giggled. "For one, Dad's boss couldn't accept silly preschool stories about animals living together in an imaginary world, and that crushed me. Second, it seemed like too much work."

"To be fair, you were in the first grade when that happened, but now that you're older you better understand how it works. If you wanted to try again though..." My heart welled with hope. I'd never seen her nearly as passionate about writing as I was, but it would be fun to try persuading her. We could share each other's ideas and build each other up, maybe even write a bestseller together.

She waved a hand. "Nah, drawing's way easier for me. I feel more at peace."

My shoulders sagged. "Yeah, I thought so." I kept the disappointment behind my words hidden with an understanding tone. Writing wasn't for everyone, and that was fine. "Hmm, what if you put your mind toward being an illustrator? Lots of writers would love to have a talented artist like you around." Sure, it wasn't writing, but at least this way we could still work together... like Ben and I used to.

She blushed at my compliment. "Aw, that's really sweet of you to say."

"Think about it! You and I could make some cool things!" My eyes sparked with inspiration. "Wouldn't that be something?"

"Yeah..." Her smile dropped, a solemn frown taking its place. "What was the difference with Dad's job? He had a camera, and a notepad, just like those people at the funeral."

I bowed my head slightly, as I returned to my depressive state. "He was writing for a nature magazine," I explained. "They wanted to know about all the different creatures in the world, how people live..."

"But what about the forest? How come he never wrote about that? With all those rumors..."

I pondered how to word my response, then breathed another sigh. "Rosella... If you remember, I told you that there are people in this town that don't quite understand the forest the same way we do. They think it's a dangerous place." *Because it is, but that's beside the point.*

"But they don't know what it's like there unless we tell them," Rosella argued. "For instance, if they met Great Granny Felan and Fenris, they'd see they're really nice!"

"That wouldn't matter," I stated firmly.

Rosella sighed. "I wish we could live with Great Granny Felan and Fenris. It's way better in the forest."

"I know..." *It's the safest place for you away from all the creeps and cameras...* A shiver ran down my spine. *But it's also the most dangerous, and I promised Ben I'd continue to protect you no matter what...*

Neither Rosella or the town of Hollow knew what existed beyond those trees, and though it was important the townspeople never found out, I was more worried about Rosella finding out. She hadn't shown any signs of realization yet, and as long as she didn't linger in those trees long, she never would. At least, that was what I hoped for.

As long as she doesn't hear her, Rosella will never have to leave me, I thought. *I just have to keep her safe, and as far from the trees as possible... But not too far, or else Mom will get suspicious.*

CHAPTER 1

I T'D BEEN TWO YEARS since Dad died, two years lonelier than usual in this house. Never did I imagine him sitting in his office, pale as the curtains draped over the window behind him, his beaming grin unaffected by his deteriorating health, being the last time I'd see him alive.

I spent most of my time up in my room the entire first week since the funeral, either curled up in bed or seated at my bay window, crying. I felt guilty letting my mother see me suffer when she was stressing over things too, so the only time I ever freed myself from self-imprisonment was when I went to the bathroom, and visited Great Granny Felan Sunday of that miserable week. Other than that, it was just me in my bedroom with a tray of food left at my door by Mom three times a day.

"'Just keep your head up, Ro-Ro.'" I quoted the last words my father ever said to me while stuffing my books in my backpack. "I know, Dad... I am."

Despite the gaping hole still prominent in my chest, I forced myself to be strong for my mother, especially when I finally stepped into her office and found her sobbing at her desk the day I ended my confinement. Scattered papers strewn about the room, it took me no time to realize they were important legal documents regarding Dad's final expenses.

I couldn't help with the bills or annoying reporters that snooped into our personal lives. I also couldn't stop the rumors that spoke of how my mother planned my father's death so she could profit off of it, or that Great Granny Felan had poisoned him with some concoction so as to induct him into her "secret cult" that, for some reason, people believed in. But the one thing I could give her? Grief, something that she already had more than enough of. And yet, Mom still made sure I was clothed, fed, and protected, despite all the stress.

A tear streaked my cheek as I glanced at the black rubber bracelet around my right wrist, a gift from my father on my thirteenth birthday, and a faint smile graced my lips. In cursive white letters it read, "Blossoms in Bloom".

Fitting, don't you think, Ro-Ro? After all, our family name is Bloom! As soon as I saw it, I just knew you had to have it.

"Yeah, Dad... It's very fitting." *You insisted on taking Mom's name, but people only ever saw you as Benjamin Walsh, "the Exploring Writer".*

My days of exploring the world are over, Ro-Ro... It's time I explore new territory, right here in fatherhood. People may not understand that at first, but I'm sure they'll come to accept it eventually. I can always find time to travel, but I only have one chance to see my baby girl grow up.

I wiped the back of my hand across my wet eyes and face, then checked my desk to make sure I hadn't left anything. It was where I used to work on my art, until Dad died.

Your mother and I gathered some wood from the trees. Turns out I'm quite good with an axe, though sanding was a little difficult. Still, the splinters and blisters were worth it for you, Ro-Ro.

I rested my palm against the desk, and my eyes explored the curving rings that lined the smooth wood, as my fingers grazed over the thin cracks etched into it. *This was a gift to me on my ninth birthday...* My wandering gaze fell upon the sketchbook atop the desk, the thirtieth in my possession. *It's been... two years.*

I hesitantly picked up the sketchbook and hugged it to my chest. Like the rest stuffed in my closet, countless hours of practice, from simple sketches of hands to colorful illustrations of scenery, resonated within. The work in this sketchbook dated back two years, maybe a little further. Holding it felt like reattaching a lost limb, or like finally adding the final piece to a puzzle that'd been misplaced for a long time.

"You're actually taking it with you?"

I did my best to ignore the nauseating pit in my stomach, as I peered over my shoulder and found Mom standing in the doorway. "Yeah. I, uh, actually thought about drawing in it again recently. Ya know, I was pretty shocked by how many pages I'd used up. I mean, there are still some left, but..."

"Your father and I always supported your passion," Mom said, "especially him."

I gave a light chuckle. "Remember when he caught me stealing some of his blank computer paper from his desk when I was little? He joked that he knew there was a 'paper gremlin' hiding somewhere. He just...

didn't expect it to be me." A slightly pained snicker slipped my lips. "I started crying."

She snorted. "Yes, then he told me he felt bad for teasing you, and started leaving stacks of paper out on the coffee table for you every few days."

The corners of my mouth wavered as I fought to keep my voice steady. "You and Dad both did a lot for me, but I feel embarrassed praising him for most of the work. You played an equal part." Unshed tears blurring my vision, tension gripped tightly to my shoulders, and my fingers curled into my sketchbook. *But if it were a contest, I have to admit he'd win for sure. He never failed to make me smile.*

Mom rubbed at the sleeves of her turtleneck, a worried glint in her brown eyes, as she kneaded her lips into a thin line. "Your father's always been the overachiever... At any rate, he'd be glad to see you pick up your art again."

I glanced down at my sketchbook and sighed. "Yeah..." *Two years sure is a long time to waste.*

"So..." An excited look sprang to her face as she returned her gaze to me. "On a lighter note, I got a good deal with a publishing house for my next book."

"Traditional, right?" I asked. The change of subject relieved some of the pain our conversation inflicted upon me, and my shoulders loosened. "First time you went indie, second time you're changing lanes."

"Yes. I don't know how long I'll stick with it," Mom said, "but I like it for now. Plus, I got a nice big check."

I cleared my watery eyes as a snicker slipped. "Wow, guess that means we're livin' fancy now."

"Yeah, I guess so." She slipped her hands in her jeans' pockets. "I honestly thought we'd be stuck with ramen noodles and water, what with everything that went out, but your great-grandmother was quick to jump in..." She again kneaded her lips together, her eyes darting to their corners.

"You know how she is," I said with a faint chuckle. "Thanks to her, we have plenty of vegetables and meat to live off of, plus some nice soups, when needed. She's basically our personal grocery store."

"That she is." Her face fell into a blank expression. "But thanks to your father, we'll be more than sittin' pretty... To tell you the truth, that's how I got into the traditional publishing business."

"I know that. I was in the room when you got the phone call. They were all excited that you emailed them."

"Yeah, and they were willing to pay me whatever necessary to publish my future stories..." A low sigh brushed her lips. "I guess that makes me a bottom feeder..."

I shook my head. "Don't feel guilty. Dad's death definitely had an impact on your books, but you didn't plan that. It just happened."

"I just don't want to look like I used his death as a meal ticket," Mom argued. "He was the one who spent years working with me on my debut novel, and now that he's gone—"

"If you're going to mention Georgia Morse, she failed to bury your career in the dirt because you didn't back down. And you and I both know that Great Granny Felan isn't what she's made her out to be."

Mom scowled at me, though her gaze quickly softened at the sight of my flinch. "I can't wipe it from my mind," she uttered calmly. "She smeared me, Hollow's Storyteller, and your great-grandmother, into the muddiest of gossip. I almost didn't make it out of the negative mental space it put me in, and it was frustrating. I'd just started making somewhat good money with my fantasy-thriller novel, and then this jealous woman decided to toss her hat in the ring of reporters to feed lies to the public. Right after your father's death, no less..."

"I know, and she used the forest as leverage." I positioned my sketchbook at my side with one hand, and pinched the bridge of my nose with the other. "This is why I hate gossip and money, because people tend to use both to hurt others."

"Now, I can't confirm if she actually *paid* anyone to publish those claims," Mom countered, "but I firmly believe she did. She knows *a lot* of well-trusted sources."

I cocked a brow. "Right, and that's why you're convinced she's also *giving* herself to others."

"Again, don't know if she's ever paid anyone, but you have seen the way she acts, the way she dresses." Mom groaned. "She thinks that all she has to do is hike her leg..."

I placed my free hand against my hip. "Okay, but in the forest, nothing like that exists. You just go out, hunt, pick berries, grow your own plants, and just live. You don't have to worry about the gossip or going hungry, and you can't shield your crimes with money."

"And like I told you, I was raised out there," Mom said. "For the umpteenth time, you can't just uproot yourself and reside within the trees. You don't have the experience that I do."

"But Great Granny Felan's doing it," I argued. "She's not a coward! She's willing to face whatever's out there head-on!"

Mom's turtleneck swallowed her neck as she shrank into herself, her shoulders raised.

"Sorry." I shamefully looked away. "That was uncalled for."

"No, it's okay," she mumbled.

"It's not. I mean, I don't believe the twisted fable this town's weaved about the forest or Great Granny Felan. You and I have been in there hundreds, if not thousands, of times. But that still doesn't give me the excuse to be nasty toward you."

"Oh, Rosella..." Mom swatted a careless hand to the air. "Really, it's fine. I wasn't offended. And as for the town, I don't want you worrying about it."

I knelt down to my backpack and slipped an arm through the strap, a frown on my face. "Forgive me for sounding like a complaining liberal, but I don't understand why we can't have peace, like in the forest. And don't tell me it's because that's just the way the world is, or some other complicated excuse."

Mom strode toward me and brushed a gentle hand down the side of my face, as a comforting light illuminated her brown eyes. "It's okay, sweetheart. Like I told you, when you're old enough, you can do what you want."

A playful smirk teased my lips. "What if I want liposuction, or a piercing?"

"Like I said," Mom stated, as a firm frown sprung to her face. "When you're old enough. Just... Just promise me you won't let any boys sneak around that cutie booty." A smile betrayed her stern expression when I uttered a surprise snort.

Cheeks flushed bright red, I gently slapped at her. "Mom!"

She threw her arms around me, and nuzzled her cheek to the top of my head. "You know what I mean."

I laughed. "Yeah, I know."

"I'm serious. Focus on getting your degree first, then settling down in a place where you're comfortable if it's not here."

"If you mean what you say, then..." My eyes fled to their corners. I wanted to continue with, 'I want to live in the forest with Great Granny Felan and Fenris after I graduate,' but the words refused to surface.

"You know something? I can't get over how much you really look like your father, and share bits of his personality." She didn't seem to notice my inner conundrum as she tenderly combed her fingers through the locks of blonde hair resting over my shoulders, a dreamy spark in her eyes.

"You really think so?"

"I do. His spirit is thriving within you." She tapped the tip of her finger against my nose. "As he always said, you are the prettiest rose ever seen."

My heart fluttered with joy. "Thanks, Mom."

"You're welcome. Now then, we better get going. You've got school in an hour, and I need to get to the library."

My sneakers padded softly against the carpet as I followed my mother out of my bedroom, and down the hall to the stairs. Dad always told us to hold onto the wooden railing since the carpeted steps could be slick, so Mom and I made sure to do that before heading down. It only took one time for me to slip as a toddler and suffer Dad's gentle twenty-minute lecture to make it habit, but even then he'd remind us before we got within five feet of them.

"Your father would be proud of us for remembering," Mom said, as if she'd read my mind. "What do you think?"

"Oh, for sure," I responded.

She gave a laugh upon her trot to the kitchen after hitting the bottom step, and scooped her car keys off the counter. "Ah, well... I got a lot of books to reorganize at the library today, plus some decorations for fall to prepare."

"Maybe while you're there, you can get some writing done," I suggested. "Being surrounded by books is good motivation, right?"

"Yeah, sometimes." She eyed me with suspicion. "Your father once gave that same idea in order to get rid of me for the day. Wound up coming home to a new cat."

"Hey, I'm just trying to help," I said, and meandered over to the front door. "If you do plan to do some writing, I'll see if Susan can stop by to pick me up after school." I felt something stroke my leg, and I looked down to our cat Pooter. "Oh, and if you remember, you immediately fell in love with this little guy."

Pooter meowed with affection as I bent down to pet him, and he rubbed his face into my palm.

When I rose back up, Mom planted a kiss on my head, her straight golden-brown locks bouncing against her back. "Alright, let's get going. We got a busy day today."

"Right." I smiled down to Pooter. "We'll see you later, buddy."

The cat blinked his large blue eyes as he swiftly threw his tail around himself.

"Okay..."

I followed Mom outside to the van, and waited to hop in as she unlocked it for me. I slipped into the front passenger side of the vehicle, while she came around the other and climbed into the driver's seat. Once we were buckled in, she put the key in ignition.

We rolled out of the driveway, and went down the empty road lined with trees at either side. Speed gradually blurred them together in a patch of greenery, a decent view I enjoyed far more than the bland array of buildings and streetlights within the town. I wished that it could last longer, maybe even forever.

I released a tired sigh when the exit rose into view, and glared at the stop sign positioned to the far right. *May as well be a meek attempt at telling us to stay out.*

"Hey, don't you have a math test today?" Mom asked.

I shuddered at the question. I hated math, as it was a difficult subject.

"Your teacher said that your grade should rise back up to a 'C' if you pass."

God, I don't wanna get into that right now... Looking to deter from the uncomfortable topic, I thought up an easier one to bear. "Man, I'm glad

I found my belt. Keeps these jeans capris up better. I mean, I got wide hips, but my body just can't seem to find the 'perfect' fit."

"I know what you mean. I have the same issue."

Thankful she accepted the bait, I continued the conversation. "Yeah, though you are smaller than me."

"I still have to wear a belt," Mom said. "I just have to tighten mine more."

I snorted at her response. "Thanks for rubbing it in, Mom."

Her face paled. "I-I'm sorry. I wasn't trying to be rude."

"I'm just joshin' you," I said, and gently nudged her with my elbow. "It's okay."

"Well, I just…" She nibbled at her bottom lip.

"What?" I asked.

"Usually when we talk about that stuff, it makes me feel bad."

"Yeah, but you don't make fun of me or anything, unlike…" Anxiety traced down my back like a tempted knife at the thought of my high school bully. "You know…"

Mom's hands squeezed the steering wheel, her lip curled in a snarl. "That damn brat… Her aunt's ego crawled so far up her ass she's basically a carbon copy."

I recoiled at that response.

"Ugh, sorry," she uttered. "I'm just so over her bullshit, especially the name-calling. How many times has she thrown the 'fat pig' insult at you? Like a broken record, damn it."

"I'll be fine," I murmured. "I got Sophia, she'll protect me." I turned my head to the window, so as to hide my frustration. *Timid little Rosella, always depending on her bestie to be her shield.*

"Just… be careful," Mom said. "I don't want you out after dark."

"I know, I know."

"We've got a decent system here, but some badges don't shine as bright as others."

Oh great… This again.

"As you mentioned during our earlier conversation at the house, money talks."

"I wouldn't go that far," I said. "I'm not saying I'd put it past Caroline or her aunt to live dangerously, but I don't think officers are that stupid."

"Some of them are," Mom warned. "Believe me, I've witnessed a few drooling over Georgia's thigh. She's surely taught her niece some of her tricks..."

I shook my head. "I know I'm gonna regret asking this, but I'm curious. You're not... calling either of them... what I think you are, are you?"

Her knuckles turned white as her grip tightened around the steering wheel, an irritated groan slipping her lips. "Sweetie, I'm not calling anyone anything. I'm only referencing their behavior. Georgia is... not the best influence, and based upon what I've seen of Caroline..." Worry surfaced to my mother's face as she gnawed at her bottom lip.

"Well, since we're giving opinions here, I feel like you're being a little too judgmental," I said calmly. "I mean, we've walked around the house together in only our undergarments before, and seen each other, yet you don't think that's wrong."

"Okay, but that's..." Mom rubbed a hand over her face. "Ugh."

"It's not like it's every day, Mom. We just happen to run into each other while looking for clothes sometimes. I'm sure other mothers and daughters have done the same thing."

"That may be true, but we only do that at home," Mom added.

"So, you just prefer stuff like that to stay at home?" I asked.

"I am going to forever regret this conversation, aren't I?"

"You're the one who started it."

Mom blew a frustrated gust of air from her lips. "Lemme put it to you this way. The world doesn't need to know *everything* about us, the same way the world doesn't need to know my opinion about Caroline."

"Okay, but assuming things about someone without actual proof isn't right. That's what the town does to us, and now you're doing it to Caroline and Georgia."

Mom's eyes widened a little, but settled again as she gave a tired nod. "Yeah... I guess you're right."

"Don't think I'm trying to bully you into having a different opinion," I told her. "Because I'm not. I'm only trying to figure out what you mean." I sighed at the woman scowling over her shoulder at us, as the van slowed to a halt at the stoplight. "I know that it's weird of me to defend Caroline. It's just that, every time I see someone being judged, I get worked up over it because I know how it feels."

"Rosella..."

"I just want them to take time to understand us," I went on. "I'm not saying we should put out our personal business for the world to see, just to look at the situation from every angle. Like you once said, we do something harmless that they see as strange, and then accuse us without question." I motioned at the air with a hand. "Like the other day, when you were at the grocery store sniffing fruit because it looked a little funny. People kept pointing fingers at you and whispering amongst themselves. Honestly, I think they did it just because it was you. If it were someone else, they wouldn't have bat an eyelash."

"Oh, I'm sure they'd bat an eyelash at any mother and daughter walking around the house together in only their undergarments," Mom muttered, as she glared at the rearview mirror. "Like the woman we just passed."

"Yes, but—"

"Sorry, I let my sarcasm slip again. Anyways, you want people to gather all the facts before making a judgement call, but what you also have to understand is that not everyone will. That's just how it works." She stiffened. "As you just saw, even I've done that."

I rubbed at the back of my head as I sought out the right words. "I guess... I'm just very sensitive to gossip then. We have to go through it every day, and it's irritating. When I see someone else going through it, it bothers me because it's literally the same thing."

"Yes, and you pointed that out," Mom said. "Very clearly."

"So, why were you doing it?" I asked sternly, "when you go through the same thing?"

She kneaded her sealed lips together, her face in a hard frown.

I clasped my hands together in my lap with discontent. "I rest my case I suppose."

"It's because we're all human," Mom abruptly answered. "Your father's gossiped about people he doesn't like before, and he's told me he's not proud of it."

"But Dad also kept an open mind," I pointed out. "He never judged anyone at first glance. He always got to know them first."

"He met both Georgia and Caroline before he passed..."

I bowed my head. "Okay, but like Dad said, it's never good to openly judge someone based on appearance… I get points for at least trying to be nice the day Caroline and I met, even though she came at me with claws out."

"I know," Mom answered gently. "And, like I suspect, it's because of her aunt. She raised her to dominate others, not to work well with them."

I cocked a brow at her words. "You mean, she raised her to be a bully?"

Mom's face went blank, as she pulled the van to a stop once more and put it in park. "Nevermind, this subject matter is too mature for you, so let's not bring it up again."

Suspicion sparked an arousal of curiosity in my mind, but I ignored it, and opened the passenger door. "Thanks for driving me," I said and stepped out, backpack in hand.

"Hey."

I peered over my shoulder. "Yes?"

A faint smile graced Mom's face, but it wavered on the edge of a frown. "H-Have a good day, okay? And if you feel sick or anything, go and see the nurse."

I relaxed a little at that comforting thought. "Yeah, Patricia is pretty nice."

"Alright, have a good day."

I shut the passenger door, and gave Mom a wave as she drove off. I silently observed the retreating van until it was completely out of sight, and then proceeded toward the many stairs leading to the school's entrance.

"Hey! Rosella!" A pale girl with an ebony ponytail waved down to me, then folded her arms over her small chest. "Up here!"

Just try to have a good day today, I thought. *You can do it.* I raced up the steps to greet my best friend, my protector, the only person who bothered to be around me. "Hey!"

Rosella… Rosella… It's… It's me…

CHAPTER 2

I HURRIED UP THE steps of the school entrance, eager to meet with my best friend, my only friend in Hollow, Sophia Mitchell. In stark contrast to me, she was tough and handled herself, but she never went after anyone unless they came at either me or her first.

Sophia chuckled as she watched me double over from the jog up the steps. "So, you ready to go in?"

"Yeah, sorry..." I eyed the black tank top she was wearing, and my thoughts wandered back to the conversation I'd just had with my mother. "Is the school really okay with that?"

She cocked her head. "With what?"

"Your tank top."

She examined herself. Paired with her top of choice were black skinny jeans and sneakers. "Yeah, why? You've seen me dress like this for school before. In fact, I remember you asking me on the first day."

"Well, I mean..." I struggled to find a response without bringing up my awkward conversation with Mom, and mentally kicked myself. *Stupid question, Ro. Mom doesn't see Sophia the same way she does Caroline...*

"Everything okay?" Sophia asked me.

"Yeah, fine," I lied. My gaze dropped to my shoes, a sheepish look on my face.

Sophia waved a careless hand to the air. "Look, I've told you before, I can't pull off 'cute' like you do."

Trying to play off my stupidity, I forced a smile and shrugged. "Y-Yeah, you're right. Guess I was worried about nothing, haha!"

"I'm serious, Ro! Like that babydoll top you're wearing? It's adorable on you! Whereas on me, it'd look weird."

"Perhaps..." I mumbled.

"Trust me, it's okay. As long as I keep myself covered here..." She smirked, and grasped at her breasts. "I'm fine."

Embarrassment flamed my cheeks, my eyes bulging at her mortifying act. "Sophia!" I hissed. "Stop that!"

"What?" She frowned. "People know I got boobs. Big deal."

"Yeah, but…" I dropped my voice to a whisper, as my eyes drifted to the onlooking students meandering around us. "Y-You really shouldn't do that in public. Otherwise, people are gonna get the wrong idea."

Sophia laughed, and released her grip. "Whatever, come on, let's go!"

I meandered into the school with my eyes to the floor, while Sophia strode in with her head held high, a proud grin across her face, and together we traversed the enormous gathering of students. Though there was plenty of space to navigate an easy path, I never enjoyed this early morning commute. Being in the commons area, surrounded by lots of people, it always made me feel like I was being squished into a can of sardines. It was a big space, yes, but not big enough for me to feel at peace, unlike the outdoors or the mall.

Thankfully, Sophia led me through the crowd no problem, and I breathed a sigh of relief as we approached a quiet corner of the large commons area, away from the chaos.

"So…" She cocked her head, and turned around to face me. "What's up, Ro? Clearly something's bothering you."

I sighed in defeat. *No point in hiding from her…* "I, uh, had this interesting conversation with my mom this morning, and—"

"Weeeeeell, what do we have here?" An obnoxiously loud voice rang throughout the commons area, and fear coursed through me like a shot of ice in my veins. "If it isn't the 'weirdo duo'."

Sauntering over was Caroline Morse, with her long, perfectly curled red hair, flashy manicured-nails, and slim purple dress that left her lower thighs slightly exposed. Known as the "queen" of the school, as well as Georgia Morse's pampered niece, she lacked grace in favor of glorifying her distasteful personality. Like Sophia, she didn't care about what others thought of her, which was probably the only good quality she possessed.

"Hey, Rosella, remember when you asked me about what's acceptable in school?" Sophia asked aloud, then shot a glare at Caroline. "Well, *that's* not."

Caroline put her hands on her hips. "Huh, thought the school exterminated *all* the insects. Guess they missed one." Her nose to the air with her self-defined pride, she scoffed at Sophia's ensemble. "Psh, you look like some cheap Barbie knockoff," she remarked, her words dripping with aggression, and then turned her focus on me. "Still the same little wallflower, huh, Rosella? Very fitting, I must say, Gloomy Bloomy."

I foolishly opened my mouth to retaliate, but her cocky smirk sent me fleeing behind Sophia. Just like always.

"What do you want?" Sophia spat back.

With a tilt of her head, Caroline lifted her left foot to stroke the bottom of her three-inch heel. "Like these new shoes I got? My auntie bought them for me." Her glossy red lips pursed into a plump kiss, and she fluttered her perfectly-brushed eyelashes.

A couple of snorts from behind caught my attention, and I hesitantly peeked over my shoulder. A few girls were watching, their hands over their mouths as they leaned in close to each other.

Well, that didn't take long, I muttered in my thoughts.

"Flaunting your shit like the self-proclaimed bitch queen you are, just like always," Sophia retorted. "Don't you have somewhere else to be? Kissing up a jock, or perhaps..." Amusement teased the corner of her sneaky smirk, and she finished with a mischievous air, "...kissing somethin' o' his?"

Too late, I thought, with a disgruntled face. *Now it's on.*

The girls behind me broke out in a fit of giggles, eager for the excitement.

"Pfft." Caroline rolled her eyes, her hands planted to her taut hips. "I'm no skank."

Sophia raised a brow. "Well, with the way you present yourself, how else am I supposed to think?" She gestured at her with a hand. "I mean, look at you. You're deliberately showing yourself off like some fuckin' first-class show pony, and based upon what I heard, David Grayhill's been meetin' you under the bleachers twice a week since last month."

"So what? I gave him a little..." Caroline slunk back into a seductive lean. "... *shoulder massage.*" She coiled a bouncy lock of her curly hair around her index finger. "I got him wrapped around my little finger here."

Out of the corner of my right eye, I spotted a boy with some others a ways from us. They were playfully slapping at his arms as he snickered back at them, his hands raised in self-defense.

"Oh sure!" Sophia countered, and I looked back to her. "And I bet he's got you wrapped around his little— Ouch!" She rubbed at the spot on her arm I'd pinched.

"Stop it," I hissed. "Seriously. Let's just go."

Caroline scoffed at us. "You wouldn't know the difference between a dick and a cucumber, *Mitchell.*" She spat Sophia's last name like it was venom.

"At least I keep my legs closed," Sophia muttered.

My mouth fell agape at Sophia's response. I'd never witnessed her stoop to this degree before. Usually it was a simple spat, and that was it.

To make matters worse, she wiggled her pinky finger. "I bet it does this when you touch it, like a little worm." She stuck her tongue out at Caroline's burning scowl.

"Urgh, retract that slimy slug before I tear it outta your mouth!" Caroline snarled. Her face turned bright red, giving her hair the impression of flames.

"Oh, someone's gettin' feisty, dishin' out the fancy words, I'm so scared." Sophia stomped forward, putting her nose only centimeters from Caroline's. "Better watch yourself, *Morse.* I don't take condescending whores like you lightly."

Caroline gave a curt laugh as she mirrored Sophia's sharp gaze with confidence. "We'll see, won't we?"

"God, I'm so tired of you getting away with your bullshit," Sophia shot back.

"Whatever." Caroline flicked her wrist at her. "I'm going now. Toodles~!" She whipped her fiery head and stormed off, and the blessed fading of her clicking heels graced my relieved ears.

Sophia pressed her thumb to her nose and wiggled her fingers with her tongue out, then turned to me with a warm smile. "Come on, we better get to class." She gently grabbed my hand. "We got a math test to prep you for."

As I hesitantly followed after her, I took notice of the dozens of eyes locked on us and shuddered. "Soph, why did you do that? Seriously..."

"Ro, come on. I've been biting my tongue long enough. She had it coming."

I bowed my head in an attempt to ignore the bystanders. "I-I get you wanted to insult her, but you really went the extra mile this time."

Sophia sighed. "Rosella, I'm tired, okay? You saw the way she struts around, like she owns the damn place. It's one thing to have extreme self-respect, but to haul yourself around like you're a trophy? And throwing yourself on whatever's breathing?" She shook her head. "I'm sorry, but I don't respect people like that."

"Mom did kinda tell me she thinks Caroline dresses like a prostitute," I said, "and that her aunt is teaching her to do all that stuff."

She snorted. "I'm not surprised, what with how she acts. I mean, I personally don't care how she dresses, but that's just me. I just wish she'd cool it with the showing off. It's so annoying!"

"What about when we were outside?" I challenged. "When you grabbed your boobs?"

"At least I wasn't trying to grab anyone's attention," Sophia argued. "Like I said, people know I got 'em, but that doesn't mean I'm going to show them off."

"Yet you said..." I fiddled with a few strands of my hair while dodging Sophia's questioning look. "... people knew you have boobs."

"Because they do know," she said, "and the purpose of my shenanigan wasn't to show off." Her voice fell to a whisper. "And I was covered..."

"Caroline was covered. I mean, she showed off, but..."

Sophia uttered a groan, and slapped at her forehead. "Ugh, Ro, just let me stew in peace, okay? Sheesh..."

I wrung my hands together. "I'm sorry, I didn't mean to make you mad." *Please don't be mad at me. You're the only person here that I can actually talk to, the only one in town who understands me.*

She patted my shoulder. "No, I'm sorry. I just... I get annoyed easy when interrogated for stupid comments I make."

"I can understand how that feels," I mumbled.

"Seriously. It's like that one time when your mother sniffed some fruit at the store. People thought she was snuffing it to get high or something."

I frowned. "Wait... Is that what happened? I thought they just assumed she was being weird."

"I heard different," Sophia said. "I found out at one of my neighbor's houses yesterday. They were talking about it with my mom."

"Oh."

"Anyways, getting back to what we were talking about..." She lowered her voice again, as we entered our first class of the day. "Caroline's attitude is what bugs me, not her fashion choice. And sure, I speak my mind at times when I shouldn't, but like everyone else, I don't give a damn."

"That's kinda what I did this morning with my mom," I whispered. "She holds certain opinions that I don't quite agree with, nor understand."

"So that's how this came about." Sophia cocked a brow. "I can see that. She was raised out in the forest, right?"

I nodded. "Yeah, she was."

"I mean, I guess it makes sense that way. She didn't get to see what the world was like until she was much older." She rolled her eyes. "My mother... Hoo boy, is she... somethin' to talk with about stuff like this."

"Mmm, I think my mom responded the way she did because she hates Georgia, Caroline too since she behaves like her aunt."

Sophia rubbed at the back of her head. "True... She really has it out for Georgia, huh?"

"Ever since she tried to smear her name in the dirt," I grumbled.

Sophia clapped a reassuring hand to my back. "Well, know that I like you guys, and won't ever gossip about you."

I nuzzled my head against hers. "Thanks. I know I can always trust you."

"Ro, this is gonna sound a little outta left field for me, but staying home all the time and away from people is a life of luxury in a world like this." She sighed. "However, that's not exactly the best life either..."

I swallowed the nervous lump that rose up my throat at those words, and stiffly nodded.

Sophia seemed to notice my troubled expression, for she gently squeezed my shoulder, and uttered an apology.

"It's okay," I said. "Really."

Our first hour teacher didn't have anything for us to do, so I resigned myself to brushing up for the third hour math test with Sophia's assistance, though second hour wasn't nearly as luxurious. I had to suffer discouraging insults scrawled on paper, courtesy of Caroline, since we had that class together.

Rather than make constant trips to the garbage can, and possibly alert the teacher, I paid Caroline no mind and slipped the several balls of paper she dropped onto my desk into my backpack every time the teacher turned her back.

"Oh, thank god," I whispered when the bell finally rang, and sprang from my seat like it was boiling hot. Between Caroline and my math test, I'd choose the math test any day.

"Ro!" Sophia poked her head in the doorway, as students flooded past her. "Hey, you ready to go?"

"Yeah, one sec! Just gotta grab a folder." I leaned down to pluck my folder of notes from the compartment under the desk. As I did so, my backpack slipped, and the contents spilled out. "Shoot!"

"Oh no!" Sophia ran over. "Here, let me help you."

"No no no! That's not necessary..." My voice faded from my throat, as she picked up a couple wads of paper.

"Ro, what are these?" She unballed one of the sheets, and a fiery glare melted the confusion from her face.

"Please," I begged. "Just let this go. It'll be fine."

She shook her head with disapproval. "Ro..."

I gave her a pleading look, my hands clapped together at my chest. "P-Please... Don't."

"Miss Mitchell?" my teacher called out. "What are you doing here? I don't have you until sixth hour."

"Sophia..." I watched helplessly as she went up to my teacher and revealed the note to her.

Sophia pointed to Caroline, and then Caroline whipped her head in their direction as she paused mid-exit.

In a panic, I stuffed the folder of notes into my backpack, scooped up the remainder of my things, and bolted from the room. I bumped into Caroline on the way out, but ignored her as she spat an insult my way.

Anxiety hit its peak, as I rocketed down the hall and stumbled into third hour. I felt like the biggest coward to ever roam the earth, and the sturdy lump trapped in my throat threatened to slip my lips when Sophia walked in several minutes after class had started. Disappointment evident on her face, she plopped down in her seat, her squared jaw set in a hard frown as she mumbled something inaudible to herself.

Nothing was said as our teacher went on about staying quiet so everyone could focus, and as the test was placed in front of me, I cautiously glanced at Sophia. Her scowl was so strong, I was surprised her eyes didn't scorch her paper, and it only got worse when they met mine. God, I wanted to crawl into a hole and disappear upon facing that monstrous glare.

My head jerked back into original position as I tore my gaze from hers, my heart galloping like a racehorse in my chest. *She's pissed at me... I know she is.*

Trying to read through a wall of tears proved difficult, and I struggled through my math test over the course of that grueling hour. As I got to the end, the bell rang, and I wrote down a random answer, not caring if it was right or wrong. I hastily scrambled together my belongings, before stumbling over to my teacher's desk to drop off the test, a terrible feeling in my gut that I'd probably flunked it. But I held out a wink of hope that I'd earned a passing grade, just in case.

Sophia lingered by the doorway, waiting for me, and her expression softened upon my approach. "Hey."

I recoiled under her stern gaze and whimpered.

"Are you okay? I, uh, saw you struggling..."

My eyes cautiously wandered to her face, and my shoulders relaxed at her apologetic expression. "Y-Yeah," I said. "I think I did okay." *By some miracle.*

She rubbed her fingertips at her temple. "God, I wish I could be more level-headed like you."

I uttered a dry laugh. "You don't want a head like mine. It's a mess."

"No, I mean, I wish I could avoid conflict more easily, like you do." Sophia motioned a hand at me. "Ya know, just keep to myself, and ignore the idiots."

"Honestly, if you did, you wouldn't be you," I joked.

She blew a frustrated huff of air between her lips. "Rosella, I... I told Ms. Garbs what happened."

My eyes averted hers once more. "Yeah, and I bolted."

"Ro, you know that I've always got your back," Sophia said calmly. "I don't mind fighting your battles for you, but you need to be there to explain your side of the story. Caroline played the whole thing off as some kind of 'framing scheme', and even though Ms. Garbs insisted she'd talk with her about this, you and I both know that won't do any good. At some point, you're gonna wind up like the others."

"Others?" I frowned. "What do you mean?"

She pinched the bridge of her nose with a scrunched brow. "I'll tell you later, it's not important right now. As for what is, you have to stop letting her push you around." She nodded ahead. "Come on, let's get to fourth hour, then go to lunch."

Since we were part of the second lunch group, Sophia led me to our next class, a resting period during the school day. Kinda like study hall, it was a time for students to sit around and either chat for a bit, or do some homework, while the first group spent their time in the cafeteria. After their lunch break, they would enter their fourth hour resting period. while we took ours.

During our wait for lunchtime, I pulled out a book to read. Sophia, meanwhile, looked over a music sheet with words on it. She told me once that she'd been part of choir for some time, so I assumed that was what it was for.

"Lunch bell," Sophia said as it went off. "Let's go get some munchies!"

I nodded, and packed up my things. "Right."

Spotting a pair of students holding hands with their linked arms stretched as we left our classroom, Sophia and I sped around them, and hurried down the hall toward the cafeteria. Sophia made a comment about how annoying that was, but I shrugged it off. I was starting to get pretty hungry, and I wanted to savor the meal I'd made for a bit before shoving it down near the end of lunchtime.

"Hi, Patricia!" Sophia called, as we walked past the school nurse's office.

"Hello Sophia!" The school nurse, Patricia, kindly waved back. "How are you doing?"

"Good!" Sophia nodded to me. "Just heading to lunch with my girl here."

I waved at Patricia. "Hello."

She beamed at the two of us. "Always nice to see you two together, have a nice day!"

"Always!" Sophia's smile vanished once her back was to Patricia. "Ya know, she asked me about you. Said she hadn't seen you in a while."

I nodded. "Yeah, I usually go to her when I need ibuprofen for stress headaches or menstrual cramps. Dealt with this month's period during the weekend, since the first and second day are always the worst. As for my stress headaches, there actually aren't that many anymore."

"That's good to hear," Sophia said. "Kind of shocking, though. With Caroline always breathing down your neck, I'm surprised you're not addicted to those pills." She shuddered. "God, I hope that never happens."

"It won't," I assured her. "Promise…" I glanced past her, and my stomach dropped to the floor. Seated at a nearby table, Caroline was laughing with a group of guys and one other girl. She didn't notice me, but I wasn't willing to wait for that to happen and bolted.

"Rosella, wait up!" Sophia trotted after me. "Geez, what's gotten into you this time?"

"Nothing, just wanted to make sure we got this table." I looked around. We were practically on the other side of the cafeteria, and Caroline's table wasn't even visible from this spot.

"Alright." Sophia seated herself, and set her binder on the table with a paper bag. "I guess you saw her?"

"Yeah, but she can't see us here, so we can eat in peace." I unzipped my backpack as I took my seat, and pulled out my lunch container. It had a delicious salad with ranch dressing and chopped up pieces of carrots.

"Psh, who cares," Sophia muttered, as she retrieved a saran-wrapped sandwich and large bottle of water from her paper bag. "She's got money and fancy clothes and a wide vocabulary, but she doesn't have a good head on her shoulders like you." She pointed to me. "You, Rosella, are a good person, and she can't take that from you."

I ducked my head between my shoulders. "Good doesn't make me strong, Sophia…"

She rested a hand on my shoulder. "C'mon, don't be so hard on yourself."

"Soph, I'm not... I'm not brave like you are. I've always been... by myself."

"Ro, c'mon now, you've not been alone out here for two years now." Sophia gestured to herself. "Remember?"

I waved a hand at her. "Look at you, you don't have to carry a backpack full of books, or folders with tons of scribbled notes, because you have a good memory. You have a nice look, and you know your way around people, and there aren't any rumors burying you alive." I pounded my elbows into the table, my hands clutched at my head, as my eyes watered.

"Hey." Sophia scooted closer to me. "Hey, Rosella..." She rubbed a comforting hand against my back. "Ro, come on, don't cry."

"I'm not crying," I grumbled. "I just... I have a little something in my eye." I hastily drilled my knuckle into my wet eye. It ached in retaliation.

"Ro, I know it's hard," Sophia whispered gently. "Some days are good, many are bad, but I promise you, you're not alone. There are others that have personal issues too." She shrugged. "They may not relate to yours *per se*, but that doesn't mean you can't try finding others who understand you. I mean, you got me, and even though I don't relate to your particular set of problems, I understand you. At least, I hope I do."

"You do..." I rested my chin in my hands. "If I hadn't met you, I wouldn't be sitting here at all..."

"If I remember correctly, your father helped encourage your mother to let you follow me to school."

At those words, memories of me and Dad wearing Mom down resurfaced in my tired brain. "Though I'm sure Dad could've done it himself, he didn't want to do it behind her back..." I blew a huff between my lips. "I spotted you, one day, playing in the schoolyard, when he and I were on our way home from somewhere. I stared through the car window with big eyes, and saw you running around, laughing and cheering. If I'm not mistaken, that was 'recess'."

"Yes, it was," Sophia said, and chuckled. "It's cute that you remember."

"Yeah..." I wrung my hands together in my lap, a faint blush to my face. "That day when I saw you there, playing and laughing with the other kids, a drive of curiosity I never knew I'd had awakened inside of me. It was like a whole new world had opened its door to me, beckoning me toward it."

"Well, not to add salt to the wound, but you're not trying hard enough," Sophia stated, her words laced with disappointment. "All you've accomplished these last couple years is getting enrolled and claiming one friend."

Dread swarmed my heart, and I brushed aside another tear from my eye. "I know..."

"So, change it."

I hesitantly glanced at her. "How? How can I?"

Sophia's lips drew a hopeful smile. "I can help you figure that out. Like I said, I'm here for you when you need me." She reached over, and brushed a lock of my hair behind my ear. "I will always be there to help you up when you get knocked down. You're way too precious to lose, Rosella."

I rested my hands on the table. "I know you mean that, but I can't always have you protecting me."

She gently grasped them, and sighed. "Rosella, look at me."

My heart fluttered like a pair of dragonfly wings as I witnessed the fiery passion ablaze in her emerald eyes, and my cheeks grew hot. "S-Sophia..."

"Ro, I love you more than anyone. You are my best friend, and that makes you important to me." She squeezed my hands. "I have *always* got your back. Whatever you need, I'll do what I can to help. That will never change, but what should is your gloomy attitude."

I laughed. "It's easier said than done."

"Then do something about it, otherwise you may as well be beating a dead horse. Settling on 'good enough', with just one friend, hanging out at home... That isn't going to work anymore."

"Yeah..." I freed a hand to wipe my eyes and said, "Oh, I forgot to tell you. Mom's got a new story brewin'."

A look of intrigue flashed across her face. "Ooooooooh, you'll have to snag me a copy, I wanna read it sometime."

"I'll see what I can do," I said.

Sophia and I worked on our lunches in silence after that. We had roughly ten to fifteen minutes left, and we didn't want to waste any more time. I ended up finishing first, and after putting my lunch container away, I got up to use the bathroom.

"I'll be back in a minute," I said.

"Alright, have fun."

I chuckled at her comment. "Pfft, okay."

I hurried across the cafeteria and over to the girls' bathroom, where I slunk into the first stall to relieve myself. I fixed my jeans capris when I was finished, and turned to leave when the familiar clacking of heels echoed beyond the stall. My heart felt ready to leap up my throat, as they stalked into view at the five-inch gap between the door and floor.

"Hey, open up," Caroline's voice snapped, her sharp tone cutting like a knife through the air.

A whimper stifled in my throat, but I strangled it to silence.

"C'mon!"

Cautiously, my shoulders gripped by fear, I approached the door. "Wh-What do you want?"

"Open the damn door!" she barked.

"N-No," I stammered. "Not a chance. Go away."

"Ugh!"

I witnessed the hasty retreat of Caroline's heels and, against my better judgment, slowly undid the latch. I creaked open the door and peeked around it. I didn't see Caroline, so I deemed it safe, and breathed a sigh of relief.

I exited the stall, and started toward the sink to wash my hands, but then froze. Her clicking heels dominated the floor, as she slunk into view behind my reflected frame of fear, her glossy red lips curled in a menacing leer. I flinched with each step she claimed in my direction, her hands to her hips as she towered over me, and through the mirror, our eyes were locked.

"I wanna talk to you about your friend," she sneered.

I shook my head. "I-I am sorry... She can be a bit of a loudmouth, huh?" *That's right, Rosella. Drag her down with you...*

A ferocious snarl between her clenched teeth, Caroline growled. "Someone needs to put her in her place..."

I cowered beneath her burning glare. If looks could kill, I'd have already dropped dead.

She bowed her head slightly and, as if for show, a shadow cast over her face. "You looked like you wanted to make her shut up... Why didn't you? Huh, fatty?" A fleck of spit shot to my head, adding to the insult, but rather than let loose a weak sob I worried at my bottom lip.

She grabbed my wrists from behind and twisted them, forcing a cry to slip out of me. "You're such a weakling," she whispered, her breath grazing my ear. "Without protection, you're nothing."

"Caroline, please..." I begged. "That hurts!" The unnerving pain surged through my muscles, and settled deep into my bones, forcing me down to my knees.

"Fat pig... You better hope I don't get my hands on her." She clutched a scruff of my hair and yanked. "Ugh! You're so irritating!"

Searing pain scorched my scalp, and I hissed between my teeth, as I felt several strands of hair tear from my head. "Ngh... Ah!"

"Maybe I'll find someone to hog-tie her like an animal. Or better yet..." A bone-chilling smile sculpting her crimson lips, she hooked her glossy nails further into my hair. "Maybe I'll call up some buddies of mine to drag her sorry ass out to that forest and strip her naked, hang her by her ankles, and use her as their personal punching whore."

"P-Please! Stop!"

I clawed at her wrist in a feeble attempt to free myself with frantic hands, though they quickly retreated to my sides upon her piercing my head. A burning itch ignited at my scalp, and I grimaced at the faint trickling of what I assumed was blood. All the while, my arms hung limp at my sides, useless, helpless, like me.

"I bet they'd enjoy that... They can relish in her screams, maybe paint the trees with her blood..." Caroline's threat cut deep, emotional lacerations to my heart, her brown eyes lit with frightening truth. "How about that, huh?"

"Ngh..." I squeezed one eye shut, my teeth ground together.
Stop it!
Caroline growled in my ear. "God, she pisses me off!"
"C-Caroline," I whispered.
No!
Without warning Caroline shoved me to the side, right into the stall, and a pained grunt crept from my throat, as my neck jerked back and

forth from the impact. My body fell to the floor, my vision clouded in a haze, and my eyes rolled into my head, as my chin nuzzled the cold, hard surface.

No! Rosella!

Uh... Oh god... It hurts... My head... Endless waves of pain drowned my pulsating brain, and I thought for sure it'd implode.

Caroline spoke up again, but it was like I had cotton balls shoved in my ears.

I can't... make out what you're saying... You need... to speak... up...

Rosella, just hang on!

My head spinning, I forced my throbbing eyes shut, and focused on alleviating the sharp, nerve-busting ache behind them. I could barely hear the groan that emitted from inside me, as I wrapped my feeble arms around myself.

"... hell!? Ro! Ro!"

"Ugh... Soph..." was all I could muster.

"Rosella!"

The eruption in my skull worsened as a pair of arms jostled my shoulders.

"Jesus, what happened to you? I saw Caroline just now! She stormed outta here like a bat outta hell!"

I sensed my knees buckling as I was pulled upward. "Ugh... Sorry..." My hand aimlessly wandered just in front of my face. "Just... had a bit... of something... Where... Where is...?" My floundering hand managed to find my head, and my fingertips crept along the top to the back. Surprisingly, the painful lump wasn't sticky with blood.

"Rosella." Sophia snapped her fingers in my face, drawing my attention back to her.

"Caroline... Little scuffle..." I hesitantly tilted my neck, and my spine jolted from the sensitive ache rattling my skull. "Oh god... Ow..."

"Seems like more than a little scuffle..."

"Please... Don't." I put up a weak hand. "I'm not..." I winced. "I don't want more..."

"That bitch isn't getting away with this," Sophia growled. "Come on... Let's get you to the nurse's office, okay? She can check you out."

In a daze, I allowed Sophia to gently guide me out, my feet stumbling over each other as we went.

"Bitchell better keep her mouth shut if she don't want my cock shoved down her throat," an unknown male voice called out. "I'll put her in her place no problem."

I dumbly glanced around, and immediately regretted the action as my vision teetered. I about spun to the floor, but managed to clutch Sophia's shoulders, and pull myself up.

"Why don't you shove it in a meat grinder and shred a few ounces, Dale?" Sophia's words bit down like a rabid dog, clear ferocity in her tone.

"You wanna take me on!?" the dude, who I assumed was Dale, challenged with an edge of his own. "Come on, let's go Bitchell! Right here!"

"Oh, believe me, it's on!" Sophia dared. "Meet me in ten at the staircase, and we'll throw down. I'll kick your ass so hard I'll launch it five years back!"

"Bring it!"

My hands blindly clung to Sophia's tank top as I was abruptly jerked to the side.

"You hit like a puny twerp!" Sophia shouted. "That the best you can do?"

"Watch me!" her assailant roared.

"Come at me, see what happens!"

Suddenly, I was flung from Sophia, and my back hit the cold, hard wall. My spine crackled with sharp jolts of pain, and I slumped to the floor in a crumpled heap with my eyes closed.

"Ro! Shit! Get the hell off me, you bastard!"

I heard some grunting from Sophia, and then there was a sharp yelp from what I guessed was the guy she called Dale.

"Ah! F-Fuck..."

A crowd of hushed mumbling gathered around us, like the excited chattering of bats in a cavern, further provoking my already frayed nerves. All whispering amongst themselves, I didn't need my eyes to know the pointed fingers were there, all poised like rifles prepping shots.

Gossip as their ammunition, they opened fire, and bullet upon bullet of shame struck me, leaving my anxiety to bleed from my prattled mind.

"Get lost, all of you!" Sophia snapped. "God!"

"What the bloody hell is going on here!?"

My rattled spine quaked with fear at the booming voice of our principal.

"Alright, I wanna know what happened, and I wanna know right now!"

CHAPTER 3

I SCREWED UP, *BAD*. Once again, I let my temper get the best of me, only this time I thought I was going to be suspended. Before, I only ever got minor scoldings from Mr. Howley, the principal of our school. All the more reason why I didn't give a damn, as he reeled both mine and Dale's asses in for our scuffle. Unlike Dale, who was squirming in his seat beside me, I wasn't a coward when facing Mr. Howley. He might be good at intimidation, but it didn't work on me. I could easily take the man down if I wanted to.

I won't, I reminded myself. *I'm not like Caroline.*

"Does this *look* like a boxing gym to either one of you!?" Mr. Howley roared. "I mean, seriously! Both of you! This is unacceptable! Absolutely *horrendous!*"

I lowered my head as thoughts of Rosella sprung to mind. *She got badly hurt because I wasn't there. Why the hell did I let her go alone? God, what was I thinking...*

"You both are lucky I won't expel you right here and now," the principal went on.

I rolled my eyes. *Right, but you'll let Caroline get away with her shit.*

"Sh-She kicked me first!" Dale pathetically argued. "Why am I in trouble!?"

"You idiot! You know why!" I snapped.

Dale snarled in my direction. "Ya know, you're right! It's because of you, Bitchell!"

My temper reignited like a raw flare-up, and I glowered at him. "You listen here, chump! You were the one who came at me with a fist of fury!"

"You started it!" Dale snapped back. "Tellin' me to meet you under the stairs."

"Dale, you were the one throwing threats at Rosella and me! Talkin' smack about shovin' that worthless worm in your pants down our throats!"

"Enough! Both of you!"

His golden-brown eyes draining of color, Mr. Howley's anger-laced voice rang throughout the office, prompting both me and Dale jump in surprise. He slammed his hands on his desk, and it shook with abrupt force as a thin crack raced across the wood. Dale and I stared wide-eyed at the damage, shocked that the desk was still standing.

"Huh…" I mumbled. "Guess you're, uh, stronger than I thought…"

With a huff, the principal smeared his dark brown face. "I…I am putting both of you in detention," he whispered, and stared us both down with a threatening glare. "For two weeks. Got it?"

"I can live with that," I stated nonchalantly.

"Two weeks!? Come on!" Dale exclaimed. "I got a game comin' up! I can't afford…" He clamped his mouth shut as Mr. Howley's piercing grey eyes flashed silver in his direction.

"You are bloody lucky you're only getting two weeks of detention," Mr. Howley growled. "If I were in charge, you'd be in for a much worse punishment…"

As the principal uttered those words, his silver eyes fell on me, and I stared back with a challenging glare of my own. He might've had Dale by the balls, but I sure as hell wasn't giving in. I was a fighter compared to that moron.

A fool you are… Defying me all these years…

I rolled my eyes at the intrusion of my so-called master's voice. *You don't scare me. Get lost.*

Your time will come…

I groaned. "Look, can I go now?" I put my hands on my hips, and nodded to the dope next to me. "I don't care if you make Dale your fucking plaything, but I got places to be."

Mr. Howley cocked a brow at me, a vein pulsating at his temple. "And just where might that be, young lady?"

I crossed my arms over my chest. "The day I spill my guts about my business is the day you admit that Georgia Morse's hush money's been payin' your bills. Just because you're a Husk like the rest of us don't mean you get a free pass on society's guidelines. Unlike Georgia, who I'm sure got the beefy end of the stick, you're stuck managing the few of us here. Hell, I bet you wish the tables had been turned when you both demonstrated your abilities." I gave him a sly smirk. "Sorry, but super strength don't cut it for our precious lord, Ashen."

Mr. Howley's jaw twitched as his head looked ready to explode. The sight amused me.

I got up from my seat. "Whatever, I'm out. I'll be there for detention. At least I'm noble enough to serve my time, unlike this dickhead."

Dale's jaw dropped as he watched me exit the office, and I stuck my tongue out at him. Meanwhile, Mr. Howley's expression went blank, as he resumed speaking with Dale. Since I was out of earshot, I couldn't make out what they were saying, but I figured it was about Dale's behavior and nothing more.

Ashen had Georgia put Mr. Howley in charge of Dale, Caroline and me some time after they'd met, but that didn't stop me from continuing my act of defiance. I wouldn't do what Ashen wanted me to do. I wasn't like them...

Defective... Reject...

I ignored the irritating whispering in my head as I continued walking. *You can't control me. I'm my own person.*

Ever since birth, I was stuck under Ashen's close surveillance, just like the rest. The way it was explained to me, we were humans claimed at the start of life by whatever the hell this thing was. I was out of the loop, since I chose not to attend the many meetings held, opting instead to try my best at being normal.

It was hard, trying to keep a random vine from shooting out of my finger on accident, or causing a dead root to sprout from the ground. If the other kids I was around, the 'normal' kids, saw any of that shit, they'd have turned tail and ran for sure. But I kept my powers under-wraps, because I ignored them, and as the years passed on they seemed to have faded out of existence.

You are defective... You always have been...

I scoffed at my master's annoyance. I didn't care what Ashen thought of me. I made my choice, because I was in cha—

"!"

I stopped dead in my tracks, as my hands suddenly went clammy at my sides. My head teetered a little to the side, and I had to take a step forward to keep from falling backwards.

Oh god... My tongue feels like sandpaper... I scrunched my nose in disgust as I sought out the nearest water fountain. *Water, I need water.*

My stomach bunched in knots, the beads of sweat trickling down my forehead. I felt like I was gonna be sick unless I got some water, somewhere. Stumbling about the hall, on my frantic search, my heart ran rampant in my chest, as my tongue began to burn. It was so dry, and the roof of my mouth felt scaly. A scorching rash crawled up the walls of my throat, choking me. Water, I needed water, water to quench this ungodly thirst.

A wheeze of relief escaped my strained esophagus when I spotted a water fountain beside a row of lockers upon rounding the corner, and my desperate hands clung to it so tightly my knuckles turned white. I practically threw myself over the water fountain, clamped my mouth around the metal piece in desperation, and pressed my thumb hard against the button. Fresh, crisp water poured over my tongue, and quickly soothed its irritation.

God... Much better! I screwed my eyes shut, as I continued sucking in as much water as I could. *Haven't felt like that in a little while...*

Gradually, my stomach settled, the painful rash in my throat went away, and my mouth moistened up again. I hesitantly pulled myself away from the water fountain, and breathed a heavy sigh. I felt better again.

"Sophia?"

I peered over my shoulder, eyes wide. "P-Patricia!"

"Sweetie, are you okay?" she asked me.

I struggled for a response. "Y-Yeah... Fine."

Patricia rushed over to me. "Sophia, you look white as a sheet!"

I cocked my head with a frown. "I do?" *Crap, she can see it... Hopefully she's still dumb enough not to figure me out.*

Patricia rested the back of her hand to my forehead. "No fever..." She put her hands on her hips. "Still, come with me. You look like you need a minute to rest, and perhaps someone to talk to."

I gave a tired laugh. "I'm not getting out of this, am I?"

"I'm afraid not, dear. I'm far too good at my job."

Yeah, that's what I'm afraid of...

As far as I knew, Patricia had no idea what I really was, but as we meandered down the hall to the double staircase together, I worried about whether or not she debated on examining me closely. I wasn't afraid of going to her for help, though she seemed sharp as a whip, and the last thing I needed was to blow my cover of being a typical highschool student.

Thankfully, when we reached her office, she instead asked me how my day had been before the incident, and I confessed to her about the terrible exchanges between me and Caroline.

"That bad, huh?" she asked.

"Yeah, I totally blew it. I stressed Rosella out so damn bad, and I feel awful about it, but man I really wanted her to have it." I gave her a sheepish smile. "Glad I got off easy with two weeks of detention after kicking Dale."

She gave me a sly wink. "Doesn't hurt to have a little backup yourself."

I cocked my head. "Did you...?"

"I may have had a word with Mr. Howley before you were called in," Patricia said. "While you were sitting in the hall, awaiting your sentence."

I gave a curt laugh. "That's a good way to put it, actually."

Patricia nodded, as her grin fell into a frown. "And as much as I hate to disappoint you, Dale is going to be fine."

I snorted. "That's, uh, actually... yeah." Rather than let my mouth fly further, I decided to keep quiet. Not just because I'd already gotten myself into enough trouble today, but also to keep Dale's existence as a Husk a secret.

Patricia sighed as she rounded her desk. "Oh, Sophia..."

"Say, how is Rosella?" I asked abruptly, hoping to deter her attention from Dale. "Will she be okay? I've been thinking about her the whole time."

"She's on her way to the hospital. I did a quick checkup, and though I don't think she's terribly hurt, she needs a proper examination." Patricia eyed me curiously. "Sophia, you recall when we first met, right?"

"Yes, I remember," I said. "On the very first day of high school, Rosella threw up from anxiety, and I got to be her escort."

"And when you rounded the corner for the office, I heard Caroline say some..." A look of discomfort took hold of Patricia's face. "... undesirable things. I've heard things like that during my school years too, but goodness…"

"Apple doesn't fall far from the tree," I muttered. "Her aunt's no better. She's teaching her niece how to walk all over everyone." *And how to control them…*

Patricia wrung her hands together. "Okay, but you could just *ignore* her."

My jaw went stiff, and I ground my teeth together.

"Your mother told me that you're like Rosella's bodyguard." Patricia chuckled to herself, as she sorted through some papers on her desk. "She said that you were a tough nut to crack, and that deep within that thick, cold shell, there was something soft and warm. She's not wrong."

My eyes dropped to the floor. "Uh huh."

"Sophia, I've known your mother for quite some time, since we work in the same place together, and she's told me a lot about you. Truth be told, I enjoy her company."

I eyed her suspiciously. "Patricia, where are you going with this?" It wasn't that I didn't want to hear what she had to say, but because she mentioned my mother, I was feeling a little apprehensive.

Patricia seated herself at her desk, and gave me a sympathetic look. "Grace told me how hard you work to be the best you can be. You're one of the 'straight-A students with incredible talent.' You could be looking at Harvard University in the future. And yet, you always look for trouble. Why is that?"

I breathed a sigh of relief. *Oh good, she doesn't know.* But then another thought crossed my mind. *Except now I have to deal with the shit Mom's drilled into her head…*

"Sophia?"

I shrugged. "I don't let people boss me around. If someone comes at my throat, I go for their legs. Can't reach my throat if they're only a couple feet tall."

Patricia laughed. "Eh, that sounds like you."

"What can I say," I said. "Stubborn as a bull, that's how I roll."

"This is the first time I've heard you say that line, and I'm sure it won't be the last."

"Little mantra I tell myself sometimes," I said, with a smirk.

Patricia interlocked her fingers, her elbows propped on her desk. "I guess you don't want to be put in a box then, huh? You want to show people you're not just some 'egghead', right?"

"It's not really that," I told her. "I just..." I crossed my arms over my chest. "I don't know. I just... Eh."

"Can't really explain it?"

I shook my head. "Like I've said before, I don't like being pushed around, and I most *certainly* don't like when Rosella gets picked on. She is the sweetest, kindest person I've known for years, and I'll be honest, I want to be more like her. But at the same time, I want to be tough. If I don't show some form of dominance, then people are gonna think I'm a pushover, which is what Rosella is."

I felt terrible for saying that, but it was the truth. Rosella was used to being by herself or with her parents. She never took the time to go out and explore, even though her dad encouraged it, and somewhat her mom even though she was the one at fault for Rosella's timid nature. I couldn't blame Chloe for wanting to shelter her. She wanted to protect her, especially since Rosella was... special.

I knew deep down what Rosella was, but she didn't know, and it wasn't like I could tell her. I couldn't even admit what I truly was, and yet, somehow we were the best of friends who, in her eyes, told each other everything.

But that's a lie, I thought to myself. *Because I'm keeping things from her...*

"Sophia?" Patricia seemed to be awaiting my response.

"You never judged her outright, did you?" I asked. "Just asking, out of curiosity."

"Well, no," Patricia said. "I am aware her great-grandmother lives out in the forest, which is deemed a dangerous place, and I know of the silly rumors revolving around her, but I know Rosella has nothing to do with that." She wrung her aged hands together. "Sometimes, you hear strange noises, and a few times people have gone missing, but I've never met or seen her great-grandmother, and with the way I heard Rosella talk about her the first day of school, she must be a really nice person."

"Rosella's never told me how or why she lives there," I said. "And I've never seen or met her either."

"As far as I know, dear, no one has. At least, no one outside of the Bloom family's circle."

"No one except for Benjamin Walsh, the top-notch explorer who literally dropped everything in order to settle down with the mysterious Chloe Bloom." I scoffed at my wording, having taken it straight out of a magazine.

Patricia nodded. "I followed Benjamin's articles closely, and like everyone else, I was surprised at his sudden decision to abandon his travels in favor of a smaller job."

I gave a huff. "Patricia... Why do people care so much about stuff Rosella's family has done? There was literally no harm done. The guy found this woman, fell in love with her, and settled down. So what if her family is secretive? So what if this guy just dropped everything? So what if he was way older than her mother? Does it really matter that much?"

"For some, it does," Patricia said. "They take it personally, like you with Caroline when she goes after Rosella."

I balled my hands into fists at my sides. "That's so not the same! My reasoning is because I want Rosella to know I'm there for her, to protect her when her mother can't. And Caroline? My god, she's garnered so much attention I am *baffled* at the fact that she *still* hasn't been expelled."

Patricia gave a tired sigh. "I think the most recent case was a girl whose head she'd threatened to pour pig's blood over because of some personal affair between them."

"Yes!" I slapped at my sides in irritation. "The girl made out with a boy named Marcus Thompson, and because of that, Caroline threatened to turn the girl into Stephen King's *Carrie* for god's sake! And then, here's the kicker!" I gestured the air with both index fingers. "Caroline literally paid, *paid,* two guys to stuff two rat corpses into this girl's bra, and then *lock her* in her friend's locker! If the girl's friend hadn't forgotten something, I'm telling you, she would've been trapped there all damn day, because no one would've noticed."

Patricia nodded several times. "Yes, yes, I remember it all."

I furiously tapped the toe of my shoe to the floor. "So?"

The nurse hesitantly tugged at the collar of her uniform. "E-Even then, nothing happened. And believe me, I-I tried to tell them to do something, but…" Her green eyes darted to their corners. "I don't know how to explain it, dear. I mean…"

I was about to continue, but then clamped my mouth shut upon realizing how useless my tangent was. Caroline was very good at the power she'd been gifted, so of course nothing would be done about it. And here I was, mindlessly raging to a poor, confused woman who had absolutely no idea what the hell was going on behind the scenes.

Like Rosella, I thought. *She has no clue either…*

"There really is no point in being positive," Patricia mumbled after a minute of silence passed. She gazed down at the papers atop her desk, her eyes devoid of emotion. "If you really want to know what I think, I believe this entire town is cursed."

Amidst the shock that struck me, I feigned confusion at her words. "What… What do you mean?"

"I've seen things going on that you would think would raise a few eyebrows," the nurse continued. "And yet, no one does anything. They just pin the blame on either the forest or the Bloom family, and leave it at that, even that Morse girl's behavior."

A chill coursed down my spine at her words, but I kept a straight face.

"Sophia, I may have only known you for a little while, but, out of everyone here…" Patricia raised her head, and our eyes met. "You are the most honest of them all. You are that little piece of resistance that defies this town's regime, whatever that is."

My heart sank. "Patricia, I…"

Her expression suddenly went blank, and when I heard the clearing of Mr. Howley's throat behind me, I knew that was why.

"Sophia, you should be attending your next class," Mr. Howley told me. His tone was quite stern, almost threatening.

Patricia nodded. "You'd better hop to, missy."

"Right." I peered over my shoulder as I slipped past Mr. Howley. "Um, thanks Patricia, for checking up on me. I'll try to talk to you again soon."

I left Patricia alone with Mr. Howley, who abruptly shut the door behind him, as soon as I'd stepped out. I didn't want to leave her alone. I wanted to stay with her, to stand by her like I did with Rosella.

She's more right than she realizes, I thought to myself. *This town, that forest… Caroline's behavior toward Rosella…* I glanced over my shoulder, and sighed. "Patricia will be fine," I told myself. *He won't hurt her... Everything's okay.*

But I wasn't. Though I knew Patricia definitely was, I spent the rest of my day worrying about Rosella. Since I had detention, I couldn't call her because students weren't allowed to use their phones in detention, nor could I have my mom drive me to her house because, well, *I had detention.* So, I got to spend an hour in a quiet ass room, with a few other people, Dale included, doing absolutely nothing.

Seething with rage, Dale and I never locked eyes with each other, so as to avoid the temptation of ripping each other to shreds, especially with witnesses around. However, if we were alone, I'd have surely whooped him in minutes, because I didn't need the help of our bullshit master, unlike that pathetic weasel.

I shot out of my chair, binder in hand, when the damn bell finally rang, and I made a beeline for the stairs leading up to the second floor. I wanted to be as far from Dale as possible, lest I wanted to get myself in more trouble.

Just as I rounded the corner at the top of the steps, I spotted a certain someone standing several feet away. My sneakers screeched to a halt upon the glossy tiling, a fresh scowl on my face.

"What do you want?" I snapped.

Caroline stood with a blank expression on her face, her hand on her hip.

"Look, I got places to be." I marched forward, but then stumbled back as her hand shoved me in the chest.

A menacing shadow fell over Caroline's face, her glaring eyes narrowed. "I know what you're doing," she uttered in a low, sharp tone. "You think you're her shield, just like her guard dog."

I mirrored Caroline's expression. "'Course I do. It's the only way to keep her safe from you."

She uttered a sharp laugh. "Oh, really? A thin, scrawny twig of a weakling like you..." She jabbed a harsh finger into my chest with each word as her curved lips spread apart, revealing her unnaturally white teeth. "I wonder how long it'll take for you crack when our master Ashen comes for you."

Like before, I stood my ground with narrowed eyes. "At least I'm not pimping myself out."

A lustrous giggle slipped from the red head's wicked grin. "I give the boys what they want, and they give me what I want..." Her brown eyes flickered to silver, then back to brown again. "And that's *power*. I enjoy watching them bask in their euphoria, when they're most vulnerable, so that when I come down on them, they're forced to bow before me."

I frowned at this. "You give them what they want, and you like it?"

"Please, I could care less about their feelings or needs. They're nothing but tools." She placed her hands to her chest, and slowly slid them down her sides. "All I care about is satisfaction for myself, and with a body, mind, and power like mine, I can get whatever I want."

"So even though they're living beings with emotions, you don't care?" I argued, despite already knowing the answer. By this point, I was tired and running out of good snappy comebacks.

"Don't you wish you could control people? I bet you do." A sinister gleam sparked in her brown eye as it drained of color again. "Like with Dale, for instance. You lured him in with his enjoyment of taunting you, and then when you cracked down on him, you felt powerful..."

"That idiot deserved to be put in his place," I muttered. "I was fucking tired."

Caroline took another step toward me and, slowly, raised a hand to my throat. "Right, but again, you can't tell me it didn't make you feel good."

I resisted a flinch as she stroked her fingers over my skin, and squared my jaw in resistance. "Except I didn't resort to Ashen's magic, because I don't need it. It's nothing but poison in our veins." *As tempting as it is to try using it on your prissy ass...* But I couldn't, because I resisted Ashen's influence for years.

"That why you're the weakest link, right?"

I cocked a brow. *Damn bitch must've read my expression, since she can't read minds.*

Caroline cocked her head, as her nail traced an invisible line across my throat. "Ya know, I could easily take you out with one hand tied behind my back..."

"You don't scare me," I snapped. "You might have the rest of this damn school under your wicked spell, but it doesn't work on me." A smirk broke across my face. "And it seems Patricia's resistant too. She knows something's up, told me so herself."

Caroline's nails traced the slight dip into my collarbone. "Who needs her anyway? The boys are way more fun, and easy, to manipulate. They give me so much for so little, unlike her. All it takes is a little spark, and then they're putty in my hands." She let loose another giggle. "My auntie always said that the rush was her favorite part, and since we're not human, there's no harm in it."

I recoiled in disgust, and stormed around her. "You're vile, you know that?"

"Say what you will," Caroline called after me. "Deep within the both of us are power-hungry beasts waiting to be awakened. We use different approaches, but in the end, we're the same."

I glared over my shoulder. "No, you're just a toxic leech feeding off of people's emotions, and I'm a person with immense self-respect."

Caroline's burning scowl failed to scorch my bravery as I gave her a defiant smile. "Just you wait, Mitchell. Your time is coming, and I will take you down. That cowardly weed is nothing without you, and once you're gone, I can bat her around all I want."

A sneer replaced my triumphant expression, as I balled my hands into fists and looked away from her. "You like to play with people's emotions for your own pleasure, and use them for your sick and twisted needs. That makes you as gross as Ashen and Georgia." I stomped a sneaker on the first step. "They won't win, and she will take back what's hers. As for you, I sure as hell hope you stop and think about your actions. You're letting yourself go down a dark path. You don't care one bit about yourself."

"Control is what I like best," Caroline stated. "Like Auntie said, you learn through experience, and I have."

"You don't get it!" I whirled around to face her from my spot on the step. "You're the one who's being controlled! They're *using* you!"

Caroline's eyes narrowed. "Auntie would never use me. She's been nothing but good to me." She raised her hands and clenched them. "She taught me, Mitchell, how to channel my powers, and to use them to my greatest advantage. With this gift, we can make this entire town bow at our feet."

"I was talking about Ashen, but I wouldn't put it past Georgia," I snapped.

She lowered her fists to her sides, and squared her shoulders, that vicious scowl locked on me. "You're a fool for not realizing your potential, for denying your powers. But it's fine. Makes it easier on me."

I shook my head. *She has no idea what she's doing to herself, and she doesn't care.* I turned on my heel and continued up the stairs in silence.

"You will see, Mitchell!" Caroline shouted. "You will regret running away from your position!"

Caroline's words haunted my mind the rest of the way to the art room. I was nothing like her, yet I was the same as her. But I'd fought against our master's curse for years. Caroline may have embraced it, but not me. I wasn't going down like Rosella's father, or anyone else.

Benjamin fought off Ashen's curse for as long as he could, I thought to myself. *He was a brave soul for a regular human, and as long as I'm here, I'll keep fighting for his daughter.*

I tucked away my thoughts as I entered the art room, where I found my mother packing away some boxes. My chest tightened as my eyes fell upon the copy of Chloe's book on her desk, but I pretended to ignore it. Her obsession with Rosella's mother was peculiar since they barely talked, but rather than bring up the sore subject myself, I let my mother suffer in silence.

"Hey Mom," I said, "sorry for being so late."

She gave me a disapproving look. "Sophia, you wanna explain to me why you got detention? Mr. Howley and Patricia both said that you kicked a guy today, and before that you got into it with Caroline. Again."

I groaned. "Mom, I had to do something, Rosella—"

"Sophia Cheyenne Mitchell," my mother roared, "how many times are we going to have this talk!?"

I bowed my head. I knew this was coming. "I'm sorry, Mom... I'm not leaving Rosella. She's my best friend, and I love her."

"Sophia, you don't understand."

"No! You don't understand!" I exclaimed. I threw my head back up, and my emerald eyes sparked with rage. "Rosella needs protection,

Mom! I can give her that! I know you said you didn't want me around her because of the danger involved, but I don't care anymore! I can't just sit here! She needs me!" A tinge of silver warped my vision, and I took a breath. Quickly, it returned to normal.

My mother's jaw clenched, like she was biting back a response.

"I will protect her," I said, my sharp voice barely above a whisper. "No matter what it takes, I won't let anyone hurt her." I turned on the toe of my shoe. "Now, if you don't mind, I need a ride home, unless you plan on making me walk."

"Now, why would I do that?" she countered.

"Because you and I have been at odds lately, and unlike Rosella, I can take care of myself."

"Sophia, I just want to protect you. Don't you understand that?"

I breathed a sigh to calm my frayed nerves. "I do, but I'm not worried about me. I'm worried about her." I peered over my shoulder. "I've stuck by her side all this time, and I'm not about to abandon her now."

CHAPTER 4

Chloe

TODAY HAD BEEN ONE of the most exhausting days of my life. Rosella was already anxious, and then got attacked at school, had to take a trip to the hospital. The doctor said she'd be fine, but my poor baby's neck was sore, and she had a concussion.

I sat at the kitchen table, my eyes settled on the warm mug of coffee in my hands, a small bag of medicinal powder beside them.

"Is Rosella really going to be okay?" a small voice asked.

I looked up to see Susan, my assistant at the library. "She will be fine." I eyed the bag of medicinal powder. "Just don't tell anyone about Mom's herbs."

Susan came over and sat next to me, a big ball of fur in their arms. "I, uh, stopped by your house today because I forgot my laptop here, but then Pooter came out, and I couldn't just leave him." They stroked a hand over his long, silver fur. The cat meowed in response.

"I appreciate that." I rubbed a hand into my eye. "God, Susan... That brat really took it too far."

"I know you're mad," Susan said. "Really, I get it. But you need to be more careful. You already almost got yourself in a mess once before."

I gave a huff. "For the last time, I didn't touch her. I simply went to speak with Georgia like an adult."

"But Rosella told me you—"

"I didn't touch her," I grumbled.

Susan shied away at the harsh tone in my voice as they brushed a lock of their short brown hair behind their ear. "Rosella was only talking to me because she trusts me... Please don't be mad."

I gave them an apologetic look. "I'm sorry. I didn't mean to snap at you. I'm just... a little stressed."

"You still haven't gotten over that incident Georgia pulled," Susan mumbled, "have you?"

"She smeared both mine and Mom's names in the tabloids as a means of revenge," I pointed out, "which played both positively and negatively into my career."

Susan cocked their head. "How so?"

I gave a tired sigh. "Lots of people came out to support me because they liked my work, which prompted a boost in sales. Then I got the haters, who either tossed my books into a fire or gave them away. For those who gave their copies away, that perked the interest of others who decided to share my work. People who bought my books got yelled at for supporting someone who lots said was terrible, but they didn't care and fought back, and well..."

"It became an endless cycle that is still continuing."

I shifted uncomfortably in my seat. "I got the sharp end of the knife in the heart, because I'm Chloe Bloom, the person who's secretly hiding a cult witch, and is now making money off of her late husband's death."

A veil of silence fell over Susan and I at those words, and as Susan mindlessly ran their hands through Pooter's long fur as he sat atop their lap, I found myself meandering through one of the many gut-wrenching experiences haunting my mind once again. Ever since I was a little girl, I'd had an active imagination, always in search of something new to discover, and long after I'd settled outside the forest, I revealed myself as the first ever writer to be based just beyond the town of Hollow, as well as the lucky one who got to work closely with Benjamin Walsh, the Exploring Writer.

His vast knowledge of exploration fed my starving creativity just what it needed, and helped me craft my first ever published story just before he died, a dark fantasy/horror novel about a cursed forest, and a group of inhabitants' souls trapped inside. Though it took years to make, because of him, I honed my love of writing into a respectable craft, and I loved it. I had something that was mine, and not directly tied to the forest. Though, when I openly admitted it being my inspiration, people took it that way.

Deep down, I knew that I would always be connected to that place. It was where I was born and raised, up until I was eighteen, when Benjamin and I married and got a place of our own. Even though I considered it home, I came to loathe the trees, seeing it only as a prison. And then I came to hate them upon discovering the evil that not even Rosella knows of...

She can't ever find out, because then... she'll want to go back, I thought to myself. *I can't let her go. I don't want her to. She's my only child...*

"F-Forgive me for asking this, but when exactly did the 'cult' rumor start again?"

Dread settled like dead weight in the pit of my stomach as Susan's voice tore me from my thoughts, and I felt the blood drain from my face. "When Georgia revealed her so-called 'evidence' to the world, a bunch of expertly-crafted pictures made to look like actual photos in false connection with both the shoemaker and Sarah Mitchell's disappearances, after people found out that Rosella went sneaking off that one night when..." I sucked in a sharp breath, a lingering sob at the edge of my wavering lips. "No one even knew of Rosella's existence until that dreadful event happened, and I honestly don't even know *how* they found out about that, because no one was there except for Ben and Fenris."

"Hey, it's okay." Susan reached over to grasp my sweaty fist as it quivered upon the table. "Chloe..."

I pointed toward the glass door leading out to the backyard with my free hand. "Out there, in the trees, gossip doesn't exist. Money doesn't exist. It's just you and the wildlife. That's the kind of life Rosella wants, the kind of life I used to have..."

"But that isn't the only thing that exists out there..." Susan's hazel gaze wandered to the glass door as well. "Because, what happened to Ben..."

A chill ruptured my spine, and I swallowed the lump that rose in my throat. Too much had been said already. I just wanted this to end. I wanted to sleep.

"Chloe?"

I hastily cleared my throat. "It's getting late, Susan. You should get home. I don't feel comfortable with you this close after dark."

"Right, right." Taking the hint, Susan immediately set Pooter on the kitchen floor and got up from their seat. "I... I really should get going."

I looked to them with concern. "You'll call me when you get there, right?"

"Of course, always!" They smoothed out their dress, then smiled at me. "If you need anything, just give me a holler. I'll do my best to assist you."

"Thanks Susan, I appreciate that."

They paused at the kitchen doorway, their back to me. "Chloe…"

"Yes?"

They peered over their shoulder. "Today… Do you think those events happened for a reason?"

I shrugged. "If you mean Caroline, then yes."

Susan nervously squeezed their shoulder. "So, you've got that sneaking suspicion too…"

I wanted to deny Susan's guess, but it was difficult. Whether Georgia was a Husk, I couldn't be sure. Anytime I tried to think her over, my mind became hazy. But Caroline was different. I could easily piece together my suspicions of her, despite the same lingering fog that threatened to cloud my mind, though I had no proof to confirm my suspicions.

And that's even harder to figure out, I thought. *What is it that makes a person a Husk? Fenris told me that they were people like me, except they could use dark magic…*

"Rosella still doesn't have a clue, does she?"

I flinched at Susan's bold, interrupting question. "N-No… She… She doesn't."

"Chloe…"

"Before you say anything more, nothing will happen to her," I stated, with a rather abrasive tone. "She will stay how she is, right by my side. And once she graduates from Hollow High, I can begin preparations to move her."

"Wait, you can't mean…" They whirled around on me with a baffled look. "Chloe…"

"I have a few years to look for a place that's not too far away," I said. "Mom and Fenris will learn to understand."

Susan looked as though they wanted to argue it further, but they knew better, and instead turned their back to me again. "Chloe…"

"Yes?"

They bowed their head. "I don't agree with this method. It's not fair, it's stupid, and you know it."

I looked away from them, and bit my tongue to avoid saying something I'd regret.

"Even if you take her away from here, there's no guarantee that she'll be perfectly safe. Think about what happened with Adrienne, and that was *outside* the trees."

"Susan." I uttered their name with a sharp edge to my voice. "Leave."

They gave a sigh. "I'll see you tomorrow."

I continued sipping on my lukewarm coffee, as Susan left the house without another word. When I heard them close the front door behind them, I set down the mug and smeared a hand across my wet eyes, then got up and went to the living room. I meandered through the darkness to the wall of photos, where I found myself staring at one in particular. It was a shot of me and Ben together in our wedding attire. We were so happy in this photo, so excited to live our lives together.

"You gave up so much for me," I said. "You were a successful writer touring the world. It was your dream to explore every inch of it, and you gave up your lifetime career for some measly journalist work that, though an excellent paying job, detailed only a *fraction* of your fascinating experiences, all so you could stay close to me. And you didn't even know me that long..."

I don't know what it is about you, Chloe. I just can't leave you behind. I'm afraid that if I do, I won't ever see you again. I won't ever find anyone like you either, because I don't want anyone like you. I want you, and you alone. That's why I'm choosing to stay, so I can be beside you. I love you, Chloe.

"To think that if I hadn't gone against Mom's request to stay within the trees, away from society... I would never have met you."

Seeking independence at sixteen, I went against Mom's request to stay within the trees. I'd grown bored of the same old scenery, and wanted something new and refreshing to explore, despite her warnings that there was an entirely different world I wasn't prepared for on the other side of the trees, that I would be mistaken as someone I'm not...

And she was right. That night I snuck out after she'd gone to bed, it was frightening, wandering into town without a clear sense of direction. I'd never experienced the horrific sounds of honking cars or bright lights shining in my face before, and there were so many people... pointing and staring at me... claiming that I looked like...

It's her! Isn't it? That same battered girl who was running through the streets, screaming.

The same girl who darted into the forest! Just like the shoemaker's wife...

One of Mom's biggest concerns was that I'd wind up like Adrienne, that I'd run into the wrong stranger. And based upon how I was treated, I expected that to happen, so I turned around to flee the scene... But then I bumped into the arms of a kind soul, and as he wrapped me in his jacket out of courtesy, I felt a warm seed of security sprout deep within my heart that grew over the night we spent together.

He was gentle with me, as he asked if there was anyone he could call to come get me. Unsure of how to answer, I told him no, and that I was a visitor from out of town, which was basically true. However, he knew there was more to the story, and offered to take me back to his hotel room with him in order to get away from all the excitement around us. I said yes, even though, in the back of my mind, my mother was screaming my name and begging me to come home.

It was foolish of me to follow this random stranger back to his hotel room. He could've forced himself on me, just like what happened with Adrienne. But he didn't do that. He kept his word, and it was that night I learned he was an honest man with a big heart.

My name is Benjamin Walsh. You may or may not have heard of me, but they call me "the Exploring Writer". I take tours around the world, detailing my experiences, with lots of photos as proof. I've discovered sights many are too afraid to explore, having gone deep-sea diving in the coldest of artic waters, trekked the hottest fields of sand. Hell, I've even walked across hot coals just for fun. I've seen it all. But what about you? I know of this town's history, and was even warned to avoid it, but I couldn't turn myself away from the famed 'evil forest'. I had to see for myself what it was like... and based upon that look on your face, I'm guessing you're from there. So tell me, who are you, and what is your connection to that forest?

"Sharp as a whip, just like Mom.... You could easily read just about anyone. But you never snooped without good reason..." I uttered a pained whimper. "Why couldn't I read you equally well? You said it right to my face, and I still didn't think to act..."

Chloe... I can't keep doing this. I'm just sitting here, rotting away. I... I don't want Rosella to see me like this, but I don't want to keep hiding from her either. She thinks I'm pushing her away. I love you both, and I hope that someday you'll forgive me for this.

I made sure to look either down at the floor or at one of the walls, as I traversed the downstairs hallway. Otherwise, I would've peered at his office door, the place where I found him slouched in his chair the following morning after the last night we spoke. It was closed when I awoke, and when he didn't answer as I called out to him, I knew that something was wrong. And when I opened the door, I held back a scream so as not to alarm Rosella...

I kept her upstairs as the paramedics examined Ben's body. They ruled it a suicide by overdose, because it was, though they pondered why his corpse looked oddly skeletal. The shadows under his eyes were so dark, they appeared sunken into his skull, and his skin was dry and crinkly. I did the best I could to lie, and said that it must've been some underlying condition he had that I didn't know about. But I did know. It was Ashen's curse, only I couldn't tell them...

The buzzing of my phone suddenly caught my attention, and I pulled it out of my pocket to answer. "Hello?"

"Hello? Chloe? Are you there?"

My eyebrows rose. "Mom? What's wrong? You never call past nine at night, unless it's an emergency..."

"Chloe," Mom answered on the other end, "how is Rosella doing? You left a message for me asking if you had the right medicinal powder, the one for headaches and sore muscles? I wanted to tell you that you did, so long as it was the white powder."

"Oh, yeah, yeah, sorry. I called while she was being checked out. She has a small concussion, case of whiplash I think, and... something else. God." I brushed a hand through my hair. "Caroline just thrust her into the bathroom stall. Surprisingly, she only has bruises, and a few cuts to her scalp, but I guess that's because of..." I refused to finish my sentence. I didn't want to think about that.

"That powder I gave you should take care of things," Mom continued on anyway. "Just keep her home for a few days because that stuff will make her drowsy. If she winds up sleeping the whole day, no need to worry."

"I know," I said. "I made sure she ate something before she took it. I anticipate she'll awaken probably sometime around noon, or a little later tomorrow, but then go back to sleep."

"Sounds about right. If she's feeling better by Friday, then hopefully you'll make it by Sunday. Even a week's time feels like forever."

"I know," I said. "Oh, and, uh... Is Fenris going to be there this time? It's been a little while."

Mom sighed. "I know. It's been two years..."

I nodded slowly, a quiet sob sealed behind my lips.

"I still see him all the time, but he always makes himself scarce around you two. He's a lot like Benjamin, always wanting to hide his pain."

"Ben is the reason why he's hiding, isn't it?"

Silence lingered for several seconds on the other end of the call, and then there was another sigh. "I will see what I can do, Chloe. I can't force the issue, but I will do my best to help him come around."

"Mom..." My voice quivered uncontrollably. "I-I... I am really worried about Rosella. Caroline really hurt her today."

"We'll talk about that more when you get here Sunday," she said. "If you stop by, that is. And if not this Sunday, then the following. For now, please don't do anything rash."

"Okay, I will hopefully see you then."

"Alright, goodnight dear."

I hung up with her, set the phone down on the table, and headed for the stairs. I wanted to check on Rosella to see how she was doing, and to my relief she was sound asleep in bed. I left her be, and headed back to my room. I was exhausted from today, and sleep was exactly what I needed.

Chloe, promise me you won't give up. You'll keep fighting alongside her.

Ben's fragile plea echoed in my mind, as I doubled over from the wave of nausea washing over me, and braced myself for the vomiting. When nothing happened, I cautiously rose back up again.

Please, don't let her wilt in the darkness... Keep her safe.

A stray tear grazed down the side of my face. "I promise, Ben. Just... promise you'll forgive me too, someday."

Using my knowledge of his detailed experiences, I knew of a few safe places far from here. It was just a matter of choosing. I still had a few years to go, which was more than enough time. Mom and Fenris would come to understand...

CHAPTER 5

Rosella

I SPENT MOST OF the next few days asleep, having only woken up a couple times a day to use the bathroom and sip some water. In the beginning, even opening my eyes was a challenge. It was like someone had glued them shut. My head also throbbed, a lot, and my legs were so heavy that it felt like I was wading through a thick body of watered-down glue.

Thankfully, the discomfort did not linger, and I smiled to myself as I sat up that Friday, knowing Great Granny Felan's remedy had done the trick. My bruised wrists had healed, and the pain of moving around was gone.

"Hey, you awake?"

I looked over to see Mom standing in the doorway, Pooter in her arms.

"You were out a lot of the time," she said.

I yawned, and looked to my bay window. "What time is it? Mid-morning?"

"Almost eleven," Mom said. "More like late morning, early afternoon."

"I see." I carefully slipped out of bed. As I expected, I felt totally fine, though my legs were wobbly from lack of use.

"You feel like eating something?" she offered.

"I think so," I said. "Just gonna stretch a bit more." I again threw my arms high above my head, then bent over. "Aaaaaah... There we go, all good."

Mom set Pooter down, and he rushed over to rub against my legs.

"Hey buddy." I kneeled down to pet him. "Guess you were worried, huh?"

The Maine Coon blinked his bright blue eyes at me, and gave a soft meow.

I laughed. "Yeah, I missed you too." I glanced over my shoulder at my mother. "I think I'm gonna take a quick shower, then meet you downstairs. Even though I didn't move around much, I did sweat a little. Plus, it's been a few days..."

"Alright, sounds good." She turned on her heel. "See you in a bit."

Pooter followed Mom downstairs, while I gathered together a fresh set of clothes and went to the bathroom. It felt nice having a steady cascade of slightly steaming water rain over my weary joints and down my back, and for the first few minutes, I relished in it, before squeezing a generous pool of shampoo into my palm.

I took my time massaging every inch of my scalp with soapy fingers, my head just out of reach of the water, but not my back. When I was finished, I made quick work of gently smoothing my hair back as I washed it clean of the shampoo, then set to lathering up my curvy body.

I came out of the shower feeling refreshed, having shed a thin layer of sweat and fatigue, a cloud of steam misting around me. I patted myself dry with the towel, slipped on the clothing I'd picked, then combed my hair. I found Pooter seated in the square gap in the wall next to the entrance of the kitchen when I came downstairs, and I beamed at him.

"Do you think living life as a cat is easy?" I asked, as I settled at the table.

"I don't know, maybe." Mom grabbed two slices of bread, and slipped them into the toaster. "How was your shower?"

"Very good," I said. "Took my time with it, enjoyed it."

"Good!" She peered over her shoulder. "I figured you were gonna be a bit, so I made myself some coffee. Once I heard you hit the stairs, I got out the bread."

"Yeah..." I observed our cat from a distance. "Hmm..."

"Something on your mind?" Mom asked.

I mindlessly waved a hand. "Nah, just wandering thoughts."

Mom shook her head. "I know what you're thinking. If you were a cat, you wouldn't have to put up with anything."

I turned to her with a shy grin. "Yeah, I guess so. It just seems so nice, lazing around all day, without a care in the world."

A nervous look crossed her face, her eyes darting to Pooter. "I'm sure it is. But we aren't cats. We're humans, and we must coexist with the rest."

I gave a tired nod. "Yep."

Mom wrung her hands together, as her concerned gaze settled on me. "Rosella, are you okay? Tuesday was..." She went silent at the sight of my raised hand.

"I am okay," I said. "I mean, it was upsetting, but at least I'm okay."

I hadn't had time to really think about what happened. I went from standing in front of the sink to being slammed against the bathroom stall. And now, I was here at home, having lost a few days to sleep. So, how could I be okay? Physically, I seemed fine, as Great Granny Felan's powder worked. But mentally? I had no idea.

"I think I'm okay," I said again. "Though, a little confused... Not sure if I'm scared, or sad, or even angry. I mean, at the time, I was definitely scared. But now, I think I'm just confused." I folded my arms, and rested my chin atop them. "I don't know. I don't really want to think about it. I just wanna have a nice day with you, Sophia too if possible."

Mom opened her mouth to say something, but was interrupted by the toaster. She pulled a plate down from a cabinet, plucked the toast, and placed the pieces on a plate before handing it to me.

"Thank you so much," I said, and gingerly took a bite. "Mmm, so good. Feels like I haven't eaten in years."

Mom chuckled lightly. "Well, you certainly slept a while, so I can understand why."

"Hey, Chloe? You here?"

My mother and I both looked toward the entrance to the kitchen. A head popped around the corner, and to my surprise, it was Sophia.

"My mom just dropped me off, and is heading back to school now. She'll pick me up later." Sophia glanced my way. "Hey Ro, been a while."

"Soph!" I got up from the table, and went over to hug her. "I'm so glad to see you!"

"Glad to see you too." She gently squeezed me. "Oh, I missed you so much."

I rested my chin atop her shoulder. "What happened to you Tuesday? After what went down between me and..."

Sophia pulled away from me with a sheepish look. "Got detention for two weeks for kicking Dale, thanks to Patricia going up to bat for me. She'd persuaded Mr. Howley to lower my sentencing."

"How come you're here, then?" I asked. "Today is Friday."

"Teacher work day." She gave a sly wink. "Figured I'd take the day off to spend time here with your mom."

"She's been wanting to read some of my stuff," Mom said, as she came over to us. "I told her it was okay."

"That's cool," I said.

"Yeah." Sophia threw her arms over her head. "Too bad we can't go out to the mall. It's pretty nice out today."

I made a pouty face. "I wanna go to the mall."

"Well, maybe after you spend a little more time recovering, we can go," Sophia said. "For now, you need to stay home and rest."

I looked over to Mom. "Do I have to wait? I've been cooped up in here for a few days now. I'm itching to stretch my legs." I bent my knees to demonstrate.

"Sweetheart, you just woke up," Mom argued. "And you stretched upstairs."

"I know," I said, "but I really want to go out."

Sophia cocked a brow. "You know you're still around people, right?"

I sighed. "Yes, but at least I'm in a bigger space, and I have plenty of things to distract me."

Truth be told, as much as I hated having tons of eyes on me, I really enjoyed being at the mall. At least there, it wasn't super crowded, and there were plenty of stores to look through. Even if I didn't ever buy anything, I enjoyed examining things, maybe even gather some ideas for art.

"I've already wasted most of my week sleeping in bed." I meandered back to the table. "I want something good to come out of it."

"Yeah, but..." Sophia made a questioning look. "What about your injuries? Last time I saw you, you were hurt pretty bad."

I showed her my wrists. "Everything's healed up now."

Astonishment surfaced to her face, as her jaw dropped a bit.

"All thanks to Felan," I said proudly.

Sophia cocked her head, but then her eyes lit with understanding. "Oh! You mean your great-grandmother."

"Yeah," I said, and gave my best friend a pleading look. "So, Sophia, do you wanna go to the mall with me? I'd love to spend a little time with you before Monday."

Her face suddenly went blank, and then her eyes widened as they darted to their corners.

I raised a curious brow at her reaction. "Soph?"

"S-Sorry! Um… I, uh, gotta use the bathroom real quick. Be right back!" Sophia bolted from the kitchen, her sneakers pounding the floor as she went.

"Wonder what that was about?" I murmured.

"Not sure." Mom shrugged, and put her hands on her hips. "Well, at any rate, I guess it'd be alright…"

I beamed at her. "Really?"

She gave a hesitant nod. "Sure, but I'll be supervising from a distance."

I nodded. "Thanks, Mom."

"You're welcome." She came around the table to hug me from behind. "And if anyone gives you trouble, I'll be there, okay?"

I took hold of her hand. "I know. You're always there for me, and so is Sophia. I'm not worried."

I scarfed down the rest of my toast, and guzzled a glass of milk, much to Mom's dismay, but I didn't want to waste any more time. Sophia said she had detention for two weeks, and so I wanted to spend every second I could get with her before she was to resume her sentencing.

Having already sported a comfortable t-shirt and shorts, I threw on some sneakers, and waited for Sophia to return. Several minutes passed, and soon worry pricked at the back of my mind. Was she okay?

"Hey, sorry!" She came running out of the bathroom with a bright smile on her face. "Had a surprise shit to release."

I about choked on the bit of oxygen I'd abruptly sucked in.

"Never… heard it put quite like that before," Mom uttered quietly. "But, anyway, shall we?"

Sophia nodded. "Yep! Let's go!"

We followed Mom out the door, and piled into her van. She made sure Sophia and I were buckled in at the back before pulling out of the driveway, her focus now on the road.

"Say, wanna go check out that new store that opened up?" Sophia asked, as we entered town. "I hear talk it's a café, and it has lots of great treats for us to try!"

I bounced in my seat with merriment. "Ooooooh, a café at the mall? Sounds awesome."

"Mhm." As Sophia turned to her passenger window, a strange look settled on her face.

I paused mid-bounce, concerned for my best friend. "Hey, you okay?"

"Huh? Oh, yeah... I'm fine." She looked to me with a slightly different expression. "Hey, you said that your great-grandmother gave you something, right? To help you with your injuries?"

"That's correct," I said.

Sophia tilted her head. "What's she like, anyway?"

"Hmm, well..." I stroked my chin as I thought of how to describe her. "I'd say that she's a master of medicine, since she knows her stuff when it comes to mixing herbs and other things. Once, she crafted an ointment that cured an infected blister I had on my arm in three days flat, even though the doctor my mom took me to see said it would take weeks to heal with the proper antibiotics. It was sore and itchy, and the yucky stuff that came out made it even worse." I rested my hands behind my head. "I used to wonder why Great Granny Felan didn't become a doctor, but then I realized how restricted her abilities would be."

"How so?"

"Well, she handles medication in a different way. She mixes powders together, and throws in flower petals, sometimes even pours in strange liquid..."

"So, they'd assume she's cooking up drugs?" Sophia asked.

"Yeah, like crack or something." A frown settled on my face. "If the world were flexible, Great Granny Felan could surely assist millions struggling with healthcare, but she has to keep her work hidden since, like I said, some would either deem her practice illegal without thorough investigation, or nurture it with greed rooted in their wicked hearts." I rolled my eyes. Hollow might've been a simple tourist town, but that didn't mean a weed or two wasn't growing in the yard.

"Oh..." Sophia's eyes darted to her passenger window. "So, uh, the blister just vanished, huh?"

"Yep." I recalled our initial conversation with a nod. "Like I said, took only three days."

"Wow, that's impressive."

"Felan is something else," Mom chimed in. "I can't say I fully understand, but I'm hoping to learn enough before too long myself."

"You mean, you're actually learning?" I asked. "How come you never told me?"

"Well, I..." Mom's nervous expression stared back at me through the rearview mirror. "I guess... I don't know. I just think it might be a good idea."

"Okay, well, if you're learning then maybe I should too," I offered. "It's a good skill to have."

Mom gave a meek nod. "Sure." She didn't sound sold on the idea.

"I don't know, I feel like it's a good idea..." I turned my attention to my window. "Just a thought."

The rest of the drive to the mall was shrouded in awkward silence, but the excitement of the day returned when Mom pulled into the mall's parking lot. Sophia and I had quickly unbuckled the moment she'd slipped into a spot, and together we hopped out of the van as it was put into park, then waited for Mom to join us.

"Whatever you girls want, I'll pay," Mom said. "I got plenty of cash to spare." She turned to the side, and revealed her small black purse.

"That's super sweet," Sophia said, and pointed at the side pocket on her cargo pants. "I brought some cash from helping one of my neighbors, so I should be able to cover something."

"So, it's an allowance?" I asked.

Sophia nodded. "That's right. Do you not...?" She glanced at Mom, then back at me.

I shook my head. "No. I never had a need to buy anything since Mom and Dad always bought things for me. And Great Granny Felan's a pro at knitting."

Mom shuffled her feet, an embarrassed expression on her face. "I never got around to teaching Rosella much about money because I'd been so busy with writing."

"It's okay," Sophia assured. "So she's a little late to the game. At least she's not burning it, unlike me." She eagerly winked at me. "Save it up, sis. You're gonna be glad you did."

I effectively hid my confusion with feigned understanding, as a curious thought crossed my mind. I'd recalled watching a movie where a character mentioned burning money, and then actually set their cash on fire. My eyes widened as an image of Sophia running around flaming dollar bills surfaced next, and I held back a gasp. No, Sophia wouldn't do something so dangerous...

"Alright! Let's go inside!" Sophia sped off like a kid charging into a candy store.

Pulled from my thoughts, I ran after her. "Sophia! Wait!"

"Geez! Hang on," Mom called.

The mall was probably the biggest place in town. It mainly consisted of clothing stores, but others housed either electronics or jewelry. Out of all the stores, I particularly enjoyed looking around this one called Clover Alley. They sold things like stuffed animals with backpack straps, plushies, little keychains with anime girls on them, graphic t-shirts, figurines. Basically, anything that I could "geek out" at, or get super excited over.

Unfortunately, that didn't stop the dozens of eyes honing in on us like lasers targeting an intruder as we entered the store. Mom and I kept our heads slightly bowed, while Sophia pretended like nothing was happening.

"I'm gonna go check out some keychains." Mom gave a small nod toward the rails of keychains at the back left corner of the store. "If you need me, that's where I'll be..."

"Okay, we'll be over here then!" Sophia suddenly snatched my hand, and I jolted in surprise.

"Oh? Wh-Where are you taking me?" I asked, as she tugged me along.

"This way." She led me over to a rack of hoodies and shirts. "Let's see what we've got here..."

While Mom busied herself in the back, away from most of the other customers, I set my sights on the different hoodies before me. Truth be told, I had quite a few, plus an array of sweaters. But that didn't mean I couldn't find another to add to my piling collection.

"Sweater weather is my favorite time of year," I mumbled under my breath. I was nervous about others possibly listening in on my conversation.

"You have, like, what, twenty sweaters?" Sophia guessed.

I shrugged. "I'm not that picky with clothes, but sweaters and hoodies are most comfortable, and they go great with leggings and sneakers."

She cocked a brow. "I thought you hated leggings because they felt too tight on you?"

"That was the one pair my mom got me from that thrift store," I said. "They were too small, and the material made me itch."

"Ah, gotcha." Sophia continued glossing over the rack of hoodies, and her mouth tilted in an awkward frown. "Hmm, nothing here peekin' my interest. You?"

I shook my head. "Not yet."

"Damn... Oh, look at this one!" Her eyes lit up with glee as she pulled a black hoodie with a cute anime-style cat on it. "This one's really cute, and it's not too expensive."

"Why don't you get it then?" I asked. "They have it in your size, and it's also got the thick sleeves with writing on it. Oh, and it's got ears too." I pinched the soft cat ears stitched to the hood with my thumb and forefinger. "So cute."

She chuckled. "Yeah, I'm sold, and so is this hoodie. How about you? See something you like?"

"Hmm..." I skimmed over the many hoodies decorating the rack, and a specific one caught my eye. "I think... this."

"Oh, nice choice!"

I plucked a light grey hoodie from the rack. It had wolf ears on the hood, and on the left breast of the hoodie was a pink heart, while along the sleeves were the words, "Moonpaw". I took a peek at the tag, having recognized the name.

"Moonpaw is a good one." She looked at the tag on hers again. "Oh, this one's from a different brand. Also, the sleeves on this say, 'Nya Nya Hey!' on them."

"Hmm, mine is softer than yours." I experimentally kneaded my fingertips into the fabric of my chosen hoodie. "It feels like cotton, but it's airy and cool."

"They're supposed to keep you nice and warm, but they got this technology where you don't burn up while wearing it or something." Sophia reached into her cargo pants to pull out her wallet. "Alright, we're getting these."

"Hey, Sophia..." I nervously wrung my hands together. "What exactly are you going to do with that?"

Sophia gave me a puzzled look. "With what?"

"Your money," I said.

She raised a curious brow whilst retrieving some cash from her pants' pocket. "Uh, spend it? Why?"

"Well, I..." I stroked a bit of hair behind my ear. "I was just..." My voice trailed off, my eyes widening as she pulled something else out of her pocket: a lighter.

"Shoot, how'd this get in here?" Clutching the small bit of cash in one hand at her side, she used the thumb of her other to spark a flame from the lighter. "Huh."

My eyes widened. "Sophia..."

"Ro, you okay?" Sophia quickly extinguished the flame. "It's okay, no one's looking."

Panicked, I snatched the lighter from her, and held it at my chest. "No!" I whispered. "Don't do that!"

"It's okay Ro," she said. "No one saw it, and it was just a little flame. No big deal."

I hastily stuffed the lighter in my pocket.. "Are you kidding me!? This is a public place, a-and..." My eyes darted to their corners. To my surprise, no one was looking at us. Instead, they were focused on Mom, who was still observing the keychains.

"What?" Sophia asked. "If you're worried about me smoking, I don't do that. Occasionally, my mom does, but it's rare." She put up her hands. "Still Ro, I don't know how that got in there, and like I said, I don't get involved with cancer sticks."

My eyes averted her worried gaze. "It's not that. It's..." I worried at my bottom lip. There was no way I couldn't be blunt about it.

"It's what?"

"I thought, for a moment, that you were maybe going to set your money on fire," I admitted, and returned my gaze to her. "You said you burned your allowance, and since you've got it in your other hand, I guess I thought... you were going to burn it."

Sophia's face went blank.

"So... Sophia?"

The corner of her mouth twitched, and she broke out in a small fit of laughter.

I stood there, dumbfounded, by her reaction. What was so funny about setting her money on fire?

Sophia wiped a stray tear from her eye. "Oh, honey! You... Oh man."

"What?" I asked. "Why are you laughing?"

She shook her head. "Ro, have you never heard the expression, 'spending money like it burns'?"

"Uh..." I cocked my head. "I once saw a movie where this guy actually burned a whole wad of cash, and I thought..." I frowned at her as she stifled another chuckle.

"It means that I spend it a lot," she explained. "My allowance goes by so fast, like flames burning through wood. I 'burn' through my allowance super quick."

"Oh... You mean, you don't..." I buried my blushed face in my hands. "Oh god, I'm such an idiot."

"No, you're fine!" Sophia patted me on the shoulder. "It's okay, Ro. You just misunderstood."

"I thought you were going to set your money on fire," I muttered. "That is more than a misunderstanding. That is utter stupidity."

"To be fair, I was holding an actual lighter," she pointed out.

"Still..." I dug the heels of my palms into my eyes. "God..."

Sophia chuckled. "It's okay, really. Hey, come on, don't be so embarrassed."

I shook my head, and turned away from her. "Stay away from me, I don't want you catching my idiocy."

"Ro..." Sophia sighed. "Come on, give me some joy, won't you?"

"No."

She sighed again. "Please? I'm sorry if I hurt your feelings. I thought it was silly, but nothing more! I promise, I wasn't making fun of you."

"It's not that, it's the fact that I misunderstood you..."

"Oh, you silly goose, come on!"

I shook my head again.

"Alright, guess you forced my hand..."

I squeaked as a hand suddenly scribbled across my pudgy middle. "Hey!" I hugged myself. "Stop that!"

Sophia lightly grazed my side. "Nope!"

"Hey!" I wiggled away from her as the corners of my lips curved up.

"Aw, don't be so bashful!" Sophia teased me with a gentle pinch to my neck. "You're fine!"

"Knock it off!" I said with a laugh, and slapped her.

Sophia snickered as she struck my stomach again, and I squirmed in a fit of genuine laughter. "There we go!"

"You're so-ho-ho mean!" I complained through a fit of giggles as she mischievously stuck her tongue out at me. "I mean, I appreciate you making me feel better, but still!"

"Alright, lemme make it up to you by buying you this hoodie then." Sophia pointed at the wolf hoodie I still held in my hands. "Is it a deal?"

I nodded.

"Alright!" She threw an arm over my shoulders, and squeezed me softly. "And hey, don't feel bad for not understanding what I said."

"My issue was that I'd seen it on TV before," I explained. "And because I didn't fully understand the expression. And your version was worded different."

"No wonder." She nuzzled her head against mine. "Well, you'll be happy to know that I don't burn my money."

I giggled. "Should be more careful when letting my mind wander."

"It's okay." Sophia pointed toward the front of the store. "Alright, let's go pay."

I eyed the cashier as we approached the desk. They had a blank expression on their face, their glassy eyes locked on me. I shuffled in place as I averted their uncomfortable gaze, then nodded to Sophia. She looked to me, then back at the cashier, and tilted her head.

"Um... Excuse me," Sophia said aloud, "we're ready to pay."

A smile suddenly sprang to the cashier's face, like they'd hastily thrown on a mask right in front of us. "Oh! Yes, of course!"

Sophia looked like she'd swallowed a bout of anger, her jaw stiffened at their reaction, but she kept her tone level. "These hoodies, I'd like to pay for them."

"Let's see..." The cashier gingerly took the hoodies from her and scanned them. "Okay, with tax included, that's $40." Their eyes wandered to me again, and the corner of their lip curled a bit.

"Hey girls, think I found something." Mom came up behind us. "Found this cute little keychain." Her voice went silent for a moment as she locked eyes with the cashier, and then she cleared her throat. "Um, hi there. Just came over to pay for this."

The cashier's brow curled into a deep frown. "Chloe Bloom? Was a little surprised to see you walk in here, but utterly shocked to see your daughter."

Mom's jaw unhinged, a strained expression now on her face. "What's that supposed to mean?"

The cashier shrugged. "Oh nothing, just thought you'd rather keep your daughter locked up, instead of out in the public."

My eyes widened at their abrupt response, and when I looked to my left, I saw rage festering in Sophia's. *Oh no... No no no.* My hand hesitantly reached over to take hers, but retracted when her fingers curled into her palm.

"And uh, how do you know which one of these girls is my daughter?" Mom asked calmly.

"It's easy to recognize her from the pictures released after the funeral," the cashier stated matter of factually. "She's also the only girl we know who has her hair cut at the back, with shoulder-length locks at the front." They gave a sarcastic snort. "Again, surprised to see her since it's not often we get to. I guess you know what the presses want."

Mom rolled her eyes. "So you're one of those people who think I wanted to make a quick buck out of my husband's death, and that I use my daughter as a bonus promotional piece."

"Like dangling a carrot before a hungry rabbit." The cashier cocked a brow, a challenging glint in their eye, as a wicked leer cracked their lips. "Everybody wants to know more about you all, especially after the little stunt she pulled all those years ago."

As if she'd read my mind, Sophia dropped the question before I could. "What are you talking about?"

The cashier pointed to me. "Why, that night she wandered into the forest by herself, and her late father had to run in after her."

I glanced over at Mom questioningly, who'd gone stiff as a board with an unreadable expression.

"So what? She got a little curious," Sophia went on. "Kids like to have a little fun on the dangerous side sometimes. I've snuck out many times before myself at night without telling my mom."

The cashier frowned at her. "You're surely one to preach that, aren't you, young lady?"

Sophia didn't seem to understand what they were implying, as a confused expression sprang to her face, while a dull look of irritation crossed the cashier's.

"I guess I have to spell it out for you. It's illegal to play with fire within this building, let alone within this store. I understand you enjoy living dangerously, but that behavior will not be tolerated here."

Panic rose within me, and I shook my head. "She wasn't playing with it!" I blurted out. "She was just..." I fell silent with embarrassment, as Mom rested a hand on my shoulder.

"I can assure you that these two girls mean no trouble," she continued for me. "Please... Leave them alone. Direct your disgust toward me."

The cashier cocked their head with a look of suspicion. "That's pretty interesting coming from someone who possibly killed her husband. And how about your mother's secret cult?" They looked from Mom to me, then Sophia. "Ya know, little girl... It's rumored that Miss Bloom here has been keeping her daughter locked up indoors. Wasn't sure if she was holding her hostage, or preparing her as a sacrifice."

I silently stared, dumbstruck, at the cashier. Who the hell was this person to think such things, and what the hell were they talking about?

Sophia aggressively drummed her fingers atop the counter. "Can we please hurry this along? Just let us pay for our shit so we can leave."

"Right, of course." The cashier nodded with a displeased frown. "Not safe to keep a pyromaniac around for long. Might set the whole store ablaze."

My face flared red at the cashier's infuriating comment, and my brow furrowed.

The cashier seemed to take notice of this, and locked eyes with me. "Oh? Did I strike a nerve?"

"Alright, listen here pal!" Sophia suddenly slammed both hoodies on the counter. "I don't know what your fucking problem is, but I've had enough!"

I backed into Mom's form, and she threw her arms around me. In turn, I grasped tightly to her.

"God, people like you just... AAAAAAAAH!!!!"

I couldn't explain what happened after that, but out of nowhere, the sound of thunder rang out, the cash register toppled to the floor on its side, and a flurry of dollar bills rained down around us, all while the counter split in two. The cashier stumbled back several steps, their face drained of color as their eyes bulged.

As Mom pulled me away from the wreckage, fear spiked in my nerves as my galloping heart caught in my throat, my widened eyes glued to the destroyed counter, and my jaw dropped to the floor. How in the hell...?

"Shit..."

Her voice catching my attention, my eyes darted in the direction of Sophia hastily tossing her two twenties toward the shambled remains of the counter. She appeared completely unfazed by what just happened.

"Thanks, have a nice day." Sophia's ponytail whipped the air with a quick turn of her head, and she stomped out of the store. "Customer respect my ass!"

I returned my gaze to the baffled cashier. "S-Sorry... I, uh... S-Sorry." I turned on the ball of my sneaker and shot after Sophia, with Mom hurrying close behind me.

"The nerve of some people!" Sophia exclaimed as we caught up. "Can you fucking believe that?"

"S-Sophia, sweetheart, you should've..." Mom's horrified gaze wandered to me. "Uh..."

I gawked at her with silent questioning. *What the hell just happened!?*

"Ro."

I jumped back as something brushed my arm, and I realized it was Sophia handing me my hoodie. "Here."

"O-Oh... Th-Thanks." I gingerly accepted the hoodie from her, though I avoided her gaze in favor of the floor as the memory of the incident played over and over again in my head. *It just broke... How...?*

I glanced around. The mall wasn't shaking. No one was running around in a panic. So, it couldn't have been an earthquake. So, what else could it be? Did anyone outside the store even take notice? Did they feel *anything*?

"M-Miss..."

A rush of anxiety coursed up my spine at the sound of the cashier's voice behind us, and I peered over my shoulder.

There, the cashier stood several feet from us, a nervous expression on their paled face. "Y-You forgot... to pay..."

"Right, the keychain." Mom fished out a few dollars from her pants' pocket, and strode toward the cashier, prompting them to jump back a few steps.

"D-Don't come any closer!" They threw their hands out. "J-Just..."

Mom held the money out to the petrified cashier. "Just take the damn money and go."

They hesitantly reached a quivering hand toward Mom's, snatched the money, and ran off.

Once the cashier was out of sight, Mom came back and threw her arms around both me and Sophia. "Come on... Let's go get something to eat."

Awkward silence filtered the air, though no one paid us any mind, as we exited the mall. It was a quiet drive through town, the only words uttered being confirmation of a pizza place to dine at. When we arrived, Mom instructed us to take a few moments to settle our nerves before stepping out, so as not to arouse suspicion.

"Alright..." Mom stepped out first, then looked to me and Sophia. "Let's just forget about what happened back there. Okay?"

I nodded meekly, and glanced at Sophia. "Soph?"

She seemed to be lost in her thoughts, a strange look on her face.

"'Kay, let's go inside." Mom took me by the hand, and in turn I grabbed Sophia's, effectively startling her out of whatever it was she was thinking about.

We entered the pizza parlor as calmly as possible, though when people laid their disgruntled eyes on us and began whispering amongst themselves, I couldn't help but think that they knew of the incident, and were now gossiping about it. Mom reassured me with a slight shake of her head, however, and the tension in my chest disappeared with an immense sigh of relief.

Sophia and I seated ourselves at a booth nestled in a back corner of the pizza parlor, while Mom stood in line at the front. Neither one of us said anything, though my eyes kept wandering back to her.

Another minute of this painfully drawn-out silence went by before, finally, I forced myself to speak up. "Sophia, what are you thinking about?"

As if someone had struck her with a hot poker, Sophia violently jolted in her spot beside me with a horrified expression on her face. "R-Ro, I-I'm sorry."

I gave her a nervous look. "What... What?"

"I-I-I'm sorry!" she stammered. "Really, I am!"

I frowned. "What... What do you mean?"

Her expression went blank, then screwed into one of fear. "I... I..."

Sophia

Think of something to say, you fool!

Rosella was staring back at me with upmost confusion, and I had no clue how to play this off. God, I screwed up so fucking badly. Fuck, I didn't think I could do that! It just happened! Was it because I didn't learn to control my powers? If so, how the hell could I even use them? Perhaps they were just unstable...

Rosella... She was beyond baffled, I knew she was. She was looking around the damn place, surely thinking that maybe an earthquake had happened or something. And that *fucking* cashier. What absolute dipshit shoved a stick up their ass? God, I was so mad I about spit fire, and if I could've, boy howdy I would've!

I angrily whipped my head around, my ponytail smacking the back of my neck with the motion. *They were deliberately trying to get under my skin, just to get a rise outta me!* My emerald eyes narrowed as a flash of silver sparked across them. *I saw it, too. That glint in their eye, but it wasn't like mine. The way they stared at me... I didn't pick up on anything, so...*

"Sophia?"

I squirmed in my seat like a mouse caught in a trap. I'd totally forgotten about Rosella. "Uh... Well..." My eyes darted to their corners. "Well, you see—"

"Alright, I placed our order."

"Chloe!" I abruptly called out. "Hey."

Rosella's mother was now approaching, a suspicious look on her face at my reaction. "Yes?"

"S-Sorry!" I drummed my nervous fingers atop the table, and nibbled at my bottom lip. "I'm sorry, just... Uh..." I screwed my eyes shut. *Fuck, stop apologizing!*

"Sophia, are you okay?" Rosella's hand came down on my shoulder, and it took every ounce of strength not to leap from my seat in surprise.

I pressed my arms as tightly to my sides as possible. "Y-Yes," I lied. "I'm fine. Really." *No you're not! You're sweating bullets!* I cringed at the dampness beneath my armpits. *God, so itchy and warm...*

"Sophia?" Chloe seated herself across from me. "Are you... Are you really okay?"

Eyes still squeezed shut, I gave a hesitant nod. "Y-Ye..." I cut myself off when I felt the tingling of my tongue. *No... No, not again! Fuck.*

I hid my hands under the table as I balled them into fists, my shoulders squared. Oh god, the scorching heat on my tongue, it was getting worse, like particles of sand wedged between every individual taste bud. Damn, it was itching, so so much, and as badly as I wanted to scrape it along my teeth, I knew that would only make it worse.

It fucking burns, I muttered in my thoughts, but resisted the urge to squirm. I had to stay still, just pretend I was fine until I could get to the bathroom and quench my unnerving thirst at the sink.

"Here, Sophia."

I cracked one eye open, then both as I swiped the glass of water presented to me. I guzzled down the soothing liquid fast, then slammed the bottom of the glass to the table. Just like that, the fire had been extinguished. Much better...

"Mom! Mom, is she okay!?"

Alarmed by her words, I shot a look at a frantic Rosella, then Chloe. Compared to her daughter, she was calm and collected.

"I think she's just a little overwhelmed by what happened," Chloe answered coolly. "Do you feel better now, Sophia?"

Rosella gawked at me with upmost concern. "Yeah, are you okay?"

Playing it casual, I rubbed at the back of my head with a laugh. "Y-Yeah, I'm good! Just... a little out of it I guess."

I knew my response was shit, but Rosella didn't question it and instead rubbed a comforting hand up and down my back. I couldn't resist the fluttering of butterflies in my stomach as I felt her fingers graze along my spine, though I kept a straight face and thanked her for the gesture while secretly melting in the palm of her hand.

After that little stunt I pulled, I don't deserve this, I thought to myself. *But it feels nice... And I didn't mean to do it...*

"So," Chloe piped up, "I think we should talk about what happened at Clover Alley."

My heart leaped up my throat as I rose out of my shallow pool of euphoria, preventing me from uttering a sound.

"Sh-She's always been outspoken," Rosella stammered. "Stubborn as a bull, that's how she rolls. But..." She looked from me to Chloe, and then back to me again. "Mom... What... What *did* happen back there?"

I felt my cheeks flare hot as fire at her question. *Shit... Tell me she's not...*

"Sophia." Chloe cocked her head at me. "Where is that lighter now? Out of curiosity?"

"I-I have it." Rosella gingerly retrieved it from her pocket, and handed it over.

"Rosella panicked when I lit it because she thought I was gonna burn my money," I mumbled, with a shameful bow of my head.

"I see..." Chloe slipped the lighter into her pocket. "Well, let's be more responsible next time, okay? Lighters are not playthings."

"Y-You're right. I apologize for that, and for making a scene in there."

"It's okay. We all make mistakes."

As she uttered those last words, I couldn't help but flinch when her brown eyes narrowed slightly in my direction. The way they stared back at me, it was like they were trying to search for the truth I was scrambling to hide from her, and she knew exactly where to find it. As our gazes wandered to the empty glass before me, it didn't take long for me to connect the dots.

I felt the warmth that Rosella sparked drain from my cheeks. *She knows it was me, doesn't she?*

"Mom..." Rosella dropped her voice to just above a whisper. "How did that counter break? No one was touching it, but we were standing there. What if people think we did it?"

I clenched my fists in my lap. I wanted to scream out that it was my fault, and that I didn't mean it, that it was an accident. I had no control over that.

"I'm scared," Rosella went on, an anxious look on her face. "What if people start saying that we committed witchcraft or something in that store? We... We can't go back there." She hugged her sides. and screwed her eyes shut. "It's not fair. We didn't do anything wrong..."

Chloe wrapped a comforting arm around Ro's shoulders, and rested her cheek against her head. "It's alright, sweetheart. Really..."

Rosella groaned as she rubbed the heels of her palms into her eyes."No it's not. This town's been hellbent on pinning every single thing on us. Ever since Georgia Morse opened her big mouth about that stupid shoemaker story..."

I frowned at her words. "What story?"

Her hands fell away from her face, revealing her puffy red eyes. "You know, the shoemaker story..."

"Wh-What does that entail?" I asked nervously.

"Some fable people made up," Rosella grumbled, as she waved a hand at the air. "And I don't believe a word of it, nor Georgia's claims that she was responsible for what happened to the guy, if he was even real, or Sarah Mitchell."

I shuddered at the mention of Sarah. "She has the same last name as me and my mom." My eyes dropped to the table. "I... I did ask Mom once about it. Ya know, to see if maybe there was a connection, but she denied it."

Mom never liked when I brought up Sarah. She always became erratic, screaming that it was all Chloe's fault that she died. I never came to understand this reaction, though I at least learned to dodge the topic.

But why blame Chloe? I thought to myself. *What did she do?*

Chloe suddenly shot up from her seat. "I'm gonna go check on our order."

My eyes were glued to Chloe's retreating form until I heard Rosella clear her throat, and I looked over to her with a concerned expression as I grasped her hand. "Hey, you okay?"

She nodded tiredly. "Y-Yeah."

"You sure?"

"I'm fine." Rosella pressed the heel of her free hand to her left eye yet again, a pained expression on her face. "I just... wanted to have a good day today."

"Hey, Ro." I squeezed her free hand. "Rosella, don't let what happened back there ruin the mood."

"But why did that happen?" she asked, worriedly. "The counter just snapped! And even if we weren't there, people are gonna assume we had something to do with it."

"And if anyone comes for you, I'll protect you. Just like always." I stared her down with a calm frown. "I've got your back, Ro. No matter what." My eyes drifted back to the empty glass of water, and I shuddered. *Stubborn as a bull, that's how I roll. I'm not backing down. Ever.*

CHAPTER 6

"OKAY... YOU READY?" MOM asked me.

I beamed at her. "Yep. I'm still full of yummy waffles and chocolate milk from breakfast, so energy is strong."

Twirling on the ball of my shoe, three layers of white linen blossomed out beneath my soft, ivory dress, and a vibrant red cloak, with white fur trimming that nicely framed my smiling face and body, splayed out behind me. This ensemble was a gift I'd gotten from Great Granny Felan a year ago. She first designed the whole outfit on paper, then asked me for my measurements, and set to work. It took her three months to complete, which kinda surprised me. But of course, I didn't know how long sewing something like that usually took. Knowing her, it was a cinch.

A pair of adorable wolf ears stitched to my hood wavered as I pulled it over my head, and I tied the thick red ribbons under my chin into a bow. "I remember when I first asked her what it was, and she sang, 'Oh, I'm just making you a little something~!'" I fondly pinched the furry trim of the cloak at either side and, like an amused child, swung from side to side. This caused the tail attached at the back of the cloak to tap against the back of my knees.

"Don't remember if I told you, but the threading was created from cotton, flax, and a couple other plants she grew herself." Mom laid her hands atop my shoulders, a faint smile on her face. "She's also got a closet of collected fabrics from over the years that she's kept nice and neat."

Great Granny Felan had developed a strong green thumb long before I was even conceived, and though I myself could tend to flowers, I lacked the vast knowledge she had. Watering plants and feeding them fertilizer was one thing, but creating unique flowers out of existent ones? That piqued my interest.

"I'd love to craft something like this one day," I told myself. "Not sure I have time right now, but maybe later down the road..."

"Rosella, you've got all the time in the world." Mom nuzzled her cheek to my head, her fingers interlacing the golden locks draped over my shoulders. "You just have to believe in yourself. There's more there than you realize."

I smirked over my shoulder. "Yeah, I guess you're right. Can't go wrong with Mom's intuition."

A joyful spark danced across her brown eyes. "Ha, alright then, let's go." Mom grabbed her backdoor house key, while I handled the basket of goodies.

"Hope these cookies work," I said.

"The medicinal powder I threw in the batter is a supplement to her aching joints, so they should." Mom sighed. "She's been having a hard time getting around lately."

"She looked fine to me when we saw her last."

"To you, yes, but when you had your back turned, I saw her stumble on her way to the kitchen." Mom opened the back door and slipped out. "She won't admit it, but she needs help sometimes."

I stepped out with her. "I wouldn't worry about it. If she really needs something, she'll ask."

Mom closed and locked the back door behind us. "Front door also...?"

I nodded.

"Alright."

We made haste through our fenced backyard, the grass crunching softly beneath our shoes, and paused at the fence's door, side by side with linked hands. A gentle stir of wind rustling the trees before us, their leaves whispered amongst one another as if beckoning us toward them. We answered their call as we stepped out of the safety of our backyard, and the fence's door swung silently behind us.

Rosella, come on... It's me... I'm trying to reach out to you. Can't you hear me?

A sudden chill coursing down my spine grew stronger the closer we came to the entrance, and not because my mother's hand had tightened around mine. She always got like this whenever we approached the forest, but I never did. This place was a whole other wonderful world beyond the town, the wonderful world I felt I truly belonged in. The sun's warm beams seeping through the trees, its gentle kiss of warmth against my fair skin... The chirping of the birds as woodland critters scurried about, and the hushed excitement of the bristling leaves... All of this was heaven compared to the bustling town of people, honking cars, high school drama, and the infectious gossip.

"It's so pretty out here," I said, whilst admiring the greenery. I breathed in the crisp, clear air, and exhaled. "Ah, relaxing..."

"Hmm?" Mom uttered. "Oh, yeah, it is..."

I glanced at my mother, and a confused frown crept across my face. "Mom?"

A shadow clouded my mother's expression, the light of the sun deflected from her dull eyes as she nodded tiredly. "It's nice."

"Mom."

A dim flicker of light sparked her gaze, and she glanced my way. "Yes, dear?"

"Are you okay?" I asked. "You look... troubled."

She nipped her lower lip with hesitancy. "...I'm sorry. I'm just antsy being here with you." Trembling, she stopped in her tracks, and averted my stern gaze.

"Mom?"

"Rosella, I don't want to trouble you with this."

Steaming with frustration, I lowered my head with a furrowed brow as I thought back to the incident at the mall. "It wasn't our fault that damn counter snapped in half like a bread stick... but people are saying it was, aren't they?"

Mom sighed. "It's alright if they come for me about it. I only ever get real upset when someone tears into your great-grandmother, or you. Like the incident with Caroline... It's not the first time she's targeted you, and that particular incident was the first time she actually laid a hand on you. I'm worried that things will only escalate further." She glared at the ground. "I mean, on your first day in school, she called you a fat pig ready for the slaughterhouse."

I groaned. "Yes, and when you tried to get justice for me, Caroline threatened to drown me in the toilet, after she played the middle school principal like a fiddle." A nauseating lump formed in my throat as I thought back to that day she'd cornered me in that empty hallway, no witnesses around.

Mom's expression hardened into slight ferocity, a fiery glare crossing her face. "Then you understand how dangerous being around her is... I mean, you do have Sophia, but..."

"But what?" I asked.

She shrugged. "Oh, I don't know. I was thinking, perhaps... we might need to relocate."

My eyebrows rose. "R-Relocate? What are you saying?"

"I just feel uneasy being in this town, what with everything going on. I'm worried for your safety."

I shook my head. "Uh, I... I can't just up and leave!"

"I didn't say that."

Worry pierced my heart like a shard of glass at the thought of losing Sophia. "I-It sounds like you are, though. I mean... Sophia is my best friend, my only friend outside. If I leave her..."

"Rosella." Mom paused in her tracks, her hands on her hips. "I didn't say that we should uproot ourselves tomorrow. I'm just saying that we need to consider some better options. And it's not like we can't tell her where we're going."

Several steps ahead, I came to a stop and peered over my shoulder. "Do you remember how it was Soph and I met? It was during a writing event at the old library, if you recall. Dad encouraged you to go because you wanted to meet other writers, and when I got bored you led me over to the kid section where Sophia happened to be."

"I remember that," Mom said. "You two got to talking, and that was when I ran into..." She bit her bottom lip. "Ngh, at any rate, Sophia's your only friend because I kept you locked away for years. I should've listened to your father and not been so clingy. I'm sorry."

Her words triggered another painful memory still fresh in my mind. It was after I'd met Sophia that the pain had begun to fester in silence, burning my lungs with each inhale, choking me for years. Unable to stop the sting in my heart, I'd struggled to keep the emotional swelling under control.

"We only saw each other every once in a great while," I continued quietly. "There were a few times when we bumped into each other during outings, and a couple times when she actually got to come over, and then that time I saw her at recess... And I... I got attached to her." I glanced down at the ground. "She was the first kid in town who wasn't pulled away from me, or acted disgusted when around me. And after everything she told me about her life, I realized I wanted that too..."

I was twelve when that fuse of frustration had shorted out and exploded at the dinner table. I couldn't hold it in anymore, and I scorched my mother with the fiery rage I felt for feeling like a prisoner in the house. Through the puff of awkward smoke that lingered after, I found Mom appalled by my outburst, while Dad gawked at me.

For a few days, Mom and I didn't speak. At first, I thought that she was angry with me, but Dad assured me that she felt I needed space to cool my head, and once the heat had settled, she'd ask if I was okay. When she did, we all sat down to talk...

I choked down a whimper. "He died a few days before I was to start middle school... I was looking forward to telling him how it went, not that it wound up going well..."

Mom heaved a tired sigh. "I know..."

I turned my back to her. "Then you understand how badly it hurts to even think about losing Sophia by moving. I'd already lost Dad... I don't want to lose her too."

Mom and I continued on in silence for the next several minutes, the only source of noise being the continued chirping of the birds and crunching of the dirt at our feet. Under the canopy of the trees, Mom became distracted by the wilderness while my mind wandered back to my homeschool days, and I found myself wading through a pool of nostalgia.

Writing in those notebooks, listening to her dish out history facts, spelling lessons, and equations for eight grueling hours, Mom did this with me every day without fail. She was a good teacher, having been a mostly straight-A student throughout school and retained a master's degree. Her lessons were generally easy to follow, though sometimes I did struggle, and during those times she'd patiently work with me until I got it no matter how many hours or days it took.

"You are the reason I remember the fifty states," I uttered, "and the periodic table, and the difference between apostrophes and commas. Because you kept me close, I was able to focus, and get a decent education without worry." I ran a hand down my right arm-warmer sleeve and gazed upon the white paw print stitched into the palm. "But I have to admit, it was a lonely time for me, until Sophia turned up in my life."

"She was a game-changer," Mom murmured.

I nodded. "I remember when we had our first sleepover about a year after we'd met. We were both eight years old, and it was one of the best nights of my life. We got to stay up late watching movies, playing games, and stuffing ourselves full of junk food."

A snort slipped Mom's lips. "I don't know how you both didn't get sick from all that."

"Us either. But you know, the best part was when she told me all about her experience in school. It was mind-blowing." I halted in my tracks again. "And like a piece of candy just out of my reach, the thought of attending public school taunted me for years, until you finally let me have it, despite the risks."

A painful expression took hold of her face as Mom stopped beside me. "But you understand, right? Why I did what I did?"

"Of course I do, because you wanted to protect me."

She didn't say anything to that.

"Look, I... I am glad you're there for me... but I can't..." I heaved a tired sigh. I didn't want to argue about this anymore.

Rosella, don't be upset with her. She knows she can't keep you forever...

"We're here." Mom's words abruptly brought me back to focus. "See it?"

I spotted Great Granny Felan's cabin ahead, and I took off without warning. Finally, we were here.

"Wait Rosella!" Mom called.

I ignored her. The entire walk had been nothing but dreadful. I needed my retreat to happiness, and the only place where I could get that was at Great Granny Felan's.

I abandoned my troubles at the bottom of the steps, my red high-top sneakers squashing them upon the first creak. Excitement carried me to the wraparound deck at the top, the wooden railing decorated with a line of paper lanterns, the cabin roof's edge trimmed with more. Two windows resided on each side of the front door, a rocking chair to the left.

I paused at the top step upon spotting a striped curtain of fabric draped over the railing. It had several colorful rows of diamonds and dots set in a haphazard pattern. I reached over to stroke it, and found the material to be a little stiff, almost like straw. I smirked at my great-grandmother's hard work, then turned to the door and, with a hearty rap of my gently clenched fist, waited for Great Granny Felan to answer.

"Who is it~?" I heard a muffled voice call beyond the door.

"It's me~!" I sang back. My grin widened as I heard a musical giggle beyond the door.

A few moments passed, and then a sweet seventy-eight-year-old lady was standing in front of me. "Rosella!" She threw her thin arms out, a beaming smile on her face.

"Great Granny Felan!" I happily accepted her embrace.

"Oh, I've missed you sweetheart!" She lovingly pecked my cheek. "Oooooh, it's been too long!"

I laughed. "Aw, I missed you too."

"Mom~!" I heard my mother approach behind me, and I glanced over my shoulder. She looked kinda frazzled, but seemed otherwise alright.

"Chloe!" Great Granny Felan hugged her next. "Please, come in!"

I followed both her and my mother inside. "I can't wait to show Great Granny Felan what we've brought."

"Well, come into the kitchen then!" Great Granny Felan toddled on ahead, Mom trailing just behind. "I'll get some tea ready."

A soft, intricately decorated rug greeted us upon entry into Great Granny Felan's spacious living room. Adorning the walls were an assortment of family photos, some with us three and Dad, others with just Mom and Great Granny Felan, and a few photos of Mom and Dad on their wedding.

On the coffee table in front of the old floral couch was a potted white rose with green leaves tinted a faint shade of pink. Beside the couch stood a large silver-barked tree thriving with beautifully patterned cherry blossoms. Tiny magenta and purple specks dotted their dark ruby-tipped petals spread wide.

"That one must be new," I said, observing the cherry blossom tree. "I guess Great Granny Felan figured out how to make them grow." I approached another potted plant, a bright blue three-petaled bloom with four thin green filaments, each tipped with a cluster of white anthers.

"I wouldn't touch that, you don't know if the petals or stamen are poisonous," Mom warned. "Ugh, I remember when your father pricked himself and fainted from that cactus..."

"Yeah, but Great Granny Felan said he'd be fine, just a little woozy..." I chuckled. "But then he threw up over the deck railing, actually got Fenris on the head."

Mom laughed. "Oh yeah, I definitely remember that. Poor thing had to have a bath."

"Yeah." I glanced at her. "Say, how does Great Granny Felan do all this? I remember finding some of the flowers she's grown in books, but..." I cocked my head at the cherry blossoms. "With the cherry blossoms, you find those in... Asia? Yet they're here in the US..."

She winked at me. "It's a special concoction your father helped with, Rosella, and unlike most people she uses it for harmless fun..." Her expression faltered a bit. "As well as for more important purposes."

I nodded. "Right, like the powder she made me."

"Exactly," Mom said. "That was made from ground up jasmine, California poppy, and a pinch of snodaful."

"That stuff that looks like snow?" I asked.

"Correct. How do you think she makes all her medicine and flowers?"

I admired the potted rose on the coffee table. "I wonder when she'll be able to teach me her ways. It's so fascinating."

"Perhaps one day." Mom looked to the left, at Great Granny Felan's bedroom doorway. "Rosella, I'm gonna sneak through there to the bathroom. Be right back."

"Alright."

I saw Mom off, then approached the small entertainment set where Great Granny Felan's large flatscreen TV was, and found myself admiring the family photo above. Mom, Dad, Great Granny Felan, and a very small me were all smiling in the photo, the beautiful ocean serving as the background.

I remember this... I was five years old, and it was my first time at the beach. Burying Dad in the sand, running in the water with Mom... I chuckled fondly at the memory. *Great Granny Felan kept mostly to herself under the safety of shade with her umbrella, though the towel didn't do much for her as a seat. She kept complaining about the towel bunching up under her, but Dad kept fixing it for her. Dad...* My smile faded. It still hurt, looking at photos, watching videos, thinking of him, the urge to plea for his return... *Reminiscing only reminds me of the pain.*

"Rosella?" Great Granny Felan called. "Are you coming, dear?"

I shook off my grieving thoughts. "Oh, yeah."

Great Granny Felan was waiting for me at the kitchen table, a dancing twinkle in her soft amber eyes. The warm sunlight pooling in through the screen door behind highlighted the strands of silver hair escaping her neat bun, and bathed her in its cozy golden glow. Accompanying her were the few hibiscus trees placed intricately about the kitchen, and several hanging pots of ivy spilling over with colorful blooms.

Once I turn eighteen and graduate, I'm moving out here and building myself a cottage. Great Granny Felan and I can be neighbors, and she can show me how to grow and decorate my new home with plants, like this. I eyed the tallest hibiscus tree of the bunch next to the screen door, and the extensive, leaf-decorated vines that crawled along the top of the cabinets. *I wonder if I could try growing something like that.*

Great Granny Felan adjusted a frilly wrist cuff of her floral-patterned dress with an aged liver-spotted hand, a smirk accented with gently-crinkled dimples on her face. "How are you, sweetie? Oh, and speaking of sweeties..." She eyed the basket. "What's that we got here?"

I placed the basket upon the table and removed the white cloth, as I seated myself across from her. "We got the loaves of bread from the local bakery, but we made the cookies from scratch."

"Good. I'm glad you're getting the hang of baking." She proudly bumped a fist against her chest. "*I* always had a knack for baking, but it's nice to know I'm not the only one."

I gave a slow nod. "Yeah, baking is fun."

"Something wrong, dear?"

I fiddled with the tail of hair at my left shoulder, avoiding her gaze. "Oh, it's nothing." The truth was that I was still thinking about the conversation during the walk here, but I didn't want to bring that up. "Um, Mom once said that you were having some trouble moving around lately, so she thought these oatmeal cookies and bread would help." I silently prayed Great Granny Felan would take the bait, rather than pry into my thoughts.

"So she sprinkled in a little something?" she asked.

I nodded. "Yeah, she said it's supposed to help your joints."

She snagged a cookie from the basket with one hand, and batted the air with the other. "I'm fine, dearie. She don't have to worry about me."

"Are you sure?"

"Of course. I might look old and frail, but that doesn't mean I am."

I observed the dark crescents beneath her eyes, and the small cracks in her skin. *Just like Dad...*

"Hey, Mom." My mother suddenly walked into the room and sat to the left of my great-grandmother. "What's going on?"

"Oh, Chloe!" Great Granny Felan beamed at her. "Rosella and I were in the middle of idle chit-chatter." She tapped a finger to her rose-tinted lips, a hardened frown etched into her face. "Rosella tells me that you, Chloe, told her I was having trouble getting around."

Mom's eyes fled Great Granny Felan's interrogating gaze. "Um..."

"Is that true?"

She scrubbed at her sweater sleeves. "Well... You see..."

I sat there, nervously watching the two, as they engaged in their standoff. I felt bad for throwing Mom under the bus like that. Last thing I wanted was to cause a rift between them.

Great Granny Felan crossed her arms over her chest. "Chloe, I'm waiting."

"Mom was just worried about you," I piped up. "So please don't be upset with her." I squeezed one eye shut, the other locked on my great-grandmother.

Her stony expression lingered for a few seconds before fading into one of understanding. "Well, I guess that's okay."

Relieved, I plucked a cookie from the basket and took a bite of it.

"I'm sorry, Mom. I just..." My mother clutched the crooks of her elbows. "You live in this dangerous place, and with each passing day you're one more closer to..." Her voice trailed off, a look of discomfort on her face.

"It's alright, Chloe," Great Granny Felan assured. "Like I told Rosella, I'm not ready to pull the plug yet. I still got plenty of spry left in me. You both make it sound like I'm some ol' trout ready for the home."

"A trout?" Mom questioned.

"'The home'?" I asked.

"Just some funny wording." Great Granny Felan blew it off with a wave of her hand. "Anyway, how are you two doing? I know that I always ask this, but ever since Benjamin's passing, I can't stop thinking things."

"It's been rough, but I know that Ben's up there watching us. Rosella sometimes has dreams about him, too. Don't you, darling?" Mom focused her attention on me. "Rosella?"

I put up a finger and finished chewing the cookie stuffed in my mouth. "Mmm..." I gulped it down. "It's actually been some time, but when he first died, there were a few nights where I had this dream about my father. They were never negative, just cryptic. I always found him standing in a field of flowers, staring at me as I tried to run to him." I set the half-eaten cookie down, and motioned at the air with my hands. "I never closed any distance with him. He just stood there with a blank expression, those *empty* blue eyes staring back at me. And then, next thing I knew, I was awake in a cold sweat, and my heart felt like it was being squeezed."

Not usually one to dream, it was a strange occurrence I thought was brought on by grief I'd stashed away. Seeing my father silent, and with a blank expression, was abnormal, as most times he was smiling, and always had a thing to say, whether it was a joke or just a compliment about the weather. He was a genuinely cheery person, but just before his passing, I'd started seeing less and less of him, hearing less and less of his words, despite his attempts to remain who he truly was.

I jumped with surprise when a cold hand fell over mine, and looked to see Great Granny Felan staring intently at me.

"Say, have I shown you the little leaflings I'm currently growing?" she asked.

I cocked my head. "Leaflings?"

Great Granny Felan clapped her hands together. "Oh, good! You stay right there! I'll go get them." She rose from her chair and approached the back door. "I'll be just a second!" She slipped out with a hearty hum.

I got up from the table myself and glanced at Mom. "I think I'm going to step out for a minute. Just tell Great Granny Felan I needed to get some fresh air."

She nodded to me as she grabbed a cookie for herself. "Be careful out there, okay?"

"I know, I will."

I walked back through the living room and, as I opened the door, the soothing fresh air grazed my face like a gentle caress. I strode down the creaking steps, my eyes falling shut as I embraced the crunching of leaves. Smiling, I slipped under the cabin, and latched onto one of the sturdy supporting stakes. I gracefully spun around it on the toe of my shoe, giggling as my cloak and skirt splayed out around me, then yelped in surprise when my foot slipped.

I crashed against the hard, leaf-littered ground on my rear, and cringed as it throbbed from the impact. "Ouch!" I positioned myself on my knees and crawled out from under the cabin. "Ugh, geez…"

"Rosella! Are you okay?"

I looked up to see Great Granny Felan peering over the wooden railing. "Yeah, I'm fine!"

"Okay dear, I just… I thought I heard you say, 'ouch!'"

"No, I'm alright, promise!"

Great Granny Felan nodded, then disappeared from view.

Upon my knees, I shaded my eyes with a hand as I looked up to the bright sky. The clouds were scarce, leaving plenty of room for sunlight. This was my happy place, where I could easily be at peace with myself and forget everything. Here, in the trees, was where I truly belonged…

This is your home… and no one can take that from you.

I frowned at the intense rustling of the underbrush across the clearing, and my eyes widened when I found a mesmerizing pair of illuminating blue eyes staring back at me. My sneakers failed to gain traction against the floor of leaves as they scurried out in front of me. I froze mid-escape attempt when the glowing eyes began to move, and then a large creature gradually emerged from the trees with four ginormous paws, each with a set of large black claws. His strong front legs hanging at his sides, his glistening silver fur shimmered in the sunlight. An elongated muzzle tipped with a large black nose, his frowning maw revealed two rows of sharp white teeth certainly capable of ripping things apart in seconds flat.

Eyes locked as he dropped upon his front paws, I found myself, face to face, with the wolf.

CHAPTER 7

Fenris

T HE SWEET, COMFORTING AROMA of clary sage and rose wafting my nostrils, my tail thumped excitedly against the ground as I watched her vibrant red cloak flutter gently around her like a pair of angel wings. I adored the little show before me, how she danced about the cabin's stilts like the child she was, but when she fell, I shot up in a panic, fearful that she was hurt.

I want to see her. I need to see her... Unable to stop myself, I made my presence known, my nose quick to seek out drops of blood. *Oh good, she's* unharmed. I fell back on my rear, and swished my tail from side to side as Rosella silently scrambled to her feet. "Little Rose... It's been a long time."

She blinked a few times, then slowly raised a hand. "Fenris..." A blush granted her rose-tinted cheeks a tender glow as the sun's warm rays illuminated her beautiful golden hair, and a look of joy flashed across her face. "It's... It's really you!"

I happily accepted the comforting presence of her palm against my head. It melted away the cold, unbearable loneliness from my heart.

"I can't believe it! How are you doing?" she asked me. "It's been two years."

"Rosella..." I stared into her big, round blue eyes. If I looked close enough, I could make out the curious light they shared with mine.

Her face fell into a frown, and just like that the light was gone, her gaze having lost its luster. "I missed you," she murmured. "I missed you so much. After Dad's funeral, we came to visit, but you weren't there. Great Granny Felan said that you needed some time to yourself."

Guilt weighed me down with its phantom pressure, and I lowered my head. "My sweet Little Rose, I am so sorry I abandoned you. I hope you can forgive me one day."

"Fenris..."

She gingerly slipped her arms around my neck, and I nuzzled my face into her chest. Her tiny fingers kneaded deep into my fur and massaged my neck, a comfort I'd gone without for far too long. I lowered my ears, content, at peace.

"Fenris, I promise, I was never angry with you, so there is no need to ask for forgiveness. You were hurt by Dad's death as well. I can't be mad at you for that."

I whimpered. *Chloe told her he'd died in his sleep, but it was those pills... He just wanted it to stop.*

"Mom told me that he was very sick," Rosella continued, "and that simple medicine couldn't cure him."

The corners of my maw drooped further. "Yes, I recall that."

Rosella pulled away with a frown. "Fenris... Great Granny Felan's medicine didn't help him either, did it?"

I bowed my head. "It... It wasn't strong enough, no."

I refuse to put Felan through any more guilt, especially since she's suffering the curse herself! I am strong! I will fight this! I will beat this! This damn curse won't be the end of me!

Those words were the last Ben ever spoke to me at the end of his three-week visit, before his health took a nosedive, and he faded away a few days later. Chloe and I had given up on trying to convince him to stay that day he made his proclamation, and though Felan wasn't happy about it, she didn't argue. She never did. If someone really didn't want to do something, she wouldn't bother them. But it wasn't that Chloe and I wanted to bother him, we just wanted to help him, because his willpower wasn't as strong as he made it out to be...

Don't think about it, I thought to myself. *He did what he knew he had to do. It's not your fault that he died... It's not...* My eyes caught sight of Rosella's wrist and the wristband attached to it. *Always protect her, just like I promised... But how can I when I must stay within these woods?*

"Fenris, you're awful quiet," Rosella said. "More so than usual. Is something wrong?"

"Rosella, how are you holding up?" I asked. "I heard that you got into a fight with someone."

She nodded meekly. "I'm okay. Great Granny Felan's medicine cured me."

When I caught wind of Rosella's predicament, I was livid. I vented to Felan about how I wanted to run out there and see for myself what had become of my Little Rose, but at Felan's urging, I backed off. That fiendish girl could easily track me anyhow, and so could the others, if I set foot outside the trees. No matter how much it pained me, I had to stay concealed.

Fenris, these trees will protect you, so long as you never leave them. This place is your home, and one day we will take it back. Until that time comes, the Vessels must stay away, for once they're pulled in, there is no exit for them. And you know as much as I do how much more dangerous this place is than out there.

I heaved a sigh. *Felan was right that day, and at least Rosella can come and go as she pleases...* My eyes narrowed. *That is, until Felan is to enact the emergency measure.*

"Fenris?"

Having realized I was staring at the ground, I looked up and found Rosella's concerned gaze. "I'm sorry, Little Rose, did you say something?"

"I heard Mom calling you," she said. "Are you going to talk with her?"

I gave a curt nod. "Of course. Will you follow me, please?"

Rosella nodded back. "Sure."

We walked back to the cabin together, where we found Chloe waiting for us at the bottom of the steps. She ran over to greet me when we got close enough, and I lapped at her face as she attempted to throw her arms around me with a laugh. It was nice knowing I could still amuse her, despite my two-year absence.

"You don't show it often, but I enjoy seeing that inner pup," Chloe said with a playful grin. "I've missed you, but never forgotten about you."

A whimper slipped my lips, as she nuzzled her head against mine.

"It's so good to see you again," she whispered.

"I know," I said. "My sincerest apologies for leaving you."

She wiped at her wet eyes with her sleeve. "It's okay. You were still around, just out of sight."

"Ah, see you've kept your word after all!" Felan peered over the railing. "How's about you come up here? Got some things we need to talk about."

My eyes flashed to Rosella hurrying up the steps. I waited until she was out of earshot at the top, then turned to Chloe. "Does she know?" I whispered.

Chloe shook her head, her smile gone. "I never told her. I couldn't."

I sighed. "Oh, Chloe..."

"I know, I know." She ran a hand through her long brown hair. "I just... I'm scared, Fenris. I don't want to lose her too."

"I understand, but we must make haste. There is only so much time." I maneuvered around her and started up the steps. "We can't hide the truth from Rosella forever."

Chloe didn't say anything as she followed behind me.

"The curse has already claimed Ben's life, and soon it will claim Felan's..."

Chloe still didn't say anything.

"She has to know what's to come, when this forest finally—"

"I know, Fenris," Chloe interrupted.

"The Lurkers are vulnerable to the sun, and powerful under the moon," I continued on anyway, "and Rosella must stop them, as much as I hate to admit that..."

Chloe strode up to my side and rested a hand to it. "They are lost, Fenris, and no longer part of this forest. Like Benjamin, they're suffering the pain of the curse, and it's up to us to free them."

"Mom? Fenris?" Rosella appeared at the top of the steps. "Great Granny Felan's bringing out some lunch for us, meatloaf and mashed potatoes! Better hurry or it'll get cold."

Chloe laughed and hurried ahead of me. "Alright, we're coming."

"You don't have to worry about me," I called. "I devoured a hefty buck early this morning, and caught a couple of rabbits just before you came that I can fetch a little later."

Rosella nodded. "I'll leave a little for you, just in case. I know you like Great Granny Felan's cooking."

I chuckled. "Your generosity never wavers, Little Rose."

Seated at a table on the left side of the deck, the girls engaged in idle chatter while I rested comfortably on the right. Despite my large size, it was just big enough for me to only take up half of the space.

"Here you go," Felan whispered as she set a small bowl of meat and potatoes, another with cold water in front of me. "Indulge a little with us, won't you?"

I snickered. "Oh Felan…" Like Rosella said, I enjoyed Felan's cooking, perhaps more so than a fresh catch after a good hunt. And though I couldn't live off of it, it was nice to savor.

"So, Fenris…" Rosella peered over her shoulder. "I was wondering if you'd like to take a walk after lunch. We can catch up with each other."

"That sounds like a wonderful idea," I said. "Is that alright, Chloe?"

Chloe nodded. "I don't see why not."

I caught sight of the worry in her eyes, and I reflected it back to her. "We'll stay close, I promise."

Still a bit concerned, she looked to her daughter, but then sighed. "I… I guess a walk would do you both some good."

"Awesome!" Rosella's warm expression eased my nerves, but not enough.

How will she react? I thought to myself. *I expect her to be confused, but what if she's scared? She's so used to the life she's got now.*

Talk to her, Fenris. She needs to know. It's the only way I'll be able to reach her. Please…

I closed my eyes, and gave a tiny nod. *I will do my best. As both hers and your noble wolf, I will carry out my duty as promised. You made me a Guardian for a reason.*

"Great Granny Felan, do you think you'll be able to teach me how to grow plants soon?"

Rosella's question made my ears perk at attention, and I strained to listen more closely.

"Well, sweetheart," Felan responded, "using Snodaful can be tricky. But I suppose I could try teaching you sometime soon."

"Do you really mean that?" Rosella asked.

"Of course."

Rosella bounced in her seat with a joyous grin. "Yay! I'm so excited."

Felan chuckled. "Now now, don't get too excited. I need to make sure I have some good samples your father gave me."

Out of the corner of my eye, Rosella's eyes widened in curiosity.

"It's difficult to explain unless bluntly. This forest... It holds more power than the town could ever grasp, and it was entrusted to me." Felan glanced my way. "Fenris can give you a better rundown during your walk."

Chloe, who'd been silent the entire time, suddenly shot up from the table. "Please, excuse me." She sped around the table and along the side of the cabin.

"Chloe!" I called out.

"It's alright Fenris," Felan said. "She's having a difficult time, just as we expected. She will be okay."

Rosella frowned at Felan. "What's wrong with Mom?"

Felan patted her great-granddaughter's hand. "Don't worry about that for now, dear. Finish your lunch."

Rosella seemed like she wanted to push the issue, but decided to keep quiet and worked on her food instead. Felan and I followed suit, and when we were all finished, she set to handling the dishes while Rosella and I took our walk. As we came around the front of the cabin, Chloe was nowhere to be found, though the clear scent of honeydew I picked up from her indicated she was back inside.

"Rosella, there is a lot we need to talk about," I said. "I should proceed slowly, so that you don't get lost."

"Is it bad?" she asked worriedly.

"No..." *Not all of it.*

"It's okay, Fenris. You can tell me." Rosella leaned into my side. "Lead the way, won't you?"

As we walked down the steps at a leisurely pace, I kept a straight face, despite my stomach twisting in anxious knots. There was a lot that Rosella didn't know about, and if I didn't tell her now, it would only hurt her in the long run. But there was the fear of her being either angry with me or afraid of me that kept gnawing at my conscience. What if she got the wrong idea because I was away for two years? And what about the fact that I'd only seen her once a week for six years? Sure, six years is much longer than two, but it wasn't like we got to really talk.

Every time she'd paid a visit, it was always about something like cartoons or art. Art was an easier topic, as Rosella used to show Felan and me many pictures from her sketchbook, and I could just nod with amusement. But then, when Ben died, all of that stopped, and Rosella's demeanor changed.

She hasn't brought up art once, I realized. *In the span of two years...*

"Fenris... It's been really lonely since Dad died."

I looked over to Rosella, but didn't say anything.

"I miss him." She shuffled a foot into the dry leaves that littered the ground. "It's not the same."

My ears went flat to my head, and I hesitated on a response. *I could tell her about what happened to him, but it might be too soon yet... Where should I start? Think... Think.* "Rosella, have you ever heard of the story regarding the shoemaker and his wife?"

I wanted to knock my head against a tree. Such a strange question out of left field that was. Sure, it played an important part in all of this... I sighed. There was no better way to start the conversation, and now it was too late to turn back.

Rosella's eyebrows arched with curiosity. "I asked Mom about it once. I was about six years old at the time, and I heard someone making comments about it. When they mentioned Great Granny Felan's name, I became curious."

"How much do you know?" I questioned. *Hopefully this goes over well.*

She stroked her chin, an inquisitive expression on her face. "Well, Mom told me that sometime in 1950, Great Granny Felan was married to a nice man whom she lived in a decent house with a built-in shop. Great Granny Felan was the baker, and he was the shoemaker. Both were kind spirits, full of hope and blithe." She fell silent, and nervously grasped her arms.

I felt a claw puncture a stray leaf on my left paw, and I lifted it to examine it. "Back in the day, things were much cheaper, so making $5 a day was comfortable living for them," I continued for her. "Though, success was difficult to come by in the beginning..."

"Even though sales were scarce in the beginning, they gave bread and shoes to the poor for free," Rosella went on. "One day, however, the shoemaker's kindness got the best of him when he decided to go out and collect berries for Great Granny Felan's pies. He could find none at any shop, so he sought out the forest just beyond."

"There, he found many berries," I said while shaking the leaf from my claw. "And then..."

"While he was picking the berries, he thought he'd heard a child's giggle, but found no one." Rosella kicked at a few leaves, and watched as they meekly sputtered out in front of her. "He told Great Granny Felan when he got home and, still concerned, opted to go out and find said child while his wife was safe at home. A man with a kind soul, he felt awful knowing a child could be out there, alone and afraid... Several hours passed, and he hadn't returned. Though worried, Great Granny Felan held out hope that he'd soon return. Those hours turned into a whole day, and then a few. She began to panic."

I lowered my head. "The town heard the screams of agony, and Felan went into hysterics."

"She ran after him, into the trees, the villagers begging her to stop."

"But it was too late, for she was already gone." My ears pressed further into my skull as I looked to the trees. "Her mind consumed by the forest, her body set out to reunite with it." *I remember all of it. The terror in her eyes... Screaming like a banshee... I almost didn't make it in time to save her.*

"That story is nonsense," Rosella muttered. "It's just a made-up fairytale to make Great Granny Felan look like she was some crazy old bat. Hell, I don't even fully believe the shoemaker himself exists. I've never seen pictures of him, and Great Granny Felan never talks about him."

Hearing those words made me want to shut down her outburst, but I stayed silent, as I feared arguing would only upset her further.

"And now, thanks to Georgia Morse's meddling, people think she sacrificed him to some demon overlord, and that she did the same to Sarah Mitchell when she vanished."

I spread my maw in a thin line. *Chloe really hasn't told her anything. And as much as I wish to preserve her innocence, I can't... I need to find a way to calm her down, so it's easier to reason with her.* I looked over to her, then frowned. "Rosella?"

Beside me, Rosella had suddenly gone stiff. Her eyes wide, her small hands shook at her sides.

CHAPTER 8

Rosella

I COULDN'T UNDERSTAND WHAT happened. It was like my legs had up and decided to stop working, and my voice had vanished from my throat. I felt something prick my back, and my hands suddenly raked up and down my arms. There was nothing, nothing there despite the prattling up my shoulders, the coiling around my neck. My fingers searched for something, anything. Nothing. The air, air suddenly felt so thin. Things were spinning around me. My chest tightened.

Oh god! Air, air, I need air!

I scrambled my feverish hands through my hair. Goosebumps, goosebumps everywhere. I had to get rid of them. I tore through my scalp, scrabbled my hands across my stomach and over my sides, swatted at the prickles biting my neck. Something was crawling inside me, had to get it out!

My nails frantically scoured up and down my arms once more, trying like hell to get rid of whatever it was that had burrowed into my skin. So, so itchy, like someone had rubbed it raw with sandpaper. And the whispering, it sounded like cicadas were burrowing into my ears. I tried to plug them, but it was no good. I could still hear them!

Who is making all this noise? I wondered. *And why am I so ITCHY?*

"Rosella!"

I gasped in surprise at the sudden rush of oxygen to my lungs, and as I doubled over, the uncomfortable itching and nonstop whispering vanished.

"Are you alright?" Fenris nudged me with his large nose. "Rosella?"

My arms snaked around myself. *Wh-What just happened? The hell...?*

"Rosella, are you okay?" Fenris asked again. There was a sense of urgency to his tone.

"Sorry," I said. "Must've felt a cold chill. Mom once said that if you got a sudden chill, it was because a ghost was passing through you. But... it didn't feel like... a ghost."

"Do you need to rest for a minute?" Fenris offered his side to me. "We can sit if you'd like."

"No, I'm okay." I gave him a reassuring smile. "I'm okay." I frowned. "I just... I don't understand what happened there."

A stern look settled on the wolf's face, and he glided around me, as if drifting just above ground. "What do you think happened?"

I followed his fluid movements, our eyes locked. "I... I don't..."

The wolf paused at my side. "Tell me."

"I..." A response lingered at the tip of my tongue, but it wouldn't come. I'd completely lost track of my thoughts.

"Go on," he pressed.

"I... I don't know," I said in a panic. "Wh-What do you think?"

The wolf stilled. "I think..." He lowered upon his haunches. "You should hop on my back."

My eyes widened. "Wh-What?"

"I said to hop on," the wolf requested again with a sterner tone.

"Uh... What...?" *He's never asked me to do that before.*

"It's alright," he urged, "just do it."

"Are you... sure?" I asked dumbly. "I mean..." I fell silent at his curt nod. *He's not going to ask again.*

"Rosella..."

Hop on. You can do it.

"O-Okay. I guess it'll be alright."

"If it grants you comfort, you have my word that you will be safe." He gave me a reassuring nod. "I promise, you can trust me."

Trust him, I thought. *Of course I trust him. I... I've known him long enough.*

Six years had gone by since Fenris came into my life quite suddenly. I thought it was pretty fricken cool, and the fact that I had to keep his existence secret was even cooler. I had something the town did not, a special treasure that I could safely enjoy without anyone ever knowing.

Remember, Rosella, do not tell anyone about Fenris. He is here to protect us, and only us. He cannot protect anyone else because they don't see him the same way we do. He is trusting you with this secret, and so you must trust him with your life.

Great Granny Felan's words echoed in my mind, and I nodded somewhat confidently. Though our relationship was a little different than it was with Sophia, I could trust him equally so.

Though not once in the six years I've known him has he ever offered this... I nervously tiptoed toward the wolf. "O-Okay, Fenris. I'll try to be gentle..."

A quiet rumble rattled his throat.

I hesitantly clutched his soft, silky fur. "If I pull, will that hurt?"

"Not at all," he assured. "It takes a lot to inflict pain on me."

"Okay." I hugged his neck and, standing on the tip of one high-top sneaker, raised my leg.

"Go on," he urged.

"R-Right." I attempted to swing my raised leg over his back. It came down, quite hard, on the back of his neck, as I slid myself around a smidge. "Crap." My strained muscles tightening further and further with each second I was stuck in this position, I awkwardly scrambled up and flopped onto his back.

"Make sure you're settled," he uttered. He sounded completely unaffected by my shenanigan.

"R-Right." I jostled my rear while sitting myself up, my exhausted legs snug around his sides. "Urgh... O-Okay." I scooted myself up his back a bit and gripped his neck. "Okay... Now, wh—"

I didn't get the chance to finish my sentence because Fenris suddenly darted forward, and a gust of wind was shoved down my throat. It blew back my hood with abrupt force, as I pressed myself into the wolf's body and squeezed my eyes shut. It was like I'd been thrust into a tornado, the wind was so strong.

"Open your eyes, Rosella!" he called. "Look at what's before you!"

I tightened my grip on his neck in response.

"Relax, my dear, you're alright!"

"Ngh! What are you talking about!?" I dared crack open one eye. "What... Ah..."

I was amazed by the sight before me. The trees looked like smears of earthly paints on a canvas, and they were going by so fast. The ground rolled at a breakneck pace, as if Fenris was moving it. Exhilaration flooded my lungs within the rush of fresh air, like a newborn babe taking their first breath, my eyes wide with wonder.

I cautiously rose up just enough to see over his head, and gasped as Fenris swiftly dodged a tree so close to us that, had it been an inch over, we would've smacked right into it.

The wolf howled with amusement as his paws pounded the speeding dirt. "No worries, Rosella! I know this forest well."

"Wait, where are we going?" I eyed a particular tree closing in on us, and my heart leaped up to my throat. "Uh, Fenris!? We're gonna hit it!"

Fenris ignored me and lowered his head.

Fearing the worst, I hugged to his back as tightly as possible. "Fenris! I— *Whoooooooaaaaaaaaaaa!!!!!!!!!!!!!!*"

Rather than striking the tree head-on, I found myself clutching Fenris' back for dear life as he literally *ran up* the tree. My eyes bulging, I screamed again and, in consequence, caught some of my hair in my mouth. One hand still firmly glued to Fenris, the other set to fishing out the blonde strands grazing the edge of my throat.

"Rosella?" Fenris asked. "Are you alright back there?"

I choked out the last bit of my hair and screamed. "This is crazy!!!!!! I am going to *die!!!!!!*"

"We're almost there now!" Fenris cried.

I kept my mouth shut so as not to risk swallowing more of my hair as it whipped at my face again. *'Hop on my back,' he said! 'You will be fine,' he said!*

"Hang on!"

'Hang on,' he says! WHAT DO YOU THINK I'M DOIN' HERE, WOLF!?

Out of nowhere, as if what I'd already experienced wasn't frightening enough, Fenris began to slow down.

OH HELL NO! WE'RE GONNA FALL! Ignoring the chance of choking on my hair again, I voiced my protest. "Fenris! Are you crazy!? You stop, and we're gonna... We're gonna..." My voice trailed off, and my jaw dropped.

"Here we are, Little Rose. My sincerest apologies for the stressful ride up." Fenris carefully steadied himself atop the branch. "Don't worry, I understand the term, 'precious cargo'."

A meek squeal slipped my lips as the wolf ducked his head, and I clutched at his neck to keep from sliding forward.

"Rosella, it's okay."

"I-I..." My eyes were glued to the frightening view before me. That tree branch looked awful thin.

"Gently straddle my neck as you scoot your way down. You can do it."

"This is crazy..."

I did as Fenris instructed me to, but it wasn't easy. The fear of slipping off and falling to my death weighed heavily in my conscious, though it faintly shrank when the toes of my high tops touched the branch. My arms stuck out at either side of me as the wolf's head slipped out from under my legs, and I slowly lowered myself to my knees.

Heart racing in my chest, my hands grasped the thick tree branch so tightly my skin burned from the biting bark as I settled upon it. My feet felt nothing but the air beneath them as they swung out in front of me.

"Just relax." Fenris seated himself upon the branch next to me. It swayed with his weight, his tail dangling behind him as he bunched his paws together underneath him.

"Eek! Don't do that! I'm gonna fall off!"

"If you fall, I will catch you. I promise."

I opened my mouth to retaliate with a snappy comeback, but instead found myself drawn to those hypnotic, ethereal blue eyes. Contrasting the sun's glaring rays, a moonlit hue illuminated his bedazzled irises, captivating me in his luminous gaze.

"I remember how much you adore the trees, so I brought you to them as a means to further indulge in their beauty."

I tore myself away from his luring eyes and stared upon the branch in silence. My fingers grazed over the coarse, rigid bark as my nails traced the nooks and cracks etched into it.

"So, how are you feeling?" he asked.

"Really?" I looked back to him with a cocked brow. "That's what you wanna ask me?"

A mortified expression sprung to his face. "How insensitive of me." His ears fell flat to his head. "My apologies."

"No... I..." I searched for the right words, and then gave a hearty chuckle. "Sorry. I just... I never thought I'd find myself at the top of a very tall tree. If you were to tell nine year old me that she would meet a talking wolf capable of riding her up a tree, she'd call you crazy."

Fenris snorted with amusement, then locked eyes with me again. "Do you feel even closer now to the trees than you did before?"

I struggled for a response whilst entranced by those alluring eyes. They were as vibrant a blue as the daytime sky.

"Take a look at what's before you," he whispered. "Tell me what you see."

As much as I wanted to indulge in the beauty of his addicting gaze, I forced my focus between his eyes.

"Not me, the world before you."

I shamefully lowered my head. "I'm sorry. One thing that bothers me is when someone gawks at me, and here I am doing it to you."

"It's alright," the wolf mused. "If it helps, I didn't think you were gawking." He motioned at the air with his elongated snout. "Now then… Take a look, won't you?"

I hesitated.

The wolf gave me a judging look. "Is trust not your forte today?"

I shut my eyes. He couldn't stare me down if I shielded my view.

"I take it as truth then…" A gentle sigh, one of patience, exhaled from his large maw. "I was right in my course of action, for it seems that you lack the skills needed to attempt understanding of others' intentions."

I opened my eyes again, blood suddenly boiling with anger. "Hey, listen. You weren't locked in a house for years because your mother was too nervous to let you face the public. You don't struggle to make friends at school because you're afraid that they'll judge you too quickly and worry about them talking behind your back. You aren't some outcast just trying to fit in!"

The wolf's furry brow rose.

"I… I am so sorry," I mumbled quickly. "I don't know where that came from." I tore away from his gaze, embarrassed. "I… I…"

My thoughts broke apart at the breathtaking view before me. The clouds swam in the sky above as the burning sun flared like a powerful beacon of light over the emerald field of trees. In the distance, a few birds glided through the air and engaged in a synchronized swirl. A sight like this was hard to come by, and I was lucky enough to experience it.

"Beautiful, isn't it?" Fenris asked.

"It looks like the birds are dancing," I said.

"Perhaps they are…" Fenris chuckled to himself. "Wondrous little creatures…"

I nodded slowly. "Yeah…"

"Rosella, don't let them fool you."

Confusion crossed my face, and I peered over at the wolf. "The birds?"

Eyes narrowed, his soft gaze hardened into a cold stare, though their comforting light remained.

"Fenris?" I ushered.

"Some of the creatures of this forest," he specified. "Some of them fear me and the sun, for they are vulnerable to our power." He glanced at me from the corner of his eye. "The sun kills them slowly, but surely. A swift take-down is better, but it's a good alternative when you lack a weapon."

"I... I'm not following."

"The Lurkers, Rosella... They prowl the night, in search of either their next meal or potential sacrifices."

"'Lurkers'? Sounds like a band or something." I made a face. "And 'sacrifices'... Makes me think of the rumors about Great Granny Felan."

"I've heard. Distasteful, but I cannot give my opinion unless I wish to be revealed, and I do not." His gaze softened once more, as his head turned my way. "Rosella, there's a reason I brought you all the way out here, and it's because I don't want your mother interrupting us."

My brow furrowed. "My mother?"

The wolf sighed. "As you just confirmed, she's kept you in close sights for a long time. In fact, she was afraid of you even knowing about me."

I gave him a questioning look. "Why would she want to keep your presence a secret from me, besides the fact that she felt I was a little too young? Are you not actually a wolf? Are you, like, actually a demon or a god or something?"

"That's pretty far-fetched," he said with a chuckle, "but one answer should suffice the curiosity your multitude of questions bring. I am not a god nor demon. I am... what you would call a 'protector', or the official term, 'Guardian' of the forest."

Intrigued, I maneuvered a little closer to him. "What does that entail?"

"This forest is full of magic," the wolf explained. "I have been around for quite some time, and that is because I am one of several Guardians who have been assigned to protect it."

I cocked an eyebrow. Fenris had never disclosed anything like this to me, or much of anything really. Usually, it was me who did most of the talking, and he would listen in silence.

"This forest, in a sense, birthed me," he went on. "It is my home, but as I said, there are... dangerous forces that lurk within it."

"You mean, like those 'Lurkers' you just mentioned?"

"Yes."

I winced at the canines peeking out from under his curling lip. "A-And, uh, how does this play into the rumors?"

The wolf settled himself again with a deep breath. "The shoemaker..."

"What about him?"

He stared back at me with a stern expression.

"No way... No." I shook my head. "No, that can't be true. There's no way. People made up that story just to make Great Granny Felan look..." My words faded to silence as the wolf bowed his head.

"I know you don't wish to believe, because the town is the one that spoke of it, but you must."

"But, that story!" I protested. "It's just a fable! Great Granny Felan hasn't ever talked about the shoemaker or shown evidence that he existed. And everything that Georgia Morse said is also a lie."

"Wouldn't the town say the same to you if you told them I existed?" Fenris challenged.

"Well, yes, of course! But you're real!"

The wolf raised his nose to the air, as a gentle breeze combed his fur. "What we choose to hear, and what we choose to believe, are two very complicated things. Some choose to hear only good things and believe in them, while others choose to hear only the bad things and believe in them. But some choose to hear both, thus making it harder for them to choose what to believe is good or bad." He flicked an ear, as a thoughtful look graced his face. "However, there is also the matter of *who* they choose to hear from, and believe."

I winced as the wolf turned to me and leaned in close, his muzzle pointing down as we locked eyes again.

"Ask yourself this..." he breathed. "Do you feel too uncomfortable believing in the town, or do you feel most comfortable believing in me?"

"Wh-What kind of... What kind of question is that?" I asked, utterly confused. "Please, elaborate."

Fenris' eyes darted to their corners, in the direction of the view before us. "Take this tree we're sitting upon. You were absolutely terrified of the ride here. You were nervous to even climb onto my back. I know, because I saw the fear in your eyes. But you trusted me."

I frowned. "Okay, but—"

"If the people of Hollow were the same as me," he interrupted, "you'd deny them your trust."

My eyes widened at his challenging words. "Okay, but Fenris, I've known you for years!"

"Yes, but you've also known the town for years," he pointed out. "Actually longer, you know."

"O-Okay, but y-you don't point and stare, and mindlessly spread gossip about us, like they do. You are my friend, and you always tell the truth, so..." My words trailed off, as the mental lightbulb went off in my head, and the wolf cocked a furry brow at me. I fell right into his paw, and just gave him exactly what he expected.

"Now do you see where I'm going with this?" he asked.

I pressed my lips into a thin line. I didn't want to answer.

"I see... I will give you time to mull over this."

Fenris resigned himself to silently watching the clouds above, leaving me to wrestle with the tangle of thoughts jumbled in my head. Choosing to hear either good or bad things only, and choosing to believe only in one or the other... That much, I knew, was bullshit. The world isn't just good or just bad. It's both.

But when it came to *who,* I'd choose Fenris over the town any day, though he never had anything bad to say, if much of anything at all. He never said much, staying mostly quiet, until today. The one time he is vocal, and he says that the town is telling the truth... To me, what the town was saying about the forest was bad, but he was saying the same thing, even though I was comfortable confiding in him, and trusted him...

My face fell into my hands, as I gave a defeated sigh. This whole conversation was complex, but the conclusion was simple. Fenris always spoke the truth. So that meant, for once, the town of Hollow was in the right, even though I didn't want to admit it...

And because it regards the forest, now... I don't feel as safe in it. This world used to be my happy place, but with my view of it now tarnished, I was afraid to trust it. *But what about Fenris? I still trust him...* My fingers spread apart, and my eyes darted to their corners, to the wolf.

"Rosella?" He was giving me a questioning look.

I nervously looked back up at the wolf, and nodded. "I... I believe you, Fenris. If you say there are evil creatures here in the forest, and that the shoemaker's story is true, then I believe you. Which means..." I blew a gust of air from my lips, my brow furrowed. "I have to believe the town. However, I still don't believe that Great Granny Felan is either running a cult or caused the shoemaker's death. I also reject the notion that she prompted Sarah Mitchell's disappearance, especially because you do..." As I spoke those last words, I flinched at the unsettling doubt creeping into my conscience. *No, stop it. He is part of this forest, but that doesn't mean he's 'evil'.*

The wolf didn't seem to notice my unease, or perhaps he did, but chose not to show it. His ears were perked, and he seemed a little surprised by my answer, though I could see his tail wiggle just a bit, as if he was satisfied.

Easily fooling me if he can read me, I thought.

"Do you have a better understanding now?" the wolf asked.

"I do, but... I have one more question." I turned away from him, as a solemn frown settled on my face. "Why would you not tell me this sooner?"

He uttered a low whimper. "I... I wasn't sure how you'd respond. I didn't want to upset you."

I dared to glance at him, and immense regret trampled my doubt.

Guilt was etched into the wolf's furry face, his ears flat to his head, his maw pulled into a deep frown. He was clearly refusing to look at me, as if he was ashamed.

I gave a sigh. "Fenris... Since you've chosen to be honest with me today, I feel it's fair I be honest with you too." *Or as honest as I can be I suppose, because I'm too ashamed to admit being wary of you.*

The wolf craned his neck slightly, and his gaze hesitantly flickered to me. "Oh?"

I pulled my hood over my head, and shrunk into my cloak. "After Dad died, I dropped art like it was a rock sinking into the ocean. And on top of that, I've been struggling in school. I've only made one friend within the last couple years, because I'm too afraid to engage with others."

"It's definitely hard adjusting to a world you are unfamiliar with," Fenris said.

"Yeah, it is, especially when I'm a frequent target of harassment by one particular person, and every time I'm in trouble, my only friend swoops in to protect me. I... I don't want to depend on her saving me all the time, but it's so hard because, like I said, I'm scared."

"Rosella, it's hard to fit in, but it's even harder when you don't at least try."

"A fierce blow to the heart there," I muttered.

"I'm sorry," he murmured.

"No, it's okay, I needed to hear it again."

"Again?"

I nodded. "Sophia told me basically what you just said. She also said she'd be there to help me. But like I just said, I don't want to keep depending on her. I need to be able to stand up for myself, to go out and see the world with a brave face like my father did." I looked back to the wolf, and found him reflecting my troubled expression. "He used to go to all sorts of places and meet all kinds of people, whether good or bad, and he still came out okay."

The wolf ever so slightly adjusted his bearings atop the branch, his action reminding me to check if I was steady. "I see. I am so sorry you are struggling."

I bowed my head, my eyelids quick to block the view below. "It's... difficult at times, yes, and I know it's because I let my fear control me. I just... When I meet someone new, I lock up and assume they either won't like me or toss me uncomfortable questions."

"But you are comfortable with Sophia," Fenris guessed. "How long have you known her, if you don't mind me asking?"

"A very long time, since I was little," I said. "We met at the old library, not the replacement one Mom owns. It was during an event... She's the one person I feel safest with out there..." I fell silent at those words and squeezed the branch I sat upon. The incident at the mall had suddenly come crawling back to mind. *The timing, right as Sophia blew up, and then the cashier's counter breaking...*

"Rosella?" Fenris gently nudged my head with his nose. "Something else is bothering you. Can you tell me?"

I shook my head. "I... I don't know if..."

"You can tell me, Little Rose."

"It's okay, Fenris. Really, it's nothing."

"It's about the incident at the mall, isn't it?"

My head swiveled in his direction, my eyes wide. "H-How did you...?"

Fenris gave me a sad look. "Felan told me after Chloe told her."

"Sh-She told Great Granny Felan?"

"She did."

I wanted to avert my gaze to my shoes, but the nauseating sight of the ground dozens of feet away wasn't any more appeasing, so I was forced to face the wolf head-on.

"Rosella, it's okay," Fenris assured me gently. "Really."

"N-No, it isn't. We were being gawked at, and then right as Sophia got all huffy with the cashier, the damn counter broke apart and..." I looked away from him.

A prolonged silence settled between us. Not even the birds had anything to add. So during this time, I sat there, mulling over everything that'd been exchanged, and how to proceed. This conversation with him, it was different. He was never this talkative before. Why the sudden change?

He said he had important things to tell me, and he did. But now he's asking about Sophia...

"Rosella, Felan said you'd started school... in the middle. Did Sophia help with that?"

There he goes again. I took a deep breath, and then answered. "It's called middle school. It comes before high school. And yes, Sophia was there to help. I was nervous about it, but also kind of excited because it meant I could learn stuff and make new friends, like her. Though, that plan fizzled out upon meeting Caroline..."

"And Caroline is...?"

"The person who consistently harasses me on a daily basis," I muttered.

Fenris nodded. "I see. And what about Sophia? Do she and this Caroline know each other?"

"Yeah, but I'm not sure how long." I returned my gaze to him. "Ya know, Sophia once told me she literally dropped all of her original friends just to be with me."

Fenris' ears perked up yet again, a look of sheer surprise on his face. He almost seemed... astounded, like it was unbelievable.

"It was a couple years ago when she told me," I continued. "She said that they weren't her real friends because they were 'shallow'. Not sure what she meant by that, but..." I shrugged. "I don't know."

Fenris didn't say anything, his expression unchanged.

"That girl would do anything for me," I continued. "And it really bothers me, because not only did she lose friendships I'm sure she worked hard to keep, but again..." I gave a huff. "I sound like a broken record at this point."

"Do you know for sure she worked hard to keep those friendships?" Fenris asked, a hint of urgency to his voice. "Did she say so?"

"All Sophia told me was that they were shallow. She wouldn't talk further about it."

"I see..." His tone had a slight edge to it, arousing my curiosity.

"Fenris?" My eyes darted to their corners in direction of the wolf. "Is... everything alright?"

He looked around, then sighed. "Well, I hate to cut this so short, but I feel that we should head back now."

"Oh, y-yeah, I... I do kinda want to get down." Tempted to look, I stretched my neck, then wandered back into the comfort of the wolf's gaze.

"Though I am certain this will be difficult, you must put your trust in me to help you." Eyes connected, he silently questioned me with a look that said, "Do you trust me to get you down?"

In response, I pulled my legs tightly to my chest and, slowly, began my ascension with wobbly ankles.

"Focus all of your weight to your upper body."

My hands tight to the branch, my torso caved into my rib cage as I mustered a powerful inhale.

"Okay, now stay calm... Very slowly pull yourself up. There you go."

I spread my arms out at either side of me as Fenris crouched in front of me.

"Just tiptoe toward me." He bowed his head. "You can climb over this way."

You can do it... I thought to myself. *Just breathe, and then go.*

Following his instructions, I crawled atop his head and over, my heart a flurry of rapid beats in my chest, but I stayed focused. My fingers clawed into his soft silver fur, and my knees burrowed into his neck as I journeyed to his back. I finally exhaled the overwhelming amount of oxygen trapped in my lungs once I was seated securely atop his back. I carefully spun myself around so I was facing forward, and breathed a heavy sigh of relief.

"There, now." He chuckled. "I know that was frightening, but you did wonderfully."

I clung once more to his fur, my body sliding as he stood up on his two back legs and turned himself around.

"Whoa!" I cried. "Whoa... Whoa. Okay! Oof!" I bobbed up and down, my arms and legs spread wide as I hugged his back.

"My apologies," he urged. "Are you alright?"

"Y-Yeah, I'm good."

During the few seconds Fenris spent galloping down the tree, my elbows were hooked into his neck, my legs plastered to his sides. But I remained calm. Fenris told me I could trust him, and he proved it when we reached the bottom without a scratch on me.

He had me back at Great Granny Felan's in minutes, where both she and Mom were shocked to see him gracefully skid to a halt before them. I hopped off of his back, thankful to again feel the ground beneath my feet.

I sheepishly greeted both Mom and Great Granny Felan, as Fenris planted his rear to the ground, his tail wagging vigorously. "H-Hi Mom, Great Granny Felan. Fenris here took me out for a ride."

"I see that." Great Granny Felan eyed him with an amusing grin. "And, uh, just where did you two go?"

"Through some of the trees ahead. He actually climbed up one, with me on him, and we got to sit at the top…" I threw my hands behind me. "It was actually pretty cool."

"Goodness! Well, I am glad you two had fun." She put her hands on her hips, and a hard frown surfaced to her face. "Why, Rosella, you walked out before I could show you those leaflings."

I gave a laugh. "Right, sorry about that. Why don't we take a look at them now?"

CHAPTER 9

A CALMING AMBIANCE GRADUALLY surrounded us as a sheet of darkness draped over the trees, and the rising moon shed its pastel light upon the clearing whilst the sun was laid to rest for the day. Barely visible, the silent paper lanterns wavered in a rhythmic dance, a brush of wind manipulating their routine.

Great Granny Felan peered over the deck railing. "You ready?" she called down.

"Yeah!" I shouted back.

"Alright!"

With the press of a button, the paper lanterns burst to life, and the trees broke free of their eerie shadows as they welcomed the light that embroidered the cabin's roof and railing. It was an enchanting sight to behold.

"Looks like they're all in working order," Great Granny Felan declared. She put her hands on her hips. "Best be gettin' on home then."

"Do you have all the lights on?" Fenris asked.

"Yes, even the ones at the trail." She pointed toward the trail ahead. "See 'em?"

"I do." He beckoned for me and Mom to hop on. "It's time to go, you two."

"This is cool," I said while scrambling over his side.

Mom swiftly jumped on behind me. "I've missed it."

I peered over my shoulder to her once I was settled. "You've ridden Fenris before?"

She nodded. "We used to run around the forest together."

Fenris chuckled. "It was quite amusing hearing your mother squeal every time we almost hit a tree."

Mom frowned at him. "Hey, you told me you understood what 'precious cargo' meant. That didn't mean you could tease me!"

He snorted. "I wouldn't have let anything happen to you."

I laughed. "He told me the same thing, and kept his word."

"Enough chatter, hop to wolfy." Great Granny Felan suddenly appeared at his side and patted him. "Must be off before it gets later."

Fenris nodded. "Of course, Felan."

Mom and I cued Fenris with a pair of nods, and he charged into the forest at a brisk pace, the trail of paper lanterns as his guide. The ride back wasn't nearly as frightening, if at all. There were a few dangerously close trees that zipped us by, but I trusted him to get us back home safely, and he did.

We reached the edge of the forest in minutes, and as Fenris decelerated to a casual trot several feet from the exit, he slipped out of the trees and toward the backyard fence. The wolf came to a halt just before the fence's door and awaited our dismount, his tail wagging gently behind him.

"I guess this is goodbye for now, old friend." Mom hopped off of his back, and came around to rest a hand against his furry cheek. "I'll miss you."

He tapped his nose to her head. "Please, do not be sad. I am always here for you and Rosella."

Mom gave him a quick hug, then tore herself away and darted for the house.

I cautiously slid off of the wolf, and faced him with a concerned gaze. "Are you... okay?"

Worry played at the majestic wolf's eyes as they met mine. "I am, but how about you?"

I nodded. "Yeah, I'm fine." I looked over my shoulder. "But I'm concerned for Mom. She was crying."

Fenris shuffled his paws around, as he tore his gaze away from me.

"Fenris?"

He angled his head, a shadow cast over his face. "Rosella, heed my warning and stay away from the forest after dark. Also, do not, and I repeat, *do not*, enter it on your own. Do you understand me, Little Rose?"

A little frightened by his serious tone, I gave a hesitant nod. "I promise."

Satisfied, the wolf backed away, and spun himself around. "Until we meet again then…" He sped off into the trees and, just like that, he vanished as quickly as he'd arrived.

For a minute I just stood there, waiting. Maybe he'd forgotten to tell me something and would come back. Or, maybe he missed Mom so much he didn't want their time together to end.

"Hey, Rosella?" Mom called. "You coming?"

"Yeah." I wandered back to the house, an inkling of disappointment dripping from my response.

"Since we haven't had dinner yet, I'm going to make something quick."

"Alright, sounds good."

With a tired nod, Mom walked away.

I lingered at the back porch, unable to break my gaze from the trees. *I want to see him again,* I thought. *And I don't wanna have to wait another two years for that to happen.*

A beautiful resounding howl echoed beyond the trees, and fascination played at my upturned face. Content, I meandered back into the house. I had to trust his word. I'd get to see him again, and when the time came, I'd sit with him, and dig into every inch of his mysterious aura until I found what I was looking for, like an archaeologist seeking a legendary fossil beneath the piles of dirt with nothing but a soft brush.

For the first time today, he let me into his mind, and I learned a lot. But I knew there was more.

"Hey, Mom." I found her at the kitchen counter, her back to me. "What do you think Fenris does during the night?"

"I… I don't know," she whispered.

I frowned. "Are you okay? You're not still upset about our… conversation, are you?"

She turned around with a strained expression. "Rosella, why don't you go wash up while I prepare some leftover pasta."

"Mom…" I raised a concerned hand. "You look upset. What's wrong?"

"It's nothing, Rosella. I'm just tired."

I shook my head. "I'm not buying that."

"Rosella…"

As much as I didn't want to, I had to play the strongest card in my hand. "Talk to me, or I'll tell Great Granny Felan on you." I crossed my arms over my chest. "Come on. Please."

Mom groaned as she pounded a fist against the counter. "I-I'm stressed about work and I've run into writer's block with my newest book. I'm also worried about your great-grandmother and the forest…" Her voice nervously trailed off on the last word. Both hands coursing her face, a few tears evaded their capture.

"Hey, if something's bothering you, tell me."

She sucked in a quivering breath. "I'm thinking about entering the forest… alone, after dark."

My eyes widened. "What!?"

"I know, I know. Just hear me out for a second." Mom clasped her hands at her front. "I'm sure Fenris mentioned something about 'Lurkers'."

"I mean, he told me a little about them. They hate the sun. Oh, and he's a Guardian." I frowned, and crossed my arms over my chest. "And, uh, he also told me that you wanted to hide his presence from me."

Her face paled, as a look of fear flashed across her face. "H-He did…"

"Yep, and that the town's rumors about the forest were true. I didn't want to believe it, but…" I sighed. "I trust his word, so I…" I fell silent as she put up a hand.

"Nevermind, forget what I said."

I gave her a look of suspicion. "Mom? What's going on?"

She shook her head, and turned back to the counter. "Go wash up. I need to prepare dinner."

"But—"

"I *said* to go wash up."

I winced at Mom's sharp tone, and backed away, concerned. "M-Mom…"

She didn't acknowledge me as she went rummaging through the cabinets.

I whirled around on my heel, defeated. *Guess this conversation's over.*

And I was right, as scrambled thoughts of endless worrying became the bane of my restless night. Mom didn't speak a word at dinner, and then she locked herself in her office afterward, leaving me to toss and turn in bed all damn night.

I cursed the sun when its light finally peeked through my bay window, and I debated whether or not to call off school. However, I didn't feel like spending yet another lonely day in this house, so I opted to bite the bullet and endure the silent (and quite awkward) ride to school with Mom.

We didn't acknowledge each other the entire way, though I gave a quick glance over my shoulder as she slowly drove away. With a shake of my head, I turned around to face what lay ahead of me for today.

"God..." I whispered under my breath whilst sluggishly stumbling into the school. My head was pounding from lack of sleep, and my eyes kept threatening to fall shut. "Ugh..." I eyed the nurse's office as I wandered by it. *Maybe I should stop by to see Patricia...*

As if on cue, she poked her head out of her office doorway. "Hey, Rosella! Mr. Howley gave me the word this morning about Caroline. Can't say I'm not happy about it."

"About what?" I asked dumbly.

She beamed at me. "Caroline's not here today, and won't be anytime soon. Says she's got suspension for quite some time."

Some of the dread weighing upon my shoulders vanished at those words. "That's... nice to hear. Seriously."

"You okay, hon?" The corners of her mouth dropped into a frown. "You look a little tired."

I gave a slow nod. "Uh, yeah... Got a lot of homework to catch up on."

Patricia stepped out of her office, her arms crossed over her chest. "Rosella..."

Yes?"

She rushed toward me, concerned. "Are you sure you're alright?"

I sighed. "No, I guess not... I, uh, kinda had some trouble sleeping last night. Got a headache from stress."

"What kind of stress?" Patricia asked.

"Math," I lied. "It's exhausting for me." I closely observed Patricia's reaction, hoping to hell that she'd bought it.

"Well..." She stroked her chin. "Why don't I give you some ibuprofen then? That should help."

The left corner of my mouth curved up. "That would, thanks."

She nodded and disappeared into her office for a moment. When she returned, she beckoned me over for the medicine and small paper cup of water in her hands. "Here you go."

I gingerly took the water and pill from her. When I was finished, I handed the cup back to her. "Thanks, again." I turned on my heel to walk away, but was stopped by Patricia's hand to my shoulder.

"Rosella, are you truly alright? Caroline struck you quite hard last week."

I peered over my shoulder and dismissed her worry with a carefree wave. "I'm okay, really."

Patricia cocked her head. "Yes, but…" She looked confused.

My eyes darted to my wrist and I let my hand fall back to my side. "Great Granny Felan gave me something," I said and nervously rubbed the back of my head. "Heh."

"Oh." She thoughtfully stroked her chin. "Interesting. From the looks of things, I figured you'd be out for at least a couple of weeks."

I frantically sought for a response that would put a speedy end to this increasingly difficult conversation. "W-Well, she, uh… She is good at making medicine with plants. I don't know if you know this, but it's possible to do that." I ground my teeth together. *You idiot, now she's going to question it further!*

"I guess that makes sense."

"I-It does?" I stammered, then shook my head. "I mean, yeah! Of course it does. Ha!" I rocked on my heels, my hands fumbling with my backpack straps as I hoped she'd ask no further questions.

"I've read articles about plants being used for medicinal purposes," Patricia said. "I take it since she's lived out there for a long time, she knows how to use them."

I nodded hesitantly.

Patricia beamed at me. "Alright, well, if you ever need anything, feel free to stop by."

I gave a relieved grin. "Thanks, Patricia. I'm sorry for being such a handful."

With a wave of her hand, she chuckled. "Oh, you're fine dear. It's my job to look after the students."

"Well, I find you to be quite generous." I bid Patricia a pleasant morning, then turned away with a heavy sigh. *That was way too close.*

"Hey! Ro!"

I walked over to greet Sophia upon hearing her voice, but paused when I spotted Dale, out of the corner of my eye, with a group of other boys. Right as he opened his mouth, Sophia took position with a threatening glare, and he backed off while flipping her his middle finger. I gave a sigh at their interaction, but said nothing.

"Real mature, dickhead." She swatted the air in his direction. "Ugh, and keep that putrid gym sweat to yourself."

Dale snorted, and clutched his front. "Putrid, huh? That's funny, comin' from someone with fish clenched between her legs."

"Come on," I muttered, and dragged her away before she could ignite another fight. "He's not worth it, and you know it."

She blew a gust of air from her lips, but didn't protest.

"Would you too terribly mind helping me with my math homework?" I asked. "I'm sure there's a lot."

"Sure thing, Ro." Sophia cocked her head as she looked me over. "Hey, you okay? Your eyes look a little... droopy."

I gave a tired nod. "Yeah... I didn't get much sleep last night." *Not actually at all, but at least my headache's starting to let up.*

We both arrived at the school an hour before the day was to start, so Sophia suggested going up to the library. I had several pages of equations from the book to work through, some of which were word problems, so working in a quiet setting was obviously the right choice. My only hope was that I wouldn't fall asleep.

As we walked through the hall, my legs wavered a couple times, and I almost fell flat on my face. Luckily, Sophia was there to catch me, and even offered to help steady me with an arm around my waist. She went on to ask if I was coming down with something, to which I responded that I wasn't. I was just feeling a little rundown, which was partially true.

"Okay, you can take pictures of my notes so you have them for later," she told me when we finally reached the library on the second floor. She led me over to an empty table and pulled a chair out for me.

"Thanks, Soph," I mumbled while pulling my phone out of my pocket.

She took a seat next to me. "No problem. Just make sure it's not blurry." She opened her binder and sifted through a neat stack of papers. When she found them, she pulled them out and placed them in front of me.

I pulled up the camera on my phone and positioned it to snap the first shot. "Man, I'm real glad you spared time to teach me how to use this thing, even though it's not often that I do."

"I've noticed," Sophia said with a chuckle.

"Ugh, thank god you've got decent handwriting too."

"Yeah, it's a gift from Mom. I also know how to write cursive real well."

"Same..." I managed to get the first shot in decent quality, so I moved to the next sheet, but paused to look at Sophia. "Hey, can I ask you something?"

"What's up?" she asked.

"I was wondering if you could tell me your thoughts on something personal..." I set my phone down. "See, I..." I interlocked my fingers and pressed my palms into the table. "Did I ever tell you about a peculiar dream I had about my father?"

Sophia raised an eyebrow. "I don't believe so. Are you struggling still?"

"No. I just... I don't know, I'm curious to know your thoughts."

I didn't know where I was going with this as I was super tired, and it was a random topic to bring up. But I couldn't tell her anything about Fenris, as much as I wanted to. She was my best friend, and I knew I could trust her. But I gave my word.

It is nice to gain some of her wisdom, I thought. *Maybe she can shed some light on this at least...*

Sophia tapped my hand. "Ro?"

I dumbly blinked a couple times. "Right, sorry. See, there were a few times where I had this strange dream. I'd be standing in a field with him far from me, but when I try to run to him, I don't go anywhere, and he doesn't speak. We just stare into each other's eyes. Then, out of nowhere, I wake up sweaty and scared." I turned to her with hope, and searched her eyes for answers. "What... What do you suppose that means?"

"Hmm…" Her face went crooked with confusion, her brow cocked and lips scrunched under her nose.

I patiently awaited her answer during the minute of silence that drifted between us, the fear of her lacking wisdom weighing further and further upon my mind with each passing second. Ugh, again, I felt like I was being too dependent on her. So desperate to seek comfort from her, even with something she couldn't exactly "fix".

"Well… You see… Um…" She cradled her jawline with her fingers curled over her cheeks, her elbows to the table. "Shoot…" Defeat draped its ugly shadow over her face. "I don't know. You don't usually dream a whole bunch, and I don't either… I hate to admit it, but you might be asking the wrong person here."

I bowed my head in disappointment. "I get it. It's okay," I mumbled, my voice void of emotion. *I can't depend on her for everything, nor can I be upset with her.*

"I'm sorry, Ro. I wish I could help. I mean… I don't know. I don't know your dad well enough, so…"

"It's okay." *I am not mad at you. I'm mad at myself.*

"I guess."

I took a deep breath, and then gradually released it. "Okay… Back to work. I got a lotta stuff I need to do today." I picked up my phone again and resumed taking photos.

"Ro…" Sophia lowered her head. "I'm really sorry I couldn't help you."

I set my phone down again, but didn't look her way. "It's okay, Soph, really. I'd rather you be honest with me than not." *Don't be upset with yourself. You didn't do anything wrong.*

Out of the corner of my eye, Sophia flinched, her mouth pressed in a straight line.

"Wow, these look complicated," I said, hoping to abandon the awkward tension I'd caused. "Lots of words."

"They're… They're really not too terribly difficult once you get the hang of them."

"I suppose not." I shot her a concerned glance. "Um, you… alright?" *Of course she's not. Why would you ask that?*

"Yeah, why?" she asked.

"You seem a little down is all." *Of course she's down, you moron. You made her feel bad for not being able to help you. You depend on her too much, and now look what's happened.*

Rosella, it's okay. Please, don't beat yourself up. If anyone is useless, it's—

Sophia pulled back her bangs with a nervous blow of air. "I... I don't know, I guess I've been cooped up in my head a little too much lately. Not sure what's up, I just feel kinda... bleh, like you." Eyes crossed, she stretched her mouth with her tongue out.

I giggled. "You look ridiculous."

She reset her face into a blank expression. "Yeah, but you know what I mean, right?"

"Kind of, yeah. I got like that just the other day too, when I was thinking about the years I was homeschooled, and about how you admitted that you felt I wasn't trying hard enough."

"Oh shoot." Fear further corrupted her already pained gaze. "I didn't... I didn't mean to hurt your feelings. I'm really sorry."

Rather than spill the truth, I instead swallowed it back down and drank in the lie that teased my tongue. *I've already troubled her enough with my neediness.* "It's fine. It didn't bother me." The guilty aftertaste reeked of bile at the back of my mouth and cursed it dry. *What a dirty lie... She told me to tell her when I was scared, because she's my best friend and wants to be there for me... Ugh, I deserve to scarf down pounds of sand as punishment for all this trouble I'm weighing upon her.*

Rosella, stop it. You're better than that.

Sophia's relieved expression taunted me without her knowledge, and part of me felt it was a necessary evil. Last thing I wanted was to be more of a burden but, like me, she preferred the honest truth, and nothing but.

And I need to give her that... I took a deep breath. "Okay, I'll admit... It did kind of bother me."

Worry took form on Sophia's face. "Rosella, I'm sorry. Really."

"No, I should be the one to apologize." I turned to face her directly. "Sophia, I always depend on you for pretty much everything, and I-I shouldn't do that." I forced myself to look her straight in the eye as my hands fumbled in my lap. "I'm sorry for being so... dependent."

She snorted. "Rosella, it's okay. I don't mind."

I shook my head. "No, it's not okay. I should... really try doing better."

"Ro." She placed a hand over mine. "It's okay. You are my best friend, and I want you to stay that way, forever." A comforting gleam twinkled in her emerald eyes, and she nuzzled her head against mine. "Please, tell me when something's wrong, even when it's not a big deal. That's what I'm here for."

"I know, I just..." I averted her gaze. "I just feel like maybe you're right, and maybe I'm not trying hard enough because I choose not to. Sometimes it's exhausting to try, and sometimes it's not, but backing out is the easy way out. I need to... figure things out for myself at some point, instead of piling everything onto you. Like, last night... I brought up a sensitive topic with my mother, and it didn't go over well."

Sophia pulled away from me, though her hand remained attached to mine. "What do you mean?"

I opened my mouth to tell her about yesterday, but paused. As much as I trusted Sophia with my secrets, I swore not to say a word about Fenris or the forest, and I especially couldn't tell her about Mom's shocking proposal to move.

"Is this about what happened at the mall?" Sophia asked abruptly. "If so, like I said, I am really sorry about that too."

Jumping on the topic that'd save me, I quickly nodded. "Y-Yeah, I think that's what it is. I mean, she told me that she was struggling with writer's block, but I think she's stressed about that and other things." I stroked some hair behind my ear as I looked down. "However, she won't tell me, so I..."

"Don't know how to help her?" Sophia finished.

I nodded silently.

"Okay..." Sophia pondered this for a minute. "Okay, well, lemme help you at least a little, okay? Maybe... Maybe something that's been on her mind all this time is finally starting to show, and she might need some space." She patted my shoulder. "You don't have to take this advice though because, honestly, there's a chance that I could be wrong."

"Yeah, maybe," I said. "But it feels like I'm experiencing what I went through with Dad. Just like him, she locked herself in her office last night, refusing to talk to me."

"And if it bothers you that much, come to me so that you have an outlet," Sophia urged. "She might be housing personal demons, but that doesn't mean you should be forced to do the same." She squeezed my hand. "I'll be here when you need me, Ro. And when your mother is ready, you can be there for her."

I stifled a sob as my eyes began to water. "Ya know, it's really hard, going through this. All I wanna do is be a kid, make friends, hang out. But no one is willing to peek around the trees, and that's why they won't found the path to my heart..." A crippling smile formed on my face. "Well, no one except you, and I'm extremely grateful for that."

The passionate spark within Sophia's eyes dimmed a little, a frown settling on her face. "But if you're harboring your pain, how can I help you?"

I pressed my lips together with a hesitant nod.

She sighed. "Look, if you don't want to feel so dependent on me, then set out for some more friends. Otherwise, you're just stuck with me being your rock. And I'm fine with that. So, let's finally put all this worrying to rest and get back to work, okay? You got quite a bit to catch up on."

"Sorry, I didn't mean to waste time," I said.

"You didn't. You opened yourself up to me, and I gave you what you needed to move forward."

Sophia's words stayed with me throughout most of the school day. Whether I gained more friends or not, she really was always going to be my rock. And like both her and Fenris said, if I wanted more support, then I would have to try looking for it. Otherwise, I had to deal with only her being my go-to for venting.

On the upside, since talking to her, much of the stress weighing me down had been lifted, and my headache gradually dissipated, so by the time my favorite class of the day came up, I was feeling better.

"Alright... Time for art class." I took my assigned seat upon entry to my seventh hour class and set my backpack beside me. "Let's see..." I pulled out my personal sketchbook and sighed. *Forgot my classroom copy. Guess I'll have to use this one.*

"Rosella? Rosella Bloom?"

My head shot up at the sound of a somewhat familiar voice, and I peered over my shoulder. "Yes?"

A tall boy, with sandy blonde hair and tan skin, approached with a sheepish smirk and waved a hand. "Hey there."

I raised a curious eyebrow. "H-Hello... Marcus." *Marcus Thompson? Why's he talking to me?* I remembered Sophia mentioning something about Caroline having dated Marcus, and my eyes widened in fear. However, I quickly settled them so as not to give myself away. "U-Um, hi."

He rubbed at the back of his sandy blonde head with a nervous face, his olive-green eyes quick to flee my questioning gaze. "I guess you recognize me, huh?" He stuffed his hands in his pockets. "I, uh, was wondering if Sophia told you about the party."

I tilted my head in response, already wary of his intentions. "Party?"

"Y-Yeah," he stammered. "It was a little gathering I hosted on Sunday." His eyes hesitantly found mine. "Sophia was there, actually. Don't know if she told you."

"Oh." I shook my head. "I'm not a party person and I've told her that before. I prefer quiet places myself, since I get too nervous in large, tight-knit crowds. Even if I'm with someone I know, it makes me feel claustrophobic."

"Understandable." Marcus sighed. "I, uh, heard what happened with Caroline last week." He scrunched his nose. "God... Can't believe I was ever involved with her."

Before I could stop myself, I scoffed at him. "Why would you be involved with her at all? If what she did is true, and I'm sure it is, that sure says a lot about you."

Marcus looked taken aback by my response and, quite frankly, so was I.

Crap, not the best approach, idiot. I shrank back on my stool and sank my head between my shoulders. "S-Sorry, I didn't mean to... come off like that."

"It's okay," Marcus said with a shameful expression. "Caroline and I had actually been friends for a long time, even dated a little, so I totally understand your reaction."

I looked away from him with an uncomfortable face. "Oh..."

"Oh shoot! Did I make it worse?"

Apprehensive, I flinched back and avoided his line of sight when he reached a hand out to me.

"Oh, uh..." He quickly retreated his hand behind his back. "Uh... If you're worried, I promise you that I'm no longer involved with her, especially after what happened to that one girl. Ya know, the one who got the... rats... in her bra..."

Set further on edge, my shoulders stiffened. He was only a foot away from me now.

"Unfortunately, I didn't have proof to help her," he went on, "but I heard she's doing better at least..." Marcus shook with discomfort. "I'd never been so mortified and scared for someone... I told her to say something, but she wouldn't listen and backed out."

My eyes darted to their corners. "And?"

"I told Caroline I didn't want to be involved with her at all anymore," he finished. "I've avoided her ever since."

My thunderous heart pumped anxiety through my veins as he inched a little bit closer to me.

"I'm really sorry," he insisted. "After I heard what happened to you last week, I couldn't stop thinking about you or any of the other people Caroline's tormented in the past." He sighed again. "I can tell I'm making you uncomfortable. I'll leave you alone." Marcus started to walk away.

"Marcus, wait." I shot up from the table. "Wait, please."

He peered over his shoulder.

"Look, I..." I wrung my hands together as I thought back to what Fenris said about trust.

I was right in my course of action, for it seems that you lack the skills needed to attempt understanding of others' intentions.

Marcus here hasn't said a single nasty thing to me, and now he's trying to take the blame for something he isn't at fault for... "Marcus, I'm nervous about making friends and you seem to understand that. I guess... I guess I'm just apprehensive because I only ever go to Sophia for help." *And that's true because we know each other well.*

"She told me once, during one of my parties," Marcus said, interrupting my thoughts.

"How come she was there?" I asked.

"She wanted to see what I was up to. Told me so herself. Also gave me a warning not to mess with you, or she'd mess me up."

I stifled a laugh. *That sure sounds like her...*

Marcus uttered a dry snicker. "I know, pretty in character for your friend, huh?"

"Yeah, but she really shouldn't be doing that." *As dependent as I am on her...*

He shook his head. "Hey, I was hanging with Caroline Morse. I could totally understand her actions. Sophia's, I mean." He scuffed the toe of his sneaker into the floor. "Though, if it makes you feel better, she said that she was only coming off strong because she really cared about you. Gave me this long haul of a speech about how talented and kind you are, and that if I took the time to get to know you, I'd see it."

I fought back a few tears welling in my eyes. "She really said all that, huh?"

Marcus' concerned expression returned. "Hey, are you alright?"

"Yeah. Yeah, I am."

"You don't look fine. Your eyes are watery."

I tried to shield my tears from him with a hand blocking my face. "Really, I'm okay."

"Why don't we step out for a minute?" Marcus offered.

"I don't think that's necessary," I said. "Really."

"If you say so." He turned around again. "I'm gonna go take my seat."

I gnawed at my bottom lip. *Come on. Try, just try... This is your chance to show someone, besides Sophia, who you are as a person. And if he tries anything, then prove that you can stand up for yourself!* Without warning, I shot up from the table. "O-Okay, just for a minute."

Marcus' eyes widened as he whirled around to face me. "Oh?"

My shoulders stiffened as I approached his side. "It's just for a minute, right? Come on, let's go."

I was really doing this. I was actually leading this guy outside of the art room, of my own accord. Before I could stop it from happening, we were lingering close to the art room door, only a few feet from it, with a clear view of the teacher's desk. This gave me comfort as Marcus plopped down a few inches from me, so that if I really had to run, I wasn't far, but...

The only trouble is that the teacher isn't in the room, I thought to myself.

"Rosella, are you sure you feel comfortable doing this?" Marcus asked. "I only offered because you seemed like you needed a minute to recuperate, and some of the other students were around, so I figured you didn't want to be gawked at."

I hugged my legs to my chest. "I, uh, haven't done this before, so I guess that I took the opportunity when I saw it." I twisted my face in confusion. *The hell does that mean?*

Marcus crossed his arms. "Well, I promise you that I'm not plotting anything, if that's what you're worried about."

My eyes crept to the corners, Marcus barely in view. "Really?"

"Well, yeah... I'm not like Dale, or David, or Cheyenne, and I'm especially nothing like Caroline."

"I guess I kinda know Dale," I said. "But that's because of last week. As for the others, I'm guessing they're friends with Caroline... She's really the only one who picks on me."

Marcus gave me a suspicious look. "Is that why we're doing this? Because you want to see if I'm actually like them?"

I shook my head. "No, I just..." I shrugged. "I wanted to try something new, sitting with someone else, besides Sophia." Cautiously, I allowed my arms to loosen a bit. "In case you didn't know, my family's name is a popular toxic topic."

"Because of the rumors?" he guessed, albeit nervously.

"Yep," I answered bluntly. "So normally, no one likes to be around me unless it's to ask me about the rumors, or see if they can get any sort of truth out of me. It's not often though, since my mom is the usual target. Mostly here at high school, people just whisper around me, occasionally call me a freak or something, while Caroline does the actual bullying, which is weird because she does all this terrible stuff, and yet no one does a thing about it when they are aware it's happening."

He nodded slowly with a pondering face. "Not to ignore what you just said, but your mom used to live in the forest, right?"

I sucked in a sharp breath and, with a hesitant exhale, I continued. "That's right. My great-grandmother Felan raised her, still lives out there."

"I thought I'd heard about someone living out there," Marcus said. "I wonder if she knows about the twins that were found yesterday."

"What twins?" I asked.

"You didn't hear?" His eyes widened. "It's been all over the news since yesterday evening. Everybody's talking about it."

I shrugged. "Didn't hear about it. I don't watch the news."

Marcus sighed. "Well, I didn't catch the names of the two girls, but they supposedly came from a place somewhere in town for girls who have nowhere to go. The discovery was first announced yesterday evening. It was said their bodies looked like they'd been mauled by an animal." He shuddered. "A horrible way to go and, worse yet, for me, I think I knew them."

They came from that place... It's a prison there.

I cocked an eyebrow. "Is that so?"

"Yeah, if I'm correct they're twins who were a lot like Caroline, but maybe worse?" Marcus cocked his head. "I remember meeting them a couple of times at the park. Seemed to be their favorite place to hang. The few times I interacted with them, they seemed real snooty."

"Just think, even more ammunition for her to use against my family," I muttered. "Ya know, because the cult stuff about my great-grandmother isn't enough." My voice cracked at the end of my words.

He scooted closer to me. "It's okay, Rosella."

A sensitive ache pierced my nasal cavity, prompting a responsive wince. "It's just super stressful for me to deal with, and the only outsider who understands is Sophia."

"Yeah, I get that," Marcus said. "You know, she told me you were homeschooled for most of your childhood."

Hearing those words, they made me want to scream in his face with all this built-up anger, though I was quick to remind myself of how illogical that would be. No matter how much I was poked and prodded within my cage, I couldn't lash out at my provokers. That was asking for more trouble, but god it was tempting to just let the madness ensue.

I didn't care as much about myself or whatever happened to me as much as I did about Mom and Great Granny Felan. Mom was already trapped under society's microscope, what with being the town's local celebrity. And Great Granny Felan, even though she was safe among the trees, hurtful words could still reach her.

This town doesn't feel like home because it isn't, I thought. *The trees aren't fickle. They don't point and stare, and the whispers they share are of good faith... And they listen without interruption.*

"Ya know, if you ever need someone when Sophia's not around, you can come to me," Marcus said. "She was right. You seem nice and... pretty lonely."

Still involved in this dwindling conversation, I peered at him with a pained expression. "Yeah, it is pretty lonely when you've only got one friend to talk to."

Marcus lowered his head as his eyes fled my gaze. "I'm sorry... I... I guess..."

Guilt clenched my heart. "Sorry, I didn't mean for that to slip out."

"No, you're right when you're right." Marcus bravely looked back at me. "I'm sure it's difficult being in your situation, but unless I'm in your shoes, I can't truly understand."

My mouth fell slightly open. Was I hearing this right? Did he really just say what I thought he said?

"Respect and understanding are two things you seem to value more than anything, and I think everyone else should too." His eyebrows knitted into a frown. "I guess you could say that was the breaking point for me and Caroline. She never respected anyone unless they were to her standards." His stern expression softened. "If... If you'd like, I'd be more than willing to lend a hand or whatever you need, anytime you need it. I know Sophia's your go-to, but it's nice to make more friends you know?"

My heart welled with hope at those words. "I... I think I'd like that. Very much actually."

Marcus beamed at me. "Awesome." He stood up and extended a hand down to me. "Well, guess we should get back to class."

"Yeah." I gingerly took his hand and allowed him to pull me up. *This boy seems nice. Maybe it's not a bad idea to give him a chance.*

I was paired up with Marcus for a project when we returned to class, and as the hour flew by we took this opportunity to get to know each other better. I learned that he liked art as a hobby and enjoyed reading in quiet places, much like me. He also liked to read comic books, which sparked a chance to share my interest in manga, to which he admitted he hadn't read before, but was open to trying.

"Alright, class dismissed!" our teacher called amid the bell chime.

"Dang it, guess we'll have to hang again another time," I said. *And who knows when we'll get to talk again anyway...*

"I'd love that!" Marcus exclaimed.

My eyes bulged. "R-Really?"

"Yeah, of course! You're pretty cool, Rosella."

I found myself grinning back at him. "I'm... really glad to hear that." *I guess... I guess this is okay. The more I interact, the more I'll gather about him.*

"Good." He stood up. "Rosella... I know you're not fully trusting of me, but maybe over time, we can become friends. I just hope it'll be before I graduate, since I'm two years ahead of you."

My heart welled with hope. "Marcus, that would mean a lot to me, seriously."

"Sadly, you'll still be stuck with Caroline..." His expression faltered at the thought, but then quickly reformed. "Nah, I'm sure you'll be okay."

"Yeah." *We'll see...*

"Rosella." Our teacher popped up in front of us. "Hey, can I talk to you for a minute?"

Confused, and a little disappointed, I nodded sadly. "Yeah, sure I guess."

"I'll see you around, Rosella." Marcus waved a gentle hand. "Bye."

"Yeah, see you." I turned back to the teacher. "Um... Is everything okay, ma'am?"

"It's Ms. Mitchell," she reminded me, and sat down on a stool. "I wanted to talk to you for a minute." She put up a hand when I opened my mouth. "Don't worry, I'll write you a pass for your next teacher."

Settling back onto my stool, I gave her a strange look. "Alright."

"How are you doing?" she asked.

"I'm a little overwhelmed with schoolwork," I said, "but I'm catching up."

Ms. Mitchell shook her head. "I know that ain't all true."

I nervously fiddled with a lock of hair draped over my shoulder. "I guess you're more observant that I thought."

"You got that right." She stood from the table and approached one of the back windows, her hands clasped behind her. "So, what's going on?" When she turned her head, her long black ponytail, held firm with a blue ribbon, whipped over her shoulder.

"Well..." My eyes darted to the left. "I decided to try making more friends today. Marcus seems like a good candidate."

"Yeah, I noticed you two at the beginning of class," Ms. Mitchell said. "That's why I paired you up. Glad you were open to it, Rosella. As comfortable as you are working alone, you really need to start trying to socialize with the other students." She whirled around with a solemn face, her sneaker squeaking as it scuffed the glossy floor. "I know this is random, but does your mother know about the murder that occurred recently, the one about the twins?"

A look of surprise sprang to my face at her question. "H-How come you're asking me this?"

"Well, I know she comes from the forest, and if I recall from an interview, she once said she isn't a fan of the news."

I shook my head. "Yeah, we don't usually tune in unless it's about the weather."

She fiddled with one of her overall shoulder straps. "Is she hiding things from you?"

I shuffled upon my stool. "I'm sorry, I—"

"Rosella," Ms. Mitchell cut in, "I've known your mother for quite some time, since we were kids. I happened to encounter her one day when I was wandering around in the forest. She popped out from the underbrush. Scared me."

My eyes widened. "Wait, really?" *Strange, she said that no one ever got close to her except for Sarah.*

"We met only a few times, since I wasn't normally allowed near the trees." Ms. Mitchell's narrowed eyes brandished a steely edge. "I think Chloe knows more than she's letting on. There's something evil brewing in that forest, and I know for a fact that she's aware of it, your great-grandmother too."

I recoiled at my teacher's prying. "Ms. Mitchell, I... I think I need to go." I gathered up my things and stuffed them into my backpack. "I don't want to be any later than I'm sure I already am."

"Rosella, I want you to convince your mother to book a meeting with me," Ms. Mitchell requested, "and you are welcome to join in, Sophia too."

I frowned. "Your daughter... Why would she need to be involved?"

"If something important needed to be said, then one should step up and say it," Ms. Mitchell uttered in a stern tone. "I taught that to her myself, and since you're her best friend, I feel she should know. Plus, you seem comfortable when she's around..." A suspicious look settled on her face. "Isn't that right? You tell her everything, don't you?"

I hastily zipped my backpack shut and threw it over my shoulder. "Ms. Mitchell, I don't know what's going on here, but if you're worried about me corrupting your daughter or hiding things from her, then I promise you I'm not." I again surprised myself at using such a strong tone, however Ms. Mitchell seemed unfazed.

"Just try to get your mother to come see me, tomorrow perhaps." Ms. Mitchell gave me a curt smile. "You can do that, right?"

"I'll see what I can do," I said.

"Good." My teacher strode past me and toward her desk. "Now then, I'll write you an excuse note. Off you go to eighth hour!"

CHAPTER 10

Frank&Creg

"**G**OOD GOD ALMIGHTY, THIS is gonna take us forever to go through."

A tired man in his early forties grazed his sore fingertips over his raw scalp as he ruffled his messy, dark brown hair for the umpteenth time. Having been in the detectives' office area within the police station all damn day, scouring over the same documents over and over again, his exhausted mind was running the same circle of thoughts.

"Frank, it's late, go home and see your wife. She's bound to have forgotten your face by now."

"Thanks for the encouragement," Frank answered, "appreciate it."

A wheezing chuckle broke out in the middle of the empty office.

Frank snickered as he peered over his shoulder. "What? You're not bein' helpful!"

A slightly shorter and bulkier man about Frank's age strolled into his sight. "Sorry dude. I'm just tryna make sure your marriage stays intact."

"It's okay," Frank assured. "Cathy understands."

"I hope so, for your sake."

"Hey, Creg, come look at this." Frank offered a paper. "I think I found somethin'."

Creg wandered over. "Jesus, man. Don't take this the wrong way, you're whiter than this sheet. Lookin' like your blood sugar's low or something."

"Heh, funny you mentioned that. My doc says I might be on the verge of diabetes unless I cut back." Frank snorted. "Yeah, right, like that'll happen."

"Still, better watch that, or else you'll arouse suspicion." Creg pointed at his own two eyes. "Those dark rings you got goin' don't look good either."

"I know, I know." Frank waved him off with a hand. "I'm too tired to be scolded right now."

"I'm just trying to help."

"I'll head home in a bit. I wanna take one more crack at this." Frank shuffled the various papers littered across his desk. "God, where the hell is..." His voice trailed off as he watched Creg easily find the document amongst the pile. "Smart ass."

"You're welcome!" Creg joked as his partner humorously snatched it from him.

Frank shook his head. "You gonna help me or not?"

His solemn frown chased away Creg's amusement. "Alright, lay it on me."

"Take a look at the passage I highlighted there."

Creg wriggled his nose as his grey eyes scanned over the section in bright yellow highlighter, his dark brow raising curiously. "Really?" He looked over the paper at his partner. "Didn't see that comin'."

"Happened upon it while I was scanning over that damn document for what feels like the millionth time." Frank groaned. "God, I'm so tired."

"Sorry, I'll hurry this along. What does this section here have to do with the twins, exactly? I mean, from what I understand... Oh wait. Hang on, I think I see what you mean." Creg put a hand to his short black hair. "Damn."

"You see it?" Frank asked.

"Unfortunately." Creg slapped the paper down on Frank's desk. "Fuck... We had a lead there. Guess she was one step ahead of us."

"Child services did a full-sweep of the place a couple weeks ago, and they found nothing." His elbows propped on the table, Frank swiveled his hands out at either side. "*And I mean nothing.* All the shit we scrambled together over the last few months, she must've thrown out. And remember that room we found? With all the words just..." He waved his arms above his head. "Ya know, just, plastered everywhere? And that table with the restraints? Wasn't there, they said. Room was supposedly clean as a whistle. Said it was for storage."

"She even managed to erase that one girl from existence," Creg observed. "There's not a single mention of her in here. All *seventeen* girls are accounted for, and they're 'clean and healthy'. If I stand corrected, there were *twenty-one*, and most of them were not clean or healthy."

"The day we went there to gather intel, Georgia's niece was present, and she said the one who mysteriously disappeared barely went outside." Frank crossed his arms. "I'm telling you, even if that damn hag didn't kill the missing one, she definitely killed Georgia's niece and the twins."

"We'll find a way to pin her," Creg muttered as he rubbed the back of his head, an irritated look on his face. "Plus, there's the matter of keeping the press out of any more of this, especially with Georgia missing as well. I'm telling you, news of her disappearance has been a real dog and pony show."

"They're also still hot about the shooting that happened a few months ago, which is what started the whole fiasco with the shelter." Frank let his head fall in his hands. "That woman looked like she was about to pull the trigger on that kid..."

"Frank, you were trapped in the heat of the moment. What the hell else could you have done? If you hadn't acted, that kid could've died." Creg pointed at his partner. "Thanks to you, he's back with his parents, who were worried beyond hell on earth about him."

"I guess," Frank mumbled.

"Trust me, you didn't murder the woman," Creg said. "If anything, she's free of the demons runnin' around in her head." He sighed. "As for the one that's missing..."

"I was told that girl made a mad dash..." Frank closed his blue eyes and exhaled. "No pun intended there, that's how Georgia's niece worded it. She said that the missing one *made a dash* for the forest the day I shot the woman that instigated the hostage situation."

"Reminds me of the shoemaker's wife," Creg added. "She bolted for the forest too."

"Yeah, I remember." Frank glanced at the paper Creg effortlessly found for him. It was a snippet of the article about the twins. "That hag in charge of these girls is hiding the terror she's putting them through, and Georgia's niece, the one person who opened up to us, was our one good witness. I mean, I never liked the brat or her aunt, but..."

"Let's not think the worst yet."

"It's kinda hard not to," Frank pointed out. "And then, to top things off, all that 'cursed evil forest' bullshit..." He shrugged. "I got enough of that from the bible-thumpin' maniacs who raised me, and as much as I hate to admit it, they aren't wrong."

"Hey," Creg warned, "careful now. Your wife hears you talkin' like that, and you're sure to be lit ablaze."

Frank waved a hand in agitation. "I wasn't trying to be offensive, and Cathy would never do something like that. I don't have anything against religion. But my parents... They shoved so much of their Jesus-lovin' antics down my throat that I once tried to summon an actual demon just to get away from them. I drew my own pentagram on the backyard porch. I did the research, yet somehow it didn't work!" He pounded his trembling fists to his desk. "I thought maybe they'd throw me out so I could finally get away from them. Instead, I got beat for it!"

Creg, unfazed by his partner's outburst, came around to put a comforting hand on his shoulder. "You went through eighteen years of that shit, Frank..."

"And it was rough," he muttered. "I had no one to depend on except you, but you know me. I don't like being a burden on others."

"I know, but you gotta remember that we've always been together," Creg said. "You and I always had each other's backs, but everything changed the day you met Cathy. Unlike your parents, she doesn't force her views on you, and you learned not to be afraid of her."

"I still can't go to church," Frank said. "Even thinking about one makes me want to vomit."

"That doesn't make you a bad person, and you know it."

A tear pricked at the corner of Frank's eye. "I know..."

"And look at me, man." Creg spread his arms out. "I found someone to love myself, even got two good grown kids out of it. Both of them are gettin' ready to leave high school and go to college. Just like you, I found someone else I could trust, and just like you I didn't feel like a burden anymore. At least, not to you."

"But we can't tell them what's going on in that shelter. Cathy would go into hysterics, and Ivy..." Frank shuddered. "God, Ivy..."

"I'm not worried about her," Creg said. "Ivy's a smart girl, and I understand that when the time comes, she must leave the nest, and I can't stop her." He gave a sigh. "Monique and I are happy to have raised her, and Aaron has enjoyed having her around, but we've all accepted that Ivy can't be with us forever."

"Right..." Frank's eyes met Creg's. "I just don't want what's happening to those girls to happen to Ivy. You saw the maimed remains of those twins... And the way that woman just... just..." He hissed through his teeth, irritated. "She was so calm about it..."

Creg shook his head. "If you get too emotionally involved..."

"I'm not getting too involved!" Frank snapped. A vein threatened to pop from his temple, his face beet red. "I'm not!"

"You are," Creg insisted. "You haven't slept in over twenty-four hours, you're incredibly stressed, and you miss your wife. Seriously, go home."

"God, fine." Frank hastily scrambled together the jumbled mess of papers into a rough stack. "I'm tired, you're tired." He took a deep breath. "And no one else's here to take over."

"Go home, sleep in," Creg urged. "Take the day even. Please, I encourage it!"

Frank snatched up his coat from his chair. "I'll consider it." He rubbed his fingertips into his burning eyes. "I need a shower."

"Alright, well, I'll see ya again soon." Creg took a peek at his watch. "Lord, it's just after eleven..."

"We've been cooped up here so long we lost track o' time," Frank called back as he exited the office.

"Right, right..." Creg went over to grab his coat from his adjacent desk. *Ivy...* He bowed his head. *Sweetheart, when the time comes...*

"Holy shit!" Frank cried. "Creg! Creg, come here!"

Creg's head shot back up, eyes wide. "My god, what now? Seriously man, you need to..." His voice trailed off when he rounded the corner of the doorway, and his stomach dropped.

Frank was stiff as a board a few feet from his partner, a look of horror on his face. "You see this... right?"

Creg nodded meekly as he approached. "Yeah... I see it."

Both detectives stood in shock at the layout before them: the words 'FOOL, CONTROL, BROKEN, MADNESS, DEFILE,' and 'LIES' marred the hall's ceiling, walls and floor in crudely-scrawled font.

"My god..." Creg whispered. He felt a chill course down his spine when his eyes locked onto the word 'FOOL'. *No way we are... We're making the right decision, letting Ivy go...*

"It's just like that room." Frank examined one of the vandalized walls. Suspicious, he reached into his pants' pocket, and retrieved a stray white glove.

"What are you doin'?" Creg asked.

Frank worked the glove onto his hand, and gently tapped his finger against the 'F' in 'FOOL'.

"Might wanna be careful," Creg warned, "tampering with evidence like that."

"Dude, this is fresh."

Creg ducked back as his partner's finger was thrust in front of his face. "Whoa, hey now!"

"This..." Frank's breathing hitched. "It's got the right consistency of blood, but it's black..." Frank experimentally kneaded together his thumb and forefinger. "Kinda chunky, too." *The fuck is this?*

Creg looked over the wall once more. *Clearly not paint...*

Hmm... Frank went to place his gloved hand against the wall, but thought better of it, and retreated it back to his side. "God... Look, I didn't want to do this, since we haven't spoken in years but, eh, she might be resourceful."

Creg tilted his head. "You mean..." *Grace Mitchell?*

"Yep." Frank pinched the bridge of his nose with his ungloved hand. "Haven't seen her in years. Honestly, I didn't think we'd ever cross paths again after that night." *If you remember, she showed up on my doorstep with a baby bundled in her arms.*

Creg nodded. "Yeah, it's certainly been a time, hasn't it?"

Frank shook his head. "Grace told us that her sister died in 1980..."

After she escaped from that god awful place several years later.

I knew Grace was here in town the whole damn time. And yet, I couldn't find her.

Creg patted his shoulder. *Hey man, don't beat yourself up over it.*

Frank looked to him with a pained face. "Dude, really wish you'd just let me stew in peace."

"I'm sorry for snooping constantly," Creg said. "But hiding our feelings from each other will only make things more difficult."

"Yeah, I, uh, noticed you were thinking of Ivy again," Frank admitted.

"I was... But I'm not letting Ashen get into my head." Creg set his face in a hard glare. "Ivy doesn't know yet what she is, but I'm certain she will soon. And when she does, I need to do what I can to help her."

"You're a force to be reckoned with for sure." Frank looked down at his gloved hand. "Ugh, I feel like I need to wash my hands. It feels like this gunk is seeping through my glove."

"I'll go with you."

The two men meandered down the hall to the respective restroom. Frank yanked off his glove, and set to washing his hands at the sink, Creg beside him. When they looked into the mirrors, they found their exhausted reflections staring back at them. Bags of wrinkles bunched under their irritated eyes, a faint line of red curved across their bottom lids, evidence left behind from constant rubbing and the drive to stay awake.

"God, I feel like I've aged about fifty years," Frank said.

"Even though you look more like it's been twenty," Creg said with a chuckle, as he turned the faucet in front of him, then pumped some soap from the dispenser into his palm.

"Cut me some slack," Frank retorted. "I'm tired."

"Sorry."

Frank shook his head. "It's fine. I'm fine. I just need a good night's rest. We've had a long day today." He cocked a brow at his partner. "Scared of a few germs too?"

Creg laughed. "Nah, just like the way the soap makes my hands feel." He thoughtfully lathered his hands. "Makes my skin soft, like Monique's lotion. Kinda nice."

"You been using your wife's lotion?"

Creg nodded. "Yeah. It's real nice. Cocoa butter lotion." He frowned. "But for some reason, it smells like almonds to me."

"Strange..."

"Yeah..." Creg shook his head. "Anyway, outta curiosity, what was the name of Georgia's niece?"

Frank frowned as he tried to remember. "Um... I don't know... Carol... Caroline, I think?"

"Caroline Morse?" Creg guessed.

"Yeah!" Frank gave his partner a questioning look. "Why? I mean, I know Georgia ain't innocent, but I'm not..." He fell silent as his partner put up a hand.

"Georgia made herself out to be a popular writer who dug up people's secrets and shared them with the world like she was merely ripping off a band-aid," Creg explained as he finished washing his hands. "Always looking down her nose at you, she thought she was the queen and everyone else were her peasants." He went over to the paper towel dispenser, and Frank followed. "With me so far?"

"Yes, but we know this already," Frank said.

"I don't like putting people down, but she was snarky and bitchy, and greedy. Remember that one case we investigated? She'd forged some checks in the name of some billionaire that came here on vacation. Can't think of his name, but she wrote out two million dollars for each one."

"I remember. But again, what does that have to do with anything?"

Creg stared his partner down with a steely gaze. "She never served jail time, even when the guy discovered his money missing, figured out that she was the culprit, even reported her to the police, and it's all because she knows how to manipulate."

"Of course she does," Frank said, as he tossed his paper towels in the trash bin, "because Ashen gave her that ability, except neither planned for the billionaire bastard to be immune to her tricks. So, she killed him, even made his death look like a suicide, a safety precaution on her part. Ya know, just in case there were others like him."

"Right..." Creg cocked a brow. "Apples don't usually fall far from the tree, now do they?"

Frank stroked his chin as he processed his partner's words, and then his eyes lit with understanding. "Her aunt is talented in manipulation, and since power runs based on bloodline, surely she's taught her niece how to play her cards a certain way."

"Exactly." Creg sighed. "Makes me wonder about Grace, though..."

Frank crossed his arms over his chest. "How so?"

"Well, Grace has never revealed her powers to us." Creg rubbed at the back of his head. "For all we know, she could be the one manipulating this town with magic, and not Georgia or Caroline. Plus, there's that infant she had with her. You and I both know that child wasn't hers."

Frank pressed his lips into a straight line, but didn't say or think anything.

"From what I understand, the child is going to Hollow High, and Grace is almost always there so she must be an employee, perhaps a teacher." Creg's eyes narrowed. "And we still haven't figured out how Grace came to get her hands on her. Maybe she's the one doing all this?"

"She said that the girl's parents were murdered," Frank said. "And I know Grace wouldn't have the heart to do that. Her sister Sarah may not have been around her long, but Grace always followed her philosophies of kindness to the letter." *Always lend a helpful hand when you see another in need, and never judge a book by its cover. And never, ever hurt another, no matter how much they hurt you, because you will only become like them.'*

Yes, yes, I remember. Creg sighed. "I personally believe in her words myself, though I've only had to go against them a few times. Some views are meant to be broken at times, as much as my mother would hate to think..." He put his hands on his hips. "So then, if we really talk to Grace, do you sincerely think she can really help us? We haven't seen her in years, so we don't know how much bullshit got into her head while she was trapped in that shelter."

"She was a victim too," Frank countered, "so even if she's not the same kind, happy girl we once knew, we still have to help her. And remember the disheveled appearance she had when she showed up that night. She was trying to hide the same fear the others still trapped had in their eyes, despite the tattered clothes on her back and the visible bruises." He put a hand over his chest. "We just have to find a way around the captain because he'll think we're crazy if we go to him."

"Right." Creg nodded confidently. "Alright, I guess that leaves us with no other option but to talk to Grace. I just hope we can trust her." His eyes lit up. "Unless..." *What about—*

"No, we can't." Frank put his hands up. "No way."

"Frank, she could help us put a stop to this."

"Creg..." Frank's shoulders sagged. "It's too dangerous. She's literally on the opposing side."

Creg nodded warily. "I know, but if you recall, we were told we could trust her."

Frank shook his head. "I don't think so."

Creg clutched at Frank's shoulders, their eyes locked in a hard stare. "We were freed from Ashen's control, so it's only fair that we cooperate."

Frank hesitated on a response. *Fuck...*

"I know you're still holding out hope for Grace." Creg's expression softened. "And we will try to help her. But we've got to gather some more allies, even if we don't fully trust them, because you and I both know they can help us." He gave Frank a pleading look. "Please, I need you with me. I don't want to do this alone."

"You're not, because I'm here," Frank said.

Creg nodded slowly, and dropped his hands from Frank's shoulders. "You've been my friend since we were kids. For the first few years, I kept wondering who it was that was calling for help, why I was the only one who could hear you. And then, I found you cowering under a tree in your backyard, and I climbed that damn fence because it was fate. Many years, *many,* go by, and we wind up on the force together. Sure, Ashen pushed us to do it as their spies, but at least we were still together."

"Ten years here," Frank mumbled.

"And hopefully many more, because you and I came to love this job," Creg went on. "But the point here is this: we fought hard, together. Ashen's influence may have been a pain to deal with, but we were still together."

"Yeah..." Frank snorted. "It's nostalgic, thinking about it, actually. Even takes me back to that time when your neighbors thought you were hitting the fence between your houses on purpose."

"Ah yeah. They told my poor, sweet mother that they were gonna send the cops over to straighten me out if I didn't cut that racket out. Couldn't blame them, though. It was pretty noisy." A mischievous grin broke across Creg's face. "That damn dog o' theirs wouldn't shut up." He humorously imitated a big dog barking, and Frank broke out in hysterical laughter.

"God, stop, you're makin' me cry!" Frank wiped a tear from his eye. "Ah... geez."

Creg snickered. "Eh, good times for sure. However, the real kicker for me was that time you grew a damn tree in the middle of your backyard, and some o' the kids started calling you "Beanstalk Frank" because it literally rose to the clouds."

"Yeah, they wanted to try climbing it in order to see how high it went," Frank added, but then his grin fell into a frown. "My parents weren't too keen on it, though." He shivered at the memory of his father belting him, the phantom sting of the marks fresh in his mind.

"Sorry, I didn't..." Creg reached out a hand to comfort him, but Frank shooed him off.

"It's okay," Frank said quietly. "It's all in the past now. I got a nice wife, who is a church-goer, but she's kind and loving." The corners of his lips faintly curved upward. "I feel so damn lucky to have her..."

"I'm sure." Creg stretched his arms above his head with a yawn. "Aaaaah, well, anyways... No more being forced to do things we don't wanna do, no more listenin' to Ashen's degrading whispers." He breathed a heavy sigh. "No more fearing death when we become increasingly thirsty..."

"God, I haven't thought of that in a long time," Frank muttered. "As a kid, that scared the hell outta me, because I thought for sure I was on a one-way ticket to hell, no thanks to my parents. I probably guzzled enough water for twenty people in two minutes." He grunted. "Ugh, regretted it though since it caused major stomach upset."

"Not me, thankfully," Creg said, and gave his partner a concerned frown. "Getting back to finishing our initial conversation..."

Frank nodded dejectedly. "No need to wear me down further, I'm tapped."

"I understand the risks, but you and I both know the rumors Georgia manifested about Chloe Bloom are bullshit." Creg looked again into Frank's eyes pleadingly. "We already failed to save some lives. Let's not let the body count rise higher."

Frank put his hands on his hips. "Fine, I'm in. I'll call you tomorrow, or whenever I get up. We can make plans to see Grace, then find a way to Chloe."

"Sounds good." Creg clapped a hand to Frank's shoulder as he slipped around him.

"Creg?"

He paused and looked over at Frank. "Yeah?"

"Do you really think we'll stop Ashen and their curse?" Frank asked.

Creg gave him a confident smirk. "As long as we stay strong, I'm sure we will."

A tear sprang to Frank's eye, relief gracing his face. *Thanks man, for always picking me up when I'm down.*

Creg nodded. *Hey, you were always there for me too.* He turned to walk away. *You and me, we make the team, and that's all we need.*

CHAPTER 11

I MADE A BEELINE for the art room that Wednesday after school, my hand tightly gripped around Sophia's wrist as I pulled her along with me. Today was the day of the meeting Ms. Mitchell scheduled, and I was extremely nervous about how she was going to approach Mom. And of course, as she mentioned, I felt most comfortable with Sophia present.

"Rosella!" Sophia cried as she hugged her binder to her chest. "Slow down, girl! Geez, why're you in such a hurry!?"

"It's because our moms booked a meeting for today! C'mon!" I slid through the doorway and, spying my mother seated at one of the tables, I gave a heavy sigh. *She's actually here...*

Mom stood up upon noticing us, her brow furrowed with worry. "Rosella, did you run here?"

"She practically flew up the stairs!" Sophia complained. "She was skippin' 'em two at a time, like she had a fire lit under her ass!"

Dragging Sophia over to a pair of stools across the table from Mom, I threw off my backpack with my free hand and set it on the floor. "Like I said, Ms. Mitchell wanted to have a meeting today." I glanced at Sophia. "You know, your mom."

"And you decided to wait for me?" Sophia asked. "Even though I had detention for an hour?"

"She wanted us to come to the meeting too," I said calmly, though secretly nervous.

"O-Oh." She looked down at my hand, albeit shyly. "U-Um, could you let go now?" Her eyes darted to the right. "U-Unless you don't want to, which is fine."

"Oh! Sorry!" My hand tore away from her wrist like it was burned, my face hot with embarrassment.

"It's fine." Backing away, Sophia went over to set her binder on her mother's desk, then propped herself up on the desk, a weird look on her face. "So..."

"Hi Rosella, hi Chloe!" Ms. Mitchell abruptly entered the room with her hands working to adjust the blue ribbon in her tied-up hair. She crossed her arms over her chest when she was done.

"Good afternoon, Ms. Mitchell," I said.

She chuckled. "Rosella, it's after school. Please, call me Grace, won't you?"

A light blush dusted my face. "R-Right. Sorry." My eyes dropped to the floor. "Uh, Grace."

"What am I, chopped liver?" Sophia joked.

"No, you're my daughter," Grace affirmed.

Sophia cocked her head. "What's going on? What reason did I need to be here so badly that I almost had my arm dislocated?"

I mouthed a quick "sorry" to her, and she snorted with amusement.

"Yes, what's this about?" Mom crossed her arms over her chest as she eyed Grace with a curious expression. "You and I don't talk much."

"Well," Grace said as she clapped her hands together, "Rosella said that she was worried about you, and I am inclined to feel the same way."

My stomach dropped at the mention of my name, my head quick to follow as Mom's gaze darted to me.

"Funny you should mention that," she went on. "I'm actually okay. Right, Rosella?"

I gave an abrupt nod. "Y-Yes, it's all good."

Truth be told, when I went to Mom about Grace's proposal, she wasn't exactly thrilled. I could tell because her jaw was clenched so tightly, I thought it'd snap right off her face. To my surprise, however, she agreed to call her, and next thing I knew a meeting had been scheduled Wednesday after school.

"Rosella and I have our issues at times," Mom continued, "but we worked things out."

"Yeah..." I rubbed at my arms. "But you and I haven't talked much since Sunday." I dared a glance at my mother, and to my immense relief, there was a glint of understanding in her brown eyes.

"Your daughter really wants to know what's bothering you," Grace said. "You really shouldn't keep her in the dark, Chloe."

For a moment, what looked to be a scowl directed at Grace had formed on Mom's face, but it disappeared as quickly as it'd come.

"Gracie..." She rubbed her hands over her jeans. "Don't take this the wrong way, but you have no business being in ours. And dragging your own daughter into this, that's ridiculous."

"Well, they *are* best friends," Grace countered, a challenging edge to her words.

She seems awful pushy about this, I thought. My concerned gaze fell upon Sophia. *Seems I'm not the only one who's noticed.*

From her place on the table, her eyes were glued to Grace, an intense look on her face. It almost seemed like she was rather irritated with her mother, and though I was curious, I kept quiet.

"At any rate," Grace added, "don't you think you'd be better off just coming clean with her?"

"Look, I came here because I thought you wanted to talk with *me* only," Mom retorted, "not drag Rosella and Sophia into this." She threw one leg over the other, and interlocked her fingers atop her knee. "So, are we going to talk this out like adults, without the kids?"

Grace squared her shoulders, her stern frown set hard. "I suppose so." She glanced at me and Sophia. "I also guess you're more of a coward than I thought."

Her gnarly comeback made both me and Sophia nervously look each other's way.

Nostrils flared and eyes wide with rage, Mom sprang out of her seat, hands slamming to the table, startling me.

"Rosella, I think we should give them some space," Sophia piped up.

"Agreed." I sped for the door. "We'll be outside if you need us!"

Sophia and I retreated, leaving Mom and Grace in their unsettling standoff. Once we were a good several feet away, I leaned against the wall and cautiously peered at the entrance to the art room. Grace was standing in the same spot we'd left her in, her expression unchanged, but she wasn't talking.

"Okay, what's going on?" I asked. "Seriously. I've never seen them like this. In fact, I don't think I've ever seen them interact except for a few words' exchange."

Sophia shrugged. "I don't know. The most I've seen is brief eye contact, nothing more."

I sighed. "'Kay, so what do we do now?" I could just make out their voices, though I was too far to eavesdrop.

"We just have to wait for them to talk it out." Sophia smirked. "Wanna head to the library? We got some downtime since it seems they're gonna be a while."

"I guess." I looked to the art room. "Crap, I left my stuff in there..."

"That's fine, we can just read or something," Sophia offered. "Or, ya know, talk."

An idea suddenly popped into my head. "Wait, hang on. I need to go to my locker. Follow me?"

"As long as you don't yank my arm off," Sophia muttered.

I gave a laugh. "I promise."

We walked to the other end of the hall, where my locker resided. Sophia asked me what it was that I was looking for, but then she saw what I'd pulled out, and I reflected her excitement as I hugged my sketchbook to my chest. I had something special to show her, my first real drawing in two years.

"I threw this together yesterday," I said. "It didn't take me too long."

"It's been a while since I've seen you carry it." A gentle glow of hope illuminated her emerald eyes. "I'm glad to know you haven't given it up."

I glanced down at the sketchbook through a faint wall of tears. "Well, I know my father wouldn't want that for me."

She linked an arm through the crook of my elbow. "Well, let's go check it out."

We hurried through the second floor of the school to the library. Once we got seated, I quickly flipped through the pages of the sketchbook. It'd been so long since I was last excited to show a drawing to someone, and it felt amazing. For the first time in a long time, I felt whole again, despite the ongoing stress around me.

"With last week being so crummy... Man, I am so glad that I got my inspiration back." I found the page. "Here it is." My heart welled with excitement, I proudly propped the sketchbook up so she could see it clearly.

Sophia's eyes widened. "Wow! This is so good!"

I beamed at her. "Thanks. I worked really hard on it."

I knew it'd be okay to show her the sketch of Fenris and "Little Red" sitting on the tree branch. The kick I needed to get back into drawing, I just couldn't get the experience out of my mind. Usually, when an image lingered longer than a few hours in my head, it ended up seeping onto the paper. Channeling an idea into my pencil came naturally to me, though it required the guidance of my hand in order to bring the sketch to life, thus proving to be a difficult task to carry out.

Art was a serious venture for me. Over the years of suffering hand cramps from holding the pencil too long, back pain caused by several hours spent seated at my desk, and bins overflowing with balled up mistakes, I chipped away at my imperfections and sculpted a high quality-level talent that many claimed would be thirsted for in a professional studio. However, all that came to a halt when my father died. Without his praise, his light, I felt lost in the dark recesses of my mind.

Ro-Ro, this is so good! Look at you, our little artist! You're growing up so fast, kiddo.

I shelved my passion, and thought I'd never find it again. My fingertips intricately traced the dusty pencil lines. *School was a bit of a rough start for me, and despite locking myself up in my room, my workplace, I never spared a glance at my tools or the desk he'd helped prepare for me.* I sighed. "I've spent only a few hours on this, probably a new record for me."

"Ro..." Concern flashed across Sophia's face as she gently raised a hand near my face and stroked over my cheek. "Hey, you okay?"

I nodded while staring down at the sketch, a tear pricking my eye. "I was just thinking about my dad. It's been two years since I drew in this thing. I mean, I used it the other day in art class because I forgot my class sketchbook, but I don't think that counts."

Sophia's smile returned. "All three of you possessed a passion for creativity, and you shared it with each other."

"Yeah." I ran my fingers over the paper. "I, uh, have to touch up the wolf's ears before debating whether or not to risk destroying it with ink and paint." A fearful thought. One slip of the hand, and then it was all over.

"You're pretty skilled in watercolor, so use that," Sophia suggested. "I think it'd look nice."

"Yeah, me too."

"Man..." Sophia rested her elbows on the table and cradled her chin in her hands. "I really hope your art gets into museums or official galleries someday. Artists I follow online would surely kill for your skills, and with said skills you'd surely make millions."

I rolled my eyes. "No way, I'm not *that* good. And besides, I'm not in it for the money."

Sophia shook her head. "Sure you are! You're gonna go far, I just know it."

"Hey! Rosella, Sophia!"

Both mine and Sophia's heads shot up as Marcus suddenly came strolling around one of the bookshelves, his hands in his pockets. "I didn't expect to see you two here."

"Oh, Marcus." Sophia's demeanor changed, a solemn expression on her face as she squared her shoulders a bit.

"Hi Marcus," I murmured shyly. "Um, I was just showing Sophia a sketch I drew." I turned the sketchbook in his direction so he could see. "What do you think?"

"Wow, that's amazing!" A sparkle of interest shone in his eyes. "How'd you nail something like that?"

"I don't know," I said, "guess I got inspired." My heart bled with unending fondness for Fenris, but I couldn't tell either of them that. *I hate lying to Sophia though...* My eyes crept to their corners, in her direction. *But I promised to stay silent. Just a small stain on our friendship, nothing more.*

"Man, I wish I was that creative." Marcus stirred me out of my thoughts as he seated himself with us. "Sophia is very lucky to have you around, Rosella. You're, like, the coolest person ever!"

A hot blush flared my cheeks at his praise. "O-Oh, you're just saying that."

"No, seriously!" He beamed at Sophia. "Isn't she amazing?"

"Yeah, she is," Sophia said. "I really want her to go to art school when she graduates. She'd be the most popular one there, except she wouldn't let that go to her head. Unlike some people..."

"Yeah, true." Marcus' voice dropped to a whisper. "Hey, speaking of Caroline..." He lowered his head a bit. "Have you guys seen her at all?"

"No, not since the day she cornered me," I said. "Why?"

"I was just asking because I went to her house the other day to try and talk with her…" Marcus winced at Sophia's glare, and shielded himself with his arms. "Hey, let me explain first!"

"Give him some time to speak his case," I told her. Deep down, I was a little upset too, because he told me the other day that he wanted nothing to do with her. However, I decided to give him the benefit of the doubt.

Marcus reluctantly settled his hands back on the table. "So, I went to her house to try and talk with her. I wanted to see if maybe I could help her realize the errors of her ways." He blew air from his lips. "If I had to describe her myself, I'd say she's like a plant born from a greedy seed."

Sophia snorted. "Oh my god, that's exactly what she is!"

"No, seriously!" Marcus exclaimed. "She was raised rotten. But anyways…" His voice returned to a whisper. "When I got there, her aunt said that she wasn't feeling well. Mind you, I live close by, about five houses down from her, and the fact that I hadn't seen her at home…" A prominent shade of fear entered his eyes. "I'm worried, you guys. I think something happened to her."

Concerned, I set my sketchbook down. "What do you mean?"

Marcus' eyes fled to their corners. "Not to add salt to the wound…" His eyes darted to me as he dropped his voice to the point where we could barely hear him. "But I wonder if she vanished into the trees…"

I leaned back in my chair, hand clasped to my chin. "I honestly wouldn't be surprised, Marcus. I mean, it looks like a big place. However, I'm not too keen on that because, well…" I gently tilted my head to the side. "I haven't exactly explored much of the place. I only go so far."

Sophia rested her cheek against her fist, her elbow propped atop the table while her other hand danced in front of her chest. "Not that I'm agreeing with him, but I did read in a newspaper article that child services stopped by the shelter those twins were staying at and found nothing." She cocked a brow. "If something did happen to her, she might be hidden there."

"I heard about that," Marcus said. "My mom says that she doesn't trust the woman in charge because of 'shady' stuff goin' on, and it's got me wondering what she means by that. Is that woman secretly harvesting their organs, or does she have trained animals she's keeping somewhere? I mean, those twins were found torn to shreds. What if *she's* the alleged 'witch' of the forest?"

Sophia shot him another glare. "Seriously?"

I shook my head. "I hate to admit it, but you can't rule that out. There really could be someone keeping corpses within the woods, and if so, that's definitely gonna put a damper on my family. I honestly think the whole 'witch' thing is nonsense, but I wouldn't be surprised if the bodies were dumped there and animals got to them." I banished the shameful thought of Fenris at those words. *He would never do that. I know he wouldn't.*

"I hope for your sake the reporters go easy on you, if they come for you." Marcus reached across the table and grasped my hand. "And don't worry, I'll be there for you."

I resisted the urge to jump in surprise at the comforting touch of his warm palm against mine, and hoped to hell and back that he couldn't see the blush dusting my face. "Um... Th-Thank you."

"I'm with Marcus," Sophia piped up. "And if anyone comes your way, Rosella, know I'll be there too." As she rested a hand on my shoulder, my face grew hotter, my heart aflutter.

I looked to Marcus, and then Sophia, with a grateful face. "You're really sweet, both of you."

"... back here with her friend."

All three of us were caught off-guard when the librarian abruptly appeared with two men behind her. I effortlessly hid my disappointment as both Sophia and Marcus' hands tore away, my need for comfort abandoned. The lingering feel of their individual grasps would have to suffice.

The librarian nodded to the two men, then left them alone.

"Greetings you three." The shorter one, a black man with a faint mustache, stepped forward. "My name is Creg Kenneth. I'm a detective." He dipped a hand in the pocket of his trench coat and flashed his badge. "This here," he motioned to the man beside him with his badge, "is my partner, Detective Frank Stormer."

The taller one, a white man, mimicked his partner's actions with a curt nod.

Why do their names sound oddly familiar? I pondered. *I recognize their faces too... I'm sure I've seen them at least on TV before, but...* I tapped the tip of my finger to my lips. *Hmm.*

"We were wondering if we could ask you a couple of questions," Detective Kenneth stated. "Is that alright?"

"Sure." Marcus looked to Sophia and me. "Ladies?"

"Yeah," we both answered at once.

"We really appreciate this, won't take long." The taller man scratched at his head. "We needed to know if you three have heard of Caroline and Georgia Morse."

Marcus sprung from his seat, his back to Sophia and me. "Yes! I tried to go see Caroline the other day."

"You never told us what day," I pointed out. "Maybe that's important?"

"Oh! Right..." Marcus nervously rubbed the back of his head. "It was... Monday, actually. I went there after school. I didn't see Caroline here, and when I went to her house, Georgia told me that she wasn't feeling the greatest."

"Well, we just got back from there," Detective Stormer went on. "Georgia Morse was found dead this morning by a friend."

My eyes widened. *D-Dead!?*

"What?" Marcus' shoulders slumped. "What... What are you talking about? She looked fine when I last spoke to her."

"We're still trying to figure things out," Detective Kenneth said. "As far as we know, she suffered what could be a fatal heart attack."

"Rosella!" Mom's voice rang out through the library, and seconds later she came running around the detectives. "Rosella! Are you alright?" She doubled over, hands clutching her knees as she took in several deep breaths.

"Mom!" I got up and went over to her. "Are you okay?"

"I'm okay," she breathed, then straightened up. "Sorry, I... I saw these two on my way out after noticing that you and Sophia were gone, so I started to panic, thinking something had happened."

I shook my head. "No, they just showed up. They wanted to ask us about Caroline."

Mom hesitantly waved a hand at the two detectives. "Hi there, sorry. I'm Chloe Bloom, Rosella's mother."

Detective Kenneth extended a hand, and she took it gingerly. "Pleased to meet you," he said. "I've read some of your work, immersive and gripping."

A blush highlighted her cheeks. "Oh, well, thank you. I try."

Detective Stormer loudly cleared his throat, his eyes glued to his partner.

"Right, well…" Detective Kenneth's hand released Mom's and fell back to his side. "We were just wondering if these kids knew anything about a young girl named Caroline Morse, as well as her aunt, Georgia Morse."

Mom frowned. "Why do you ask?"

"They just told us that Georgia died," I said.

Mom's eyes bulged as her face drained of color. "Wh-What?"

"Word on the street is that you two had a bit of a struggle," Detective Stormer chimed in. "Is that true?"

Mom nodded. "Yes, we did." She nervously eyed me. "Her niece, on the other hand, has it out for Rosella." She looked back at the two detectives. "If you don't mind me asking, did Georgia have a history of health problems?"

Detective Kenneth looked to her with a shake of his head. "I'm afraid we can't answer that."

Suspicion crossed my mother's face, but she didn't say anything.

"You said that Caroline went missing," I piped up. "Um…" My hand latched onto the collar of my blouse. "I… I experienced a serious confrontation with Caroline last Tuesday."

Both detectives laid their eyes on me, and I shrank back a little. Their stares were intense, almost interrogative.

"Is something the matter?" Detective Kenneth asked.

I rocked myself from side to side, hesitant to respond. I knew I wasn't being a snitch, but these two were strangers, and I was a target of Caroline's antics most times. What if they suspected I had something to do with her disappearance? The thought of being in one of those interrogation rooms crossed my mind, and I shuddered. There was no way I could handle that.

"Hey."

I jumped at the voice of Detective Kenneth.

"It's okay," he said gently, though his stern expression hadn't faltered. "Anything you have to say may help us in our investigation."

I kneaded my hands together at my chest with uncertainty. "I-I just don't want to get in trouble. I mean, I swear I-I didn't do anything to her. I-It's just... It's just that I'm a..." I gave a frustrated huff. "Y-You see, I was in the girls' bathroom around lunchtime, on Tuesday, when Caroline came pounding at the stall door. Scared, I didn't let her in. I waited until she left to come out, but then she came back and put her hands on me. She twisted my wrists, pulled my hair, slammed my head against the stall, and left me disoriented." I hung my head and threw my hands behind my back. "I... I felt helpless, and... well..." My eyes darted to my mother.

Detective Stormer cocked a brow. "So, what happened after that?".

"Rosella had to go to the hospital," Mom added. "She's okay now, but the fact that the girl struck my child..." She fell silent and buried her face in her hands.

"Caroline's always picked on the weak," Sophia said. "I've heard horror stories about her, one of which I told Rosella."

"It's not just a story, it's true." Marcus' sagging shoulders stiffened. "Caroline has a lot of enemies, sirs. Whether they would go as far as hurting her back, I don't know. Though I myself was involved in a relationship with her at the time, I broke it off when I learned of the incident Sophia was talking about."

Detective Kenneth looked to Marcus questioningly. "Which incident?"

"Caroline hired two guys to stuff rat corpses in a girl's bra and then shove her in a friend's locker," Marcus admitted.

"And also threatened to turn her into Carrie White," Sophia muttered.

"Anyways," Mom said aloud, "I homeschooled Rosella until she was thirteen because I was paranoid over her experience with the general public's treatment of us. And, well, look where that got me." She shook her head. "I was trying to do what I could to help her, yet I couldn't stop Caroline from hurting her." She sighed. "This is the first time this has happened because she mostly directed verbal insults and occasional threats toward my daughter. I'm now hesitant to allow Rosella to continue attending public school, but I can't keep her locked away at home. That's not fair to her."

Detective Kenneth's gaze softened as he gave a curt nod. "I understand that. I raised two kids of my own." A faint smile graced his face. "You just want to keep your child safe, right?"

"Yes," Mom insisted, "I love my daughter with all my heart." She placed her hands to her chest. "I know it's hard to tell because no one sees us out much, but we like to keep things private." Her pleading face hardened into a determined frown. "I will do anything to protect her, and I can also assure you that neither she or I would harm anyone unless out of self-defense. And I'll be honest, I can't provide a sturdy alibi because, like I said, I like to keep my personal life private." Her eyes wandered to me. "I don't care how much digging you do into my business, but please leave my daughter out of it."

Both detectives stood calmly, their expressions unreadable.

"I hope you understand where she's coming from." Grace suddenly appeared behind Mom, her hand resting on her shoulder. "Chloe isn't a liar." She glanced at Detective Stormer. "Frank, you know that I only stick with people I know I can trust."

Detective Stormer's brow crinkled at Grace's words. "I... I guess I'll take your word for it." He returned his focus to Sophia, Marcus and me. "I guess we're done here for now, kids. If you think of anything else, please inform us immediately, or tell your parents." His eyes flashed to Mom. "I'm sure you're willing to cooperate, yes?"

"Absolutely," Mom declared. "Whatever you need, I'm there."

CHAPTER 12

Sophia

S O, YOU'RE LEAVING TO *hang with those detectives? Why? We're all the same, why can't I come along?*

Because I need to discuss certain matters you wouldn't understand, Sophia.

Mom, if you keep shutting me out, I'm just going to keep forcing my way in.

Just stay here with Chloe and Rosella. Please.

Fine.

I splashed a bit more cool water at my face, then found my reflection in the mirror. I'd excused myself upon arrival at the Bloom house so as to replenish, though I couldn't spend too long in the bathroom without arousing suspicion from either Rosella or Chloe. I cupped my hands under the spewing sink and sipped from the water they cradled. It tasted so good.

I'm so scared I'm gonna get thirsty again, I thought to myself. *But if I drink too much at once in front of them, they'll get suspicious.*

I'd made sure to drink plenty more water when I could since last Tuesday, which was unfortunately a lot. The day I went to the mall with Ro and Chloe, I drank so much water that I thought I could've gone a few days after without a single drop more, yet I was making constant bathroom trips like normal humans. Why wasn't my heart absorbing a lot of it? Could this be a defect?

"Wonder if those detectives have this issue," I muttered. "Psh, they've got to be close friends of Mom's. She even called the one casually by his first name. Why else would they play it off with her so well? Did they even know she was there at the school?" I raised a hand to my face and frowned. "There's gotta be a reason. Maybe it's got something to do with Chloe?" I cocked a brow. "And the fact that she's letting me stay here..."

Back at the art room, I felt the seething tension from my mother. She wanted to rip Chloe apart from where she sat at that table. I should've stepped in, but instead I kept my focus only on Rosella. I didn't think my mom would hurt her, but then again, she didn't put it past herself to call Ro out as an enemy.

I don't want you spending time with her. She's dangerous. Just stay away from her.

She's afraid that Ro will send that wolf after me, I thought to myself as I grabbed the small towel residing on the sink. *Mom told me he resided in those trees, but I'd never actually seen him, only heard of him and how 'evil' he is...* I patted my face dry, then set the towel down with a confused look. *So why is she letting me stay here, and after dark too? Isn't that when he comes out?*

Mom always told me that the forest was a bad place, and that anyone associated with it was too. But Chloe and Rosella were super nice, and so was Ben. And that wolf never came after me, despite my status, yet she said that if he could smell me out, he'd surely come for me in the dead of night and tear me to shreds without question.

And absolutely, under no circumstances, are you to go anywhere near that shelter.

I shivered at those words. The shelter within Hollow, the place where the twins came from... Did Ashen order them to be destroyed? And if so, why? And what about Caroline? Marcus had said she'd disappeared on Monday, but that couldn't be right... I stopped sensing her presence on Friday, as well as Georgia's. And it wasn't possible for them to hide themselves to any of the rest of us, unless...

"The forest..." I whispered. I gripped the edge of the sink with nervous intensity. "Did they vanish into the forest? Ashen said that it would be impossible to find us if we were to wander in there because of the forest's magic."

Defying... Troublesome, you are...

"Stop it," I whispered, and clapped my hands over my ears. "Get out of my head."

You're a fool... a traitor...

"Shut up!" I pounded my fists against the sink. "You can't control me, Ashen..."

"Hey Sophia, you almost done?"

My head whipped to the closed door, heart racing. "Y-Yeah Ro, be out in a sec."

"Okay!"

I brushed my bangs back and blew air from my lips. "Okay... Just stay calm, Soph. Don't listen to Ashen or the others. You can't trust them. *Stubborn as a bull, that's how I roll... Not lettin' them get to me. I'm stronger than they are. Somehow, I'll help Rosella and Chloe fight back. I don't care what my mom says. Not anymore.*

I fixed my bangs, smoothed out my shirt, and exited the bathroom. For now, I'd just play dumb to whatever suspicions either Chloe or Rosella had. It was the safest thing I could think of, though that day at the mall Chloe seemed to know more than she let on...

I shook my head. "No, it's fine. It's fine. Just play it cool, Soph. Play it cool..." My heart fluttered as the thought of Rosella again sprung to mind. "Ro..."

Since her interaction with Marcus today at the library, I was feeling more than a little jealous. The way he caressed her hand with his, looked into her beautiful eyes, the entire scene had me wishing I was in his place. I wanted to be the one hugging her close so she felt loved, the one to lend a supportive shoulder when she needed to cry.

Ro and I hung out very little until she entered middle school, and within the two years that'd gone by, I proved to her how important she was to me. Hell, I wanted Ro to be my best friend forever, but I couldn't stop thinking: what if it could be something more? Perhaps some of this stemmed from spite against my mother, but most of it was genuine fondness for Rosella.

"I guess I'll find out soon enough," I told myself. "I love her so much..." I cradled my hands against my chest. "Rosella... No matter what, I will protect you, because I love you."

Rosella

It'd been a few hours since our unexpected encounter with the detectives at the school library. They assured me that none of us were in trouble, but the fact that they came to us specifically set me on edge. Plus, the taller one looked wary of Mom.

"I can't stop thinking about those detectives." I handed my mother the last glass to be put away for the night. "Why do you think they came to us today?"

"I don't know," she admitted. "It was definitely strange."

"The way my mom spoke to the one guy, I'm guessing they know each other." Sophia handed me a coffee cup that I somehow missed. "I wonder why she took off with them anyway?"

"So, you picked up on that as well," I said.

She nodded. "What did that guy say his name was?"

"Frank Stormer, I believe. She just called him Frank, addressed him as though they knew each other well."

Mom closed the cabinet, the sound of it clicking shut drawing our attention to her. "Well, it's after eight, so I'll have to whip up something quick. You girls got school tomorrow."

"We could order pizza," I offered.

Mom shrugged. "Beats trying to cook something. I'll get on that."

"'Kay." I turned to Sophia. "Wanna go chill out on the back porch for a bit?"

"Sure." She linked arms with me. "I actually have something that I want to talk about."

"Okay."

"You two be careful! It's dark out!" Mom called after us.

"We will!" I shouted back.

I didn't have to rush, though a gentle speed-walk was necessary to keep up as Sophia strode ahead of me, her arm hooked around mine. We were greeted with the hissing of night critters as we stepped out into the cool night air, the moon high into position above.

"Everything okay?" My arm came free, and I threw my hands behind my head, my socked feet padding softly against the concrete. "What's up?"

"It's... kinda hard to explain." Under the moonlight, Sophia looked paler than usual, though I could still make out the blush trailing across her face. "You see, I..." She raked at her arms. "Ugh, I'm sorry." She looked away. "This is really random."

I frowned. "What is it? You can tell me."

"It's difficult," she mumbled. "I mean, I've wanted to say this for a little while now, but I'm scared to."

"Scared?" *Since when was she ever scared?*

Sophia feverishly wrung her hands together, her eyes downcast with her admitted cowardice.

"Soph... Seriously, you okay? What's going on?"

She took a deep, long breath, then puffed out her chest. "Rosella... I have something really important to tell you."

"Okay..."

"I..." Her eyes connected with mine. "Rosella, I... I like you."

I beamed at her. "Well, I like you too."

She snorted. "No, I mean, I *really* like you."

"What do you... Oh." My eyebrows rose. "Oh..."

"Ro, we've been friends for so long and... I really like spending time with you. And when Caroline got all up in your shit, it pained me to see you cower in fear." She frowned. "I want to be the one who's always there for you. I want to be the one who protects you when you're scared, the one who holds you when you cry. I... I love you, Rosella. I want to be with you forever." Sophia fell silent, her lips wavering together.

"Wow... Soph." My eyes widened in surprise. "I... I really... Wow." I was drawing a complete blank on how to respond. Never, not even in a million years, did I expect something like this from her, let alone from anyone really. Romance had never piqued my interest, and I never thought anyone would even express such interest in me.

"I-I-I know this is random," Sophia stammered hurriedly. "Y-You don't have to say anything in return. I just wanted you to know. I thought..." Her eyes shot from side to side. "Uh... Ugh." She doubled over, arms dangling. "I thought it'd make me feel better to get it off my chest. I just hope I didn't make things awkward."

"N-No, not at all. I'm just surprised is all." I glanced at the backyard. "I guess... Well, I... I can't just leave you hanging, so I'm afraid that I don't reciprocate the same feelings for you. I'm just not there yet, plus I promised my mom I'd finish high school before even *thinking* of pursuing romance."

One thing my mother always wanted me to do before anything else was finish my educational journey, and I still had far to go. I remember when I first even brought up the topic of romance a year ago, just out of curiosity, and Mom told me that it was a complicated thing I wouldn't understand until I was older. She said that it wasn't necessary, that my education was far more important. Still, I pushed the subject, as I wanted to know more. I wanted to know how her and Dad became what they were, how their love for each other was so strong.

Your father wanted me to wait, because I was only sixteen when we met, but I was afraid of losing him. Granted, he did tell me he was concerned about a young girl falling for him out of the blue. But I knew I could trust him, and he proved that. And sure, eighteen was a bit young to be running into the pool of romance, but this was your father. I would never find anyone like him again, and he was the best man in the entire world. Now, don't think of me as a role model for romance. Just know that your father was a good one, and I was lucky to find him.

I smiled at the memory of my father and me seated on the back porch a few years ago. Dad had told me how nervous he was because he knew people would look at them strange, because he was twenty-six and she was eighteen when they became a couple. But they were happy and responsible, and loved each other very much. That, to me, was more than enough.

However, I promised Mom I wouldn't step into the pool of romance until my educational journey was completed, and I honestly wasn't ready to take on a relationship yet, especially with Sophia. We didn't know where we'd be two or three years, maybe more, from now. Plus, my mom would kill me if I turned my back on my word.

"Soph, I hope you understand how I feel," I said. "Maybe in the future, it's something we can explore but not now, though I will keep it in mind if we're still together later in life." I bowed my head. "Besides, I don't think Mom would be too happy with me getting distracted from my schoolwork... Not that she'd shame me for it, just that romance can be... a little messy sometimes." I raised my head and found Sophia staring back at me. "I'm sorry."

Sophia straightened herself, a look of relief on her face. "Well, I'm glad I got that off of my chest." She clasped her hands together. "Rosella, you make my heart sing with your honesty. Thank you."

I put a hand on her shoulder, and nuzzled my head to hers. "You're welcome. And thank you for being honest with me."

"Always."

"Rosella..."

Both mine and Sophia's heads swiveled in the direction of the forest. *"That is your name..."*

Sophia eyed me with a concerned glance. "Ro..."

I couldn't answer. That confusing, irritating itch I'd experienced in the forest last Sunday had come back. My chest felt constricted by an invisible force, my throat clogged with cotton balls. My fingers scrabbled at my skin, desperate to relieve the itch.

So, so so itchy! Itch! Can't make it stop! Crawling in my skin! I sucked in a sharp breath as I raked my nails up and down my neck. *God, it itches.*

"R-Ro..." Sophia's voice was faint, barely above a whisper. "R-Rosella..."

"Y-Yes?" I squeaked amid my suffering.

"Th... That..." Eyes wide, Sophia raised a shaking hand, her finger pointing toward the forest.

I squinted my eyes, trying hard to make out what it was.

"Th-That thing..."

I opened my mouth to ask what she was talking about, but closed it when I spotted a pair of familiar moonlit eyes. Despite the agonizing irritation I couldn't relieve, I shot off the back porch, Sophia screaming my name in turn.

Fenris' paw slunk out from the underbrush, then his large head and perked ears. When he saw me, the rest of him followed suit. "Rosella!" He wagged his tail, his paws nervously shuffling upon the ground. "Listen to me! You need to—"

"Rosella!" Sophia shrieked. "Look out!"

"Rosella... We've been waiting for you..."

A thunderous growl rumbled from deep within Fenris' chest, as he peered back to the trees. "It's you..." A ridge of dark silver rose above his back, his snarling lips unveiling his dangerous teeth. "So, you've decided to show your face." His nostrils flared with anger. *"I won't let you take her."*

"Rosella!" Sophia screamed again. I heard her hit the grass some ways behind me.

Fenris whipped his head back, a look of fear on his face. "Don't! Stay back!"

"Rosella... Rosella Bloom... Blonde One..."

I sucked in a frantic breath, my eyes wide like saucers as something else stalked out into the open.

This thing was massive, definitely taller than Fenris, even when he was on two paws. Barky flesh shriveled up and rotten, with flakes falling from its hands, its crooked claws curled inward and uttered an uncomfortable crackling sound.

Its legs were like decaying stalks, with thorns creeping up its thighs, its decrepit branching arms hanging limp at either side. In the center of its gaping chest was something slimy and grotesque, a still lump of muscle I reasoned to be the heart. Trickles of dark, almost black, liquid oozed out and down the sides of it.

Fear quivered my rigid spine when it leered back at me, its two rows of sharp, grimy teeth bared. A thick, wet, black mass slithered out between them and flung saliva from the creature's mouth to the ground.

This looks like something that could've been born from my nightmares! My nails continued their panicked frenzy over my arms and down my sides while my eyes locked to the sunken, bloodshot pearls embedded into its head.

The creature tilted its large, crooked head, its crown of leafless branches swaying with the movement, a chilling leer etched into its face. *"Rosella..."* it hissed. *"We've been waiting for you..."*

It's a Lurker! Run!

A sudden thought I couldn't explain popped into my head. *There's no mistaking it... This thing is a Lurker... It's come for me.* I whipped my head around. "Sophia, *run!*"

Several feet from me, Sophia stood firmly planted to the ground, her face in a frozen stare of fear.

"Damn it!" I turned tail to run, but something caught me by the ankle and yanked me to the grass. I peered down my leg to see the culprit, a slimy vine with no intent of releasing me.

"Rosella!" Fenris' claw abruptly tore the vine to shreds, freeing me from my plight. "Take your friend and run!"

At that moment, the Lurker lunged for the wolf, and together they went barreling to the ground. I had just enough time to duck out of the way, having been forced to tumble and roll to the side. I heard Sophia screaming for me, and then her hand had given a harsh tug on my arm. She ripped me from the ground, and together we began our frantic sprint back to the house.

"Mom!" I called. "Mom! We need he– Aaaaah!" Panic ruptured my nerves as my hand tore from Sophia's. Another vine had wrapped around my ankle and yanked me down as fast as the first.

"Rosella!" Taking emergency course of action, Sophia latched onto my wrist and, exercising every ounce of strength she had, engaged in a fierce "tug-of-war" with the vine.

"So... Sophia!" My muscles pulled taut at either end, I struggled to bear the searing pain of both my arm and leg being stretched in two different directions. "Sophia!" Hot tears rained down my face as her grip slipped, and I went sinking into the dirt.

"Rosella!" Sophia clambered after me. "I won't let you take her!" Unleashing a battle cry, she charged forward and pounced upon the vine.

My fingers hooking into the damp grass, dirt caked under my nails as I wobbled to a stop whilst sputtering crumbs of it clogging my throat.

"Ngh! No!"

I felt the pressure around my leg vanish, and dared a glimpse over my shoulder.

"Rosella! Run!" she called. Now ensnared by the vine, Sophia punched at the thick limb wrapped tightly around her waist in an attempt to break free. She screamed and kicked her legs as she was dragged toward the trees.

"No! Please!" My socks lacking traction, I slipped on the grass.

"Rosella!!!!" The sound of my best friend's panicked shriek was like ice injected into my veins.

"Sophia! No!"

"NO!!!!! PLEASE!!!! LET ME GO!!!!" Sophia's face contorted in a nauseating expression of fear, dread, and absolute desperation. *"HEEEELP!!!!!!"*

Terror clenched around my heart like a vise as she vanished into the wilderness, and a guttural cry tore from my throat. *"SOPHIAAAAAAAA!!!!!!"*

I stumbled for the trees, my brain on overdrive as the adrenaline began to drain from my veins. My face suffered multiple whips from bristles and branch edges as I barreled into the darkness, my muscles screaming exhaustion.

"Sophia!" I cried.

Somewhere ahead of me, she cried back my name, but I could hardly hear her.

"Sophia! AH!" My body jerked backwards as my head collided with a tree I'd neglected to see, and I tumbled to the ground. Another wave of searing pain racked my bones as I sat up, my hand clutched to my throbbing head.

"Rosella!"

I shrieked as I was abruptly thrown into the air, and landed on something soft. "Fenris! Wait!"

The wolf ignored my outcry and led me back to the safety of the backyard, where he was ambushed by the Lurker. I flew from Fenris' back to the ground, and out of the corner of my eye, I saw he'd collapsed, a splash of red spewing from his neck.

Nearby, the Lurker's tongue twisted around its bloody claws, its malicious grin spread wide.

"Fenris!" I frantically crawled over to him as he stumbled back onto his haunches. "Fenris, are you okay!?"

The wolf was breathing heavy with a tired nod. "I... I am fine... Just..." He bowed his head. "Oh..."

The Lurker raised its decaying hand and pointed toward us. *"You are finished, wolf."*

A thunderous growl rumbled deep within Fenris' throat as his lips curled into another menacing snarl, the fur atop his back rippling with agitation.

I shivered beside him, terrified of this turn of events. I was used to being helpless, but this? This was at a whole other level.

"Rosella," Fenris breathed, "you must get to safety. I will take care of this."

"No, I'm not... I can't..." I struggled to find the right response. My mind was racing in a panicked circle of frazzled thoughts, and I had no clue what to do.

"Just get out of here, please." Fenris dropped low to the ground, and on cue the Lurker mirrored his actions. "I will protect you, Little Rose. I won't let anything happen to you."

With a powerful howl to the moon, Fenris leaped forward once more, and collided right into the Lurker's awaiting arms while I just *sat* there, too paralyzed with fear to do anything. My legs just absolutely *refused* to carry me to safety, away from the unfolding carnage, my eyes locked onto the two ferocious beasts caught in a swirling blur of aggression as their claws sought each other's flesh.

I gasped as the Lurker managed another swift slice to Fenris' neck, and kicked him back several feet. Fenris slammed against the ground and tumbled toward the trees, the Lurker quick to follow on its stumpy feet in a crab-like trek. With lightning speed, and to my horror, it swiftly pinned Fenris with its bulky foot to his side.

"Fenris!" I screamed.

The wolf snarled up at his opponent from his crumpled position on the ground, his glare sharp as daggers.

The Lurker slowly raised its hefty leg. *"Time to end this."* Its foot came down, *hard,* on Fenris' side, and I clapped a hand over my mouth to muffle the sharp cry crawling up my throat.

Ears pressed flat to his head, Fenris scrunched his face as he endured the pain of the Lurker's foot digging deeper and deeper into his side, his maw spread wide as he released an agonizing howl.

The Lurker peered over its shoulder to me, and a grin dripping with malice cracked its rotting face. *"Wolf is finished. Give in, Blonde One, and wilt in the—"*

"GET AWAY FROM HIM!!!!!!!"

My eyes bulged wider than ever before as another form flew past me, her arm raised high to the moon as its light reflected off of the shining sword she grasped tightly in her hands. The Lurker, its back to my charging mother, swiftly jumped to the side and swung its claws down on her. Mom was quick to dodge its attack, however, and dropped to the ground in a ball around it.

"Fool!" The Lurker spun around on one foot, its toe grazing the ground, and managed to kick Mom in the back as she attempted to roll away.

Mom cried out from the pain as she was thrown to the side from the force of the blow, but still managed to land on her hands and knees, sword clutched firmly in hand.

"Mom!" I shot up to help her, but dropped back to the ground when the Lurker turned its focus on me, and a fresh wave of panic washed over me. *Oh no... No no no.*

"Blonde One..." The Lurker's empty eyes locked with mine. *"Prepare for demise!"*

My bulging eyes followed the enormous tree monster as it sprung high into the air, and I stared in sheer horror at its decrepit form speeding down upon me like a meteor on a crash course into earth. Helpless, I braced myself for the impact, but was shocked to find myself wrapped into a thick layer of warm silver fur. The Lurker landed atop Fenris, the brute force crushing me against the wolf's body as he was sandwiched between us.

My tears stained Fenris' chest fur as my hands sunk into it. *Please, please don't let me die here!*

"Chloe! Take it down now!" Fenris cried. "Quick! Before... Urgh! Before I suffocate Rosella!"

I screwed my eyes shut and whimpered into the thick wad of fur in my face. My lungs were fighting in a losing battle for oxygen, and my heart was pounding so hard that my chest hurt. I didn't want to die like this, not like this...

An animalistic screech tore through the air, followed by a strained wheeze, and then the crushing weight against me was lifted. I uttered a harsh gasp as my lungs embraced the rush of fresh air, and I coughed and sputtered upon the ground as Fenris lifted himself off of me.

"Little Rose!" He stared down at me with tear-filled eyes. "Are you okay!?"

Through the harsh coughing, I gave a hurried nod, my small chest rising and falling with each strained breath. "M-Mo... m..." I rasped, my throbbing heart lodged in my throat. "Fe... Ack! Augh!" A stream of bile burned my throat as it trickled down, choking me.

"Fenris!" Mom called. "Fenris, are you alright? How's Rosella?"

"She's okay," Fenris answered. "She's... Oh..." The wolf began to teeter. "Gah... Ch... Chloe."

My muscles strained from tension, they recoiled upon movement as I pulled my legs into my chest, and I rolled over. I managed to slip out from under the wolf, then jumped as I heard the soft, but heavy thud behind me. "Fenris!" I turned myself around, and reached out with anxious hands to the fallen wolf.

"Ugh... Rosella..." Faintly, his spine wavered. "Ro... sella..."

My fingers grazed over his soft, blood-soaked fur, a horrid sight blurred by fresh tears. "Oh god... Fenris... I'm so sorry..."

The wolf cracked one eye open, the luminous hue of the moon still raging strong. "It's alright, my dear." His side caved, then rose again, each breath nice and slow. "Just sore... from the bite... in my neck, and the pain in my side..."

"Fenris, Fenris, my friend!" Mom hurried over with her own urgency. "Oh god!"

"I am okay. Please... do not worry." Fenris lifted his head a little. "Oh." He scrunched up his face in pain, his teeth chattering against each other.

"Please, let us take care of you," Mom urged. "I have some medicine that Felan put together. I'll go get it." She shot up and ran back for the house, leaving me alone with the battered wolf.

"Rosella," he whispered, "you should go with her. I don't feel comfortable with you out here..."

"Fenris, I'm not leaving you!" I argued. "You're hurt!"

He gave me a pleading look. "Ro... Rosella..."

"Fenris! I got the medicine!" Mom came running back as quick as lightning, and she collapsed upon the ground in a mess of panicked heaving when she reached us. "I... Oh god..."

"You didn't have to run," Fenris rasped. "Really, I'm okay."

"No, you're not," Mom chided. "You need help."

"Your daughter needs you more than I do."

"Damn it Fenris, don't argue with me." Mom leaned over the wolf. "Let me see. Oh, okay, not too bad. It's just a small bite."

"'Just a small bite!? Are you kidding me!?" My head abruptly swiveled in Mom's direction with a glare at the ready. "How could you say that!?"

Mom whipped out a small jar of white cream she held in one hand, a towel in the other. "Rosella, I need you to hold him still."

I gave her a baffled stare. "H-How?"

"Just put all your weight into his side. That way, if he turns aggressive, you'll be out of reach."

"B-But—"

Mom gently stared me down, her brown eyes pleading in silence.

"O-Okay..." Hesitantly, I plastered myself to Fenris' side, my hands burrowed into his fur. "Fenris... I-Is that okay?"

"Yes," he breathed. "Now... Chloe."

Mom opened the jar and sunk her entire hand into the jar.

"Is that going to be enough?" I whispered.

"It should be." Mom's brow wrinkled as she looked over her cream-caked hand. "Okay Fenris, here it comes."

He nodded, his maw firmly locked.

I shut my burning eyes as tightly as possible and, for a moment, all I could hear was the consistent thumping of my heart pounding my eardrums.

"... Aaaaaaa*AAAAAAAAAAH!!!!!!*"

I tightened my grip to Fenris upon his sudden flailing, my ears straining against his unbearable wails of agony.

"Hang in there, Fenris!" Mom cried, her voice drowning almost completely in his anguish. Her arms were being tossed from side to side, but her hands firmly held the towel to his wound. "Just gotta make sure the bleeding stops!"

Fenris snarled, his carnivorous jaws aggressively snapping at the air.

My head whipped forward and back, my neck struggling to keep it in place. "M-Moooooom!"

"Just hold on, Rosella!"

"I'm tr-try-y-ying! It's hard!"

Fenris writhed violently about, his ballistic howls for mercy finally dwindling when he suddenly relaxed into a soothed, comfortable state.

Exhausted, I silently suffered the headache rupturing my skull as I lay limp against the battered wolf's side, my limbs stiff as concrete.

"Okay," Mom whispered, "he should be alright now."

I cracked open a tired eye. "You... You sure?"

"Yes. He'll probably be here for some time, but by morning, he'll be up and moving." She rose to her feet and clasped at her buckling knees. "Rosella... I need you to tell me what happened so I know how to proceed."

I looked to the forest. Somewhere in there, right now, my best friend was screaming and begging for her life while being dragged to god knows where. *No... No* way.

Suddenly, the realization hit me. Sophia... Sophia was... I looked toward the trees, and my mouth fell open. No... No no no. This didn't happen. This couldn't have... She... She was out there. Surely she would come back... No... No no no. No no no no no NO.

Another sheen of tears traced the rim of my eye, the weight of dread settling heavy upon my shoulders. "Oh my god... They took her... They took her. They took Sophia... She's gone." I clutched at my knees. "My god, they took her!" I doubled over in a full-blown panic. "I couldn't help her, and they took her! They took her away!" My eyes squeezed shut, teardrops rained down my face to the grass. "Mom, they took her! I couldn't do anything..."

"Rosella," Mom whispered.

"Mom, they took her," I croaked. "They took Sophia. She's gone! They're gonna kill her, aren't they? Please, we have to help her!"

"Oh, sweetheart." She came over and knelt down to hug me. "Honey, it's okay."

"Mom..." I sobbed into her shoulder, my tears staining her sweater. "It's my fault... I caused this... She tried to save me... but I..."

"Chloe?"

I went still as stone, watery eyes flooding.

"Gracie!" Mom whipped her head to the left. "What are you doing here? You were supposed to stay inside!"

"Chloe…" Grace's voice wavered. "Where is Sophia? I can't find her."

"Grace, I—"

"Oh god… No… No! No, it can't be! Chloe!"

I hid my face in Mom's chest.

"*Oh god! Sophia!*" Grace wailed. "*No! Nooooooo!! NOOOOOOOOO!!!!!!!!!!*"

CHAPTER 13

Rosella

*Y*OU DON'T DESERVE TO *be forgiven. She helped you escape, but you? You did nothing in return. Absolutely nothing.* "Oh god... Sophia..." *It's my fault. It's all my fault. She got me out, but when she got stuck... I couldn't help her...*

I aimlessly wandered the house upon entry through the back door. I had no clue where I was going, nor did I care. All I could think about was how I let my best friend get kidnapped. She literally sacrificed herself for me when that root or vine or whatever the hell it was grabbed me, and I did nothing.

That fucking Lurker took her... After everything she did for me, all those years of standing by my side, assisting me in my time of need, the one time she needed me...

"Come in here and sit down!" I heard Mom demand, stirring me from my troubled thoughts. "Sit here at the table and wait! Rosella!" She entered the room I was standing in. "Rosella? Honey?"

My eyes wandered in the direction of her voice. I found her a couple feet behind me.

"Sweetheart, sit down." Mom hurried over and gently took me by the hand. "Sit down on the couch."

I allowed her to guide me into the sitting position, but otherwise paid her no mind.

"Rosella... Rosella, sweetheart, oh god." Her cold hands combed back the sides of my matted hair. "Rosella... It's okay, it's okay."

It's not okay. Sophia is gone. It's my fault. She protected me, and now she's gone... My one chance to help her... The one time she needed me...

"Chloe!" Grace stormed into the living room, her bloodshot eyes flooded with tears. "This is your fault! Yours!"

"Grace! I told you to stay in the kitchen!" Mom barked.

Grace shook her head, and pointed a sharp finger at Mom, her bloodshot eyes wide with rage. "You did this! *You!*"

"Gracie, calm down. We'll figure this out."

Grace gestured toward the kitchen. "She's out there, and we need to help her!"

"We can't just go charging in there like barbarians!" Mom protested. "They're using her as bait to lure us in. Trust me. They won't hurt her."

"Sophia was always there for me when I needed her," I whispered. *I always forced my insecurities onto her. And now...*

"Rosella, I think you should lie down for a little while, okay?" Mom rose to her feet, a hand pulling me up with her. "Gracie, I'm taking my daughter upstairs. Will you please wait here for me?"

Grace didn't respond.

"Come on, Rosella." Mom held her hands firmly to my shoulders and steered me toward the staircase. When we passed by Grace, Mom wedged herself between her and me.

I was the one who let those monsters take Grace's daughter away. Mom shouldn't be protecting me from that.

"Okay, up we go..."

Each step closer to my bedroom door was one step further from Sophia, one step deeper into my guilt. When we reached the top, Mom led me into my bedroom, and the urge to protest exploded.

"Mom! We have to save her!" My fingers hooked to her arms in desperation. "Please!"

"Rosella, sweetheart, sit down." Mom's hands firmly shoved me onto the bed.

"No! We can't!" A fresh stain of warm tears washed my face. "She's my best friend!"

"Rosella, stay here, okay? Don't move."

"Mom..." I snatched her wrist. "Mom, I..." Her hand yanked itself free, and then silence followed my fractured voice.

"Rosella. Stay."

A sense of betrayal wormed its way into my heart, and my glassy eyes fell to the floor.

"Rosella, I'm sorry," Mom whispered. "I just... I need you to stay there for a bit, okay?"

I didn't say anything. I couldn't.

Mom whirled around on her heel. "I'll, uh, come back later."

I waited until Mom had shut the door behind her before letting the tears further spill. "Sophia... No... No no no." As I curled my fingers into my hair, I wanted to dig them into my chest and rip my heart out. "Sophia... No. God, no."

I watched my best friend writhe in terror, heard her scream, and I didn't do a damn thing about it. She easily pulled me free, yet I couldn't do the same for her? And her face, the *fear* in her eyes, as she dragged into the trees... I'd never seen her like that, ever. Sophia was always strong-willed, taking shit from no one. And yet, in that moment...

I'm weak and I always will be. I fell onto my side. *I'm so weak... How could I let this happen?*

Minutes ago, she was pouring her heart out to me, proclaiming her love for me, and that she'd do anything to protect me... and I turned her down. I told her I didn't feel the same way, but I never meant it this way! Never! I never meant to throw her away!

My hands smothered my face. "Oh god... No... No, this isn't what I wanted."

I want to be the one who's always there for you.

"Stop it..."

I want to be the one who protects you when you're scared, the one who holds you when you cry.

"Please."

I... I love you, Rosella. I want to be with you forever.

"So... Sophia... I'm... so sorry..."

Friends are supposed to be able to depend on each other, yet I couldn't do anything for just one. And now, I've totally blown it. The one friend I had was now in the clutches of evil monsters beyond the trees of my house, and I'd never see her again. Her life, her blood, would forever stain my hands...

I won't let you give up... I can't... I won't let them take what matters to you... I won't let you continue to suffer.

Chloe

Guilt fractured my aching heart as I listened to the muffled cries of my baby girl beyond her bedroom door, and it hurt worse than my lingering back pain. I wanted to go in there and comfort her, to reassure her that everything would be fine. But I couldn't bring myself to lie.

I knew they wouldn't kill Sophia but... "God... No..." I turned away from my daughter's sobbing. "Gracie..."

I trudged back down the steps, a cold chill at my sore back. Dread weighed heavily upon my shoulders, the harbored past unraveled beneath the mental graveyard I buried it within. Sprouting from the seed of guilt, I knew it would grow, and when the time came, the poisoned fruit of truth would threaten to spill from my mouth. But I'd choke on it, fight with every ounce of courage I had, in order to keep it down.

I knew it was too dangerous to let Sophia and Rosella stand out there on the back porch. I knew they would come for Rosella, because they wanted the power she unknowingly held. I *knew* Sophia would sacrifice herself for Rosella, in order to protect her. Like me, Sophia knew what those monsters were.

I clutched at my trembling gut. *What have I done?*

"Chloe..."

I stood at the top of the steps, my heart thundering in my chest. "Gracie... I thought I told you to wait for me."

Grace lingered at the bottom, her head hung low. "I was worried about Rosella, so I figured it'd be okay to check on her."

Though I didn't buy that lie, I stayed calm. "You don't have to worry about her."

Raw, irritated lines traced the rims of Grace's eyes as she raised her head, the streamed tears having run dry. "How is she?"

"She's fine," I stated more firmly. "Let's go talk."

"Sure, let's talk." Grace whirled around and stalked back into the living room.

She won't forgive me for what I've done... ever.

I raced down the steps and hurried over to the couch, where Grace awaited me. Through the dark void in her emerald eyes, I witnessed the resurfacing pain she'd suffered long ago. Still, I clasped my sweaty palms together in my lap and forced myself to relax, while Grace sat stiff as a board, her steely gaze locked on me.

"Grace," I began. "I'm... so sorry... I didn't know what was going on. I was in the kitchen, ordering pizza for the girls."

"You don't have to apologize," Grace murmured rather calmly. "I understand... Really, I do." She slid a hand over mine. "I know of those monsters out there. And you know that I know that place... I know how close you are to it... It was your home, wasn't it?"

"Of course it was," I murmured.

"Right, so the last thing I want to do is take that from you." Grace's fingers drummed over my wrist. "But they took my daughter from me, so..."

I shook my head. "If you're telling me to destroy that forest, you're crazy. Your daughter's in there. And it would destroy Rosella."

"Chloe..."

"You need to rest and so do I." I rose from the couch. "You can use one of the pillows here to lay your head. I'll get you a blanket."

I holed up in my office after getting Grace settled for the night, unable to sleep a wink, my mind ravaged with deserved thoughts of the worst. It was my fault, not Rosella's, that Sophia was taken. And Grace was the embodiment of my festering guilt.

I never meant for this to happen, I thought to myself. *I wanted to protect my daughter. But, at the cost of Grace losing hers? I should've told the girls to stay inside. I shouldn't have allowed Sophia to be the sacrifice. What was I thinking?*

I continued wallowing in my guilt throughout the rest of the night. When dawn finally broke across the sky, I wandered out into the backyard, my tired feet dragging through the grass to Fenris' resting point. In his place were bloodstains and bits of silver fur tainted the grass, the slain Lurker crumbling to ash nearby.

He must've moved sometime during the night. My gaze fell upon the trees. *I have to speak with him, tell him the truth.* I hung my head. *Maybe I can work something out... Maybe I can get Sophia back.* Hope blossomed within my heart. *I can fix this, and I know Fenris will help me.*

The thought of perilously trekking through the forest with the wolf sprung to mind. Riding on his back, like a proud warrior woman, on a search and rescue mission for a young girl whose disappearance I was responsible for... I was strong enough to endure the forest's inhabitants with Fenris by my side. If I could get him to comply, and I knew I could, we'd set out this afternoon. We both knew this forest in and out, so surely we'd find Sophia in no time.

But what about Rosella? My heart sank. *I don't want to lose her, and I can't trust Grace alone with her.* I shook my head. *No, I'll figure something out. Maybe Mom could take her for a few days.* I eyed the trail ahead. *And then, when Fenris and I get Sophia back, we can all return home, like nothing happened.* "Fenris, if you can hear me, please come see me immediately. I need to talk to you."

I waited for several minutes. The wolf did not turn up. Confused, I called out to him. When I got no response, I gave a sigh and hurried back into the house, where I went searching for my phone. I found it on the kitchen counter and set to dialing Mom's number, but paused when I heard a few knocks. I took a deep breath, then hurried to answer the door.

"Who the hell is..." My heart about leaped out of my chest upon discovering the detectives on my doorstep. *Shit! The hell are they doing here!?* I forced myself to relax, so as not to draw suspicion. "Oh! Hello detectives, how may I help you?"

"We're sorry to disturb you so early this morning," Detective Stormer said. "We were wondering if you had a moment to answer a few more questions regarding the incident with the Morse family."

I frowned. "Oh, is there anything else I can offer you?"

"We understand that you once personally went to the Morse residence," Detective Kenneth explained, "and that you left there on bad terms. You and Georgia Morse underwent an intense confrontation."

I sighed. "It was a couple years ago, back when my daughter first started middle school. Caroline had threatened to shove Rosella's face in the toilet and drown her. I think you can imagine how angry I was."

"Yes, but I never would've anticipated you to slap the girl in retaliation," Detective Stormer stated.

My mouth fell open. "E-Excuse me?"

Detective Kenneth put his hands up. "Ma'am, we're just trying to piece things together."

I glared at him. "And you, sirs, need to understand that I would never lay a hand on a child. I will not deny *wanting* to hit that brat, even *strangle* her for tormenting my daughter. But I would never actually go through with it." I placed my hands on my hips. "Who told you this bogus story, anyway?"

Detective Stormer hesitated at my question.

"There is more," Detective Kenneth piped up, "that we feel also needs to be discussed. We found information regarding your stay at Miss Sally's Safe House."

I shuddered, a heavy sense of unease splintering my back. "Yes… I know that place. It's a shelter for girls as young as toddlers to teens who can't take care of themselves. They do accept adults as well, but usually younger ones are found there." I forced down the prominent lump in my throat. *That place… Sometimes I think it's worse than what the forest's become…*

"From what we understand, you once found yourself there," Detective Kenneth continued.

My shoulders stiffened. *She didn't…* "Who told you this?"

"I am afraid we cannot disclose this information," Detective Stormer said.

The words slipped my mouth before I could stop myself. "It was Grace, wasn't it? She told you all of this?"

"Who?"

I shook my head. "You know who." I stared Detective Stormer down. "I am well aware that you two go way back. You're not getting anything past me." My glare loosened into a stern frown. "With everything that's happened, I'm now the prime suspect, so I will disclose that I was indeed involved with Miss Sally for a short time. But before I spill more of my secrets, I have to know you're willing to spill yours." A smile crept across my lips. *I may not be able to hide from Grace, or these two, but that doesn't mean they can hide from me.*

Truth be told, I knew full well what these men were. It was no wonder they stuck together all the time. And the fact that they also knew Grace on a personal level, came to *my* house unannounced, and of course their names. All I wondered now was why they waited so long.

"Well?" I stood before the two men with confidence. *C'mon boys, tell me your secrets. I know you were told to come here, and maybe, just maybe, you can shed some light on Georgia... There's something about her, I know there is.*

"The only way you're getting anything out of us is if you speak first," Detective Stormer challenged. "We could haul you in for suspicious behavior alone."

"Accusing me of something you know I'm not guilty of?" I retorted. "I'd like to see you try. As infamous as the forest is, as much as it stains my name, you would be the guilty party, sending a falsely-convicted mother of two to prison."

"Two?" Detective Kenneth questioned.

"I consider our cat a member of the family as well," I clarified, "my daughter too, so therefore we are cat moms." As stupid as that surely sounded to the detectives, Pooter was just as important, and I wasn't ashamed to state that loud and proud.

Still, neither detective responded, as expected.

"I'm sure you are aware that silence is of upmost importance," I went on. "I'm not saying I know exactly what it is that you two are hiding, because I may not. But I've noticed the way you look at each other, and the fact you're always together. See, sometimes I do pay attention to the news, but only when you come up. And every time your names are mentioned you're together, never just one or the other."

These two, they were always investigating the peculiar cases, like the one about the billionaire who committed suicide under mysterious circumstances. They said it was because he suffered from depression, but I wasn't buying that like everyone else. In the back of my mind, there was more to the story...

"Okay, so you're more observant that the average person," Detective Stormer concluded, drawing me out of my thoughts. "But what does that mean for us?"

"It means that you two, for all I know," I retaliated with a hard glare, "could either be plotting something dangerous, or you both possess something that works well when you're together."

Though Detective Kenneth kept a straight face, I could tell he was nervous as hell.

Good, he knows I'm not screwing around.

He locked eyes with me. "Alright, here's the deal, you tell us about your connection to Miss Sally and what's goin' on in that forest, and then we tell you about us."

"Okay, but then you also tell me about who leaked my involvement with Miss Sally. I'm certain it's Grace, but what if I'm wrong?"

Detective Kenneth looked to his partner, who nodded warily. "Alright, my partner and I are willing to cooperate."

"Oh, and one more thing..." I crossed my arms over my chest and cocked a suspecting brow. "I want to know everything about Georgia. She's not... normal... is she?"

The detectives both gave me strange looks at my slurred words.

I know there's something... there. I rested a hand to my head, my elbow propped on the other. It was hard to think about, like it was on the tip of my tongue, but I was missing one vital piece of the mental puzzle.

"We're... willing to cooperate," Detective Kenneth said again, and cocked his head. "Are you alright, ma'am?"

"Yes." My mind began to clear as thoughts of Rosella sprang forth, and before I knew it, I was clear-headed once again. "I... I just need to check on my daughter. Something happened last night, which I will be sharing because I promised you that. However, I am going to have to ask you not to say a word outside of this house, to anyone else."

"Depending on what it is," Detective Stormer said, "sure."

"No, you can't," I told him. "End of story." I turned my back to them and started forward. "Please, come in."

As instructed, both men awkwardly meandered into the house. They were shocked to find Grace lying asleep on my couch, but didn't feel it necessary to wake her, so they opted to sticking close to the door and patiently waiting for my return.

I hurried up the steps and down the hall to Rosella's room, then raised a hand to knock. However, I hesitated. What if she was sleeping? I shook my head. No, I needed to check on her. If I woke her up, I woke her up.

"Rosella? Sweetie?" I gently opened the door. "Hey, it's me… Rosella?" I looked over at her bed and my stomach about dropped to my shoes. "Oh my god…"

The sight made my stomach churn as I did a quick sweep of the room. Rosella didn't even try to cheaply hide the truth with pillows stuffed under her blankets. I could see it'd been slept on, yet it looked neat and tidy.

Rummaging through her closet, I was horrified to find my first clue there. Rosella's red cloak and a pair of gloves were gone, along with her sturdy winter boots, some cargo pants, and a couple of shirts. "Oh god, Rosella…"

I checked the bathroom next and, to my dismay, Rosella's hairbrush and special "Blossoms in Bloom" wristband were missing. "Oh no! No!"

I raced back down the hall in a panic, flew down the steps two at a time, and stumbled straight for the kitchen. I didn't want to believe that she'd really left. There was no way. She was too fragile. She could get hurt. She was my baby… I didn't want to let her go.

"Please, no!" I cried as I threw the glass door open and ran out onto the back porch.

Behind me, the two very confused detectives were yelling for me, but I didn't catch what they were saying.

I tripped and collapsed upon my knees when I hit the grass, my eyes glued to the trees. *"ROSELLAAAAAAAAAA!!!!!!"* The distressed cry for my daughter tore through the air, my throat ravaged from the erupting scream.

I wanted to charge in there, find Rosella, and drag her back to the safety of our house. I wanted to scold her for acting so foolish, and forbid her from ever leaving my sight… Instead, I lowered my head and sobbed into my hands.

Chloe, we can't protect our little Ro-Ro forever. When the time comes, she must embrace her true self. Please, let her explore this world while she can, before she has to leave it forever. Help me show her that there is some good outside of those trees.

"Benjamin," I rasped. "I'm sorry. I should've listened to you. She had a chance, but I didn't let her have it. Now, it's gone for good."

"Chloe."

I craned my lulled head to the side when I heard Detective Kenneth behind me. "Yes?"

"I found this lying on the table here." Detective Kenneth held out a piece of paper to me. "I think you should read this."

Reluctantly accepting the paper, I held back tears when I read over it:

Mom, I'm sorry. I have to help her. Sophia is my best friend. There's something inside me screaming that I can't leave her to die. I feel guilty beyond words for letting this happen. She was always there for me, so now I need to be there for her.

I know Fenris will find me and try to make me go home long before I reach Great Granny Felan's. I hope I can convince him to let me go. I guess you'll find out the answer whether or not you see me sitting at the edge of the forest.

I love you, Mom. I promise, no matter what happens, I will never forget you. Thank you for taking care of me, keeping me safe.

-Your loving Bloom, Rosella

I rested a knuckle against my trembling lips. *Rosella...*

"What the hell is that thing?"

I jolted in surprise as Detective Stormer whisked past me, and my eyes moved to the ashy remains in my backyard, where the detective was headed.

Detective Stormer, gun raised, precariously approached the Lurker corpse. "Creg... Creg, you gotta see this, man."

Detective Kenneth followed my line of sight, and he gasped.

"It won't hurt you," I called to him. "I've already killed it."

"Still, we want a full explanation of this," Detective Kenneth demanded.

My spine rippled with tension, I meekly turned myself around to face him. "How much time you got?"

"Hey, Creg! You seein' this shit!?" Detective Stormer called out.

"Yeah, I'll be there in a moment!" Detective Kenneth shouted back.

Rosella... My gaze lingered on the trees. *Please... Be safe... I'm sorry, I'm sorry I couldn't protect you... And I'm sorry for locking you away.*

Sophia

Bound to a tree, my arms held firmly above my head with a slimy vine, another wrapped around my legs, a thin layer of spider web stitched my mouth shut. I'd probably been here for hours by now, though there was no way of confirmation, as the dome of trees above covered the sky completely.

Several feet from me, a Lurker turned my way, and I wiggled in my bindings as it crept toward me. It placed a decaying hand to my quivering belly, its rotting claws threatening injury.

"You will help us," it whispered. Its voice was as dry as the crumbling leaves upon the ground.

I whimpered, my eyes wide with horror as I felt a claw graze over my navel and up my midsection. As it traced over my frantically beating chest, I gave a silent prayer that my death would come quick.

The Lurker laughed devilishly at my shriek. *"Pathetic Husk... You are weak..."*

I cringed as the Lurker's claw trailed back down my body, but I forced myself to silence. *I can't give this thing any more pleasure than it's already got. Come on, be brave. Stubborn as a bull, that's how I roll.* So I glared back at the Lurker in defiance.

The Lurker, scowling, retreated its hand. It stared me down for a good minute, hoping to intimidate me. But I refused to give in.

I knew that it was stupid to give myself up like that. But I had to, otherwise they would've taken Rosella. Just because I was a Husk, that didn't mean I was willing to drag my best friend to her death. Not even

Mom could convince me to leave her to die. She might've been a coward, but not me. I was going down kicking and screaming if I had to.

Rosella... I hope you're safe... I promise, I'll be strong. I let the tears fall once the Lurker turned its back to me. *I'll be strong... Stubborn as a bull, that's how I roll...* I screwed my eyes shut and swallowed down a sob. *Please be okay.*

CHAPTER 14

Rosella

"D ADDY!"

I don't remember when I closed my eyes, nor did I recall my dream playing out this way. Why was this time different?

I was standing in the empty field, just like before. The clear sky above, and the sun blaring down on me. The few times I dreamed, this was the place that came to mind. But this time was different.

"Dad! Daddy!"

My outstretched hand just beyond reach of my father, he stood emotionless, his mouth moving ninety miles a minute without a sound slipping past his frantic lips. It'd been so long since I heard his voice, so long since I was wrapped up in his arms.

"Daddy! I'm here! Please!" But I couldn't move forward, only wave a helpless hand before him. So close, yet so far...

The field opened beneath my father's feet, and his hand shot out for me, his mouth as wide as the gaping hole that swallowed him...

It was then that I awoke with a start, my body drenched in sweat, my heart pounding in my tightened chest. I could see from my bay window that the sun hadn't risen quite yet, so it had to be early morning hours.

As I slid out of bed, my dirty socks slipped on the carpet, and I tiredly yanked them off. "Ugh... god..." I scratched at my head and wandered over to the bay window. "...!"

I shot down the stairs so fast I was sure I skipped two or three at a time. I ran through the living room to the kitchen, and practically tore the back door from its hinges as I jumped out to the back porch, into the grass. Morning dew dampened the bottoms of my feet upon my haste through the backyard.

"Fenris!" I threw myself at him, my legs swinging out behind me as the wolf stumbled back a few steps.

"Rosella! Whoa, easy now!" Fenris steadied himself. "Okay... There we go."

I massaged my fingers into his soft, glistening fur. No trace of blood stained them, no scabbing laceration hidden beneath.

"Rosella, I sensed your distress." Fenris lapped at my cheek with the tip of his tongue. "Are you okay? How is your mother doing? And what about that other woman?"

I shook my head. "I don't know. I blacked out for a little while."

His ears drooped. "I am sorry. I tried to track down Sophia. Her scent was lost some ways past Felan's cabin."

Struggling to halt the cry working its way up my throat, I pressed my lips together.

"Rosella..." Fenris nuzzled his forehead comfortingly to mine.

"F-Fenris... I'm scared. She's my best friend."

"Rosella..."

I pulled the hood of my cloak over my head as I stood before the forest. I'd made sure that I packed what I needed in my school backpack, so my only hope now was that he wasn't mad at me, and that he wouldn't try to stop me.

It's too dangerous, Little Rose. You will only get hurt.

Fenris, please... I can't stop thinking about her. I'm scared for her. What if they hurt her? She always protected me, even from that Lurker. I can't let this go. I just can't. You heard Grace's cries. I... I can't.

Rosella! Rosella, wait!

Ignoring Fenris was foolish. But I didn't think anything of it. Hell, I had no clue what I was doing until I was standing in the mirror, freshly-showered and dressed for the crazy scheme I was about to commit myself to. Yet I kept going. I wrote out that note to Mom, left it on the kitchen table, and then out the door I went.

Clad in a black, comfortable long-sleeved shirt with a high neck and dark grey cargo pants paired with brown winter boots, I slipped on a pair of sturdy brown gloves as I glanced down at my backpack. I'd packed a box of crackers, a couple bags of trail mix, a refillable water bottle, an extra shirt, my toothbrush and toothpaste, a hairbrush. But I didn't have a tent on hand, and all else I could fit was a thick blanket and a special piece of clothing. A tear grazed my face as I thought about the special clothing, but I streaked it away.

"Okay... I'm ready." I picked up my backpack and threw it over my shoulder, then turned back to the house one last time. "Mom... I hope you get my note. I promise, I'll be back soon."

The sun was just peeking over the horizon now, which meant I was probably safe from the Lurkers. I remembered something about them hating the sunlight, and judging from how fast the Lurker corpse still sprawled out in our backyard was withering away, I estimated that it'd be nothing but soot by midday.

I paused about halfway through the backyard, my eyes glued to the tree monster's decaying form. *How do I know all of this?* I looked up and down myself. Oh god, was I really doing this?

Yes, you are. You belong in the forest. It is your home, and it is time to reclaim it.

"I have to... return," I whispered. *Return to the forest... Find Sophia, save her from the Lurkers. She's my best friend.*

She is nothing like the other Husks, Rosella. She never was.

"Sophia..." My eyebrows pulled together into a stern frown. "I'm coming. I don't know how, but I'll find a way to save you."

I proceeded forward and slipped through the back doorway of the fence, then made a beeline for the woods. My heart racing with adrenaline, I was really doing this. I was really going in there, clueless, to find my best friend and save her from what I assumed would be an army of tree monsters.

My boots crunched against the grass and twigs, the bristles of the bushes gently grazing my legs and sides. I had no trouble passing through, as my cloak's fabric was strong enough not to snag on them.

You must prevail... You can do it.

"You came."

I halted several feet from the wolf, his eyes piercing through the shadows. "Yes, I did."

"You are going to try to save her, aren't you?"

"Unless you stop me," I stated.

He won't stop you... Trust in him... He'll keep you safe.

Fenris sleeked into view. "I see... If I do?"

His icy stare chilled me to the core, but I fought against the shivering, and forced myself to stay still.

"Well?" he challenged.

"I will be sad, but I won't object," I admitted, my head held high. "I can't fight against you. You are much too strong." As much as I wanted to deny those words, I couldn't. If he really wouldn't let me go, I'd have no choice but to turn back. *So please don't send me home. I want to save her.*

"Rosella, I don't think you've ever really been afraid of me," Fenris said.

I nodded. "I feel comfortable around you."

"And I around you."

He is your friend. He will guide you. He will stay by your side.

I took a hesitant step forward. "Fenris, I can't leave Sophia alone. She's always been there for me."

He tilted his head. "Rosella, do you know what you are doing?"

"I don't know," I said. "There's something... inside of me." I clenched my hands into fists at my chest. "This forest is calling out to me. This is my home, where I feel at peace."

Tell him how you feel. Honesty is best policy with both of you... Trust him with your words.

"I know I am weak, afraid, unable to fight. But... I feel the need to help my friend." A few stray teardrops worked their way out of my eyes, and crept down my face. "I know that part of this is adrenaline rush, and that once it finally dwindles down, I'll realize how stupid I am and that this is crazy. But until that happens, I want to try because I'm tired, Fenris!"

The wolf nodded silently.

"I'm tired of being weak!" I exclaimed. "I'm tired of cowering behind someone! I want to stand up for myself for once! Stand up for others, save them! I couldn't save my father from his illness! I couldn't save Mom or Great Granny Felan from the nasty rumors! I couldn't even save myself from Caroline's bullying! But that doesn't mean I can't *try* to save Sophia from the Lurkers!" As the tears continued to rain down, I thrust my fists at my sides. "I don't want to be weak anymore! I want... I want to do something for myself, so that I can feel proud of myself. I... I want to save my best friend because she's always been there for me!"

"She is someone you've come to trust over the years," Fenris said.

"Yes!" I went on. "She never turned her back on me, so why should I turn my back on her!? And yeah, this sounds cliché, but fuck it! It's the truth! S-so, if you want to stop me, you can! But please, understand where I'm coming from!" I squeezed my eyes shut, my body racked with tremors as I took in several hasty breaths.

"I see... So, you want to become braver, stronger," Fenris ushered. "You are also trying to be a loyal friend, but you feel that in order to do so, you must put your life at risk." He sat down. "Rosella, do you trust yourself with this mission? Do you think you can do this? Truly?"

I stared down at the ground, afraid to answer. I knew what I needed to say, but didn't want to hear it.

"Well?"

Well?

"... No."

Silence raided the air as I hung my head in shame. He knew I couldn't do this alone. I knew I couldn't do this alone. I couldn't trust myself to save Sophia on my own. I wasn't the fighter I wanted to be. I was a weakling.

I had no superpowers. I had no courage. I had nothing. I was timid little Rosella, a tiny flower with a stem as fragile as glass. One simple twist was all it took to break me...

But you will grow... and you will stand strong...

"Well, we'd better be off then. Felan is waiting."

My eyes popped open, and my head shot up. "Wh-What?"

"I said that Felan was waiting."

My jaw hung open. Was he... Was he serious?

The wolf locked eyes with me. "You are unable to handle this quest alone. Perhaps, with me by your side, you have a better chance. That is, if you trust me." His solemn gaze softened. "Rosella, do you trust me to assist you in your quest to save your friend?"

I felt like crying again. I felt like falling to my knees again. I felt like this was all too much at once... But I shoved all that aside. "Fenris, as of this moment, I trust you with my life." I raised a hand toward him. "Will you join me?"

He got up and walked right into my palm. "Yes, I will gladly join you." He stared past my outstretched arm. "I promise, Little Rose, I will protect you. I will keep you safe."

"Okay." I removed my hand from his head. "Let's go."

Fenris dropped to the ground so I could mount him like before, then waited to move until I gave the signal that I was situated comfortably atop his back. "Feel free to grip as tightly as needed," he told me.

I gently kneaded my fingers into his neck. "It's okay, I'm actually quite comfortable. Just make sure to warn me before you go running up any more trees."

A lighthearted chuckle slipped the wolf's maw. "Alright, it's a promise."

True to his word, Great Granny Felan was waiting for us near her front door. She toddled back inside once she spotted us, and Fenris slowed to a walk as he approached the steps of the cabin. He hurried up the way, then lowered to the wooden surface so I could easily slide off.

"I won't be long," I said.

He nudged me with his nose. "I'll be waiting."

I nodded before heading inside. "Great Granny Felan?"

"Over here, dear." Great Granny Felan was seated on the couch. "Please, have a seat." She patted the spot next to her, then motioned to two teacups filled to the brims with piping hot tea.

I came over to sit beside her. "Thank you." I took one of the teacups and blew into it, before cautiously taking a sip. Hot, brewing chamomile steamed the way down my throat, a comfort I'd get to enjoy one last time.

"So, your mother is staying at the house, and Grace is there with her. As for you two, I am certain you will make a pretty good team. Just, be careful." Great Granny Felan sipped her tea. "Mmm, oh, hot." She set the teacup down, the corners of her mouth stretched. "I gathered a ton of supplies for you to take."

"I am sorry for phoning you so early in the morning," I said with a sheepish grin. "I know this is sudden."

"Oh no, I am very much glad you called!" Great Granny Felan patted me on the shoulder. "Though I must apologize for not answering right away. I was in the bathroom. Anyways, I packed lots of extra food for you, and also put together some special medicinal remedies in case either of you get hurt. Oh, and I have a sleeping bag for you, and a small pack of clothes for you to change into just in case. I know you brought your backpack, but trust me. This pack I put together is much better as it can hold more, and it's stronger..." She eyed the pack I'd prepared, a sad attempt at replicating survival gear.

"Yeah, I tried." I rubbed the back of my head. "I hadn't expected you to do all that for me."

Great Granny Felan clapped her hands together. "Ah, one more thing..."

I curiously watched her stand from her spot on the couch and shuffle over to the entertainment center across from it. "What is it?"

She opened one of the drawers and pulled out something. "Oh, just a little protection."

My eyes widened as I set down the teacup, then reached over to take the object in question from her. "G-Great Granny Felan..."

"This was your father's," she said. "He would want you to use this to defend yourself."

I looked over the fascinating weapon in my hands. "Oh my god... Great Granny Felan..." It was a large knife, with a thick hilt, and a blade as smooth as glass. Upon closer inspection, a set of initials were etched into the blade: "B. G. B."

"You be *very* careful with that knife," Great Granny Felan warned. "It's real big in your hands, but at least it'll protect you against the Lurkers, especially since they are afraid of that weapon. The hilt is made from the bark of these trees, the blade from magic."

Shock highlighted my face. "Magic?"

"That's right, hence why they fear it so. With help from Fenris, you'll see that it can take down dozens of them."

I carefully flipped the knife about in my hands. Magic... It sounded crazy, but I couldn't deny it. Between Fenris' existence, what happened last night... To think that nine-year-old me would become entangled in all of this...

I held the weapon to the light pouring in from the living room window, and stared in awe at the glinting initials. I could feel my father's spirit within this blade... He was with me, rooting for me.

"G-Great Granny Felan, thank you." I set the knife down on the coffee table, got up from the couch, and hugged her. "I promise, I'll return it safe and sound."

"You yourself must return safe and sound." She rested her chin atop my shoulder as she squeezed me tight. "I already lost a grandson-in-law. I don't need to lose a great-granddaughter, too."

"Heh... Right." I gave her a gentle squeeze before letting her go. We locked eyes with one another, and I nuzzled my forehead to hers. "Great Granny Felan..."

"Rosella." She cupped a hand around my cheek, a sheen of tears twinkling in her amber eyes. "Oh honey, you are so brave for doing this."

I nodded slowly. "Yeah..." I cleared my blurring my vision with a wink, as my arms fell from around her. "I love you, Great Granny Felan... I promise not to forget you."

She gave a pained chuckle. "I know you won't, dear. Just remember not to forget about yourself. And make sure you keep your clothes nice, and your things all together so you don't lose them."

I snickered. "Yeah, I'll... I'll make sure everything's accounted for."

Great Granny Felan and I stepped outside together to find Fenris performing a once-over around the cabin. We held out a sliver of hope that maybe he'd find Sophia clinging to a tree with fear, but wasn't surprised when he returned alone. We were disappointed, but not surprised.

"We'll find her," Fenris said.

"I know... I'm just worried..." I mumbled with my head low. "Well..." I faced Great Granny Felan with a determined face, my spirit regaining strength. "We're heading out now."

Great Granny Felan nodded, then threw her arms around Fenris' neck. "Be well, my friend."

Fenris tearfully rubbed his head against hers. "I promise, my dear. I will return to you, Rosella and Sophia in tow."

Great Granny Felan pulled away from him with watery eyes. "Oh, I'm going to worry so much." She managed a smile. "But I know you two will succeed."

I nervously pulled at the backpack Great Granny Felan had prepared over my shoulder. "Great Granny Felan, you're right. This backpack is way better."

"Indeed," she said. "Now you be careful, alright?"

I gave her a worried look. "You will too, won't you?"

"Of course, my dear." She rested a hand on my shoulder. "Rosella... You have so much ahead of you. No matter what happens, you will prevail as long as you don't give up."

"Yeah." I looked to Fenris, then back at Great Granny Felan. "Well... I guess this is goodbye..."

She crossed her arms over her chest. "Yes... For now."

I grasped at Fenris' side, my back to Great Granny Felan, and we proceeded toward the trees. I refused to be tempted into going back for another hug. Every precious second that passed was another precious second Sophia was in danger. Great Granny Felan would be fine. She had her paper lanterns.

I breathed in a heavy sigh as Mom's words echoed in my head.

They're using her as bait to lure us in. Trust me. They won't hurt her.

"Sophia," I whispered softly. "We will find you... Just hang in there..." I peered over my shoulder one last time, and mirrored Great Granny Felan's bittersweet grin. *This isn't goodbye,* I thought to myself, and looked to the trees that waved in the breeze. *This is a welcoming.*

Indeed it is... Rosella, you will prevail. I will make sure of it. Now, as the wolf's red, go forth and reclaim what is yours.

Sophia

I didn't recall falling asleep, though when I woke up, I noticed I was no longer tied to a tree. In fact, I was lying flat on my back, my bindings missing. I sat up with a start, and immediately regretted it with a meek whimper to myself. I rocked on my knees, writhing in agony.

A crippling muscle spasm in my stomach surged through my veins with needles of pain. I threw my arms around myself, my fingers hooded into my sides. God, it hurt so much! What the fuck was this!? I slid my hands around my stomach and shuddered. Through the fabric of my shirt, I felt a large lump.

The... The fuck!? I snatched my top with a nervous hand, and my mouth fell open. Just below my navel, a blister as black as my hair, roughly the size of my fist, was growing out of my stomach.

I grazed the infectious bump with hesitant fingers, and immediately regretted it. Nausea pierced my insides like a stab in the gut, and I threw myself forward as bodily fluids spewed from my mouth, hosing the ground in vomit. I coughed and gagged, the back of my mouth burning from the lingering bile.

"Ack... Ugh..." I ran the back of my hand across my mouth, and cringed with disgust. *God, I feel like shit. And this...* I peered back down at the blister. *Where the hell did this come from?*

"... bastards better release me! Ouch!"

A chill coursed down my spine as my blood ran cold. That voice...

"You have no idea how much you're gonna regret this! I got money, a-and... people! Yeah!"

I looked up in horror, my stained mouth agape.

Another person was suddenly dropped right next to me, those once fiery red locks now a dull, matted mess of faded auburn. "You idiots won't get away with this! I'll kick all your asses! I..."

I locked eyes with my fellow captive, mirroring the shock reflected at me. "C... *Caroline?*"

She blinked a couple times, and then her eyes bulged. *"M-Mitchell?"*

"What... What are you doing here!?" I looked her up and down. Indeed, this dirt-faced redhead in blue rags was the devilish queen of the school.

"What *am* I doing here!?" Caroline whipped her head around, evident anger returning hot to her face. "That fatty bitch plan this?"

Immediately, my temper flared, and I jabbed a harsh finger into Caroline's chest. "Now you *listen here*, you spoiled, piss-rigged pig! Rosella would *never* do anything like this, so you'd best keep your *fuckin' opinions* to yourself!" I spied a stick lying upon the ground and snatched it. "Otherwise, I'll shove this thing right up your ass! I'll bet you've just been *hankerin'* for a little *tug an' shove!*"

Caroline abruptly shuffled away from me, a fearful look on her face.

"Yeah, that's right!" I snapped. "Who's the scared one, now!?"

"You."

Blood drained from my face when I heard a low, gurgling voice behind me.

"You must be Blonde One's friend."

I cautiously glanced over my shoulder. "Uh... Huh... Ah!" I flipped over onto my rear and scrambled away from the towering tree creature before us. "Take her, not me! She's the ugly-faced loud mouth!"

"What!?" Caroline squeaked, and pointed at me. "No! She's the one droppin' curses like a sailor! Take her instead!"

"Oh, like you're Mother fuckin' Theresa!" I barked.

"Look who's talkin'!?"

"SHUT UP PUNY RED HEAD."

Caroline immediately shrank back.

Amusement played at my lips. *Ha! Glad someone's putting her in her place.*

"You. Brunette One. With green eyes. Follow."

I pointed to myself, and a frown settled upon my face. "Me?"

"Yes."

"Uh... I... O-Okay."

Afraid of angering the monster once more, I obediently stood and followed after it, my head craned to look over my shoulder. Caroline was backing as far as she could into that tree, and I trembled at it. How long had I been bound there? My arms were only a little sore, but it felt like much time had passed...

I looked up to the trees, and grimaced. Not even a sliver of sunshine could save me...Which meant... *This must be their lair.*

"I take you to leader. Explain everything."

I stared up at the Lurker with curiosity. *Oh god... Its chest looks so gross... and those eyes... Yuck!* I scrunched my nose. "Disgusting."

"Not disgusting. We are Lurkers."

"Right," I muttered.

I never knew how they got their name. My guess was it was something chosen at random. It didn't matter to me. At the end of the day, they were still monsters.

I bowed my head with shame. *I shouldn't think like that. It's not their fault they're like this. They were forced into captivity.*

"Here she is." The Lurker stopped at the edge of the clearing, where a much taller one stood facing the other way. "*Red Head is still mad. What we do?*"

"*Don't worry about her for now.*"

"*Alright.*"

I felt a chill course down my spine. *This one's different...*

Unlike the rest, rotting leaves dangling from the decrepit branches atop this one's head. I squinted to try and better examine when the creature turned around, and gasped. Within the leader's gaping chest was an aggressively-pulsating dark purple mass, a black jewel embedded in the center.

Oh god... This one... I hid my fearful realization behind a stern mask, and hoped they wouldn't pick up on it.

"*You may leave now,*" the leader said. "*I must speak alone with Brunette.*"

The smaller Lurker nodded, then walked away.

Opting to play it smooth, I glowered at the leader. "Alright, pal. What the hell is this? Why am I here?"

The creature uttered a dry laugh. "*Blonde One is important to us Lurkers. She is vital to our survival. You will assist us in her capture.*"

I scoffed at them. "I don't know who and what you think you are, but I ain't doin' shit for you!"

The Lurker leader tilted their decomposing neck, and a sharp crack rang out. "*Foolish girl. You are just like the Caroline.*"

"Screw you!" I snapped.

"*Ha ha ha... You think you are powerful, but you are not. You are a worthless Husk with no chance of escape.*" A purple light illuminated the embedded jewel in their heart. "*You shall see.*"

"Gah!" I collapsed to the ground, my hands pressed into my gut as an abrupt, hot, burning pain set my insides ablaze. Beads of sweat trickling down my forehead, I kicked my legs out in retaliation at the blistering stabs of pain ravaging my insides. *Oh god! It hurts! It hurts!*

"*You are important to the blonde one,*" the monster whispered. "*If we break you, we break her treasure.*"

I worked up a scowl against the perspiration scorching my dry eyes. "I don't care what you do to me," I growled. "Break my bones, tear apart my innards, devour my soul if you must. I will continue to fight for Rosella."

"*Foolish girl...*" they snarled. "*You are stubborn, but you will crack.*" The monstrous tree beast narrowed their sunken eyes, their jagged teeth set in an awkward slant. "*This forest is no longer hers. And once we capture her, we shall plant our seed in her soil, mark this land in her blood, and rejoice in our conquest.*"

Disturbed by the leader's words, I shuddered against the relentless churning of my stomach, and retched upon the ground. *Damn it...* I wiped my moist lips with the back of my hand. "I... I won't let that happen. I'll find a way out. And when I do, I will take Rosella someplace where you'll never find her."

The leader Lurker's frightening scowl reigned over my meek glare of determination, effectively trampling what little confidence I had. "*And just how do you plan on doing that?*"

My nervous fingers danced up and down my sides, as I bravely stayed locked in my terrifying battle of wits. "I-I have always protected Rosella when she needed me. She's my best friend. You can't take her from me. I won't allow it."

The creature didn't respond.

"Wh-Why is it that you want to hurt her?" I demanded, albeit hesitantly. "What did she ever do to you?"

They coughed out a dry, curt laugh. "*I told you, we need her in order to complete our goal. She once ruled over us with an iron fist, manipulating us into doing her bidding, but no more. We are reclaiming our brethren.*"

My nostrils flared with anger. "That is a lie! She would never, *ever*, do such a thing!" I exclaimed. "She is kind and full of warmth. She loved you all!" I locked eyes with the leader. "Don't tell me you don't remember that! *She* is your master, not Ashen!"

My outburst stirred the entire clearing. Lurkers all around snapped their branching heads in my direction, evident shock awkwardly sculpted into their haphazard faces as they paused their activities. Caroline, meanwhile, remained where she'd been abandoned, her jaw unhinged, eyes bulging.

The leading Lurker unleashed an aggressive snarl. *"You fool... You are rejecting the poison..."*

I broke eye contact with the monster out of timidness, my next words a risky shield that bore no protection, as I stared down at the ground. "If anyone's a fool, it's you... I know you're still in there... I know. Why else would you still be alive? Tell me, are you still in control? Or is Ashen forcing you to say these words? Your master... She loved you, so why would you turn on her? Did you turn on her?" I bravely raised my head to them again. "Answer me, god damn it!"

The leader was silent for several seconds, before turning on their heel. *"Your punishment cannot come soon enough."*

As the creature stalked off, their back hunched with arms dangling loosely at their sides, a nervous lump rose in my throat. I swallowed it back down, and noticed the itch. It'd been some time since I last drank some water... Would these things give any? With a quick scan of the place, I didn't see an ounce, and if I didn't have water, then...

I shook my head. "No, no no. Don't think the worst. They aren't planning to kill you... not yet." I glanced over at Caroline, who was still curled up against the tree. *If these things know better, they'll give us water soon. Unlike humans, we can only drink water to quench our thirsts. Otherwise, we'll die...*

My eyes wandered to the trees again. The Lurkers were fast, but I could easily outrun them, and with that thought in mind, I forced myself to my feet. My knees knocked together from the throbbing of my abdomen, but I ignored the urge to sit back down, and broke out in a sprint.

Get to the trees... Get to the trees, and you'll be okay.

But I wasn't. Once I got within a few feet of them, searing pain erupted deep in my gut, and I collapsed to the ground with an agonized wail. I scuffed the heels of my sneakers in the dry earth, my arms wrapped tight around me, as I broke out in a heavy sweat that drenched my entire body.

The pain subsided over the next several minutes, but I didn't dare move out of fear it'd hurt to. Heart beating rapidly in my chest, I placed a quivering hand over it to try and steady it.

"F-Fuck..." I raised my weak head to the trees, and held back a cry as the unshed tears stung my eyes. I was stuck, and as much as I wanted to see Rosella, I hoped I wouldn't. She would only be trapped here, like me.

CHAPTER 15

Chloe

"**H**ERE." I SLID THE mug across the table to Detective Stormer. "Should probably slow down, as this is your third."

"Trust me, I've run on twenty in two days," he mused. "This is nothin' for me."

I snorted. "Isn't that dangerous?"

Detective Stormer set the mug on the table in front of him. "Nah, I'm not like you. I can easily scarf down as much as I want. It's really just water that affects me. Too little leaves me incredibly thirsty, while too much can make me nauseous."

"But I thought you needed lots of water to survive?"

"Since we're no longer under Ashen's curse, we won't die if we go without water for too long, but we really don't wanna do that, because we still get 'parched tongue'." Detective Stormer rested his arms atop the table. "Honestly, it really just depends on the Husk's tolerance level. For instance, Creg can easily down three gallons once every two weeks and be totally fine. I, on the other hand, can only handle roughly two bottles of water every other day."

I nodded. "So, your partner needs more water than you do?"

"I guess. Sometimes, though, I wonder if the bastard's heart is secretly a sponge."

"Right, your hearts..." *They aren't human, so of course their bodies function differently.*

Detective Stormer rubbed at his forehead. "Oooooooh, can't believe how late it feels. It's not even noon."

That means it's been an hour since I discovered Rosella's note. By this point, she's probably long since past Mom's house. I buried my face in my hands. *Rosella... and Fenris... How are you two holding up?*

"So, your daughter... Is she coming back?" Detective Stormer asked. "It's been some time since she left."

I shrugged. "I can't say yes, but I can't say no either. It all depends on how things play out." I looked away, my unshed tears hidden.

"I'm sure you're worried sick about her." He eyed the back door. "Man, I still can't wrap my head around all that... I didn't think it was that serious."

I expected them not to know anything about their connection to Rosella, beings that they waited so long to come see me, but I was quite surprised to find out they knew nothing about the Lurkers, or anything really. They told me they weren't part of the main group of Ashen's subordinates, that they were tasked with simply observing the town.

"It's all they told us to do," Detective Stormer said. "We don't attend any meetings, converse with the other Husks, just stay off to the side and watch the world go by."

"So, you don't even know what else could exist in the forest?" I asked.

"We only know that Ashen has it out for the forest goddess."

I tapped a finger to my flattened lips, pondering what to ask next. "Okay... Then how come you were their most trusted subordinates?"

Detective Stormer shook his head. "Ashen sees all of the Husks as equals that serve under them, but I'm certain they had their favorites. But, it does have me wondering why they keep me and Creg out, since they raved about their success in connecting us..."

"Ashen always said you two were special," a low voice muttered.

I nervously peered over my shoulder at Grace. "Shouldn't you be taking it easy?"

She stood in the doorway to the kitchen, her head hung low, a menacing shadow over her face.

"Gracie..." I extended a comforting hand, but then retracted it when she whirled around and left the room.

"Quick question..." Detective Stormer threw one leg over the other, and clasped his hands atop his raised knee, a quizzical look on his face. "Does she know about your daughter? What she is?"

"She does," I admitted. "I also told her that destroying the forest would destroy Rosella, which is something I regret deeply."

Detective Stormer snorted. "Probably wasn't smart to tell her that."

I shuddered at the detective's smart-ass comment. "W-Well, no one is perfect..."

He raised a brow. "I never said anyone was."

"Hey... Uh..." Detective Kenneth poked his head through the opening in the wall next to the doorway. "Pooter here's acting like he's hungry."

Eager to step away from the awkward conversation, I shot up from my seat. "I'm so sorry, be back in a shake and a half!"

"Take your time," Detective Stormer said. "We'll be here."

"Thanks."

I left the detectives to chat as I fetched a can of wet food for Pooter from one of the cabinets. He had to have been close, for as soon as I turned around, he was sitting at my feet, eagerly awaiting his yummy food.

Pooter was the only thing keeping me sane, the only part left of my usual routine, and since Rosella was long gone, I'd have to craft a new one without her...

"He's got a special bowl here." I reached across the counter for the glass kitty bowl. Written in fancy, cursive writing was the cat's name, a gift from Ben on one of Pooter's few birthdays. I fondly thought back to Ben's reaction when he first showed it to me and Rosella.

See, it's got his name on it! Pretty neat, huh? A friend of mine made it! They're real nifty, ya know.

I refocused at the sound of Pooter's meowing. "We leave his water bowl in the corner there, near the back door." I tore open a package of moist cat food, and dumped it into the bowl.

Excited, Pooter coiled around my legs, as I attempted to walk toward the back door.

"Pooter, hang on a sec!" I stepped over the cat, and quickly set the food bowl next to the water bowl. "There you go! Goodness, you act like I'm starvin' ya!"

Pooter, purring loudly, set to work on his hearty meal.

"Geez..." I shook my head. "I swear, bein' a cat mom sure ain't all it's cracked up to be."

"What do you mean?" Detective Stormer asked. "I thought it'd be fun."

I eyed him with a curious glance. "They never said cats would be demanding, and overly-attentive, and push you around."

Detective Stormer ushered a hushed laugh, then pulled out his phone. "Ope, got a text from the wife. She's gettin' worried about me pullin' a lotta all-nighters."

"You're married, Detective?"

He batted the air with a hand. "Call me Frank. No need for professionalism."

"Frank." My grin spread a little wider. "Alright, just call me Chloe then."

Detective Kenneth extended a hand as he entered the kitchen. "Creg."

I respectfully shook hands with him. "Nice to meet both of you, casually."

"Likewise."

My solemn expression resurfaced, as my hand fell back from Creg's, and I crossed my arms over my chest. "I know how hard it is, giving up your secrets like this, but at least I have some to share too." My eyes darted from one man to the other. "You two were meant to cross paths. After all, you can only read each other's minds…"

"It's been this way since we were born," Frank said.

"And we found each other some years later," Creg added.

"Yeah…" I peered at Frank, and my heart sank at the uncomfortable look on his face. I could tell he was as nervous as I was.

"Well, we promised to share everything with you, didn't we?" Creg went over to take a seat beside his partner. "Just to recap, Frank and I are Husks, people who were claimed as humans by Ashen, and evolved from their curse. Frank and I used to serve under Ashen as part of their main army, though he and I were stationed quite a ways out for some reason. Like the rest, we possess powerful forms of dark magic handed down by Ashen themselves."

"Right, I remember all of that," I said. "And this magic… It's Ashen's, correct?"

"Yes," Creg confirmed. "They have the power to give and take it."

"Like the 'forest goddess'." I mindlessly pulled the lot of my long, brown hair over my shoulder, and combed through it with my fingers, as my eyes dropped to the floor. "She… She has the same ability, pretty much. And from what I've heard of Ashen, from you two, it's just as she warned me they were."

"Yeah, they're a real hard-ass," Frank grumbled.

"Right..." Creg's face twisted with discomfort. "I'm sorry to ask this, but I was wondering if you could tell us more about your husband. You said that the curse killed him..."

My chest tightened at the mention of Benjamin. "He... He was aware of what was going on," I said quietly. "And the only way he could cope without losing his mind was by venting to me. He didn't want to forget anything, so drinking himself into zombification was out."

"'Zombification'?" Frank questioned, his brow furrowed.

"Zombie," I clarified. "Ya know, lost drunkard that stumbles around like a zombie." I shook my head. "He'd have lost both Rosella and me that way, not that he liked to drink anyway. Only person I knew who went his entire life sober, besides my daughter."

Frank scoffed at me. "Well, I would hope so."

I blew air from my lips as I smoothed back my hair, and pretended that I didn't catch his harsh response. "Anyways, getting back to the curse, instead of 'evolving' him into a Husk, it drained the life out of him, to the point where he could no longer stand. And he couldn't defeat it because his willpower wasn't strong enough..." The lingering memory of Ben in his decrepit state drove a stabbing pain through my heart, and I blinked away the onslaught of tears. "Be... Believe me when I say that he fought hard. But now he's gone, and he got it long after my mother."

"You say she's your mother... and yet... she's not." Creg cocked his head. "I recall you mentioning her as your daughter's great-grandmother."

"Oh! Oh, right... I forgot about that part." I rubbed at the back of my head. "Right, that's about where we left off on my end before I had to step away, to check on Gracie shortly after you arrived." I shivered. "She still hasn't eaten anything."

"I'm sure she'll regain her appetite soon," Frank said.

"Based upon what you've disclosed to us," Creg added, "those things... The Lurkers, they're responsible for the disappearance of Caroline Morse, the deaths of Georgia and the twins. Now, they've got Grace's daughter."

"Yes, that is all correct," I confirmed.

Frank threw his hands up, his face scrunched in upmost confusion. "Then what the hell is this 'Felan' woman doing out there?"

I sighed. "She's sort of like one of the forest's loyal protectors."

"You mean, as a Guardian?" Creg guessed. "Ashen told us about them a long time ago. They're like us, except they serve the forest goddess."

"Y-Yeah..." My eyes darted to the entrance of the kitchen. I didn't trust sharing this information within earshot of Grace.

"Look, I can tell you're nervous about her." Frank got up and walked over to me with his hands on his hips. "She probably already knows everything because she was holed up at Miss Sally's shelter for years, before her escape." He shrugged. "And whether you like it or not, she knows what your daughter is..."

I stared back with suspicion. "You know Grace well, don't you?"

"Sort of," Frank said. "She disappeared the night her sister died. I know because she told us herself."

I bit back a sob bubbling in my throat with quivering teeth. *I didn't mean for that to happen. I just wanted to be their friends.*

"Chloe?" The detective lifted an intrigued eyebrow. "Is something wrong?"

I went over to the sink and pulled my hair back. My stomach was churning, and I felt like I was gonna throw up.

"Are you okay?" Creg asked.

I waited a minute, and though nothing happened, nausea remained heavy as a lead block in the pit of my stomach, as my vision blurred with tears.

A soft scuffing of a chair scooting across the floor resounded behind me, and then Creg's gentle hand rested on my shoulder. "I can get you some water."

I shook my head. "N-No, I'm okay."

"What's wrong?" Creg urged gently. "You can tell us."

I wiped the back of my hand across my wet eyes, as I turned myself around. "Did she... Did she ever tell you *what happened* to her sister?"

"Well..." His eyes darted to his partner, who held a stoic expression that was hard as stone.

I stared Creg down with a pleading gaze. "Creg, please..."

"When we met up with her, after speaking with your daughter and her friends at the school library," Creg uttered, "she told us a bit more about what happened. She said that you were involved in Sarah's death, but she refused to disclose further details."

I searched the man's face for any sort of hint that he was playing me, but kept up empty-handed, so I sought out a possible answer to the next question I had. "Tell me, why did you wait so long to come to me, if the forest goddess was adamant that you find me?"

Creg worried at his bottom lip, as his gaze wandered to the ceiling. "It's... It's complicated, but not important at the moment. We're here now, aren't we?" His eyes wandered back to me. "Did she ever try getting Grace to do the same?"

I nodded sadly. "She did, but Grace wouldn't listen."

It broke my heart knowing Grace was against us. It was understandable why, though it certainly made things more difficult, especially since our daughters were super close, and that shouldn't have been drawn into the conflict between her and I. They had nothing to do with what happened to her sister Sarah...

"How come your mother's lasted this long in the forest, Chloe?"

"Huh?" I dumbly blinked a couple times, and found Creg awaiting a response to his question. "O-Oh! Well, you see, she was put in charge of the forest's defenses, in case a Lurker Queen should ever arise."

"And a Lurker Queen is what again?" Frank asked, a little rashly.

"From what intel I've received, a powerful being that can grow anything she wants, and control the forest itself. She would gain the ability to manipulate it in any way she chooses, and even summon her own creatures to do her bidding."

"Okay, so that means Felan is in danger, which again begs the question: why the hell is she out there?"

I sucked in a breath before responding to the snippy detective. "She could easily turn a houseplant into either a medicinal herb or a weapon, so she's more than capable of defending herself."

Concern crossed Creg's face. "Perhaps Ashen is after her too, then."

"They are, so as a safety precaution, she has a series of UV paper lanterns to keep out the Lurkers, as well as other emergency measures should those fail."

Frank meandered up to Creg's side, his narrowed eyes locked on me. "She's his wife, right?"

"Whose wife is whose?" I questioned.

"Felan," he said with a nod, "she's the shoemaker's wife."

I bit my lip with a hesitant, returning nod.

"Rosella is her great-granddaughter, which makes you her granddaughter," Frank continued. "She lost her husband to the curse, didn't she?"

"Yes. As for my biological mother—"

"Adrienne," Frank interrupted. "Her name was Adrienne Bloom, and your father's name was Adam Shoremick."

My frown twisted with confusion. How? How did they know both of my biological parents' names? From my understanding, people only saw my biological mother as 'the mysterious girl in bloodied clothing'. As for my father, well, I had no information on him other than the fact he assaulted her.

And... I am... I wrapped my arms around myself, and tried to ease my anxious nerves with a slow, deep breath. It seemed to do the trick, but I wasn't sure how long the effect would last.

"You seem troubled," Frank remarked. "Also, a little surprised."

I nodded. "Y-Yeah." I looked to both detectives with a hard stare. "What happened to my father? Do you know that too?"

"He died about five years ago," Creg answered in a somber tone.

My fingers hooked into my forearms. "How?" I demanded. "How do you know this?"

Both detectives glanced at one another, their mouths pressed into thin lines.

"Please..." I clasped my hands at my chest. "Tell me how you know about my parents."

Creg sighed. "We...We got your mother's name from your father, because your mother foolishly disclosed it to him."

"Okay, but how—"

"And your father was a Husk that we actually knew somewhat personally."

My arms fell heavily to my sides, as the blood drained from my face, and the hairs on the back of my neck rose at attention, the shock of this truth striking me like a bolt of lightning.

"Last time we saw him, Frank and I were out for a night on the town," Creg explained, "and we happened to find him in an alley..." His face went blank, and then morphed into a look of disgust. "He was... talking to himself, drunk off his ass. Like us, he was stationed in town, though I can't remember what exactly his duty was. But I remember what he said to us, when he saw us."

"He stumbled right up like it was some casual meetup," Frank added. "Was bragging about something he'd done with this girl, and we were... Well, I don't know if we were stupid or smart enough to ask, because this information is important to you, but we could've gone without knowing..." He smeared his face with his hands, and stretched his jaw. "Ah..."

I sucked in a sharp breath, and then released it. "Wh-What did he say?"

"To put it lightly, he said he fucked her up," Frank admitted. "Rambled about how he found this 'poor little rose bud' wandering around, and he couldn't help himself to 'a little of her sweet nectar.'"

"I remember it clearly," Creg mumbled, a faraway look in his eyes. "He pointed to the corner, and said, 'That's where it happened, boys! Took her as my own...' He went on with the details, but I'll spare you those. It wasn't pretty, to say the least."

"Said that Ashen's influence is what drove his 'inner beast into awakening,'" Frank muttered under his breath, as he stared at the floor with a troubled face.

"Frank."

N-No... No way... Tears pricked my brown eyes, and I stifled a harsh sob as my knees knocked together.

"Chloe?" Creg reached out a concerned hand to me. "Hey, you alright?"

"I-I..." I clutched at my thighs, and knelt upon the floor, my head hung low.

It was troubling enough knowing that the town knew something was wrong. They'd seen her sprinting down the street, screaming while clothed in tattered rags stained red. But even worse than what happened to her was the fact that a damn *Husk* did this. One of Ashen's subordinates...

They not only had a hand in destroying my husband, and greatly damaging my adoptive mother... They helped destroy my biological mother too. They encouraged someone to hurt her...

"Hey, Chloe." Creg's hand was resting against my bicep now. "I... I know this is difficult to take in, but... at least you're not..."

Fear pierced my heart, and my head shot up, eyes wide with horror. "That I'm what!? One of you!?" I rose to my feet, Creg quick to follow suit. "I-I better not... I better not be!"

Creg put up his hands in defense. "H-Hey, we're all on the same team here, remember?"

"Yes!" I snapped. "I-I can't..." I paused, and breathed in. *They... They are not like him. They're not under Ashen's control. They... They wouldn't do something like this...* I gradually released the gust of air trapped in my lungs.

"D-Do you feel better?" Creg asked hesitantly.

I nodded slowly. "Y-Yeah... I just... I'm sorry, it's just that... It's hard enough, being a... a..." The term refused to slip past my lips. "I... I just... I... have to know... how you knew what he was." I forced each word out, my voice strained from the fear constricting my throat.

"We pick up on each other's presence," Frank stated abruptly, "unless it's within the forest. Based upon my senses, I can also safely say you are not one of us. But Sophia and Caroline both are, as well as Grace, who is leaving..." His sharp gaze honed in on me once again. "So you should be fine now."

My eyes darted to the kitchen doorway, and my shoulders stiffened as I heard the front door slam in the living room. *Gracie...*

"Tell me, did you... have a feeling that she was one of us?" Frank cocked a suspecting brow. "And if so, what about Sophia?"

"E-Excuse me?" I stammered, taken aback by his question.

"You knew she was a Husk as well, didn't you?"

Anxiety rattled me to the core at the way this detective was looking at me, questioning me. He made me feel like we were locked together in a confined room, the floor was littered with eggshells, and if I made too loud a sound then he'd lunge for me from the corner. He was far more difficult to handle, compared to his partner, who was more than willing to give me some space.

And the fact he can see right through me, I thought, *it makes me wonder if he can read my mind too.*

"Frank," Creg chimed in, a warning tone to his voice. "I don't think she knows what you're implying."

"Oh, but she does." Frank crossed his arms over his change, his expression unchanged. "So, you going to answer or not?"

Creg shot his partner a deathly glare, and I worried at my bottom lip.

"We had a deal," Frank stated. "So, fess up."

"I wasn't made aware of what Sophia was until recently," I said, and eyed Frank with an equally challenging stare that I prayed was believable. "But before I explain why, I'd like to know why you brought this up."

"Well, we lose the connection we feel to another Husk when they either die or vanish into the forest..."

A fresh wave of guilt washed over me, and I almost drowned in it. But I pulled myself out, and successfully hid my inner turmoil with a straight face. "I can promise you that I did nothing to her."

"That still doesn't answer my question," Frank stated.

I winced at the sharpness of his tone. *He's really pushing me to drop everything at once... I'm not so sure it's safe to tell him that Fenris told me his suspicions...*

I thought back to Sunday, just before Rosella and I were to leave Mom's cabin. Mom was just setting up the paper lanterns, and while Rosella was admiring them, the wolf had pulled me aside. I didn't think anything of it, despite the serious look on his face...

I had to tell her, Chloe. You left me no choice, especially now that I am aware she's been spending time with that girl... She's one of them, I'm sure of it. If you really want to protect Rosella, you will sit her down and tell her the truth.

His warning about Sophia caught me off-guard, but I ignored it, because I was upset with him for going behind my back, which was why I wanted to go back to the forest after Rosella went to bed. I knew she'd be safe here, just for a bit, and I wanted to confront him about his actions. But then I recalled when Sophia suddenly bolted for the bathroom when she was here a couple days prior, that Friday we met to the mall, and then when she scarfed down that glass of water in the pizza parlor after the event that transpired at Clover Alley... And now, knowing how Husks survive...

"You're withholding information you promised to disclose to us," Frank piped up, his searing tone yanking me out of my thoughts.

"I... I'm sorry." I scrubbed at my sweater sleeves. "It's just..."

"Why don't we answer something for a change, huh?" Creg again glared at his arrogant partner, and then turned to me with a concerned face. "Tell us something else you wanna know about us, and we'll share."

Grateful for his understanding, I breathed a sigh of relief, and shed the crippling weight of feeling cornered from my shoulders. "Actually, I'm curious to know more about this 'connection' thing mentioned earlier... If you two are able to read minds, what if one of you dies? Does the other, too?"

"No," Creg answered. "Ashen was very smart in that regard."

"We run on similar mental waves or something," Frank muttered. "We cooperate well together in the mind, basically."

"As far as we know, there are no other Husks like us, as Ashen told us themself that they'd been yearning for this opportunity for years."

I switched focus to Creg. "And you were told by the creator of the forest to find me upon being freed of Ashen's control?"

"That's right, and it seems we can trust you." Creg raised a brow. "Do you trust us?"

I hesitated on a response, and the temptation to glance at Frank taunted me.

"Chloe." Creg pulled me back to focus. "Do you trust us? I know that my partner hasn't made it easy for you..."

"Well...!" I jumped at the sound of something buzzing loudly on the counter, and my eyes flickered to my cellphone.

"Go ahead and answer," Creg said as he stepped away, then nodded to his partner. Frank did as asked, though his cold hard stare never abandoned me.

"Sorry." I reached across the counter and picked up the phone. When I saw who was calling, I answered it. "Mom? Hey, sorry. Uh…" I paused when both Creg and Frank also pulled out their phones. "Lemme find a good spot real quick."

I went over to the glass door, pulled it open, and stepped outside onto the porch. As I closed it behind me, I saw Creg and Frank pointing toward the kitchen doorway. I nodded for them to go.

"Chloe, I need to talk to you," Mom said on the other end of my line. "I'm not interrupting anything, am I?"

"No… Not exactly." *At least I'm safe from that Frank's fiery temper now.* "And if you're going to tell me about Rosella, I found her note."

"Oh… I see…"

I quivered in place at the somber tone in Mom's voice, but I kept mine steady. "Did she take Fenris with her?" I asked quietly. "And does she have everything she needs?"

"She does, dear."

"That's good." I sighed as my eyes settled upon the view ahead of me. The Lurker's corpse had almost completely faded, though a thin patch of soot remained. "Hey, I was just speaking to those two detectives, the freed Husks. They first came to me yesterday to ask about Georgia and Caroline, and now they're back today. Georgia was supposedly killed, and Caroline's gone missing." I nibbled at my lip. "They confirmed to me that Caroline is, in fact, a Husk, so…"

"Well, that would explain Caroline's behavior toward Rosella."

"It would," I said.

"What about the detectives?" Mom asked. "Are they on our side?"

"For the most part… One of 'em's a little on the prickly side, but it's probably just because he's nervous about this whole thing." I kneaded my lips into a thin line before continuing. "I-I didn't mean for Sophia to get taken. I guess… I guess I thought…" Unsure of what to say next, I slapped at my thigh in frustration.

"Chloe, you thought that Sophia would protect Rosella and she did. You just didn't expect her to get captured."

I screwed my eyes shut. *That's not... entirely true...*

"Chloe?"

"Mom, I..." I swallowed the uncomfortable lump rising in my throat. "I knew what was gonna happen... and I let it happen..."

There was a minute of silence on the other end of the line, and then she cleared her throat. "It's going to be okay, Chloe. Just, get here as soon as you can, and bring those men with you."

"A-Alright, I will."

Mom hung up before I could say anything more, so I retreated back into the house. I almost bumped into Creg upon entry, who held out some photos to me while still on the phone. Confused, I asked him what they were for, but he ignored me and walked away.

My eyes widened as I looked down at the photos. In them were shots of walls scribbled with crude writing all over.

"Chloe." Frank suddenly appeared, startling me.

"Jesus!" I jumped back a few inches. "Hah, god..." I rested a hand against my frantic heart. "What's up?"

"Captain says he's got some bad news for us back at the station, so we gotta go." He noticed the photos in my hand. "I see Creg gave you those."

"Th-These photos, wh-when were they taken?" I asked in a hurried stammer.

"Last night. Janitor's having a hard time cleaning it off. Guess words do stick sharper than a knife."

"I see." I drummed my fingertips to my quivering lips.

"What is it?"

"Come back here when you're done," I said. "I need to take you both to see Felan."

Frank's jaw jerked a bit to the left, but didn't say anything.

My heart constricted with anxiety, I clutched tightly at my chest. "Please," I begged. "I really need you two."

He gave a huff. "Fine, as long as Creg says so."

CHAPTER 16

Frank&Creg

"**A**ND THAT'S WHY I'M giving you both some time off." The captain, his back turned to the two detectives, clasped both hands behind him. "You're working yourselves like dogs."

The detectives were hit with shocking news upon their return to the police station. They were told that 'bad news was coming', straight from the captain himself, but they didn't expect this. They'd come so far on the shelter case, only to have their investigation shut down because they were working too hard, which was true, but it was for good reason. Not that they could tell him...

Frank squared his jaw, and bit back a snarky comment as Creg tightly squeezed his shoulder.

"I'm sorry I had to deliver the news this way, but any other time you're out and about the town. You're barely at your desks, and when you are I'm already gone for the night."

This can't be happening, Frank protested.

Just let him finish, Creg said. *The man isn't even aware of everything like we are.*

He's been going on for almost thirty minutes now... How the fuck can he pull a speech out his ass, when all he could say is, 'Hey, guess what? I'm pulling you off the case. Get some rest.'

Creg rolled his eyes. *You kept interjecting, which is why he's taking so damn long.*

"Anyways, to end this long haul of a conversation... You both are now dismissed. I don't wanna see you here for a while, capiche?"

"Understood, captain." Creg eyed his partner with a warning look. "Frank."

"Yeah... I'm coming."

Frank stiffly followed his partner out of the captain's office, and Creg led him down the hall leading into the detectives' office area. Out of the corner of his eye, Frank spotted his wife Cathy waiting at his desk, and his heart shot up his throat.

Don't worry her any more than she already is, Creg warned.

Frank cleared his throat, and managed a smile. "Cathy! What brings you here?"

"I wanted to surprise you!" Cathy beamed at her husband as he strolled up to her, while Creg meandered back over to his desk so as to make himself seem busy.

"Aw, well, aren't you sweet?" He pecked her forehead as he went around her, and plopped down at his desk. "Ah…"

Creg eyed his partner with a somewhat stern air, but didn't say anything as he continued to shuffle some papers around.

"Frank…" Cathy smoothed the skirt of her sundress, her brown eyes blocked by her choppy bangs as she hung her head, her small ebony locks bouncing against either side of her face. "Um…"

The detective acknowledged his wife with a raise of his eyebrows. "Yes, dear?"

"You've been restless, and lost your appetite." She raised her head, and the pained expression on her face made his heart ache. "When was the last time you ate? And have you been drinking plenty of water?"

"This morning, I got something from the snack machine, and I-I have, I promise." He sighed. "I'm sorry, dear. I know I've been working hard… Got some good news, though. Might get to spend more time with you since I've just been informed by the captain that he's cutting the cord on mine and Creg's investigation. Said we needed to take time off, no 'ifs' or 'buts' about it."

A glint of hope sparked in Cathy's eyes, but it quickly dimmed. "Oh, darling, I'm sorry. I know how serious that case is. Those poor girls…"

"Yeah, I know," Frank muttered. "It really pisses me off, because we were so close to cracking it wide open. This morning, we contacted Chloe Bloom, and she…" He shook his head. "Ugh, it's just a mess."

Creg loudly cleared his throat, and Frank looked his way.

I'm not telling her anything too deep.

Just be careful, blabbermouth. Creg sent Cathy a toothy grin. "Ah, you know that captain o' ours! Real pain in the hindquarters, that guy."

Cathy nervously wrung her hands together, a blush surfacing to her cheeks. "Y-Yes, but what about Chloe Bloom? I've heard some things about her, you know."

Creg nonchalantly brushed off her concerns with a wave of his hand. "Nah, no need to worry. We spoke with her ourselves. She's actually quite nice."

"If you say so," Cathy mumbled, clearly doubtful.

If Georgia really is still screwing around, that means she's got a shackle around my wife's mind too... Frank swallowed a vulgar comment regarding Georgia that he almost let slip.

Hey now. Creg eyed his partner worriedly. *Watch that tongue of yours.*

Frank nodded shamefully, and heaved a tired sigh. "Sweetheart, I'm real sorry I've been absent. With everything going on, I just... I'm rundown."

Cathy gave her husband a pleading look, as she clasped her hands at her chest. "You sound stressed. Would you... mind if I...?"

The corners of Frank's mouth curved slightly upward, and a warm glow sparked in his eyes. "Honey, it would mean the world to me if you prayed for me... As my wife and best friend, your love is something I cherish more than anything."

"Frank..." Cathy's gentle hands reached across the desk, and cradled his jawline. "I love you so much. I know you struggle with this, but I still believe God drew us together."

"If that's true, then I wouldn't want it any other way, especially since it makes you happy."

Cathy shook her head. "No... What makes me happy is that I'm with you, no matter what."

Frank's heart swelled with a sense of joy singed by guilt. *Cathy... I don't deserve you...*

Frank had disclosed what he was to Cathy long ago, back when they first met. He'd just gotten accepted into the academy, when he saw a man stealing her purse on his way home. He chased the thief for a few blocks, before tackling him to the ground and retrieving it. Cathy was ecstatic to have her purse back. And then, right as he handed it to her, there was that glint of understanding in her eye. She could tell, immediately, that he wasn't normal.

Your eyes! They're silver! Oh my goodness, now they're blue!

"I remember what you said when I told you what I was," Frank said, and got up from his chair. "You told me that I was a demon who'd broken free of the devil's control, and rather than wreak havoc, I discarded my horns in exchange for angel wings..." He went around the table and wrapped his arms tight around her, his chin atop her head as tears pricked his eyes. "You became the beacon of light in my dark mind that day, Cathy. So, please don't ever go out..."

"Frank."

"Seriously... Thank you for accepting me for what I am, and not disowning me like my parents did."

Cathy laid her head against his chest. "Darling, I was confused when we first met, but I took the time to understand. You aren't like the demons the bible speaks of. You have a good heart in your chest, and a smart head atop your shoulders."

He pressed his pursed lips to her head. "Cathy... I'm sorry for spending so much time away from you..."

She chuckled. "Oh, it's fine. It's your job, right?"

"Y-Yes, but... Surely, you're feeling at least a little irritated with me."

Cathy's eyes dropped to the floor. "W-Well... I guess... I am a little sad, but I'm not irritated. I just... really wish I could see you more often." A heartbroken smile cradled her lips, as she looked back up at her husband. "M-Maybe it's better this way... Like you said, we'll get to spend more time together."

"I think that's just what you two need." Creg strode up with a sullen face. "Some alone time together... at home."

Frank didn't dare look at his partner, as he knew what awaited him, and that was a look from Creg that said, 'You heard me, man.'

"Well, I guess I'll leave you two be," Cathy mumbled, as she stared longingly into her husband's eyes.

He nodded down to her. "Be safe, alright?" he asked gently. "Try not to stay out too late."

Cathy pulled away with the upturned face that blessed his life every day. "I'm going out with some friends. We're having a picnic at the park!"

"That's wonderful!" He kissed her head. "Have fun."

"I will." She looked over to Creg. "And, of course, thank you Creg, for taking care of my husband."

"You're very welcome," he said.

"Okay, I'm off!" Cathy waved to the both of them, and they returned her gesture with warm grins. "Bye!"

Frank and Creg watched Cathy's retreating form as she skipped out of the office like the spirited child she was. As she slipped through the doorway, the captain slunk into view, his shoulders squared and brow creased in a stern frown. When his eyes landed on the detectives, he shook his head and meandered out of sight, presumably back to his quarters.

"Sheejus…" Frank muttered, and rolled his eyes. "'I've got it all handled. You two go home and get some rest. I don't wanna see you back here for at least three weeks. You've both worked your asses off, so you've earned it.'" He snorted. "'It's a beautiful day, go out and enjoy the air. You're dismissed.'"

Frank, bite your tongue. Last thing you need to be doin' is puttin' yourself on probation for mouthin' off to the captain.

Please, he's not gonna care. Besides, it's you and me, remember? Frank smirked at his partner. *You and me, we make the team, and that's all we need.*

Creg gave a strained laugh. "Alright, well, guess we should, uh…" He looked around. "Guess we should get on home then, maybe hit the bar or something."

Frank clapped his hands together. "Yep. Let's go."

The two men casually took up their suit coats, and exited the office. When they reached the hall, they found that the janitor had made some progress cleaning off a portion of the wall to the right. There was still much to go, but it was a start.

Creg's brow furrowed as he eyed the wall. *I can't help this feeling that Georgia has something to do with this. Fucking Georgia.*

Thought I was the only one. Didn't want to bring it up, though. Figured maybe I was wrong, that you had a different thought.

Nah, there's no way. Why would he suddenly cut us off like that, when we're extremely close to cracking the case?

Frank stroked his chin, a questioning look on his face. *Yeah, but she's gone. So, her magic shouldn't be affecting anyone anymore.*

Yeah, all the more reason to believe something's not adding up here. Creg nodded to himself. *Let's get back to Chloe. She said Felan wanted to see us.*

Yeah, and what if she pulls something? Frank retaliated. *For all we know, she really could be a witch lookin' to trap us!*

We can't judge them outright. Besides, they haven't done us harm, unlike Ashen...

Frank sighed in defeat. *Alright, fine. I'll go along with this. But what about Grace?*

I'm sure Chloe will figure that out, Creg told him.

"Sure hope we don't get trapped," Frank whispered under his breath. "We've never met this woman, and Chloe said she could make fucking plants into weapons."

"We'll be fine. We have tricks up our sleeves, if need be."

Frank and Creg didn't speak another word as they left the police department building, and headed to Creg's car. Once they were buckled in, Creg turned the ignition, and silently drove them through town. When they reached the empty road, Frank wondered if anyone at all came through here, besides Chloe and them.

"My guess is no," Creg answered. "From what I gather, the Blooms are not a popular bunch."

Frank nodded. "Yeah, and as we've discussed, that's because of Georgia."

"Right."

"You think she's aware of Georgia, or...?"

A stern frown settled on Creg's face. "I don't know, and for your sake, I hope you don't go prying into her mind like that again."

Frank gave his partner a questioning look. "What do you mean?"

Without taking his eyes off the road, Creg sent Frank a warning look with his mind. "Because if you do, I'll kick your ass. You had no business interrogating her like that. I understand you're suspicious of her, and so am I. But she's not a suspect in a murder case."

"So you didn't see her guilt then, when I brought up Sophia?"

"I did see it, but scaring her into complying won't work. That woman's got a lot on her mind, what with her daughter missing..."

Frank shook his head with disapproval. "You can't tell me she didn't do *something* to that girl. Grace herself had said—"

"I'm just saying that we should be a little more careful," Creg stated aloud.

Frank, though irritated at being cut off, nodded in resignation. "Fine. I'll play nice."

"I'm serious. You back off. We need her as our ally, not as our enemy. She'll open up to us when she's ready." His eyes narrowed. "Focus more on your wife. She needs you."

"Cheap shot, Creg..." Frank glared at him. "Not like you've paid much attention to yours lately, either."

"Actually, I have," Creg argued. "Monique and I recently had a nice dinner together one night after work, and yesterday she took off on a trip with some friends. Ivy, Aaron and I insisted on it, since she's been stressing over everything..."

"Stressing over Ivy, you mean?"

"Yeah..." Sadness settled upon Creg's face. "Last time we spoke, Monique promised me to keep a close eye on Ivy, and I feel terrible because I'm going back on my word..."

A cloud of guilt hovered over Frank's head, and rained upon him without mercy. "C-Creg, I'm sorry... I didn't..."

"Don't be," Creg stated abruptly, as a stoic expression took hold of his face. "As far as I know, Ivy's at home, practicing her music. She's real adamant about that."

"And what about..." Frank's voice dropped to just above a whisper. "What about Nana?"

"She... She's been on edge lately..." Creg nervously shuffled upon his seat. "I still don't see her much at all, my guess being because I'm a Husk. But it's fine. As long as Ivy can confide in her, that's all that matters."

As the two men continued down the road in silence, the sun rained down upon the car in spots of light, though not enough to blind them through the windshield. It was a peaceful sight to observe while traversing the lonely road, especially with the shrouding sense of unease taunting them.

"Hey, look." Frank pointed ahead when Chloe's house finally rose into view.

Creg nodded. "I see."

Grace was seated on the front porch, her head in her hands, when the detectives left. And there she was, in the same position, upon their return.

Frank exited the car once Creg pulled into the driveway, and trotted over to Grace. "Hey, Grace, you're still here."

She lifted her head. "Yeah, I am."

He cocked his head. "I figured you'd have left." *She looks exhausted.*

Creg put the car in park and exited it. "Grace…" He came around the vehicle, and approached the woman with a nervous air. "How are you doing?"

She looked up, and blinked her tired eyes. "I'm fine."

"Is Chloe still here?" Frank asked.

"No, she stepped out, but should be back shortly…" Grace shot up and turned around, startling Frank. "You can follow me inside if you want."

Frank gawked at her retreating back until she'd disappeared into the house, then turned to his partner with disappointment. "That went well."

Creg nodded. "Let's go check the backyard."

"Why?" Frank asked.

"I wanna see something."

Both detectives rounded the corner and ventured to the back, where they noticed the Lurker's corpse had gone missing. In place of the otherworldly figure was a body-shaped patch of black that smelled of deadwood and rot.

Creg pinched his nose as it burned his nasal cavity. "Damn… Strong stuff," he grunted.

"You got that right! Shit." Frank buried his own nose in the crook of his elbow and peered over it. "Stinks to high heaven! Why the hell would you wanna investigate this?"

"That's not actually what I wanted to look at." Creg wandered toward another spot. "Look here."

Frank followed his partner. When he noticed what Creg was pointing at, his jaw dropped.

"See that? It's dried blood." Creg knelt to the ground. "And fur."

Frank dropped down beside him. "Well, I'll be damned."

"You think it's from that Guardian Chloe mentioned?"

"I don't think, I know."

"Guys!"

Frank and Creg's heads swiveled in the direction of the forest, and their eyes widened with astonishment.

Chloe came running out of the forest, her hand waving high in the air. "What are you doing back so soon?"

"We got benched," Frank called. "Boss wants us to take time off."

"Really?" Chloe came to a halt several feet away. "Yikes, sorry to hear that."

"What's going on with you?" Creg asked.

Chloe cocked a brow. "I was just coming back from my mother's." Chloe looked over her shoulder, then back at them. "I went to see her after you left. Wanted to check in on her, and make sure things were okay." She took a few steps toward them, and peered at the ashy stain in the grass. "We should go inside. Stinks out here right now."

"Ya know... You still haven't shared much about your involvement with Miss Sally." Frank squared his shoulders as his frown hardened. "You ever gonna hold up your end of the bargain?"

What the hell did we just talk about?

Frank dared a glance at his partner. *I'm just asking a question, is that alright?*

Creg's jaw unhinged, but he said nothing and instead focused on Chloe. "Don't mind him, he's just curious."

"No, it's fine..." Chloe threw her hands behind her. "That's a whole other story..."

"... Bloom... Bloom... Bloom..."

All three looked in the direction of the hushed voice. It was coming from the forest...

"She is coming... She will be ours..."

"... the fuck?" Frank mumbled.

"We need to go inside, now." Chloe snatched Frank's wrist and yanked him toward the house. "They're listening."

Creg stared appalled at the trees, while his partner was dragged away. *She's right. They're listening.*

Ouch! God, help me with this woman, please! She's gonna rip my arm out.

Creg whirled around and went chasing after the two. "Hey, Chloe! Chloe, wait up!" He followed them back into the house, Chloe quick to slam the back door right as he slipped through.

"They're listening!" Chloe clutched at either side of her head, and sucked in a shaky breath. "Damn it."

"Who's listening?" Frank demanded. "Ashen? The Lurkers?"

"They're using the Lurkers to listen in us," Chloe mumbled, as she paced the floor. "God, Rosella... No..." She smeared her face, and hung her head between her raised shoulders.

"Chloe." Creg strode over and gently grasped her forearms. "Hey. It's gonna be okay. Come on." His somber tone seemed to have worked, for she relaxed, and gave a hopeful look.

"Thank you..." she whispered to him. "I really appreciate your help." Her brown eyes began to water, and her lips quivered as she stifled a sob.

"It's okay." Creg wrapped his arms around her, and laid her head against his shoulder. "Just relax. Everything will be okay..."

A few minutes of silence fell over the trio, and during this time Creg pondered what to do next. Frank was nervous as hell about this woman, but Creg's gut told him she was trustworthy. But was it because he felt sorry for her, or because she was going through the same pain as him?

His daughter Ivy, like Rosella, played a key part in all of this. And seeing someone else going through the same pain, it made him want to sympathize, because they were in this together, whether Frank liked it or not. Georgia's claims were bullshit, and Grace... Unlike Frank, he didn't trust her. She wasn't the same cheerful girl they once knew when they were kids.

Yesterday, when we spoke privately with her, she seemed fine, Creg thought. *But then we asked about Chloe...*

The memory was still fresh in Creg's mind. Grace had offered to take them to a nice restaurant, but Frank convinced her that the local diner a few minutes from the school was fine. So it was there she'd asked them how they'd been doing, what life was like working for the force, when Creg had spied the book sticking out of her purse and asked her about it.

Like Jekyll and Hyde, Grace went from a smiling, kindhearted woman, to a threatening shadow of her former self. Creg had found the immediate change in demeanor disturbing, especially when she uttered her response in a tone as cold as ice:

Oh... So that's why you're here... I've been waiting.

Waiting, she'd said. Frank bowed his head with shame. *All that time...*

We don't know if that's what she meant, Creg argued.

Frank gave him a look. *She knew we were out there, but we were too cowardly to make the move.*

We couldn't find her, Frank. Her magic was under wraps.

Yeah, and then that night she appeared on my doorstep with that baby bundled in her arms, she was scared, helpless, lost. Frank's jaw tightened. *She was waiting for US, Creg. We knew something was going on at that place. Girls being mistreated, starved, beaten, worked like dogs... She showed us the scars, Creg. She wasn't lying.*

I didn't say she was...

"I've lost her..."

Creg looked down at Chloe. "Pardon?"

"I've lost her... My baby girl..." Chloe pressed her tear-stained cheek into his shoulder. "Rosella is gone... I'm never going to see her again..."

"Chloe..."

"I know this isn't important to you or your partner, but I appreciate you listening to me." She pulled herself away from Creg, and wiped a hand across her wet eyes. "Thank you for comforting me, Creg... It means a lot."

Creg worried at his bottom lip, and before he could stop himself... "Chloe, I understand where you're coming from. I understand your pain."

Chloe shook her head. "You don't..."

"No, I do..."

Frank's eyes widened. "Creg."

"Frank, I have to be honest with her." Creg sucked in a heavy breath, and then slowly released it. "My daughter, Ivy... She's like Rosella, and I'm concerned about her safety, even though she has her own Guardian..."

Chloe's eyes bulged. "Wh-What..."

"My wife Monique and I took her in, and we raised her as our own, alongside our biological son Aaron. We love her with all of our hearts, but..." A burning sting protruded his nostrils, as tears welled in his eyes. "We know that we can't keep her, like we can Aaron. And it's hard, because she is our daughter."

Frank stood off to the side, baffled at Creg's abrupt confession. But he said nothing. He was too shaken with shock.

"Wh-Why are you telling me this?" Chloe murmured. "I-Is it because you..."

"I want you to trust me," Creg said, "and to know that you're not alone in this." He locked eyes with her, hoping to hell and back that she'd see his honesty. "You and I are going through the same pain, but we can work together, if you'll allow it."

Chloe's jaw moved up and down, as if to say something, but she seemed at a loss for words.

The fuck did you just do!? Frank yelled. *Do you realize how dangerous telling her that is!?*

Creg ignored him, and instead kept his focus on Chloe. "I know we just met and all, but like I said before, we're all on the same team. Ashen has no control over Frank and me anymore. So... Now that I've disclosed something confidential, let alone extremely personal, do you feel more comfortable sharing things with us in the future?"

Chloe's mouth opened again, and this time she had something to say. "I... I do," she said, albeit cautiously. "I just... need some time to gather my thoughts, and... there's just so much ground to cover."

"We'll take it a little at a time," Creg suggested. "Just keep up your end of the bargain, as we've kept up ours."

Relief settled upon Chloe's face, and she nodded slowly. "Th-Thank you."

Frank observed the two as they hugged, and shuddered. To him, it was too soon to be letting their guards down to her. And deep in his heart, he couldn't help but feel a little envious. Creg was supposed to always be there for him. They made the team, and that was all they needed.

But he couldn't tell Creg that. He didn't want to expand the difficult rift between them any more than it already was, especially since he was the one who caused it in the first place. He'd just have to trust his instincts that Creg wouldn't betray him, and he knew he wouldn't.

Though he'd still refuse to trust Chloe. He was no fool. She was hiding things... and he'd find them one way or another.

CHAPTER 17

I LAID FLAT ON my back, my mind racing in a constant circle of fear for Rosella. Where was she right now? Was she okay? Did they capture her too? I had yet to see her come through those trees, and with each passing minute, I felt that sense of security would dissipate. I wasn't able to leave and go find her myself, so all I could do was sit and worry.

I spied a nearby Lurker sniffing its claws, and sighed. It'd been lingering about the clearing like the others for some time, whether just staring into space or lazily rocking back and forth.

I can't help pitying them, I thought to myself. *These creatures, once magnificent and thriving, now reduced to brainless dolls, controlled by Ashen...*

The Lurker mumbled something under its breath, then looked up to the trees with drooping blank eyes as it gently swayed itself back and forth. *"Along the wind... I sway..."* it cooed in a dull tone. *"In the midst... of May..."* The Lurker's head tipped to the side. *"To the farthest regions... to the one in my heart... May the wind carry my love... to you... when I'm not around..."* Lost in its mindless state, the Lurker fell silent for a moment before continuing its broken lullaby in a lowly hum.

I bowed my head. *If anything, these things are Husks...*

These poor, innocent creatures... There really was nothing left to them, except maybe remnants of their souls. Immortality was cruel when dealt as a punishment, and demoralizing when used to animate the corpses of a once peaceful, thriving race.

"So, let me get this straight. They want to kill her, right?" From where she stood against the tree, arms crossed, Caroline rolled her eyes. "Psh, better yet, let these things adopt her. She belongs with her freakish bloodline."

I groaned. "God, you just *never* stop, do you?"

"What do you mean?"

I lifted myself upon my palms. "C'mon, tell me. What the hell is your problem? Huh?" My voice increased in volume, anger scorching my words. "Seriously, why the *fuck* do you have to bash on her?"

Caroline whipped her matted red head in my direction with a ferocious scowl. "Why the fuck do you fantasize over that cowardly pig?"

My knuckles cracked as I balled my hands into fists. "Caroline…"

She flipped me her middle finger. "Fuck you, Mitchell. It's her fault I'm here, and why my Auntie Georgia is dead."

"And just how is *that* Rosella's fault?" I challenged. "Go ahead, enlighten me!"

Tears pricked at her brown eyes. "You weren't there! You didn't watch her spasm upon the floor, foaming blood at the mouth!" She wiped the back of her hand across her wet, glaring eyes. "Auntie Georgia meant a lot to me, ya know!"

I raised a brow in surprise. Caroline never shed a tear for anyone.

"She is the reason my auntie dropped dead right in front of me!" she went on. "Auntie just fell, right to the floor, and I couldn't do a damn thing about it!"

My expression softened at the pained tone in her voice. "Caroline… I…" My lips pressed into a thin line. As badly as I felt, I couldn't bring myself to say, 'I'm sorry for your loss,' simply because it was her. Maybe that made me a bad person…

Caroline's face went blank at my response, and then cast me a threatening glare. "It's no fucking wonder Ashen wants to get rid of you, you fucking traitor."

I snorted. *Huh, guess I'm not that bad of a person…*

"You're constantly fawning over the enemy, you've completely *trashed* your chance at power…" She pointed at herself. "Meanwhile, I took advantage of Auntie's offer to help me master Ashen's gift. She taught me how to control my magic, and build myself tall. And what about you? You're just chasing after some make-believe romance! You've wasted your potential."

"Oh sure, you built yourself tall alright!" I snapped. "So tall you come crashing down on anyone who opposes you!" Hot, angry tears burned my eyes. "And you blame it all on Rosella, because she's an easy target, right?"

Caroline snorted. "Ha! 'Easy' is an understatement! She's like a house of cards! One wisp of air is all it takes to knock her over!"

I shot to my feet. "Shut up, Caroline!"

Caroline threw her head back and laughed. "Run outta insults, have we?"

"Oh, believe me, I never miss an opportunity to shit on a cock-sucking leech with no respect!"

"Seriously? Is that all you're capable of?" Caroline put her hands on her hips. "For real, what's your specialty? I know you have one." A wicked grin broke across her face. "Whether you like it or not, Ashen is part of you."

I clenched my teeth in a snarl. "My personal beef with Ashen is no business of yours."

"I figured as much..." She combed her fingers through some of her matted hair, a dreamy spark in her eyes. "Oh well, I at least have the world bowing at *my* feet. I am cared for, loved, worshipped as a goddess..." A giggle slipped her curved lips. "Like me, you long to live free and do what you want, and put people you don't like in their place. It gives you a thrill." She raised a brow. "However, it does no good, because you threw away your power. And now that you've been cornered, you're regretting your decision immensely..."

I flinched at her words, and in turn Caroline uttered a snicker.

A smirk tugged at her lips. "Struck a nerve, didn't I?"

I bowed my head. "You're right. Your magic is far superior to mine. But lemme tell you something. I don't have to possess powerful magic in order to strike someone down. Hell, I can just as easily snap your neck with both hands tied behind my back, without magic." I shot the snarky bitch a glare I wished would kill her. "Unlike you, I don't depend on a worthless handicap."

A tinge of silver flashed across Caroline's eyes. "Wanna prove it to me?"

Another angry response almost erupted from within me, but I swallowed it back down, and instead turned on my heel. *I'm tired of this conversation. It's getting me nowhere. She's just trying to see how far she can push me.*

"Really? You're walking away from a challenge? Huh, guess you're more of a coward than that fat pig."

I scowled over my shoulder with a sneer. "Stop calling her a fat pig..."

Caroline spread her arms out, and taunted me with wiggling fingers. "Come on, Sophia! Release that beast inside you! Mine's ready to play!" A tenacious leer slithered across her lips. "I wanna see what you're made of."

My nostrils flared with irritation. *She won't get it... She never will. Just walk away. She's not worth it.*

"What? You scared?"

Just walk away. She is NOT worth it.

"Yeah, thought so. You're as hopeless as your lesbian love story."

The color of the world drained from sight as my vision faded to silver. Anger boiling at the brim, Caroline's venomous comment tipped it to spill. And now, I was ready to spill her blood. What I lacked in magic, I more than made up for in physical strength.

As I calmly whirled around to face her, she stood out in stark contrast to the colorless world. "Why don't you come at me first for once?" I growled. My head shot up, eyes wide, and I unleashed the pent-up anger inside. "Come on!"

"Alright then..." Caroline's eyes glowed a gentle purple, indicating that her vision had turned silver as well. It was a trait used to pinpoint other Husks when activating our magic.

"BRING IT!!!" I roared.

"GLADLY!!!"

Caroline lunged for me, and together, we went tumbling to the ground with hands tearing strands of hair from scalps, nails clawing at faces. As we rolled around the tree, she managed to pin me, her fist raised high. Pain ruptured my skull, my head whipping to the side as she delivered a powerful blow to my face.

"You always put her on a damn pedestal," Caroline hissed. "You think she's just the *shit!* Well, guess what? She's not!" She slapped at my breasts. "This!? This right here!? Ha! It's all for show!"

"You're one to talk!" I aggressively snatched Caroline's wrists, and kicked her in the stomach. She grunted as she flipped onto her back, her head jerking forward.

Quick on my feet, I leaped on top of her, and hugged her hips with my knees. "For your information..." I snatched both of her wrists and jerked them in opposite directions, making her scream. "I love Rosella for who she is, and would never use my looks to win her heart!" I shoved my face into Caroline's, our silver eyes locked with one another. "Is that what this is about, huh?"

Caroline let out a dry chuckle, her lips spread wide in a malicious grin. "... Piss your shit through those sandy flaps."

A new level of fury erupted within me as I prepped a fist to deliver a nasty round of blows.

Just then, a malicious cackle broke out through the clearing. *"Foolish girls... Blinded by rage, thirsty for blood, and willing to maul each other in order to savor your desires~!"*

I craned my head to the left, my frozen fist still poised to strike.

The Lurker leader lingered a ways from us with a lustrous smile, their dubious arms spread wide. *"Go ahead, relish in your useless plight. It drives my curiosity, and leaves me begging for more."*

My boiling temper rescinded as my vision returned to normal, and my fist unfurled at my side. "Take your 'hard wood' elsewhere," I snapped, and stumbled to my feet. "Oh wait, you don't have one, do you?"

Caroline snorted, prompting a sly smirk to tug at my lips, though I made sure she didn't see it. Just because her response was humorous, that didn't mean we were awkward buddies.

Meanwhile, the lead Lurker seemed confused by my words, but rather than question me, they turned on their bulky heel to leave.

I stared down their back, as the monster made their hasty retreat. *They want me to lash out, to let my guard down...* I glared over my shoulder. *Like her.*

"You still think you're in control?" Caroline uttered a curt laugh. "You've wasted your time teasing beast inside, and now it's too late to welcome it. Time to give yourself up."

I shook my head. "Whatever, I'm finding a way out of this hell hole." I walked a little ways from her, dropped to the ground, and ran my fingers over the dry, crusty soil. *I'm not dying anytime soon...* I sucked in a pained breath. *I'll find my way back to you, Rosella, and once I do, we'll go someplace far away together, where no one can hurt us...* My teeth ground my frustration between them. *Even if it means leaving everything we know behind.*

"You're wasting your time," Caroline called out. "These idiots seem smarter than they really look."

I ignored her, and kept clawing at the dirt. *I have to do something. I can't just sit here. I can't...*

If I knew her well, Rosella was back home, alone and scared. And with a bleeding heart that spilled kindness, and blessed the ground she walked on, surely she was just as worried about me. Kindness, in this world, was hard to come by. But it was also easily manipulative, especially in those who were cooped up indoors for most of their lives.

A shocking thought crossed my mind, and my eyes widened. What if Rosella actually was in this forest? What if someone, or something, persuaded her to try and find me? What if it was that wolf?

Mom warned me about the wolf... And that night we met... The night I was taken... He knew what I was.

You are not invincible. You can't protect her from everything.

I squeezed her eyes shut. *Mom...*

My mother always told me to be headstrong, to take shit from no one. She also said to be kind, to help others in need, and to give respect that's earned, while also achieving it. However, there was the one golden rule I'd promised to follow, no matter how badly my heart wanted to stray, and yet I allowed it. I couldn't help it, though. I loved Ro with every fiber of my being, and she needed someone to help her up when she fell.

And like I told her, I never turn my back on others who need me, Rosella included. Stubborn as a bull, that's how I roll. Always have, always will. Dirt spat in my face as I slapped at the ground. "Ugh... God, this is hard."

Stay away from the trees. That girl is nothing but trouble among them.

God, shut up, I thought. *Leave me alone.*

You should focus on those choir girls more!

I knocked my forehead to the dirt, my knuckles stiff. "Why can't you just leave me alone? For five minutes? Why?"

If you stay with her, you will only be putting yourself in harm's way! What if she tells that wolf about you? If he finds out where you are, he'll rip you to pieces!

My hands combed the grains of soil across the hard surface. "Just leave me alone. You don't understand." I repeated my previous action. "Leave me alone. Leave her alone. Leave us alone."

You're better off distancing yourself from her. All she'll do is continue to weigh you down.

"Ugh!" My nails bared like claws, I shoveled the earth with raw intensity, my shoulders rolling in simultaneous rhythm.

Don't get too close. Remember, she's the enemy.

Amidst the buzzing of my mother's annoying words in my head, I paused to examine my work. Not even an inch in... Raising ravaged hands, I glanced over the dirt tracing the tender cracks in my scorched fingertips. These hands, they were strong enough to punch a jock in his jaw. They possessed a grip capable of tearing Caroline's entire head of hair from her scalp.

Defending myself is easy. I'm not afraid to hurt those who hurt me, or the ones I care about. But Rosella... She could never bring a punch to the table, because she's not capable. Ro's always been kind... which is why... why I would never hurt her, no matter what.

"Oh, what, givin' up your new life as a mole?" Caroline remarked.

God, would you just shut UP already!? I mentally screamed.

"Well?"

I peered over my shoulder with an icy glare, a snarky comment at the ready.

Caroline scrunched up her nose. "Ew, what the hell is that thing on your neck?"

"What do you mean?" I placed a hand to the left side. "There's nothing..." My fingertips traced around it, a small, coarse rise in my skin. *A-Another one.*

"Uh, might wanna get some zit cream for that," Caroline said.

I ran my hand along my neck. A normal person would think it barely noticeable, but for me, it was like permanent marker on paper. Would this one grow like the one on my stomach? What if... What if they broke open, and ooze dripped out of them? Would it hurt?

No, I can't think like that. I have to be strong. I have to. I just...

"I wouldn't be surprised if that was due to spending so much time with her," Caroline uttered intentionally loud enough for me to hear. "She's such a disease to us."

"EURGH!" I sprung to my feet. "I... I..." I briskly paced back and forth, my fingers digging into my scalp. Black strands fell loose from my messily-tied hair, and teased my neck and face. "I-I-I-I can't! I can't! I CAN'T! I CAN'T DO THIS!" I clasped my hands to my head. *"AAAAAAAAAAAAH!!!!!!!"*

Like the firing of a bullet from a gun, I struck the ground with fervent pace and sped across the clearing, in a desperate thirst for freedom. Treating the earth as if it was layered with hot coals, my sneakers barely touched the surface with each feverish step. The trees grew larger the closer I came, so close I could almost touch them.

A rush of nausea abruptly flooded my stomach, and my head whipped to the left as I spat at the dirt. An agonizing stab, like a phantom knife twisting into my insides, weighed me down with anchors of pain to the ground. My quivering arms wormed around my sides, as my fingers danced in a panicked frenzy.

I wanted the ground to just swallow me up, to take me away from here. At least if I was six feet under, I'd find peace. Death... It was my only salvation at this point, wasn't it?

I guess... I guess I better... I screwed my eyes shut to fight back the stinging tears. *I can't... I can't give up... not like this... I can't give up on Ro. She needs me! I have to be there for her, to protect her! I can't... I can't give up. Not now.* I curled into myself when I felt a small rumble in my stomach. *God, I'm hungry.* I gave a dry cough and cringed. *And my throat hurts.*

I bit my tongue to negate the sob behind my wavering lips, and regretted it. My teeth grazed over my tongue in an attempt to relieve the seering itch that'd been ignited, but that only made it worse. It was like a bunch of needles prickling my tongue, it stung so badly.

I nestled my head into the earth, and smacked it with an angered hand. *Why is this happening to me? Why? I never did anything so wrong to deserve this. I know I've made mistakes, but I'm always learning from them! So why...* I hooked both hands into the soil and, dejectedly, began my progression back toward the middle of the clearing. *I feel like a corpse dragging herself to her grave... but I won't give in. Not yet... I still... have fight left in me... Stubborn as a bull...*

An exasperated grunt trekked up my sore throat, my teeth clenched as I willed myself to my knees. My limbs wobbled like I was struggling on stilts, but I wouldn't give up. Baring my nails, I stiffened my fingers into claws, so as to ravage the dirt once more, but paused. Out of the corner of my eye, I saw it, the leader's sinister grin.

I craned my head in the direction of the creature, and prepared to shoot them an insult, but held back. It wasn't the leader speaking with those dry, cracked lips, it was the monster inside of them.

"You're digging yourself a bed of doom," they cooed. *"And soon, you will be forced to lay in it."*

I ignored them, the one I refused to acknowledge as my master, and kept digging. *You're wrong... You have to be... I'm not giving up yet... Stubborn as a bull... that's how I roll...* I wiped at my clammy brow. *Just have to keep going... for as long as I can.*

The leader turned their back to me, and proceeded toward the bonfire, where a few regular Lurkers loitered around with their heads bowed and arms loose at their sides. The leader screeched at them, and all three snapped at attention.

Though I couldn't hear what they were instructed to do, I could see the pain in their eyes. *They're suffering. Like me.*

"She can't save us. We're all doomed..."

A raspy whisper prompted me to peek over my shoulder, where a lone Lurker stood pitiful and timid. Like the leader, this one had leaves, but they were silver.

"She didn't abandon us. She was forced to run... She never meant to leave us." It looked up with a sad face. *"Don't want to live anymore... I want to die... a full death..."*

I shook my head. "No... You can't think like that. You can't."

The creature raised its head, and its tear-filled eyes stared back at mine. *"Wolf friend... I wish he'd freed me that night. Had I been strong enough to step out, he would've... Tired. Don't want this anymore."* It poised a claw in front of its gaping chest. *"Done. Not... doing this... anymore. I want... to be free..."*

"Please, stop," I whispered.

The Lurker whimpered, then pointed the claw of its other hand at me. *"Dig a bed for me too, Brunette."*

I stumbled to my feet, screaming for the Lurker to stop, when two others suddenly sprung into action. In seconds, both took up either side of their struggling captive, its arms around their necks. The imprisoned Lurker roared in retaliation, and kicked its legs.

"Wh-What are you doing?" I asked.

They ignored me, and instead began dragging their flailing captive over to the raging flames of the bonfire.

"*No! Leave me alone! Let me completely die!*" the captured Lurker bellowed.

"Stop!" I scrambled over to them, and began yanking on one of their legs. "Please! Don't do this!"

The Lurker I clung to shook me off, and kept walking. "*This one defective. Must be destroyed.*"

"*Not defective! NOT DEFECTIVE!*" the struggling Lurker screamed.

"*Defective one. Begone.*"

I watched on in silent horror, as the two Lurkers effortlessly threw their pleading associate into the fire, and its screams of misery exploded throughout the clearing. The ungodly loud noise pierced my skull, and I doubled over with my hands clasped at either side of my throbbing head.

My teary eyes wandered to the flames, where I could see the Lurker's frantic hands clawing through them. They flailed uselessly for several seconds, until they were swallowed up with the rest of its body, and a rotting stench that smelled of a charred corpse tainted the air.

"Told you, didn't I?"

I didn't acknowledge Caroline as she strode up behind me.

"This is all her fault." She gave a curt laugh. "And you're powerless. Powerless, and hopeless." Caroline gracefully turned on her heel. "Well, guess I'd better leave you be. That grave ain't gonna dig itself~!"

I dropped to my knees, my gaze locked on the fire. *I can't believe this happened...* I hung my head. *I couldn't do anything... It pleaded for its life...*

You've lost control... Give up, and embrace the darkness.

I found my eyes wandering to the Lurker leader without difficulty. I could see them just beneath my matted bangs, and as we locked eyes, it wasn't the monstrous tree puppet taunting me, it was the one controlling them, as if talking behind them... Ashen, slowly breaking me down...

I glared back at the leader, but then my expression faltered, and I turned my attention back to the ground. My chest tightened, and I sucked in a sharp breath, so as to hold back a timid sob.

Rosella... I failed to contain the tears pooling at my sore eyes. *I... I never ever thought this would happen, but I'm scared. I'm so scared.* I ushered a pained hiss. *Please... I don't want to wilt in the darkness... Please... don't let me wilt in the dark.*

CHAPTER 18

T HE BULK OF OUR conversation was exchanged silence throughout the day, as I wasn't exactly in a talkative mood. My eyes dragged over countless trees, my ears drawn to every little sound around me, whether it was the smallest brush of a leaf, or a whisper of the wind. Sophia was out there, and despite Fenris' claim that she would be well-hidden, I was determined to examine every bush, look around every tree, overturn every rock.

I believe I mounted and dismounted hundreds of times throughout that dreaded search, and every failed glimpse of Sophia was a crack of the emotional whip to my heart. Like a dreary cloud looming over my head, a gloomy shadow blocked my rained face.

We still haven't found her. Where could she be?

In a trade-off with the moon, the sun eventually laid itself upon the trees, its dying light bathing their head of leaves in a shower of warmth. It wouldn't be long now. Drawn by the moonlight, the Lurkers would be on the prowl, hunting me.

What are they doing to her now? What if they're torturing her? I shuddered at the sickening thought, and forced it away. *I can't... I can't think like that. I... I have to... I have to do something. If the roles were switched, she'd be out here, right now, tearing through these trees, looking for me.*

"Why don't we take a rest?" Fenris offered, breaking me out of my depressing thoughts. "The sun is setting, and we can't carry on with no sleep, especially with the Lurkers out and about.

I rubbed a hand over my wet eye. "Yeah, I guess not."

"I can go for longer, so I'll take the first watch. You need rest." The wolf stopped. "I think here is good."

I chuckled weakly to myself. "There are literally a bunch of trees around us, have been the entire time."

"Yes, but here we have a pond to use." He gestured to the side. "It's plenty big enough for you to bathe, if needed."

"No thanks, I'd rather not. With the Lurkers out, yeah, nah." I shook my head. "I'll take the chance of rancid body odor."

"Understandable. Well, I'm going to hunt for something. Why don't you prepare a fire, and when I come back, we can talk some more?"

"Sure thing." *We've barely talked all day today, so this oughta be interesting.*

I busied myself with starting a fire, mainly as a means of distraction, while Fenris went searching for his dinner. As I drilled a stick between my palms into the pile of many others, I stumbled upon a fond memory of my first time creating a fire at Great Granny Felan's, the first ounce of positivity to my mind all day.

I was seven years old, sitting in Mom's lap, and I got so excited when the first spark happened in a matter of minutes. Mom joked that I must've possessed fire magic, and then for several days after, I pretended to be a fire wizard.

The memory sprung a smile to my face. "Good thing she kept the lighters put up," I mused. "Heh... Heh."

Thinking of Mom was hard. I up and left without telling her. It was a wonder she hadn't found me yet. Was she even out here now? She told me that she was thinking of venturing into these woods, and at dark.

Mom... I hope you're safe. I miss you. A fresh tear pricked at my eye. *I'm sorry. I'm so sorry.* I eyed the pile of wood in front of me as I continued to spin the stick, and sighed. "Better get this going, or else I won't be able to cook anything."

A few more minutes of silence passed, and then, finally, newborn sparks of light crept over the thin strips of bark, the smoke rising precariously upward. I tended to them with twists of the stick and the occasional blow, until eventually tiny specks of fire danced upon the pile. Once the embers grew to decent size, and their crackling reached my ears, I tossed the stick aside, and observed the flakes of ash ascending from them to the night sky.

I hugged my legs to my chest, and rested my chin upon my knees. "Hmm..." My ears registered the rustling of leaves beyond, and my shoulders tensed.

"My apologies for taking so long."

"That's ok— oh." My eyes widened. "Holy... crackers."

Blood smeared across his maw, Fenris licked profusely over his crimson-stained teeth, as he stepped into our camping site.

I did my best to swallow the rising lump in my throat. I knew I shouldn't have been surprised. I'd seen the graphic nature shows. "Um... Oh, hey!" I yanked my backpack closer and opened it. "I got some marshmallows here, some extra sticks too. Would you like to try one?"

Fenris frowned. "Try a stick?"

"No silly, a marshmallow." I pulled out the large pack of enormous squishy treats. "Y-You just take this..." I tore off a corner of the package, and plucked a single marshmallow. "Okay... So, you place this on the stick like this. After that, you hover it over the fire for a few minutes." I demonstrated as I went along, Fenris eagerly watching me.

"Ah, fascinating... Excuse me." He plopped down across the fire, his tongue brushing over his red lips.

I grimaced through my expression at the stains. *It's just red paint. That's all it is... Yeah. That should make you feel better.* My expression faltered. *Who am I kidding, get real Rosella. It's blood. He's a wolf...* I focused on the toasting marshmallow. With the tender flames already crisping the edges, it wouldn't take long for it to brown. "Hey... Fenris, remember when I asked you if you were a god or a demon, and you said you were a 'protector' of the forest?"

"Yes," he said matter-of-factually. "Do you have more questions to ask about me?"

"Kinda." Eyes glued to the marshmallow, I precariously spun the stick in my fingertips.

"Have I made you uncomfortable?"

I shook my head. "Just a little surprised." *No point in hiding, huh?*

"My apologies. Like you, I must eat to survive, but it was disrespectful of me to assume you'd be comfortable, or even tolerable, of it."

A curt snort escaped my lips. "I... I appreciate that, but really... It's... oh." I squinted through the embers' light. "I think this is done." I moved the browned marshmallow from the fire, and got up to approach the wolf. "Here you go. Be careful, it's hot, and the stick might jab you in the throat."

Fenris sniffed at the treat, then carefully clamped his front teeth just over the end of the stick, and scraped the marshmallow off it. He sat there with a thoughtful face, his furry brow curling into a thoughtful frown. "Mmm, interesting flavor. Very sweet. Soft."

"Good, though?"

"Yes, indeed they are." He lowered onto his stomach, and rested his head on his front paws. "Ah, much better."

I chuckled. *He's like a huge, cute dog... Well, I guess he technically is a huge dog. Wolves are from the dog family, aren't they?*

"We certainly came a long way already," Fenris said. "I don't know if you're aware of this, but the forest isn't actually that large a size, since it's right at the end of your town."

"I was wondering how much it took up." I pushed back my hood, and set to preparing another marshmallow. "Fenris, I'm curious about you and this forest."

"Oh, of course. Ask away."

"Alright." I brought the bag of marshmallows over to sit between us, though I lingered a couple feet. "First off, you said you were a protector of this place, that you were assigned to that role."

"Yes," the wolf answered.

"If I remember correctly, you said that there are other Guardians, but you divulged little detail on that." I cocked my head. "Care to elaborate?"

"I doubt any harm will come in explaining." The tip of his tail vigorously tapped the ground. "As you see, Rosella, I am not the average wolf."

"Right, and when I asked if you were a god or demon, you said no."

He nodded. "Correct, but that isn't to say that I am a wolf at all."

"But you look like one," I pointed out.

"Yes," he said.

"And you seem to hunt like one."

"Yes."

"So, you are one."

Fenris shook his head. "I am a descendant not of the wolves, but of this forest." He looked to the trees. "This place is what birthed me."

I gave him a blank stare.

"Perhaps I should explain further. You see, I sprung from the ground out of nothing, and took on the form most suitable for me." He glanced up at the trees. "The other Guardians, and the Lurkers too, all came from this forest. In fact, we all used to live here in peace."

My eyes went wide like saucers. "Y-You... You did?"

"I know, it's strange, but hear me out. Before the evil fighting to claim these trees surfaced, things were different, pleasant..." A blank expression settled on the wolf's face, a faraway look in his eyes.

"That's... surprising."

A confusing image of Fenris and a Lurker happily enjoying each other's company sprung to mind. I shuddered, as Sophia surfaced between the two of them, helpless upon her knees, cowering before their menacing forms. They were prepped to pounce, the festering hunger for her flesh in their eyes...

Stop it! Snap of it! I shook off those disgusting thoughts. *Fenris would never do such a thing! Ever!*

"Rosella, are you alright?"

I shot a cautious gaze at the concerned wolf. "U-Um, yeah. Sorry, I was just..." My shoulders tensed. How could I tell him such shameful thoughts?

"I see that I have caused some concern for you. Please, allow me to reassure your fragile mind." Fenris sucked in a deep breath, and slowly exhaled. "My dear Little Rose, before a life can be taken, it must be given, and the one who gave me the life is my master, the creator of these trees."

"Creator... and master?"

A glint of nostalgia shimmered in the reminiscing wolf's eyes. "The first time I heard her lilting voice, the sound of my master, I was only two weeks of age. I've never seen her face. But her song captivated me in its melodic embrace, and I felt such warmth, protection, in her presence. Her harmonic lull beckoned me forth, and my ears were blessed with a serenade of blissful carol."

My eyes widened in awe at his poetic description, but I didn't interrupt.

"In your terms," he went on, "she would be my mother. But to be more specific, she merely created me, along with everything else, with the magic that flourishes within this forest."

"Magic..." I glanced over the flames before me. "What kind of magic?"

"Her magic," he said. "And now a curse has befallen these woods, claimed the Lurkers, and turned them against her..." Darkness clouded

Fenris' luminous eyes, dimming them a murky blue. "At times, I hear her reassure me, encourage me that we will reclaim our home, yet never have I met her face to face." Fenris granted me a sorrowful look as his head fell atop his paws, and a small whine left his lips.

My heart grew heavy with sadness for the wolf's pain. "I'm... I'm so sorry... I..." My eyes widened as the waft of charred marshmallow finally caught my nostrils' attention, and I quickly smacked the burnt treat at the ground. "Crap!"

The wolf's ears drooped. "Oh dear, that's not good."

"Guess I should've paid it more mind." I set the stick down. "Oh well, I can make another." I reached into the bag of marshmallows, and plucked another. "Okay, there we go." A grumble resounded beside me, and I glanced back at the wolf once more. He looked a little irritated, and his eyes seemed watery as he stared at the ground. "F-Fenris..."

His fractured gaze flickered to me. "Hmm?"

I leaned to my left, toward the wolf, and my fingertips were quick to catch the starry tears that escaped his moonlit eyes. "I... I'm sorry you're enduring such pain. Please... Don't... Don't cry."

His head leaned toward my hand as a response, and I fondly stroked over the bridge of his nose with a gentle hand.

"I... I know how it feels to miss someone," I said. "You long for them to return to you, even though they can't. I mean, I don't know if this person you speak of, your master, or creator, will return to you one day, but..." I lowered my head. I felt terrible for weighing him down with my pain, when he already had enough of his own.

"Go on," he insisted.

"It makes me think of Dad," I admitted. "You know, he worked as a journalist, and every time he wrote something, he'd come to me and be like, 'Hey Ro-Ro, check this over for me, will ya? I wanna know what you think!!'" I choked on a pained laugh. "He always gave me his thoughts when I finished a piece of artwork, so it felt nice to help him in return. It was a way for us to indulge in each other's passions."

"You two were quite close," Fenris said.

I nodded. "You know, one day, I asked him why he was so intent on my exploring of the world."

"What was his reasoning?" he asked. "Are you comfortable telling me?"

I sniffled, tears already threatening to overflow. "I was… sitting on the back porch with him. He asked me if I really wanted to know, and I said yes. Do you know what he said to me?" I stared the wolf square in the face. "He said to me, 'Because the world lay out there in front of you, yet you've never gotten to see it. I want to share my experience with you someday. I want to explore the many wonders, dangers, and places never-before-seen with you, Ro-Ro, to take you on a journey through this wonderful, historical garden.'"

"That sounds exactly like him," Fenris said quietly.

"'I want to see you blossom into a powerful, vibrant bloom that stands strong against even the heaviest of winds, coldest of storms, hottest of days,'" I continued. "'Because you are my rose that never wilts. You will keep growing, learning, when you seek out the mysteries of this life.'" Tears rained down my face, as my quivering hands yanked the marshmallow-bearing stick out of the raging fire and set it on the ground. I worked to remove my right glove, my hands shaking so badly that my fingers kept slipping.

Fenris rose up a little. "Rosella…"

"The very day he told me those words, he gave me something I've always remembered to take with me. It's my most precious memory of him that I don't ever want to forget." I raised my right hand close to my face, so I could make out the writing on my wristband in the firelight. "'Blossoms in bloom,' he said, 'they stand the strongest. A powerful Bloom you will be, and may you blossom, one day, into an unstoppable force.'" I turned myself so I was facing Fenris, and held my arm out for him. "See?"

Fenris' eyes settled on the bracelet with utmost fascination. "Rosella, that is beautiful."

I nodded hesitantly. "Yeah." I cleared my tear-stained face with my other hand. "I don't ever want to forget all that he's done for me. He was a great man, a thoughtful husband, and a wonderful father." A shudder prodded my spine at those words.

"Rosella?"

"I'm okay…" I whispered. "It's just…" I rubbed up and down my arms. "I just… I became this empty shell of what I used to be, after he died. I mean, I was still shy and afraid. But I was happy because he was there." I dropped my hands. "I-I don't think I'm hungry anymore." I went to stuff the bag of marshmallows in my backpack, but paused as I looked over at the already-cooked marshmallow. "Do you want another one? That one's on the ground, so there's probably a bit of dirt stuck to it now."

"No thank you," Fenris declined. "I'm alright. Perhaps tomorrow."

"Alright." I put the marshmallows away, then retrieved the sleeping bag Great Granny Felan gave me and unfurled it. "Guess I should get some sleep… You need to focus on stuff around here anyway." I tugged off my other glove and threw both by my pack. "God… I'm tired."

"Rosella…" Fenris lightly prodded me with his nose. "Rosella, come lay next to me. I'm sure you'll feel more at ease that way."

I moved the sleeping bag over without question. "Hey, Fenris?"

"Yes?"

I leaned into his side, and embraced the comforts of his plush form. "Thank you… for listening to me, and helping me. I've never really opened up to anyone about this stuff except for Great Granny Felan, Mom, and Sophia. Of course, I told you why…"

"Yes, you did," he said. "Because you trouble yourself with the difficulty of trusting others, and that's okay. It takes time…"

"Yeah…" I rested a hand against my fluttering heart. "I-I know that we haven't really talked on a personal level until now, but I sincerely hope that I don't ever lose you. When the Lurker attacked you that night, I feared the worst. And then, tonight, you showed me that you really are more than a mysterious wolf." My fingers combed his thick, soft fur. "So much has happened in so little time, and it's scary… But I'm sure glad I met you. I don't know where I'd be without you here."

Fenris flicked an ear. "Little Rose, I am happy to hear you say that. Know that I will always be by your side."

I stared back with tearful eyes. "Really?"

"Of course." He stretched his neck, and lightly licked the palm of my hand. "You are important to Chloe and Felan and Sophia, as well as to Ben, and me."

"Fenris…" I buried my face in his fur. "Thank you."

"You are most welcome. Now..." He grazed his nose against my head. "Go to sleep. We have another long day ahead of us."

I nodded. "Be careful, and make sure you rest soon."

"I will, when the time is appropriate."

Rather than further busy my occupied mind with the counting of sheep, I claimed solace in the sea of stars littering the night sky above. It was a pretty, peaceful sight...

You see, Ro-Ro, we humans possess the technology to explore many worlds beyond our own, like another country or the moon. And do you know why? It's because of our curiosity. It pushes us to explore, to discover what's around us. Perhaps one day, you too may discover a world far beyond what any of us could imagine.

You mean, like the stars, Daddy? What if there's a place out there, full of stars?

Besides space? Haha, maybe.

Maybe? But doesn't that mean it's not true?

It's possible for it not to be true, but it's also possible for it to be true. Until you discover it, your curiosity will only grow. And the stronger your curiosity, the stronger the chance you will get to find out. All you need is curiosity, bravery too.

Bravery?

That's right, Ro-Ro. Because without bravery, your curiosity...

I bit back a gentle sob. *Won't last.*

My father was a wise man whose preaching was interrupted by sudden death. He wasn't always right, and even acknowledged that. Still, he believed strongly in his views of the world, because an open mind welcomed possibility beyond face value.

I recalled one last set of my father's wise words, before drifting off into sleep.

Curiosity cannot exist without bravery, as bravery is useless without it, and fear will stop at nothing to ensure that.

Fenris

The night sky was beautiful, a treat for the eyes when the day was done, though I harbored a hatred for the moon, despite its alluring, enjoyable glow. A silent alarm to me, it unleashed a sound only the Lurkers could comprehend, a mechanism that lured them out into the world.

I could recall the first sighting with perfect memory, the beginning of the forest's deterioration, a sign that my master's life was at risk. This place... It was the bane of her existence. The trees as her bones, without them she'd lack structure. The soil as her muscle, without it she'd have no strength. Attacking one or the other would greatly weaken her, but attacking both would surely kill her. That was why she fled, because it was the best course of action. But the outcome hasn't changed. All she did was lay that burden onto our shoulders, the Guardians...

My weary eyes wandered to Rosella, who was just starting to fall asleep. *I waited the first several years to meet this girl, despite being warned by the others not to get attached to her, because of our master's messy planning...* Itching with envy, my eyes began to droop. They craved the rest I'd granted my legs. *If I don't sleep soon, I'll lose focus.* My head again fell between my front paws, and I blew a breath of air between my lips. *But I can't rest yet. They're out there.*

I fought, with every ounce of strength I had, to combat the weighing drowsiness. Insomnia was a curse for most, though its presence certainly would've been welcomed had it been offered to me.

I've pulled all-nighters before. I can do it again... like that time I dug all those holes for Felan, so as to keep out those pesky deer nibbling at her plants. I chuckled at the memory. It was a fun time...

Fenris, you say I'm a stubborn ol' fool, but look at you! At this rate, you may as well entertain me with a game of "Whack a Mole"! You can be the mole, as you made the holes~!

Felan... I miss you.

It pained me to have to leave her behind, even though I didn't intend to stay away for long. But it seemed as though I was leaving home for good, despite not actually leaving it, because this forest was my home. And if anyone was leaving home for good, it was...

My furry brow curved into a frown, and another huff of air brushed my lips. *Rosella... She was curious as to how Felan could do so much work on her own, so she had to make up an excuse. Something about just having a ton of energy, and a powerful shovel... I'd never felt such an urge to just jump out and take credit. All those years of watching her stop by every single Sunday, like clockwork, no matter how she felt, or what the weather was like. And that one day, I wanted so badly to tell her how much fun it was digging all those holes. But Chloe didn't want that. She wanted Rosella to stay oblivious. To her, the farther she was from the truth, the better...*

Chloe worked hard to keep her safe from the evil hiding in these trees, to raise the child she and Ben had always dreamed of. But, to Chloe, that also meant me keeping my distance, until she felt it the timing was right. At first, my reveal was planned on her sixth birthday, but then that arrangement was changed to the next week, and then the next, and then into a few years. And it was all because she was afraid of losing Rosella...

But for me, it was different. Watching from the trees, I resisted the urge, countless times, to burst out from the underbrush, and run toward her like the excited dog I was. Even after I finally came out when she was nine, just by being near her, there was never an answer from the person I'd hoped would surface.

This girl is not an obstacle, I assured myself. *She is a shield... a shield with a beating heart that I must protect, but she is more than a shield to me...* My claws curled into the dirt as I endured the strong gnawing of guilt at my conscience. *My initial plan to lure her out failed, but I will not turn my back on this girl.*

Observing her actions, the way she spoke of her likes and dislikes, she was exactly like Felan, Ben, and Chloe. It took me a great while to see that, though. At first, all I saw was a fence of security to hide my master, and that if she died she'd be nothing more than a body to be collected.

My fur bristled, and I wrinkled my snout in disgust. *Terrible thoughts, terrible... I can't think like that. I don't think like that anymore. She is a part of my master, but she is also real, like me. Chloe and Ben loved her very much, like she was their own...* I gave a low whine. *How is Chloe doing now? She must be hurting.*

I peered over at Rosella sleeping soundly. This sweet little girl was Chloe's one chance at having a child to raise, and I snatched it from her with much thought, despite knowing how painful it would be for her. But she knew Rosella would have to return to the forest someday, and she'd still have Ben...

She doesn't have Ben anymore, I reminded myself. *Ashen's curse took him, and I took Rosella.* I buried my face into my paws, as my ears fell back against my head. "I'm sorry for doing this to you, Chloe. I promise to make it up to you someday."

I nuzzled myself a little closer to Rosella, then focused on my surroundings. It proved to be relaxing, and my eyes grew heavy as I drifted off to sleep...

Felan

Rocking myself back and forth in my chair with a pounding headache probably wasn't the best idea, but it was the best distraction at my disposal right now. My hands were too sore and achy to continuing sewing, and I needed something to take my mind off of Rosella and Fenris for just a little longer.

The cool night air was much more tolerable, in comparison to the sweltering heat of the day. Well, maybe it wasn't *sweltering*, but my clothes still clung to my back with sweat. To be frank, I quite enjoyed the beauty of night, even if it was a dangerous time to be outdoors. I always imagined the moon as a beautiful pearl that cost nothing to see, and with the way the trees graced its presence with their peaceful swaying, I was sure they thought the same.

"Mom, you here?"

"At the back, dear!"

Soft footsteps creaked along the floorboards, and then Chloe rounded the corner of the cabin. "Hey, I got Grace relaxed at home for the night with some of that sleeping powder. Slipped it in her water, when she wasn't looking." Chloe hesitantly wrung her hands together. "She's... doing okay it seems. Also, I got the detectives onboard."

"Good, good to hear," I said. "Was the walk here alright? It's after dark."

"Yeah, it was." Chloe placed her hands to her hips. "Mom, you told me you were busy today. I know your bedtime is near, but you can't escape that easily. Why did you and Fenris go behind my back?"

I didn't dare look her way. I knew a ferocious glare awaited me.

"Mom."

I scampered for a response, and though it was strong, it was all I could think of. "How come you forced Sophia the role of bait?"

Chloe sighed. "I..."

"Chloe, you said you knew they were prowling about."

"I didn't want them to take Rosella, and—"

"And you knew that Sophia would sacrifice herself in order to save her," I finished. "Come now, I raised you better than that."

"I-I honestly didn't mean for it to happen," Chloe argued. "I didn't!"

My amber eyes narrowed. "Never tell a lie to a wise woman who sees through sheer curtains."

Chloe approached the deck railing, and let her face fall in her hands. "Oh god... Mom..."

"I'm not scolding you," I told her gently. "I feel you've been punished enough by losing Rosella."

"I haven't lost her," Chloe retorted with a steely tone.

"My dear, I hate to admit this..." I bowed my head. "I am afraid that you won't be seeing her again..."

Her back to me, Chloe hid well the tears I was certain stained her vision.

"Fenris and I wanted to prep her," I continued. "Sure, six years old was a bit young, but the sooner the better. However, Grace resurfacing reached your ears, and next thing you knew, Sophia had become part of Rosella's world. Like us, you were only doing what you thought was best for her." I shook my head. "Even after Fenris entered her field of vision a few years later, not a single glint of recognition sparked her eye. So, in the end it worked out the way you wanted."

"What about Sophia?" Chloe whispered with quivering words.

"There is still time for her, if she remains strong," I said.

"Even though she's a Husk," Chloe mumbled.

I pondered how to proceed on with this conversation. Chloe was just as doubtful, but we couldn't give up yet. Sophia, from what I'd heard, was strong-spirited. She'd been fending off Ashen's control for years. And the fact that she gave herself up to protect Rosella, that proved further that she was a fighter.

"Where there is despair, there is hope. We must hold onto that." I raised my head up again. "I have seen no new activity as of yet, so perhaps that is a good sign. You do know what to do when the time comes, right?"

"I do," Chloe responded firmly.

I nodded. "Good. Do not stray from the course of action needed. I've been around far longer than we all thought I'd be, and I'm not about to watch you give in now. If I can hold on, so can you."

Chloe peered over her shoulder. "Mom... Rosella... If she dies, she won't... forget about us, will she? Even though she's... collateral..." She choked on a small sob.

"Her body will remain, but her piece of the spirit will be forced to return to the forest," I uttered sadly. "But she won't forget us, unless the forest is completely destroyed."

A look of discomfort settled on Chloe's face. "But she's still doomed..."

"Fenris will protect Rosella," I assured, "and if you recall, she is the strongest of the bunch. So you've nothing to fear. Now..." I pointed a finger at her. "Dry those tears. Grab yourself a tissue if need be. Make sure to snag a cookie or two, fresh out of the oven."

I resumed my silent observing of the night, as Chloe silently slipped into the cabin, and I'd join her once I'd had my fill of gazing at the stars. A tapestry of lights dotting the vast space above, I always wondered what it was like up there.

Perhaps, I thought to myself, *when I finally ascend, I'll find out.*

CHAPTER 19

Rosella

I WAS STANDING IN the field again, but my father wasn't there. Still, I called out to him. There was no response. I took a step forward... and then another. And another. And another. I broke out into a run through the endless field. There was no sound, except for my voice, no one else around, except me. And the sky was a blank canvas.

"Dad! Dad, where are you?" I called.

No response.

"Daddy!"

I tripped and fell flat on my face, or I would have. Instead, I phased right through the grass.

Rosella... Rosella, don't go down that path... No! Don't!

As I awoke with a start, I rolled onto my side, and found myself alone in a thick, bright red fog. Heart racing, breathing heavy, my head whipped to the left, and then the right. I could see nothing ahead of me. There was nothing but red. And tall, deadwood trees. All around me.

"Rosella... Rosella..."

"Huh?"

"Rosella... Rosella... Rosella..."

That voice... Why is it whispering my name? I can barely hear it. I rose to my feet. "Fenris, is that you?"

"Rosella, Rosella, Rosella."

"Fenris?"

"Rosella, Rosella, Rosella, Rosella." The whispering, it was faster, excited.

My legs suddenly began to move in tune with it, the adrenaline pumping through my veins.

"Rosella! Rosella! Rosella!" the voice chanted in a rushed breath.

Faster, faster, I urged my legs. *I have to catch up with it! I can't lose it!*

I broke into a sprint without a sense of direction, and blindly ran through the fog. Eventually, it began to clear, and my eyes gradually adjusted to the darkness unveiled before me. By this point, the whispering was burrowed so deeply into my ears, I could feel the ghostly syllables piercing my eardrums. They drowned out the noise of my boots crunching over the bones— Bones!?

I gasped when I tripped over a skull, and slammed into the ground. But this time, I did not fall through the cold, hard ground beneath me.

"RosellaRosellaRosellaRosellaRosellaRosellaRosellaRosella."

Forgetting the skull, I shot back up. "I'm coming! I'm coming!" I cried. "I'm coming!" I frantically whipped my head around. "Where are you!? I can't see you!"

"RosellaRosellaRosellaROSELLARosellaRoSELlaROsSEllaRoSeLLARoSEllA!"

My boots planted themselves to the ground. I gasped and threw my arms out.

"ROSELLAROSELLAROSELLAROSELLAROSELLAROSELLAROSELLA—"

I pressed my palms against my ears to try and drown it out. "Stop it! I can't!" I sunk to my knees, and looked to the unveiled trees. "Oh... Oh god..."

Suspended by nooses made of vines, various corpses hung from the trees by their necks, like morbid decorations. Whispering my name in a mix of intervals, their dry, coarse lips wavered at a brisk pace. Some of them swayed from the branches with their entrails spilling out, others with a missing limb or two. All were peering down at me with their sunken eyes, their eerie smiles stretched wide.

In unison, there was a clear, sickening *crack* as they each raised an arm, their fingers pointing ahead. Their whispering became a mass of jumbled noise, like dry leaves aggressively rustling against each other.

As still as they were, I followed their sense of direction with my eyes, until I found her lying unconscious upon the ground. "Sophia!" I screamed. I sprung forward, right to her side. "Sophia! My god!" I dropped to the ground, and grabbed hold of her shoulders. "Sophia! Sophia, wake up!"

Sophia didn't move.

"Sophia?"

A small bulge emerged from underneath her shirt, right at her chest, and slowly trekked down her torso.

Behind me, the corpses' garbled mess of unintelligible murmuring continued on, almost drowning out my voice completely.

"So… Sophia?" I whispered. I stared in horror as the small bulge stopped at her stomach. "Ah… S-Sophia…" I reached out a shaking hand. Terrified, I gently pulled her shirt back, and recoiled at the bulbous blister pulsating within Sophia's flesh.

Just then, her eyes popped open, and she looked straight up at me. "Ro… Ro, is that you? I—"

I let out a blood-curdling scream as the blister burst open, and a shower of red rained from above. A claw burst out of my best friend's gut and clung to my wrists. I desperately tried to yank them out of its grasp, while Sophia's frantic hands tore into her middle.

"*SOPHIAAAAA!!!!!*" I shrieked. "*STOOOOOP!!!!*" I pulled and jerked the claw firmly holding my wrists together, my actions tugging Sophia toward me.

"*Make it stop!!!! Rosella!!!!! Please!!!!*" she cried, her bulging eyes flooded with tears. Bits of flesh plastered to her tattered fingers, she buried them into her intestines, and continued to eviscerate herself.

I mindlessly fought with the claw attached to her gut, somehow managed to get my bound hands near my shoulder, and yanked super hard. This prompted Sophia to fling forward and on top of me.

Rosella! Rosella! Wake up!

"*YOU DID THIS TO ME!!!!*" Sophia roared. She clasped her hands around my throat and squeezed, her nails hooked into my skin.

Rosella!

My bound hands uselessly grabbed at her wrist. Unable to reach oxygen, I unleashed a restrained wheeze.

ROSELLA!!

I bolted upright with a sharp gasp. The cloud of blood shrouding the forest was gone, its deathly red glow replaced by the golden rays of early morning sunlight.

"Rosella!?" There was a lick to my right cheek. "Rosella!"

Still racked with fear, I flew to my feet. "Leave her alone! Go away!" I whirled around to face the one behind me. "You can't take her from me! Leave her alone!" My throat burned with each fiery wail, my eyes flaring with anger.

"Rosella…"

"Ah…" The flame of my raging temper abruptly extinguished itself. "Oh…"

A frightened expression was displayed on Fenris' face, his ears flat to his head.

"Oh god… I…" I pushed my messy bangs back. "Fenris… I'm so sorry. I…" I frantically searched for any sort of excuse I could use to break away. "I…" I winced at the threatening urge of my sensitive bladder. "I need to use the bathroom."

In a panic, I sped off for the trees, leaving a clueless Fenris to ponder what just happened. At first, I felt a bit better relieving myself, but then realized I'd neglected to grab wipes, and I cursed myself for it. Begrudgingly, I yanked up my drawers when I was finished and stomped back to the clearing, where I found Fenris with his back to me. He gave a huff when he sensed my presence, and buried his face into his paws.

"Fenris…" I came around him and crouched to his level of sight. "Fenris, are you alright?"

He grunted.

"Fenris," I urged.

"I'm sorry," Fenris mumbled. "After last night, when you saw me with a bloody face, you had a nightmare about me."

I frowned at him. "What?"

He peeked around his shoulder. "You don't know if you can trust me."

"What…" Worry clenched my heart and squeezed. "Th-That's not it at all!"

The wolf cocked his head.

"I'm sorry, I…" An unsettling weight of nausea burrowed in the pit of my stomach. "I had a nightmare about Sophia, not you. I was in this bloody fog, a-and I found her l-laying there, and she… and she…" Tears once again flooded my eyes. "I…" A few streaked down my face. "I'm sorry."

"Rosella!" Fenris scrambled to his paws and trotted over to me. "Please! Don't cry!"

I scrunched my face in disgust as his tongue ran over it again, and I wiped the back of my hand across it. "A-A claw emerged from her stomach." I winked my left eye as Fenris came at my face yet again. "Please."

He pulled away from me, embarrassed. "I'm sorry."

"It... Ugh." I cleaned my face with my sleeve. "It looked so real. I tried to help her, but she kept tearing at herself. The claw had a hold of me. And then, when I pulled, she fell on top of me." I swallowed the rising whimper in my throat. "I'm sorry. I don't wanna talk about it anymore. I'm gonna get something to eat, and then we can continue on."

My stomach argued with the bread and berries I devoured minutes after the conversation with Fenris, but I knew that if I didn't eat then, I probably wouldn't get time later. We still hadn't seen the Lurkers, to which Fenris said that they could be anywhere by this point. This further prompted my nausea to bite at my insides like a rabid dog, though I did my best to bear it.

"The pond is safe to drink out of," he told me.

"That's good to know." I rummaged through my backpack until I found a small bag. I unzipped it, and pulled out my toothbrush and some paste. "I'll take this time to brush my teeth while you hunt. And Fenris..." I gave him a stern look, and pointed my toothbrush at him. "Take all the time you need, even if it's more than a few minutes. You need to eat too."

The wolf grumbled with a shake of his head before taking off into the trees.

I sighed and went over to the pond. "Can't really blame him," I mumbled to myself. "I scared the hell out of him..." I dipped my toothbrush into the water, and squirted a bit of paste on top. Staring into my wavering reflection, my eyebrows knitted together as I shoved the toothbrush into my mouth. *I know he's worried, but that's not what I want for him.* I paused mid-scrubbing. My reflection in the water... I leaned toward it. My eyes... Since when were they pink?

"Rosella! Caught something!"

I whipped my head over my shoulder, toothbrush clasped between my teeth. *Damn, that was quick.*

Fenris peeked around one of the trees across the way. "I found a couple rabbits. Should tide me over for a while."

I gave a thumbs-up to him, then returned to facing the pond, where I was surprised to see blue eyes staring back at me. Though confused, I disregarded what I saw as my mind simply being tired, and washed off my toothbrush.

I cupped some cold water in my hands, then swished it around in my mouth for several seconds before spitting it out onto the ground. "Bleh! Okay, I just need to put my gloves back on, and stash my toothbrush." My cheeks flushed a light pink as I thought of my slightly-soiled undergarments. "I'm also going to make a quick clothing change, if that's alright."

"Okay," Fenris called to me. "I'll be waiting then."

I sighed in relief. *Good, he's not questioning it.*

I found a tree to hide behind so I could change in peace, while Fenris kept watch for any Lurkers. When I was finished and made sure I had everything packed up, I banished the troublesome thoughts plaguing my mind. Tempting as it was to wallow in my self-pity, I had to break the vulnerable cycle of treating myself like an insufferable dandelion, and prevent my weak stem from swaying flat to the ground with even the gentlest breeze of negativity.

I wanted to shed those fuzzy, anxious pieces from my mind, and carry myself upon the wind. I wanted to soar through the sky, and show the world that I too could be strong, that I could support myself, like Sophia. Her stem, it stood tall, her petals vibrant with a fierce air about them.

A sob crept up my throat, and about slipped my sealed lips. *At least, she was until that night... The Lurkers all but crushed her...*

"She is alright," Fenris uttered.

I hesitantly glanced at the wolf.

"We will find and save her." A courageous light burned bright in his radiant eyes. "And you are strong. You just don't know it yet. Everyone grows at their own pace."

"Yeah, I guess you're right." As I did another check to make sure I had everything packed, I eyed the box of crackers inside and opened it. "Sorry this isn't as good as rabbit or deer." I offered a large saltine to Fenris. "Wanna try one?"

The wolf shook his head. "Oh, you don't have to worry. Those rabbits filled me up fine."

I shrugged. "One cracker at least won't hurt, right?"

"Well... I guess not." He carefully nabbed the cracker with his teeth. "Mhn..." He swallowed it. "Ah... That is pretty tasty, but definitely not as filling as the rabbits."

"Hopefully you'll find something when you do get hungry again..." I shot a glance over my shoulder. "Looking around, I see nothing. Guess word got out to the critters that they lost two of their own."

"Jesting me for being a carnivore," Fenris mused. "Funny, ha ha."

I laughed. "Sorry, figured we could use some silly thoughts."

Fenris nodded. "Indeed." His ears perked again. "Oh, Rosella! Look!" He pointed with a paw. "Up ahead!"

"Huh?" I searched for what had grabbed his attention.

"The trail."

I spotted a dirt trail with scattered leaves after a quick scan of the environment, where the trees ahead were strictly parted. "Wonder where that leads?" I pondered.

Fenris lowered his nose to the ground. "I'm picking up something."

"Really?"

"Yes, and it's quite fascinating. A combination of eucalyptus and pine, peach blossom. Perhaps vanilla, maybe lavender?"

I cocked my head. "You're naming off a *bunch* of different scents. What's goin' on with that sniffer of yours?"

"I'm not sure." He started sniffing at the ground. "This peculiar finding is getting stronger with each step I take."

"You sure you're not smelling crackers too?" I asked.

Fenris chuckled. "I'm sure."

Okay." I looked down at the cracker box in my hands. "You want another one?"

"I'm fine for now," Fenris said. "I'd like to focus on this strange scent."

"Alright, suit yourself." I pulled my backpack off to stuff the crackers inside, then slipped it back on. "Say, what do I smell like to you? I didn't shower last night, so I imagine I reek a bit."

Fenris looked offended at my question. "You do not reek one bit to me. I envy the sweet, earthy aroma of rose and clary sage you bless the air with. Sometimes, I even pick up a hint of honeydew and chamomile."

"Huh, interesting how that works," I said.

Fenris sucked in a heavy breath. "Ah, it's intoxicating."

"Whoa now, slow down pal." I put my hands up. "We're just friends here."

"My apologies." A sheepish grin spread across his maw. "It's comforting to revel in sweet scents, especially when it's that of a familiar. Oh!" He craned an ear, and his eyes widened with excitement. "I think I hear someone calling out to us. Try and listen."

I waited. "Hmm... I don't hear anything."

"They must only be able to reach me then," Fenris said. "Still, I'm curious..."

So as not to distract Fenris, I resolved to silently embracing the comforts of the forest, while the wolf focused on the supposed voice. The birds were singing their merry tunes high above, and a cool breeze carrying the floating stray leaves brushed along my shoulders. Sunlight illuminated the towering trees with a warm emerald glow, and cast their dancing shadows on the dirt that stirred beneath my boots. It felt like this was planned, like a celebration of our arrival.

If things go well, we will celebrate. Fenris will be among us, and Great Granny Felan and Mom, and Sophia, Grace...

The last that I'd heard and seen of Grace was a distraught mother losing her child to the evil creatures of the forest. It still burned like an unforgiving lesion on my mind that refused to heal, the memory having cultivated a painful infection.

I didn't do a damn thing to help Sophia. She took on that damn vine like it was nothing, yet I couldn't do the same for her. That, and chasing after her, had done nothing. My hand balled into a determined fist. *You'll see her again, Grace. I promise.*

And that is part of why you're here, Rosella, to save your best friend, because she is also important.

"Rosella! Look!" Fenris abruptly raced forward, his paws stirring up the leaves littering the trail.

My legs quickly wore down with exhaustion as I hurried to catch up. "Fenris! Hey!"

He came to a stop, allowing me to close the distance between us.

"Whew, I can't just up and run that fast, nor that far, like you can."

"Rosella, look at this."

I doubled over with my hands on my knees. "Hang on... I gotta catch my breath." I raised my head. "Huh... Whoa."

Standing in the center of the large clearing before us was a magnificent Weeping Willow tree, with crisp pale pink leaves draped over it like sunlit curtains. Swaying in the wind, they unveiled a thick, curving ivory trunk wrapped in vines decorated with a colorful floral arrangement.

"It's so pretty," I whispered excitedly.

"It is," Fenris agreed. "I've never seen such a thing before."

"Ya know, I'm a bit surprised to see pink leaves on a tree around here."

"This one seems special, but I don't think that the leaves are the reason." His furry brow curled into a frown. "I also can't seem to hear that voice anymore..."

I approached the tree, and cautiously parted the draping leaves that blocked my view. There, I found the intricate trunk up close, and gently stroked the smooth bark creases. "It's like it's been polished," I observed. "Interesting."

Circling around, it didn't take long for me to notice something peculiar, a symbol etched into the wood: a crooked heart with strange letters encircling it. A rose looked to be blossoming from the middle of the heart, and in the center of the rose was a keyhole.

My curious fingertips grazed over the strange letters. "Hey, Fenris," I called. "Can you read this?"

"What is it?" He poked his head through the blanket of pink leaves. "Is everything alright?"

I pointed to the letters. "What's this?"

Fenris' lip curled back into a snarl. "It's the language of the Lurkers."

I gave him a frightened look.

"Hold on..." The wolf spent a minute in silent observation, then nodded. "Okay, I've deciphered it."

I bounced on my heels, and clapped my hands together. "Ah, really? What's it say?"

"This inscription is for a sealing spell."

A questioning look formed on my face. "A spell?"

He nodded.

"Huh..." I pressed my hand to the symbol. "Ah!" Out of nowhere, a blinding burst of light singed my eyes. My head became a little fuzzy, my body heavy.

"Rosella!" he called out.

"Fenris! What's going on!?" I cried out to him. "Fenris!? Fenris!" I gasped when I heard a loud noise, like a bomb going off, and I ducked with my hands over my head as I squeezed my eyes tightly shut.

"Please... Someone... Anyone..."

I cracked one eye open. *Who is that?*

"Anyone... Please... I know you're there... Please... help me... I know you heard me. One of you..."

I opened my other eye, and slowly removed my hands, then looked around me with caution. All I could see was an endless void of white. Where was this place? How did I get here?

"H... Hello?" I stood up. "Hello? Fenris?"

"Help... Please..."

I turned around at the sound of gentle sobbing, and noticed someone upon their knees. "H-Hello?"

They glanced over their shoulder. "Eh...?"

My eyes widened at the sight before me. "Oh... Oh my..."

A pale, ghostly girl, with long black hair streaming down her back, was hugging her bare arms to her pencil-thin body, a spark of fear in her grey eyes. Clad only in a musty-stained nightgown, she scuffed her bare feet into the invisible ground as she scrambled away from me.

"Ah! No, please!" A feathery voice left her ruby lips. "Stay away!"

I put my hands up. "Ah, I'm sorry!"

The girl blocked her face with an arm. "Please..." She whimpered weakly. "Please, don't hurt me!"

"I... I'm sorry. Are... you okay?"

The girl responded with a quiet sob.

Slowly, my hands drifted back down. "Hey, why are you crying?"

"P-Please..." she whispered.

"It's okay. You don't have to be afraid, I'm... I'm just a person." I gestured to myself. "It's okay."

She peeked underneath her forearm. "Y-You mean... You aren't... with them?"

"With who?" I questioned.

The girl's face went blank. "You're... You're not one of those things. You're something else entirely." Her arm fell away, and she gasped. "You are a girl, like me!" She rested a hand to her chest. "B-But how are you here?"

I shrugged. "I don't know. I just... walked up to this pretty pink tree, touched it, now here I am."

Her mouth dropped open a little.

"Are you... Are you okay?" I asked again. "What's your name?"

"You must be one of the voices I heard." The girl's eyes widened. "Oh no! Did those creatures trap you here too?"

I shook my head. "No. I just touched the tree, and then wound up here."

"Oh..." A bittersweet smile cradled her mouth. "I... I can't say I'm not happy to have someone here with me..."

"Did the Lurkers do this to you?" I asked, intrigued.

"Is that who they are?" The girl tilted her head. "What a fitting name." She flitted a hand at her mouth. "Oh! Where are my manners? I'm sorry. I haven't introduced myself. It... It's been so long since... since I've talked to someone." Her warm expression fell into a slight frown. "My name is Sarah, Sarah Mitchell."

My heart did a leap in my chest. *Sarah Mitchell!? The girl who vanished in 1980?*

A teardrop rolled down her doll-like face. "I... I'm guessing by the shocked expression on your face that you recognize me." She stifled a sob. "It's good to know I haven't been forgotten."

"H-How are you...?"

Sarah ducked her head. "I don't know. I just remember seeing..." Her voice suddenly broke off, but she kept moving her lips.

"What?" I took a few steps closer. "I can't... I can't hear you!"

Sarah gave me a confused look, then opened her mouth to speak again. However, she was interrupted by the sound of Fenris' frantic howling.

Another wave of blinding light shrouded my vision, and then I was gasping for air.

"Rosella!"

I shot up, my throat scorched from the rush of oxygen. "Ack! Ugh... Wh-Where am I?" I whipped my head around. I could see I was under the Weeping Willow tree, with Fenris staring down at me.

"Are you alright!?" he asked. "You collapsed, and your eyes rolled into your head!" He checked me over, his nose frantically sniffing up and down my body.

"Whoa! Whoa, Fenris. I'm okay." I gently pushed his head away. "Really, I'm okay." My heart sank. "I just... wish I could say the same for her."

Fenris cocked his head. "What do you mean?"

I gave him a concerned look. "It's crazy, but... I met this girl. She... She said her name was Sarah Mitchell."

Fenris went rigid, his head sinking between his shoulders.

"Fenris, are you okay?" I raised a hand to him, but paused when I noticed him flinch. "M-Maybe we should go back to that pond. You look parched."

He looked like he was about to vomit.

I hurried to my feet. "Come on, let's go..."

Together, we sleeked out from the curtain of leaves. My hand against his side, we started back the way we came. The sun was positioned in the center of the sky, indicating afternoon. Soon, we'd have to find another place to rest. I hoped it wouldn't be difficult.

CHAPTER 20

Rosella

I USELESSLY TWIDDLED MY thumbs while waiting for Fenris to recollect himself at the pond. "Fenris? Um…" My teeth kneaded anxiously into my bottom lip. The urge to question him was overwhelming.

The wolf retracted his tongue from the pond and gave a deep sigh. "Rosella, you said that girl claimed to be Sarah, right?"

"Yeah, I did." I crinkled my brow with extensive thinking. "Ya know, I didn't think about it at the time, but… Once, I came across a printed article about her in one of Mom's old folders, and there was a picture of her. She looked a lot like…" My eyes widened. "Like… Sophia…" *Back at the pizza parlor… she said…*

She has the same last name as me and my mom. I… I did ask her once about it. Ya know, to see if maybe there was a connection, but she denied it.

"Grace… and Sophia…"

"Little Rose…"

"Uh… Right!" I shook the thought from my mind, and brought myself back to focus. "When I found Sarah, if that's who it really was, she tried to tell me how she wound up there, but I was pulled back out while she was talking." I gave Fenris a questioning look. "I don't suppose I could try touching the tree again in order to talk to her?"

He shook his head. "That would be way too easy."

My face fell into an expression of anguish as the bit of hope I had fizzled out. "I guess… I guess I'll just have to wait until she decides to come back then?"

"She can't, not voluntarily."

My face twisted in confusion. "What do you mean?"

"Because of the sealing spell," Fenris explained. "Remember, I translated it."

I slapped my arms at my sides in agitation. "Great. So now, not only do I have to save my best friend from a bunch of forest monsters, now I have a ghost girl sealed within a tree who needs my help."

"I'm certain that is the case," Fenris admitted dejectedly. "Come, let us return to the tree, and try your method. Perhaps I am wrong." He dropped upon his haunches. "Hop on."

I climbed up his side, and settled upon his back. "Okay, let's go."

The ride back to the tree was much faster this time, as Fenris knew exactly where he was going. When we reached it, I jumped off of him, and charged into the curtain of leaves with lingering hope that maybe, *just maybe*, I could reach Sarah.

"Anything?" Fenris called a little ways from the tree.

"I'm touching it!" I slapped my hand to the symbol. "C'mon... C'mon..." I tapped an impatient foot. "Come on..." I waited for several seconds, then tried calling out to her. "Sarah? Can you hear me?" I waited a few more moments. There was no response. "Damn it..." Defeated, I abandoned the tree.

"Nothing?" Fenris asked.

I shook my head. "Nothing. You were right." I took a deep breath to relax myself. *I can't let myself down yet. Giving up would be a backtrack.*

Rosella... Look behind the tree... Come on.

My head whipped to the left of me. "Hmm?"

Look behind the tree.

I frowned. "Fenris? Did you hear that?"

The wolf flicked an ear, a questioning look on his face.

Wait... Can you hear me?

My eyes flickered to the left, then the right. "Seriously, you can hear that, can't you?"

"Hear what?" Fenris asked. "Is it Sarah?"

Ah! You can! You can hear me!

"Y-Yes I can," I stammered. "Wh-What is that? Who are you?"

"Rosella?"

Behind the tree, Rosella! Behind the tree!

"Behind the tree?" I circled around the giant Weeping Willow.

"Rosella?" Fenris cocked his head. "What is it?"

Look around the tree, up ahead!

I placed my hand to my chest, where a questioning warmth had abruptly sprouted. *Behind the tree...* My eyes wandered ahead of me. "Behind the tree, up ahead..."

Yes! Ahead!

"Fenris! I..." My voice trailed off, as my eyes locked on the patch of trees before me. "The tree there..." I started forward.

"Rosella? Where are you going?" Fenris trotted after me. "Rosella!"

Yes, Rosella! Behind the tree! There you go!

I approached a particular tree with a straight cut etched into the bark, and peeked around it. "Fenris! Hey, I found another trail!"

You found it! Yes! Yes!

The wolf, not far behind, started wagging his tail. "Really?"

Yes, she did! She found it!

"Rosella?" Fenris called. "Is everything alright?"

I peered over my shoulder. "I'm fine. You ready?"

He nodded. "Lead the way."

"Alright, then let's go." Paying mind to the prickly bristles of a bush nearby, I carefully slunk between it and the marked tree.

"Rosella, tell me, how did you find this so easily?"

I pondered over this. "I'm not sure. Like you, I just heard this voice in my head out of nowhere, telling me what to do. What do you think? Fenris?"

"Huh? Ouch!" The wolf flinched when a tree branch whipped him in the face. "My apologies. Oof." The wolf stumbled several steps forward as he squeezed through the small gap between the bush and tree, and shook himself out. "Oh, it's tough being my size in tight spaces."

"I can see that." I put a hand on my hip. "Anyways, I heard this voice in my head." I cocked a brow. "What if... What if it was Sarah?"

"Was she the one calling out to me before?"

I nodded. "She did mention that she heard voices, and she confirmed mine as one of them." I looked to my right as he caught up to my side, and scrubbed at my arms with gloved hands. "Fenris, i-if I actually did see Sarah, what if... Dad..." My vision blurred as I felt a tear streak down my face. "What if he's trapped here like Sarah? And what about Sophia?" My face paled at that thought. "What if—"

"Rosella." Fenris suddenly stepped into view, catching me off-guard, and I bumped into him. "Rosella, take a minute to breathe, won't you?"

I blinked a few times to clear my vision, and found myself staring at the ground.

"You've endured a lot in the last twenty-four hours," Fenris said. "The world you've grown up in has suddenly crumbled around you, and... I'm sure you're feeling more than a little lost."

I didn't say anything. He'd snatched the words right out of my mouth.

"I'm sorry you're struggling. I'd ask if I could do anything, but I know I'm only contributing to all of this."

"I... I'm..." I couldn't muster the words, "I'm fine." Because I wasn't fine.

A few days ago, I was a socially awkward girl trying to meander life in a town that did nothing but gawk and talk about my family and me, do what I could to survive high school, and decide whether or not to pursue a career in art. My dream was to own a house near Great Granny Felan's cabin, learn her ways of gardening, and fend for myself in the woods. I also wanted to invite Sophia over, live a life free of worries with her.

"So much went down so fast," I ushered. "I just... I don't know what to think. God, what was I thinking, coming out here?" I looked up at the trees towering above. "This all feels like a dream or something. I just... I don't..." I ran my fingers through my hair. *This is all too much. I don't think I can do this. I told him I couldn't. I wasn't ready for something like this. I can't... I...*

"Rosella."

The wolf's voice drew me out of my thoughts for a moment. "Y-Yeah?" I looked over to him. "What is it?"

Fenris' muzzle wrinkled. "I smell sawdust and oak."

I nervously rubbed my arm. "I-Is it close?"

"Not exactly," Fenris said, "but it's not far either. If we're lucky, we can rest there."

"That actually... sounds pretty nice." The thought of rest teased my frazzled mind, like a dessert that awaited me after dinner. "Let's take a look. It's gonna be dark before long, which means the Lurkers will be out and about."

A growl thundered in Fenris' throat.

"I'm sorry," I mumbled, and nervously clutched at the wolf's bristled neck. "I didn't... I didn't mean to make you uncomfortable." My eyes dropped to my boots, my hands falling to my sides.

"Those things won't lay a claw on you," he muttered through bared teeth. *"I'll kill them first."*

I waited for the uncontrollable chill to ravage my spine, but it never came. So I pressed a hand into his side, and gently clutched his fur again.

Fenris relaxed, the rigid line of dark silver settling atop his spine. "Ugh, I'm sorry for thinking such awful thoughts." The wolf screwed his eyes shut, his brow furrowed. "They can't take responsibility for their actions."

"What do you mean?" I asked.

"Rosella, the other night, when you were roasting marshmallows, I mentioned a curse..."

A mental lightbulb went off in my head. "Oh, yeah... I faintly remember. Something about a curse claiming the trees..."

"That's what caused them to become what they are," Fenris said. "And the only way to save them is by killing them." He hung his head. "I... I want to save them, but I've become blinded by the evil that's taken them."

"So, they have no clue what they're doing?"

"They do, but they can't help it."

"Oh..." I pondered what to say next, then laid an arm over Fenris' neck, and nuzzled my cheek against his. "Well, we all got faults, and those faults help us grow. Otherwise, we aren't learning anything." I gave a strained laugh. "At least, that's what my dad always told me."

"I suppose you're right." A hopeful air about him, Fenris slipped out of my grasp, and trotted a few steps ahead. "The smell I picked up on earlier... It is getting stronger with each foot forward, just like with the tree. Why don't we check it out?"

"Alright..."

Fenris planted his nose to the ground, deeply focused. "Okay... Let's see now..."

I busied myself with mentally counting the steps I took as we continued our walk, and I sort of fell into a steady rhythm, like I was following a dance routine. I counted each crunching leaf that graced my ears a step. One, two, three four, now five, then six, seven and eight... It was like I'd enveloped myself in a waltz, only there was no partner for me to dance with. But if there was...

For a moment, the leaves littering the ground fell silent as I forced away my guilt of denying Sophia before it could completely trample my system of distraction. *Just keep going... Don't think about it.*

I emptied my mind of all thoughts, except for the rising number of crushed leaves, and kept this up until I reached nine hundred. To my surprise, we came upon an old, abandoned two-story house some ways down the trail, and a spark of hope tempted my heart. That is, until I got a closer look at the structure, and that spark fizzled out.

"This place is in shambles," I muttered while looking it up and down.

From my viewpoint, the decrepit roof looked like it'd cave at any moment. On top of that, the front door was missing, possibly having been torn from its hinges, and the shattered windows were dressed in tattered curtains. The only things that didn't bother me were the various patches of moss staining the wood.

I slowly approached the steps. "Well..."

"Be careful," Fenris said. "It could break."

I wrinkled my nose at the scent of what smelled like either burnt wood or rotting grass. "This place smells really bad. I would hate to be you right now."

Fenris grimaced. "Yes, I have to agree with you there. This nose of mine can pick up any scent."

Locating a wooden railing off to the right, I removed my gloves, and stuffed them into my left pants pocket. "Ugh, disgusting," I muttered as I ran my bare fingers along the damp, rigid surface.

Fenris raised a furry brow. "You didn't want to ruin your gloves, though?"

With a sigh, I attempted my first hesitant step up the way to the porch, then paused at the obnoxiously loud creak. "Better proceed with upmost care."

The wood sank under the weight of my boot, and I braced myself for it to snap. When it didn't, I cautiously continued my way up, and knelt down to examine the sturdier porch when I reached the top. A rough exterior, dozens of cracks, caked with dirt, lined the ancient, splintered wood.

Looking ahead, I found the front door. It was age-old rustic, much like the porch. As I approached, I slowly reached into the right calf pocket of my cargo pants, where my father's blade was tucked safely away. I wrapped my free hand around the rusty golden knob, and turned it. The door uttered a prolonged whine as I pulled it open, and unveiled the darkness awaiting me inside.

My nostrils were greeted with a harsh contrast to the fresh, crisp air outside, a musty scent that reeked of staleness and smoke. Particles of dust shimmered in the light pouring through the open doorway, and as I stepped through, my eyes began to water from the irritation.

"Crap..." I burrowed my knuckles into my tear ducts, and winced from the scorching itch. "Lots of... dust here... Yipe!" I felt something creep up behind me, and I bolted forward, my arms up with Dad's knife held high.

"It's alright Little Rose, it's just me."

I sucked in a long, deep breath and slowly exhaled. "God, Fenris! Don't do that to me...!!"

I flinched at the abrupt flash of light that washed over my surroundings. Though dim, it provided my vision with much needed attention. I looked up to the source of the light, an enormous chandelier dangling from the ceiling a several feet above my head, and frowned at the faint clouding of dust around it.

"Time's most certainly not been kind to this home," Fenris spoke sadly.

I looked around me while slipping my gloves back on. "Yeah... Clearly."

Now that we could somewhat see, we found ourselves in a spacious, nearly empty living room. I could just make out the aged couch that sat near a silent fireplace recessed into the wooden wall, a small table with an open drawer on its side nearby. Their creeping shadows gave them a slightly ghoulish appearance, but nothing my brain could taunt me with.

I placed a hand to Fenris' forehead as he approached. "Lots of dust here, but I'm sure we'll find something interesting." I made a face at the uncomfortable stench still pricking my nose. "Ugh, smells stale."

"Indeed. On the upside, this place is fairly open. At Felan's, every inch of space is used." His brow furrowed. "Could maybe brighten up this house with some plants, or one of her hand-stitched rugs." He wagged his tail. "I'm sure she'd have a fun time bringing it back to life."

"We can discuss that later," I said. "Let's see what else is here."

We opted to explore the room to the right first, a kitchen lit only with the light of a lone window. I tried the switch by the door. Though it didn't work, I could still make out the thick layers of mold that plastered the cabinets. The sink didn't look much better, either. Rust crawled around the drain and along the faucet, and the nozzles looked to be grimy. Judging by what we've seen so far, it had to have been years since this place was cleaned.

"How disgusting," Fenris grumbled, as he eyed the state of the sink.

"Yeah, no kidding." I turned to the dusty kitchen table standing in the center, and examined the chairs in similar condition. "I bet these were hand-carved." I traced a finger over the heart cut into the back, and wiped the bit that stained my fingertip over my pant leg. "This wood's so old and stripped."

"Clean them off, add some cushions..." Fenris eyed the dingy curtains draped over the kitchen window. "Felan would probably like a different design than what's here. Grey is too plain a color for her."

"Yeah, definitely." I carefully moved one of the three chairs, and an uproarious creak rang out.

Startled by the noise, Fenris backed into one of the cabinets, and a cloud of dust showered him as a result.

"Fenris?" I turned to face him with concern. "Are you okay?"

Hunched over, the wolf's maw scrunched up, his nostrils flared, and from my point of view he looked like the big bad wolf from *The Three Little Pigs*. Hell, he could've been that wolf's hero, his sneeze was so powerful.

I shrieked as a fierce whirlwind of dust whipped at my face. "Ah, geez..." My eyes burning from the grainy sting, I did my best to soothe the itch by burrowing my gloved fists into them.

"Yuck! Ack!" Fenris jerked his head to the left, then the right. "Ugh!" He set his face in a displeased frown. "Horrible."

My hands fell away as I blinked several times. The prickling sensation lingered at their corners, but at least my eyes didn't hurt as bad. "Y-You okay?"

He squinted, his snout wrinkled with discomfort. "I... I think so." He cracked open one eye. "How about you?"

I nodded hesitantly, as a chuckle slipped. "That was kinda funny."

The wolf failed to hide the smirk tugging at a corner of his maw. "Psh, you are laughing now, but once it happens to you, you won't think it's so funny."

After recovering from Fenris' tornado-level sneeze, I followed him through a doorway in the kitchen leading to the adjacent hallway. My boots padded softly along the worn carpet, as I ran my hand along the wall. Through my glove, it felt semi-smooth, though my eyes told me it had a rougher exterior, what with the cracks and tiny bumps.

"There's a staircase," Fenris said, grabbing my attention. "And another doorway."

I looked to the staircase, then to Fenris and the mentioned doorway at my left. "We can check here first," I said. My eyes flickered to the other side, at the closed door missing a doorknob. "I'd ask if you could break down that one, but I don't want to risk the house falling to pieces."

"I doubt that would happen," Fenris said. "However, the least amount of damage caused, the better."

I nodded. "Alright, let's see what's in this room beside you."

I was surprised to find a library, complete with five rows of large windows at the back, and they granted far more light here than the chandelier did in the living room. Several rows of bookshelves, roughly six feet tall, were lined up together in the center, while the others extending to the ceiling took up the entire right wall and the first half of the left.

Sadly, though, books themselves were scarce. I found only twenty, well-hidden, among the many smaller shelves. Fenris, however, made the interesting discovery of a small resting area, with another empty fireplace and a mangy recliner at the back right corner.

I ran a hand over the top of the bronze-toned stone that framed the fireplace. "It's like a ghost town for librarians and book nerds. My mom would surely drop from anguish."

"At least it's cozy here," Fenris pointed out. "Plenty of light, and the carpet is comfortable to sit on." He planted his rear upon the floor and wagged his tail. "Ah, the fabric is so soft, and it compliments the fireplace, though I'd replace this piece of furniture with a rocking chair for Felan."

My eyes fell upon a large book sitting upon the recliner. Curious, I plucked it from its spot and examined it. "Look at these pages. They're so brittle that I could probably tear them with just a pinch." As I carefully flipped open the book, the spine crackled and hissed.

"I think I recall Chloe claiming how fond she is over certain noises books make," Fenris said. "Correct me if I'm wrong, but isn't that what you call 'ASMR'?"

"Yeah, it is. I happen to like it myself." I turned a few badly stained pages while listening closely to their crinkling. It was a satisfying sound for my ears.

"Find anything interesting?"

"Actually yes. From the looks of things, this book is filled with fairy tales." I showed it to Fenris. "See?"

A spark of amusement flashed in Fenris' eyes. "Looks like this one's the story of *Little Red Riding Hood*."

I smiled at the picture of the happy little girl in red carrying her basket of goodies. "Looks like she's heading to her grandmother's house."

Fenris uttered a low whine. "You used to do that all the time for Felan..."

Sadness speared through my heart. *Great Granny Felan, I miss your funny wording. I miss your paper lanterns, those lovely talks we'd have together...* I closed the fairy tale book and set it back on the recliner. "Ya know, I've noticed you bringing her up, a lot..."

He bowed his head. "I guess it's easy to tell, huh?"

I nodded. "I miss her too... But the old days aren't gone for good. We will get back to her soon." I turned to Fenris. "Come on, let's keep exploring."

We found another doorway, to the far left of the resting spot, that led into the hallway, so we went back out the front entrance, and up the awaiting stairs across from it. My eyes scanned over the rusty curving railing as I gripped it gently. It squeaked under the weight of my palm, though it didn't budge much.

"Where will these winding wooden platforms take us?" I wondered.

"I guess we'll find out," Fenris said.

I flinched at the threatening creak beneath my boot, and my mind drifted back to the steps leading up to the spacious wooden porch.

"Would you like me to wait downstairs?" he offered.

I hesitantly shook my head. "No... A Lurker, or perhaps something worse, could be nearby." It pained me to admit that, but I felt better with the wolf at my side.

"Very true." Based on his tone, he dreadfully agreed.

We came across a dimly-lit window every ten cautious steps up the winding staircase, a small comfort within this eerie place, though the walk up seemed incredibly long. If a Lurker really was around, hopefully it couldn't fit in this narrow space. It was so tight, I was surprised Fenris could fit.

Then again, he did prove me wrong, back when we first found the trail leading here.

"Rosella, I think I see the end," Fenris said, sounding hopeful.

Sure enough, the top of the steps crept into sight, whereupon we discovered a hallway lit with the sun's amber glow through a window at the end. Along both sides, five doors awaited our entry, two at the left and three on the right.

"Too bad that window isn't the door to freedom from our troubles," I mused. "Sucks."

"I'm sure we'll be fine, Little Rose." Fenris tapped his nose against the first door, open slightly ajar, to the right. "I'll take this side while you check the left. If I sense danger, I will come to your aid."

"Alright, and if you need help opening a door, I'll come to your aid." I stepped toward the first door on the left. "Let's do this."

As I opened the door, a loud and prolonged creak played in sync behind me, and I stepped into what I assumed to be the master bedroom. A grand, king-sized bed with four bedposts, a tattered canopy sheet draped over it, sat across the spacious room. The head of the set was pressed to the wall, a window to the right.

I investigated the dusty wooden wardrobe at the left wall, where I took note of the metal knobs on the cracked doors showing signs of longtime rust. The right one wobbled when my hand wrapped around it. To my slight disappointment, the inside of the closet wasn't all that exciting either, just a couple of coats and a pillow thrown in a messy pile.

I turned my focus to the bed, and noticed through the tattered canopy that a silk sheet was neatly tucked over the mattress. My fingers delicately pulled the canopy apart, where I found a thick blanket upon the bed. On top of the blanket was a small silver key.

"Huh, interesting." I examined the heart-shaped head, and the pair of thin metal vines intertwined around the stem. "Never seen a key like this one before."

Nothing else seemed of interest, except for the spots on the floor that spoke of furniture being arranged differently at some point in time. They were not much cleaner than the rest of the room.

I wonder if anyone lived here... My hands ran over the silk sheet. *This looks so nice... The quality isn't that bad... and the fact that there's furniture in every room so far... Someone had to have lived here.*

I initially based this house to be around a hundred or more years old. Though, upon everything we'd seen, it seemed more like sixty or seventy. However, I was surprised to find it well-structured, despite being abandoned for what I presumed to be a long time, and the furniture was in oddly decent condition compared to what it could've been.

The fact that this house was so made up, it had me wondering if this was the home of a family, perhaps a wealthy one, since there were many spacious rooms. That library was especially huge, so maybe one of them was a scholar, or perhaps someone who just really liked books.

"Fenris, nothing important in this room, except for a key I found." I exited the master bedroom. "This place seems like it hasn't been lived in for some time, huh?" I approached the second door, and gave a light push as I twisted the knob. "Shoot." I tugged on the knob, pushed and pulled on the door. But it refused to open.

"I see that someone clearly does not want others to know what is inside." Fenris came out of the second room on the right side. "If your assumption is correct, then it's possible someone who used to live here may be withholding a secret or two."

"Hmm..." I peered at the key in my hand, and attempted to insert it into the keyhole. I panicked when the tip jammed, but relaxed when it came free with a harsh tug. "Damn it, doesn't work..."

"Let's not get frustrated. I still haven't checked the third room on my side yet." Fenris' head craned to his left. "Want to look with me? The first was an empty room with a cardboard box, and the next was the washroom." He scoffed at the air. "To think that a house like this would only have one washroom, it's fairly absurd, if you ask me."

I cocked a brow at him. "I'm curious to know why you think that, when you don't even live in a house."

"I've seen Felan's cabin, and I must say, it's quite small. Based upon what Chloe told me of her house, there are a couple of bathrooms." Fenris flicked an ear, an inquisitive look on his face. "I only have what little I've seen here to go off of, but if a family of people lived here in this fairly large house, then surely two or three bathrooms would accommodate this establishment."

I nodded slowly. "Good point." I looked backed down the hall. "Well, maybe the door we found downstairs, the one without a knob, has a bathroom."

"Maybe," he mumbled.

I stuffed the key into my pocket, and meandered over to the final, unopened, door. "Okay... Let's see what's in this room, since its door does have a knob." I gripped the knob, turned it, and gave a gentle push. "Oh... It's unlocked."

The last room on the left was what appeared to be a little girl's room, and like the master bedroom, it was fairly large. Placed in between two windows opposite the wall of the doorway was a queen-sized bed, a simple white pillow propped up at the head, with a small stuffed bunny resting against it. The sheets were made of silk, with a sheer pink canopy overlay. A wardrobe stood to the far left, its doors wide open. A large chest sat across the room from it.

"Guess our assumptions were correct," I said, and took a step inside. "This place was definitely lived in. But not recently."

"I thought so," Fenris said. "I have to say, out of all of the rooms we've seen, this one feels the most put together... It's a very... pretty room..."

I slowly walked up to the bed, and through the canopy, I saw the dark red splotches staining the sheets. "Fenris..."

The wolf stood silent at the door, a blank expression on his face.

"I think these are... bloodstains." I slipped a hand through an opening in the canopy curtains, and lightly grazed my fingertips over the sheets. "If someone actually lived here..." My eyes fell upon the stuffed rabbit, and a cold chill coursed down my spine. "What if..."

The wolf shook his head. "I'd rather not think about it."

"Y-Yeah." I gave a slow, timid nod. "Yeah." I glanced over my shoulder. "Well, it's... it's safe to stay here at least."

"I suppose so." Fenris stretched his legs. "Oooooh, I'm getting hungry again, so I might go out for a quick hunt. Why don't you check the washroom and see if there's any running water?"

"Yeah, sure." I quickly followed him out of the room. "Second room, right?"

"Yes." He nodded to the door in question, and I approached it eagerly. Initially, I didn't care about bathing since entering the forest, but within closed walls I felt more comfortable.

"I wouldn't mind bathing here..." I stepped into the small space. "Oh, it's... kinda cramped... You weren't wrong, this is awful small compared to the other rooms." I turned to my right, where I about bumped into the sink. "Oh, shoot." I clasped my hands around the ceramic, and glanced at the toilet crammed next to it. "Man, it's tight in here. I mean, look at this, the bathtub is across the toilet by only a couple feet."

"It's a horrid excuse for a washroom, if I do say so myself," Fenris muttered. "Not even a shower curtain to cover the bathtub. Felan told me she had one with flowers on it."

I glanced over my shoulder, and raised a curious eyebrow. "You have quite a strong opinion on this house's layout... Are you secretly an interior designer?"

Fenris gave me a straight face. "Yes, Rosella. I am an interior designer. I use the trees to build forts, and dig holes into the dirt for pools."

I choked on a sudden snort at the wolf's smart ass comment.

He tilted his head. "That is what an interior designer is, right? I've heard that term once before from Felan, when Benjamin talked about changing the shoemaker's home into a place for him and Chloe."

I gave a hesitant laugh. "I... I think that's more like renovation or, perhaps, remodeling?"

"In that case, this whole place could stand to use either one or both." He frowned. "Is something wrong?"

I shook my head. "No, it's just... When you mentioned the shoemaker, I..." I was thinking about that conversation we had on the tree, about how I didn't believe a word of that story, until he confirmed it himself.

"That house... You did know, right?" Fenris asked.

I nodded slowly. "Yeah, I think I heard Mom talk about it." I looked to the handles on the faucet and turned them. "Well, at any rate, we've got running water here." I pulled off a glove to test the temperature, then jolted from shock upon the freezing contact. "Mother of god that's cold!" I ripped my hand from the faucet, and clutched it to my chest. "Well, so much for my chance at a shower. It's like Antarctica if it was liquid."

"I'm sorry," Fenris mumbled as he bowed his head.

"No, it's okay," I said. "You go and hunt for food. I can make this work somehow."

"Very well. I'll be back soon."

I took refuge in the master bedroom, since I was uncomfortable with the bloody sheets in the little girl's room. What happened in there, anyway? It looked like a murder scene had taken place.

No, don't think about that... Just relax. Fenris will be back soon. Just relax. I hesitantly seated myself upon the bed. My rear didn't sink, and the creaking was minimal. "Hah..." I fell on my back and stared up at the center of the canopy curtains, my hands to my chest. *Sophia... How is she doing? And what about Mom and Great Granny Felan? And Grace... I miss them all so much. I told myself I'd try to be strong, and I trust Fenris to help me.*

It'd been some time since I'd seen their faces, heard their voices... But I hadn't forgotten them. I promised Great Granny Felan I wouldn't, though I hadn't considered just how much it really hurt. I never took for granted what I had, but I so badly wanted it all back. Sure, I'd have to deal with the town's gossip, and stress at school. But Sophia's life hung in the balance, and strolling through the forest wouldn't be enough to save her.

If Sophia were in my place, she'd turn over every stone, tear through every ounce of dirt, scour every tree, until she found me. If she had to, she'd give an arm or a leg, maybe more.

But what about me? What could I give her in return for all she's done for me? Something cannot be given without something being taken... Bravery is not prancing through some trees, or going without a shower for a few days. So, in a way... "I haven't really changed at all. I'm still weak... I'm still timid little Rosella... Ha... I guess the adrenaline rush has finally worn off." Drowsiness suddenly weighed upon my eyelids. "No... I... I don't want to sleep... yet..."

Rest now... You may not believe it, but you've grown so much. You will prevail... And soon, I'll prove it, now that I have finally reached you.

CHAPTER 21

Frank&Creg

FRANK AND CREG HESITATED at the bottom of the steps leading up to the cabin. Chloe had instructed them to wait outside, as the woman who lived here had to make herself presentable. She was the one that many people of the town declared to be leading an alleged cult, particularly the religious fanatics that always drove Frank back to the car, when he and Creg were out gathering intel on incidents regarding the forest. Creg usually did fine dealing with those people alone, though he was grateful Frank at least assisted him in handling the non-religious theorists that hoarded stacks of "evidence" about their homes.

"Exhausting to deal with," Frank commented, as he scuffed the toe of his shoe against the edge of a wooden step. "Remember that weirdo with the mascot costumes? He had dozens of photos nailed to a cork board with a mapping of red thread…"

"That's not why we're here tonight," Creg told him gently. "Remember that."

"I know. I'm just saying that he was… interesting." A nervous look settled on Frank's face. "Gave me some bad vibes."

"He's just a recluse with no social experience. Remember? We did a thorough background check on him."

"Still, I'd take that overly-devout Catholic couple screaming, 'SINNERS!' any day over that crackpot."

Creg shook his head. "I don't know, man."

"Ugh, I'm sorry." Frank smeared his irritated look with a hand and sighed. "I'm tired, stressed. And I'm nervous…" His gaze wandered up the steps, where his eyes settled on the many paper lanterns that ran along the wooden railing and roof's edge. He and Creg found them to be a pleasant surprise during their walk down the trail.

"Chloe said that they're there to protect Felan from harm," Creg said. "But they sure are pretty."

"How does a little seventy-eight-year old woman live out here like this, anyway?" Frank asked. "I mean, seriously."

"Chloe says she can handle herself."

"I guess." Frank rubbed at the back of his head. "I'm thinkin' of my own grandma. When she hit that age, she was struggling pretty bad."

Creg shook his head. "God rest her soul."

"Yeah, she was a good cook with a golden heart." Frank chuckled at a memory of himself during his school days. "I remember one day for school, I brought in a bunch of cookies we'd made together. Butter pecan I think... It was our favorite." His grin faltered. "She... She never knew what was going on... because I never told her. I didn't want to lose her smile, like I'd lost Mom and Dad's that day in the church..."

Frank shuddered when another memory, a mark of trauma, came to mind. That day in the church, when he asked Father Timothy if it was possible that God may not exist, his parents were appalled by his question to the Father. Frank had never been slapped so hard in his life, let alone at all, by his own mother, and when they got back to the car, she'd demanded he spend the entire day reciting prayers of forgiveness.

"The fabric of her glove made it worse," Frank muttered.

"Hey, look..." Creg put a hand on his shoulder. "Just... Remember that your life has changed. I know it's not much saying that, but at least it's the truth."

"Which makes it mean a lot." Frank beamed at his partner. "Thanks man."

Creg gave him a hefty pat, and a satisfactory nod.

Frank glanced back at the cabin, attention caught on the gentle glow of the paper lanterns. "If Chloe said that we had to get here before the sun set, then how come we're sitting out here right now?"

Creg shrugged. "I don't know."

"7:00pm..." a small voice uttered.

Both men peered over their shoulders to see Grace lazily knocking her fist against the wooden railing, her emerald eyes empty and dull. They'd forgotten all about her during their conversation.

"Tick tock, Chloe..."

Frank frowned at her. "Grace, you alright?"

"Whatever do you mean?" she grumbled.

"Are you thirsty at all? I haven't seen you drink an ounce of water these last couple days." He cocked his head. "You haven't been around much either."

Grace shot him a scowl so threatening that, if looks could kill, the detective would've dropped dead on the spot. "And how is that your business?"

Frank stumbled back a step, stunned by Grace's response. "I-I was just... concerned, that's all. You're our friend, yet Chloe's been more..."

"More what?" Grace snapped.

"Helpful," Creg stated. He stepped around his partner, a steely gaze set hard on Grace. "We were hoping you'd be more cooperative."

"Despite her secrets and suspicious search history?"

Creg ground his teeth together at that comment. The author wasn't vocal in her personal *affairs*, though she didn't mind disclosing her personal *interests*, prompting a weed of disturbance to root itself into their heads upon learning of her search history. However, it was all for the excitement in her books.

I'm still thinking about it, Frank muttered to Creg. *She was so casual...*

I know... Creg cocked a brow at Grace. *But if anyone's sociopath material...*

She was fine when we first talked...

"Why, hello down there!" A much older woman, clad in a light blue bathrobe, shuffled into view from the top of the steps, Chloe beside her. "Come on up!"

Frank and Creg looked at each other, perplexed. This? *This* was her? The supposed *devil* of Hollow's forest?

"Gracie! You coming?" Chloe called.

"I am," she uttered in a low tone. "Just a little distracted."

Creg.

Creg whipped his head around, then hurried up the steps to join Frank at the top.

"You must be the detectives Chloe was telling me about." The older woman stepped a little closer to the detectives as they approached. "Pleased to meet you."

"Uh, hi!" Frank gingerly shook her offered hand. "I'm... I'm Frank Stormer, and this is my partner, Creg Kenneth. No need for the detective labels."

"Then please, call me Felan."

Creg gently took hold of her hand next, and kissed the top of it. "Pleased to meet you."

"Oh, what a gentleman~!" Felan fanned at her face with her free hand. "Never expected such a warm greeting for a cultist or witch, or whatever they're calling me, though I must admit, I do enjoy conjuring up... experiments." A merry giggle slipped her lips. "I would be more than happy to show you some of my work, if you're interested!"

Frank cocked a brow. *Fascinating...*

"Perhaps later." Creg casually slipped his hands into his pockets. "We were told you knew of what goes on here in this forest..."

"Yes, yes, of course." Felan beamed at the two men. "Say, how's about I prepare you boys some coffee? It's never too late in the day to live a little. I've also got plenty of water if needed, or some tea if preferred."

"You don't have to go to all that trouble, ma'am," Creg insisted.

Felan shook her head. "Oh, nonsense! Come."

Frank followed her inside, while Creg hung back to seek out Grace. He found her creeping up the steps, her head bowed.

"Creg, dear! You coming?"

His eyes locked on Grace, Creg called back to the old woman. "Yes, of course Miss Felan."

"You don't have to wait on me." Her voice barely above a whisper, Grace paused five steps from the top. "I don't want to keep you two busy."

Creg crossed his arms with a challenging air. "That's alright, we're well-practiced multi-taskers."

Grace glared beneath her furrowed brow. "Can't a woman ask for *space*, Detective?"

Creg scoffed at her. "Of course, I respect a woman's need of space. I'm simply making sure you're alright." *I've got my eye on you, Mitchell. I'm not taking any chances.*

"Respect it, then."

Creg turned up his nose. "No need to get a feral attitude with me."

The detective turned on a heated heel, his ears strained to listen for the suspicious woman behind him. His muscles tensed, his fists were stiffly planted at his sides as he stepped into the cozy cabin's living room, and a sweet, but puzzling fragrance wafted his nostrils. His arms loosened as his clenched fingers uncurled just a bit, and his curiosity lured him to the beautiful, potted white bloom, with a dusting of yellow at its sharp-ended petals, upon the coffee table. Its stamen was made up of several thin purple filaments, each tipped with a tiny blue anther. Spilling out of the pot were large, shimmering blue leaves.

Creg's focus completely shifted from Grace to the flower, as if he was locked in a trance. He'd never seen such a peculiar plant, though he'd recalled some of the books he'd read on unique flowers that existed in exotic lands he'd probably never explore.

"Fascinating, isn't it?"

His gaze shot to Chloe, who was standing by the bookshelf, a warm smile on her face.

"Be careful with those petals," she warned, "they're sharp as a blade."

Creg cautiously offered an index finger to test her words, and to his surprise, a white line had been inflicted upon barely grazing the tip of one petal. "Wow..." He examined his finger. "Could've cut it had I pressed just a teeny bit harder."

"You don't find flowers like these anywhere but here."

Creg nodded. "I'm guessing this is what your mother does in her free time?"

"That's just one thing. She also likes to knit, and watch her shows. Oh, and she loves to bake."

"This scent..." He breathed in the intoxicating aroma. "It smells like... honeydew, and blueberry, and... lavender?" He wriggled his nose, unable to fully comprehend this unique scent.

"Each one she creates is a character in her garden, and she considers their scents their personality." Chloe strolled up to the coffee table. "This one, she told me, could be something wise, with a sweet charm about it. Though, it is very much capable of defense when necessary." Her tone lost its wondrous luster toward the end of her sentence, and the playful gleam in her brown eyes faded from sight.

"Is something the matter?" Creg asked her.

"It's nothing... for now." Chloe turned away from him. "We should speak with my mother. She's waiting on us."

Creg winced when he heard the sound of the front door shut. Out of the corner of his eye, Grace sleeked past him to the couch, like a ghost haunting his shadow.

"Alright, let's go." Chloe hurried off, Creg quick to follow suit.

I don't want to be anywhere near her either, Creg thought.

"...can read each other's minds? That's interesting." Felan sat across from Frank at the kitchen table, a steaming mug of coffee to her lips. "Well, I suppose that we really aren't the only ones withholding secrets."

"I suppose not," Frank said, "and thank you for this tea, by the way. It tastes good, and it's a nice change from coffee and water." He sipped from the small porcelain teacup in his large hands. "Mmm, my wife might have some competition."

"Oh ho, well, chamomile happens to be my specialty~!" Felan giggled, her amused grin hidden behind her mug.

"Miss Felan," Creg chimed in, "my apologies for intruding upon your pleasantries, could you tell us more about this?" He gestured to the photos lying on the kitchen table. "My partner and I had taken these the night we found the vandalism."

"Thank you for leaving them." Chloe gave Creg a wink. "Very helpful."

Creg gave a bashful snort. "Yeah, of course."

Frank coughed lightly behind his cup of tea, his eyes darting between the two.

Creg nervously cleared his throat, then nodded to the photos. "I, uh, left these with Chloe so she could show them to you. As for the evidence, poor janitor's at his wits' end trying to clean it up. Still struggling."

Felan picked up one of the photos and examined it. "You were definitely smart in leaving these, as I can't assist without the evidence." She eyed the two men worriedly. "Sorry about your janitor, though. I'll send you boys home with some special cleaning fluid that should clear it right up. You can tell the janitor you found it at a small store outside of town."

"I'm sure he'll buy that." Chloe stepped into the kitchen, and looked to Felan questioningly. "What do you think, Mom? The Lurkers can understand human language, but they only write in theirs."

"That they do," Felan said. "This is puzzling for sure. See, I don't believe the Lurkers have ever wandered outside the forest."

"You sure?" Frank asked.

Felan nodded. "When Chloe stopped by yesterday, she said that you'd mentioned someone named Miss Sally." A look of unease flashed across her face. "Haven't heard that woman's name in years."

"So you know of her?" Creg guessed.

"That I do." Felan's jaw stiffened. "That... I... do..."

He cocked a brow. "If it's no trouble," he started with a careful air, "would you mind enlightening us?"

Felan interlocked her fingers, her elbows to the table. "Chloe went there of her own volition, but I'm sure you can understand why."

Frank eyed Chloe suspiciously. "She went there *willingly?*"

"I haven't gotten to tell them about that yet," Chloe mumbled, as she hid her mouth behind the back of her fist.

Felan's eyes widened. "O-Oh... I'm so sorry. I thought..."

"We haven't had the time to go over it yet," Creg jumped in. "We were curious to know more because Grace was held captive there, and when we got together, she told us that Chloe had a role in that place."

Felan nodded. "I see."

Frank and Creg exchanged eye glances upon noticing Felan's hardened jaw. She was clearly withholding information, and it seemed painful to think about. Despite this, Frank opened his mouth to ask. He wanted to know the details, and Chloe promised to share them.

Don't, Creg warned.

Frank cocked a brow at him. *Why not? Now's a good time as any.*

Creg shook his head. *I don't think so. Look at Chloe.*

Frank did as instructed, and saw her swaying nervously from side to side whilst biting on her thumbnail. Her eyes had darted to their corners, and her brow was set in a nervous frown.

"Well then, how is Grace doing?" Felan abruptly asked.

Both detectives snapped out of their focus on Chloe, and returned it to the older woman.

"She's sitting in the living room right now," Chloe uttered quietly.

Creg sent her an apologetic look. "She's... been a little difficult to deal with."

"Her daughter was kidnapped by the Lurkers," Frank explained.

Felan sighed. "Chloe said the girls were alone outside while she was indoors."

Chloe lowered her head. "I shouldn't have done what I did. I feel awful."

"Now, Chloe, remember what we talked about."

"I know," Chloe mumbled. "You told me that I'd be forgiven. But what if I'm not?"

"What do you mean, exactly?" Frank chimed in. "Ya know, out of curiosity..."

If she's talking about Grace, Creg piped up.

Frank didn't nod, though the flicker of his eyes daring in Creg's direction confirmed his acknowledgment.

"It's complicated," Felan said, and took another sip from her own drink. "Mmm..."

"Gracie!" Chloe suddenly bolted from the kitchen, her sneakers pounding the floorboards. "Come back!"

Felan left her seat, and came around the table. "Chloe! What's wrong?"

"She's heading outside! I need to stop her!"

"I'll go too," Frank offered. "Moral support. Plus, if she takes off, I'm fast." He stood from the table. "Excuse me, if you will."

Be careful, Creg told him.

I know.

"... need to talk to me!"

Frank heard Chloe beyond the front door as he hurried through the living room, and when he stepped out, he found her chasing Grace down the stairs.

"Come on, Gracie!" Chloe cried. "Talk to me! Please! I can't help you otherwise!"

Grace was halfway down, her back to Chloe. "You don't get it, do you?"

"No, I guess not!"

Grace stopped abruptly mid-step, and whirled around on Chloe. "You..." She glowered at her. "You were the one who got my sister killed."

Chloe frowned at her. "I... I don't know what you mean."

"You do too!" Grace snapped. "Ever since we were kids, you acted like you were the victim, like you were the one who'd lost something important to you! She was *my* sister, not yours!" Grace's emerald eyes welled with tears. "I watched you flee for the trees, leaving Sarah to fend for herself against those things. She was screaming for help, pleading your name! And then, you *left*."

Chloe shook her head. "Grace, I was a child then! I didn't understand! I was scared!"

"Oh, and what about Sophia?" Grace retorted. "Surely you heard her cries, or did you not understand that either?"

Chloe's shoulders stiffened. "Grace... I forced that memory away. I-I was a child then... I didn't want to remember. I didn't want to leave Sarah, but she told me to! She wanted me to get away to safety!" She glided down a few steps. "And what happened to Sophia was a fluke! You make it sound like I *told* those things to take her!"

"But you knew they were there!" Grace bellowed.

"Yes! I admit it! And it was *my* mistake!" Chloe shot back. "*I* have to live with that! *I* have to carry that burden *to my* grave, and possible carry it with me to the afterlife!" Tears raining down her face, Chloe sucked in a quivering sob, and shook a fist at her chest. "I have to deal with this," she whispered. "I can fix this... I just... need some time... I... I'm sorry."

Grace shook her head, her expression unchanged. "You ran away, like the coward you still are. My daughter is out there, right now, with those things, and you? You're here wallowing in self-pity!"

"It is *not* self-pity!" Chloe shrieked. "You don't understand what's going on because—"

"Because why, Chloe!? Because you're a liar? Because you're always hiding things?"

"Gracie... To this day, I still haven't forgiven myself for what happened to Sarah..." Chloe lowered her head. "Gracie, I'm so sorry."

"There you go again, 'I'm sorry. I'm sorry.'" Grace slipped a hand behind her back, her eyes wild with anger. "You... don't deserve to be forgiven!" She let out a harsh shriek, and charged forward.

"Grace, no!" Frank flew down the stairs and threw his arms around her waist.

Grace cried out as she and Frank both rolled down the steps, her suddenly-brandished knife slipping out of her hand.

"Are you out of your mind!?" he exclaimed. "What the *fuck* is wrong with you!?"

"She deserves to pay for what she did!" Grace screamed. "She let them first take my sister, and now my daughter! I won't ever forgive her for that!"

As Frank gagged at the sharp elbow to his ribs, his arms loosened enough for her to escape. "Damn it! Grace! Wait!"

But Grace had already bolted for the trees, her sneakers splashing through the tidal wave of leaves.

"Gracie!" Chloe cried. "Come back!" She whipped her head in the direction of Frank. "We have to go after her!"

Frank raised a hand. "Okay, just calm down. Everything will be—"

The detective was startled out of finishing his sentence. The beautiful paper lanterns lining the cabin had suddenly been yanked from their positions, flickering like strobe lights, and were flung about the clearing. They whipped over Chloe's head, as she cried out and dropped to the ground. The decorative lights, still attached to the wires, tumbled along the forest floor upon contact. When they finally came to a stop, their comforting glow fizzled out.

His thundering heart drilling within its feeble cage of bones, Frank held his breath, his muscles tensed.

"F-Frank! Frank!" Chloe's shrieking gasps resounded throughout the clearing. "A-A-Are you alright!?"

His chest inflated like a balloon upon release of his restricted breath. "I... I-I'm fine." The detective uttered another shaky inhale, and gradually released it. It relaxed his frayed nerves. "Jesus..." He paused.

Just beyond the clearing, the trees rattled their branches, a whisper among their leaves. A towering shadow teetered near the edge of the border, a claw raised.

"Chloe!" Frank yelled.

Chloe

A field of goosebumps prattled my back at the rising anxiety of the detective's voice, as he shot toward me like a cheetah on a gazelle in five brisk steps. He threw his arms around me, and sent me flying to the left seconds before the Lurker behind could grab me. I tumbled into the blanket of leaves, and rolled a few feet away, my bones racked with subtle pain.

My head spun from the impact, but I quickly recovered, and stumbled to my feet. "F-Frank!" My eyes widened at the shocking scene before me, and my jaw dropped.

The Lurker was suspended in the air, its scraggly arms limp at either side. Enormous vines, sprouting from the ground, protruded like spears through its back and chest, the fatal blow delivered at the heart.

"Chloe! You alright!?" Frank peered over his shoulder, his brow beaded with sweat.

"Y-Yeah..." My gaze wandered from the vines to his outstretched arms. "You... You did that."

"U-Uh huh." The man suddenly swayed to the side, his feet stumbling in the leaves.

"Frank!" I ran over to catch him before he fell. "Hey! You alright?"

"Ah... god..." He clutched at his head. "I don't know... I don't know what's going on. I feel... I feel so tired." Clutching his knees, he took a moment to breathe, before standing up straight again. "Okay, okay, I'm alright..."

I gave him a worried look. "You sure?"

"Yeah," he uttered.

"Chloe!" Creg's frantic voice caught my attention, and I whipped my head around to spot him leaning over the railing of the cabin. "Quick, Felan said to take this!"

"Shit!" Worried for Frank, I hesitated on whether to stay with him, or go after what Creg threw down to me.

"Go." Frank gave an affirmative nod, a stern look set on his face. "I'm alright."

I opened my mouth to protest, but thought better of it, and went over to snatch the sword awaiting usage. Personally hand-crafted by my late husband, the blade was made of pure silver and sheathing metal, the initials "B. G. B. / C. M. B." etched into the blade.

"Foolish woman... You think he is still here? He is long gone."

I shuddered at the gravelly voice calling beyond the trees, and my eyes darted back to Frank. "Y-You need to go inside. Now."

"No way." He shook his head. "You're not doing this alone." With a flick of his wrist, the summoned vines vanished in a cloud of dirt, and the slain Lurker dropped to the ground with a heavy *plop.*

"Where the hell are they?" I hissed. I looked all around me, but there was no sign of them anywhere.

"They're in the trees," Frank said. "I can see them."

I gawked at him. "You can?"

He gave a slow nod, and pointed ahead. "There."

Exactly as Frank pinpointed, sluggish footsteps thumped against the ground, and then a large decaying stump emerged, followed by fiendish claws attached to a rotting arm. A tall, monstrous tree-beast lumbered into full view, its tongue draped over its cracked teeth.

My knees knocked into each other, causing the sword in my clammy hands to almost slip out of their grip. I held my quivering weapon out in front of me in an attempt to look threatening, and positioned it as straight as I could, in the direction of my target as I locked eyes with it.

"How did you get in here?" I questioned.

"Foolish woman, you failed to notice. She's been plotting for some time." The Lurker threw its crooked head back, and unleashed a raspy howl. *"Prepare for attack!"*

Frank pointed up at the cabin. "Chloe, look!"

At Frank's command, my head snapped up, and I gasped. Four more of these things prowled the roof of the cabin. They bobbed up and down with excited panting, like bloodthirsty beasts, their slopping tongues flinging saliva that rained from their drooling mouths to the wooden shingles they were crouched upon.

Disgusted, I looked to my left, where three more clung to the stilts, their claws curled threateningly tight around the wood. I flinched at the prolonged creak.

How long have they been watching? I thought to myself. *And how in the hell did they knock down Mom's paper lanterns? Their solar energy was supposed to keep them out!*

"Chloe! Move!"

I peered over my shoulder in alarm, then dropped to the ground, my vulnerable ears exposed to the sharp pop that reverberated the air. A whistling chime grazed my throbbing eardrums.

A muffled voice called out to me, and I was abruptly yanked to my feet. "... need to... something!"

My hearing faintly returned to me, though the white noise did not let up.

"Chloe!"

"Fr... ank..." I whispered. "Ah... god..."

"Chloe!" I heard Creg seconds later, clear as crystal. "Felan is secure inside! She whipped out some kind of dust and spread it around." He came pounding down the steps behind me. "Not sure what it's for, but I'm not questioning it."

"It's a... spell Fenris taught her. It'll keep her safe as long as she doesn't leave it." My eyes fell upon the taunting Lurker that was now lying flat on its back.

"I got that one easy," Creg said. "Perfect shot."

I nodded, then glanced up at the ones atop the roof of the cabin. "You two'll take the ones on the roof." I looked to the detectives. "I'll get the ones on the bottom before they break the stilts."

Creg grabbed Frank's arm, their gazes connected. "Frank?"

Frank nervously pulled his gun from his coat pocket, and cocked it. "Creg... If we make it out of this..." His eyebrows knitted together, his jaw set in a sharp frown. "I'll treat you and your family to a nice dinner at my place."

Creg repeated his actions. "Sounds good to me."

Frank nodded. "I don't wanna rely solely on my magic. Not sure what happened, but that last strike sure left me winded."

"Strange, wonder why?" Creg asked.

"Dunno." Frank glared up at the Lurkers atop the cabin roof. "Let's get these motherfuckers!" He charged up the steps, Creg following close behind.

"Ben..." Shedding the shock of the gunshot, I pressed my forehead to the cold blade in my hands. "Please, grant me the strength to wield this once more."

I, Benjamin Gerald Walsh, take you Chloe Marie Bloom, as my companion for life. May the spirit of these trees bless us with joy.

I bit down on a sob. *I, Chloe Marie Bloom, take you Benjamin Gerald Walsh, as my companion for life. May the spirit of these trees bless us with joy...* I again eyed the fallen Lurker. *Forgive me for this.*

Adrenaline coursing my veins, I courageously raised my sword high above my head, and charged at my chosen targets with an immersive battle cry. One of the three dropped from the stilts, though it landed awkwardly on its knees with its arms out. Taking this opportunity, I swung my mighty weapon down onto its left arm. The Lurker howled with pain, as it clutched at the tattered limb barely hanging to its shoulder.

I jumped at it, and launched a firm kick to its chest, its still heart consuming my sneaker. The Lurker wheezed, and we both collapsed to the ground. The tree monster's claws ravaged the ground, as I worked my shoe out, its tongue slopping the sides of its drooling mouth.

"Don't worry," I uttered as I held the sword up high. "I'll put an end to your misery."

The Lurker's empty pearl eyes locked with mine for a split second, before I drilled my sword through it, fatally wounding the creature.

"Chloe!" Creg called. "We need some help!"

I spotted Creg struggling to reload his gun in the middle of the staircase, a Lurker clutching its injured leg a few steps above. "Shoot!" I sprung up, and darted for the stairs. "I'm coming!"

"Fools!" the injured Lurker bellowed. *"You will fall!"*

Creg ducked under its swiping claws. "Shit!"

"Creg, watch out!"

Creg stepped aside, and watched as I slashed at the Lurker's leg. "Frank shot one down!" he exclaimed. "Fell off the roof, so he went around to check and make sure it was dead!"

I nodded as I stabbed the Lurker's other leg, causing it to stumble back and fall over the wooden railing. "Creg, shoot it!" I commanded.

The Lurker, now lying flat on its back, scrambled to stand. It managed to work its way upon its knees, then glared up at the two of us. *"Y-You..."* It spat black blood from its cracked lips. *"You... are... fools."*

Creg opened fire on the monster's heart, and I watched it crumple to the ground.

"Okay, that's two down from the roof, and two from the stilts." I ran a hand across my sweaty brow. "But you said Frank shot one..."

"Guys!"

Stricken with panic at the sound of Frank's cry, Creg and I looked over the railing,

There, Frank was writhing in the grasp of one Lurker holding him high in the air, the other grasping at his legs.

"Frank!" Creg charged down the steps, his frantic hands fumbling in his back pocket for the next cartridge. "I'll help him! You get the ones on the stilts!"

I nodded. "Got it!"

Further harm to my ears proved ineffective as the next gunshot rang out moments after my departure from Creg, and my blade collided with the claws of my next target, as it approached the side of the cabin steps. I repeatedly engaged the monster over the wooden railing, my sword quick to slash its decrepit arm to ribbons.

"You won't win..." the Lurker rasped whilst clutching its destroyed arm. *"You're too late. Ashen will claim your world as theirs!"*

"Return our daughters to us!" I yelled. "They are not yours!"

I climbed up onto the railing, then jumped onto the Lurker's head and wrapped my legs around its neck. I jammed my sword into its branching cranium several times, prompting the creature to screech and moan. It clawed at my legs, thrashed its head about, anything to get me off of it, but I held on for as long as I could. However, the monster figured out a solution by ducking, thus effectively throwing me to the ground.

My spine hit the earth hard, and I cried out in pain, as my sword flew from my hands and tumbled a few feet from me. Panicking, I went to reach for it, but a tingling numbness suddenly sparked up my arms. Both went limp against my command, and I fell flat to the ground, with my torso twisted around.

"Ngh... The... The hell is going on!?" I willed my arms to move, but they wouldn't respond. "N-No..." I heard heavy footsteps behind me, and then the Lurker was lifting me up by my wrists.

It gave a weak laugh as it stared into my terror-fill eyes. *"... You... You're a coward... You think you are so... powerful... like you can take on anything. Your naïveté will be your downfall..."* Black blood trickled down the front of the Lurker's ugly face and into its mouth, where its worming tongue eagerly awaited a taste.

"You know nothing about me!" I protested. "And Grace... We'll find her! We'll get her back!"

"Brunette Woman has abandoned you... And now look at what's happened."

I winced as something wet slithered over my stomach, and I looked down. A sheer look of horror sprung to my face at the vine quickly coiling around my hips, and I struggled to break free. As the Lurker chuckled darkly, my heart pounding in my chest, I silently prayed that one of the detectives would come help me.

"It's over," the Lurker whispered. *"You are finished."*

"N-No!" I whipped my head from side to side. "No! Frank! Cr—Mmmmmmmgnh!" My cries were abruptly silenced with a constricting vine around my jaw, and I helplessly screamed through it.

The Lurker laughed again, and jabbed at my heaving stomach with a claw. *"Helpless human... No way to run now."*

I whimpered through my gag, as the monster tore a clean line through my clothes. It spread the fabric apart with two claws, exposing my heaving stomach. The vine around my hips then took the initiative, and began its menacing trek around my side, its tip tracing across my stomach.

The vine pierced straight through my navel, and I screamed into my gag as excruciating pain radiated from my gut to the rest of my body.

Oh god! Oh god, it hurts! Stop it! Stop! I whipped my head from side to side in protest. *It hurts! Please!*

The Lurker cackled at my suffering. *"So weak and helpless, aren't you?"*

I responded with another sharp cry as I screwed my eyes shut at the explosion of scorching heat in my stomach. It felt so heavy, like I'd swallowed a sack of rocks, and bounced like jelly when I swayed my hips in a panic. A sloshing sound reached my ears, and I looked down to see the intruding vine pumping with excitement.

I attempted several more frantic thrusts, each one more exhausting than the last, and my hips ached in protest at the immense amount of weight forced upon them. I prayed to god that this was all a nightmare, that I'd wake up in bed at any moment.

This can't be happening, I thought. *Please, not like this.* My chest tightened from the pressure of steaming liquid against my lungs, and I gave a muffled cough. *I -I can't breathe! N-No! Please!* My bulging eyes darted to their corners, in hopes I'd find Frank and Creg coming to my rescue, but they weren't around.

Memories of my past flashed through my mind as my eyes streamed with tears. Meeting Benjamin, going on our first real date at the museum, taking Rosella to the zoo for her birthday, sipping tea with Mom, snuggling under a tree with Fenris...

I wasn't ready to join Benjamin in the afterlife yet. I promised him that I'd continue our fight against Ashen. And what about Rosella? What if she came back? What would she do without me? And Mom... She was suffering the curse, and needed someone close by to help her. I couldn't leave her.

A gurgled whine managed to escape my bound lips. *Not like this... Please... Someone help me. Please... I don't want to die. Not like this. I can't... I can't die!* Shackled in place by heaviness, my body refused to move, and my shoulders sagged in defeat.

"Drown in your suffering..." The Lurker leaned in close to my face, its hot breath raising goosebumps to the surface of my skin. *"Drown in your suffering, and face—AAAAAUGH!!!!!!"*

Out of nowhere, I was dropped to the ground upon my knees, and the numbness of my limbs vanished. The intruding vine was ripped out of my stomach, and I shrieked through my gag as I bucked my hips into the air. I tore the vine from my face, then doubled over as gallons of black, steaming liquid exploded out of my mouth. The back of my throat burned from the lingering bile, as I splurged on the rush of air to my lungs.

My frantic hand scurried behind me in search of my sword, when a small pile of piping hot viscera slopped onto my injured stomach, and I silently thanked the gods when I found the hilt. I stuck my sword out in front of me, a curse at the ready, but froze. A Lurker, the one whom I assumed tortured me, lay eviscerated on its back, while another stood over it with a blank expression. Staining the standing Lurker's entire right arm was its fallen companion's blood, and clenched in its grip was what I saw to be a detached heart.

The morbid tree beast's empty eyes wandered to me, as it approached with an awkward limp. *"Why..."* it whispered, *"Why did she leave us... to suffer like this?"*

I quivered upon the ground, my sword still poised in its direction. It shook violently in my hands.

"I thought she was going to save us? Wasn't that her plan?"

My hand tightened around the hilt of my sword. "S-S-Stay away!" I cried. "I-I-I mean it!"

The Lurker cautiously came around my side. *"That woman paralyzed you... That's why you couldn't move."* Its hand snaked behind me, and my shoulders tensed as it pulled me close to it.

"P-Please... D-Don't..." Heart hammering in my chest, I screwed my eyes shut, and gave a silent prayer.

"You must let her go. Grace has chosen her side. She cannot be saved."

I shook my head. "No... I-I..."

"It is too late for her... Too late for us... Soon we will all die... That is why Ashen made us leave. We are too weak for the Queen. We only hinder her power."

I dared to crack one eye open, and found the Lurker staring straight at me.

"I am leaving, so my blood won't stain your hands. But know this... You are forgiven."

A stream of tears spilled down my face. *Forgiven?*

The tall tree creature released me, and stood facing the forest. *"I am going to make a bed of dirt for myself. Please do the same for my fallen comrades..."*

Arms dangling at its sides, the Lurker dragged its stocky feet through the leaves, limping toward the trees, its head hung low. Its movements were sluggish, as if it wasn't putting forth much effort, despite the sheer cries of its struggling allies not far off.

After a long haul of silence, the Lurker stopped, and looked to the sky. It was only a few feet from the trees. *"Olva, Maura, and Cree... I'm returning to you. Just wait for me."*

My eyes widened at the Lurker's words, and my heart about sprang from my chest.

The Lurker peered over its shoulder, one last time... *"Be strong, Chloe."*

I wanted to call out to the creature, to scream that it was going to be alright, that I would find a way to save it, to free the spirit trapped within. But the words wouldn't come, and instead watched it disappear into the trees, in search of its resting place.

O-Olmond...

Frank&Creg

Frank and Creg were caught in a fierce battle of wits against these two Lurkers. They seemed quite strong compared to the others, and unlike Chloe, they didn't have a sword to strike it down with.

"Fuck!" Frank thrashed about in both Lurkers' grasp. "Creg!"

"Frank!" Creg repeatedly fired at the two monsters, until his cartridge emptied. "Damn it!" *We need to use our magic! It's the only way!*

I told you, something was wrong! I don't know what happened, but it was like I lost all strength in my limbs! I felt so weak I about passed out!

"Fools!" one Lurker growled. *"You are no stronger than us! You are weak!"*

"Ngh... No!" Frank tried to free his hands of the Lurker holding them, but its grip on him held firm.

"Let him go!" Creg cried.

The one at Frank's ankles looked to the man with a sneer. *"Face it... You're finished."*

Creg's eyes narrowed as his vision turned silver. "No... Not yet."

Deep in focus, Creg channeled his energy into his heart. A spark of purple singed his fingertips, danced up his forearm, and traveled across his shoulder to his chest, where a small white light blossomed. Several dark roots sprouted from the ground, all around him, awaiting his command.

"Release him, or face my wrath," Creg warned, dropping his gun.

Neither Lurker moved.

"Suit yourself." Creg threw his hands forward, and then the roots sprang into action. They coiled around both Lurkers' limbs and yanked them back, prompting the monsters to drop Frank.

Frank screamed as he fell back to the ground. Pain ruptured his spine upon contact.

Creg gawked at his disgruntled partner for a moment, before returning his attention to the Lurkers. With a flick of his wrist, the roots hooked into the Lurkers' captured limbs, and they howled in distress, as the roots dug deep into their muscles and tore them apart.

Both creatures fell to their knees, arms hung at their sides, as the intruding roots pierced their hearts. The unmoving masses quickly shrank into themselves, giving them the appearance of shriveled-up raisins. Heads tilted back, mouths agape, they slammed against the ground on their sides.

Winded, Creg sucked in a heavy, quivering breath, and held it for several seconds as the world began to spin around him. He stumbled a few steps forward, before dropping to his knees. His legs wobbled, unable to provide support, his chest clenched tight. It was like he'd run a marathon, each breath more grueling to take than the last.

He wiped at the thick layer of sweat that coated his forehead, as he turned to his partner lying lifeless on the ground. "F... Fra... Frank," he rasped. "Frank."

"Ugh..." Frank's head lulled as his partner approached. "C... Creg..."

"I-I'm here, buddy." Creg reached a hand out to him. "How are you feeling?"

"M-My back..." Frank coughed harshly as he screwed his closed eyes. "Oh god, ow."

"Here, let me help you." Creg crawled around Frank, and slipped his hands under his partner's armpits. "I'll... slowly lift you up. Ready?"

Frank nodded, then groaned as his partner started the ascension.

"There we go, atta boy!" Creg grunted, as he helped him stumble to his feet. "Alright." He sloppily brushed the stray leaves and spatter of dirt from Frank's back. "How's that?"

Frank winced against the stroke to his sore spine. "That hurts."

"Sorry," Creg murmured. He then slipped Frank's left arm over his shoulders. "Let's... get you inside." Together, they hobbled toward the steps leading up to the cabin. By this point, Creg had mostly recovered, though his ankles felt weighed down with phantom shackles.

When they reached the steps, Frank carefully lifted one foot, then the other, and so on. "You and me..." he whispered. "We make... the team... And, that's all... we need..." His head lulled as he stumbled on the tenth to last step, Creg being quick to catch him.

"Easy bud." Creg helped steady him. "We're almost there now."

"Took a hard... hit," Frank mumbled. "I mean, I think I'm okay... but kind of dizzy."

"Yeah, same... We can rest once we get inside," Creg said.

Frank nodded. "Yeah..." He looked toward the door, eyes heavy. "I sure hope... Felan's okay. Chloe too..."

Creg nodded as exhaustion weighed in on him once again. *Damn... Limbs are goin' heavy, and my mouth's startin' to dry. Need to get us both some water...*

CHAPTER 22

Felan

I DARED NOT MOVE. Outside, the sound of firing guns and snarling tree monsters rattled the walls of my home, the multiple muffled thuds against the roof, and the creaks beneath the floorboards, taunting me with thoughts of the structure collapsing. I hunkered down into the sofa, since it was too difficult to kneel, the toes of my slippers still in the makeshift circle I'd created with the white powder. I listened closely to every bump, tap, creak. I hadn't heard any screams that sounded even remotely human, just the shrill cries of the Lurkers. But then, like hitting the "mute" button on my TV remote, the noise was abruptly cut off.

I jumped at the abrupt knocking of the front door. "Goodness…" One hand to my drumming heart, the other sunk into the couch cushions as I pushed myself up. "I'm coming! Just hang on a second. Oh!" I braced myself at the popping of my back. "Oh… thank heavens." I straightened up, and hobbled over to the door. "Thought that would be it for me… Well, kind of… Oh my!"

A pair of exhausted men stood on the other side. Frank, disoriented, bore a few tears in his suit and coat, while Creg appeared a little tired, but unharmed.

I beckoned them forth with an urging hand. "Rest your weary legs, boys. I'm sure your bones are ready to drop."

"Thank you," Creg said, as he helped Frank into the cabin. Together, they meandered over to the couch, and sunk their rears into the cushions. Frank leaned back as his eyes drifted shut, while Creg sighed, and let his head fall into his hands.

I shook my head. "Poor dears… I'll tend to you shortly." I tiptoed out the door. "Chloe?" I peeked over the railing to find her sitting in a mess of midnight crimson, her legs piled with hot, steaming viscera. "Chloe!"

Aged hands gripping so tightly to the wooden railing they ached in protest, I briskly padded down the steps, my robe floating behind me. I waded into the pond of leaves at the bottom, my eyes drifting to the lifeless body nearby. I bravely drew near, my head held high, and gasped. The darkness ailed my already weak vision, though not enough to hide the thin grey stripes burrowed in the creases of the fallen Lurker's rotting skin.

"Mom."

I looked to my daughter with concern. "Chloe..." Fear gripped my throat, choking me of further words, as I stared at the horrid sight of her sitting with sloshed Lurker guts in her lap.

"M-Mom?" she rasped, and peered over her shoulder with a bloodstained face. "Mom..." As she stumbled to her feet, the bloody mass slopped from her legs to the ground. "Oh god..."

"Chloe!" I shuffled over to her. "Chloe, are you alright?"

"I-I'm fine... But the last one..." She looked to the trees. "It's gone. It ran away."

"That's okay dear, let's just... make sure you're..." I glanced around her. "Ah, Chloe. Look." I slunk around her, and cautiously lowered myself to the ground. I felt my knees crack on the way down, and I winced.

"Mom, you need to be careful!" Snapping out of her trance, Chloe hurried over to help me back up, but paused upon inspecting herself.

"It's alright," I breathed. "Just... look at this..."

"Wh-What is it?"

I pointed down at the Lurker. There, creeping along the rim of the Lurker's empty eye, was a tear.

Chloe dropped to her knees, and with trembling hands, gently caressed the side of its head. "Its companion... killed it..."

I craned my head up to the setting sun. "I'm... sorry... Oh, Hollow... I'm so sorry..."

"G-Grace..." Chloe looked toward the trees. "Oh god... Grace... and... Sophia..."

I peered up at the cabin. "Chloe, let's go take care of the men. They must be in pain."

"I... I have to take a shower first, but..."

"Oh, of course." I clapped a hand to Chloe's shoulder, as she got back up. "We've got lots to do. First things first, we get them some water."

"Wait." Chloe dashed ahead, and went around the right side of the steps. "Mom... Mom, come here!"

"What is it?" I willed my tired legs to move. "Honey, we need to get back inside."

Chloe turned around, a stern look on her face. In her bloodied hands...

My eyes bulged. "Chloe..."

"The Lurkers were able to ambush us because the paper lanterns had been tampered with." She rubbed the wire between her thumb and index finger, the frayed end twirling a few inches over. "Someone cut these loose..."

I examined the cord as she held it out to me. "Hmm, you're right. The Lurkers alone wouldn't have been able to enter because they were UV powered, so..." A chill rattled my aged spine, and my hand flew to my mouth.

Chloe frowned in confusion. "Mom?"

My hand fell away as I locked eyes with her. "She did this. She wanted to kill all of us."

Chloe looked to the trees, terrified. "Grace was the last one to come in..."

I sighed. "Well, guess we'd better prepare ourselves." My eyes fell upon Chloe's tattered clothes. "My goodness, dear... You really are a mess! Oh, oh my!" I scurried toward her, and gently grasped her hips. "Chloe!"

"Hey!" Chloe slapped at my wrists. "What are you doing!?"

I glared at the bloody hole in her stomach. "You're hurt, you nit!"

Chloe's cheeks flushed a bright red. "Uh... Y-Yeah, but it's not bad! Really."

I shook my head. "Nonsense. This must be treated right away." I took her by the hand. "Come on now, let's get the men some water, and then treat your belly button. I've got some cream that should do the trick."

"Geez Mom..." Chloe pressed a hand over her wound and winced, a pained expression on her face.

"Don't you worry, you'll be alright."

I led Chloe back up the steps, and into the cabin. I temporarily left her in the living room with Frank and Creg, the poor dears, before heading into the kitchen to search the cabinets for my pitchers. Once I found them, I filled both nearly to the brims with cold water, then proceeded back to the living room. I gave one to Frank, and the other to Creg.

"Okay…" I turned to Chloe. "Come with me to the bedroom."

She nodded sheepishly and proceeded to stand, but fell back with a grunt.

"Do you need help?" I offered.

Her face twisted with discomfort, she shook her head, and forced herself to her feet. "I'm okay," she whispered. A hiss slipped her gritted teeth as she screwed her eyes shut.

"Oh Chloe." I slid a comforting hand behind her back, once she was in reach of me, and guided her to the bedroom. "Lay down on the bed, and don't think I'm not above tying you down."

Chloe begrudgingly did as she was told, while I fetched some medicinal cream from a drawer across the room. "

"This is the same stuff you used on Fenris," I told her. "It will burn, but since your wound is small, it shouldn't be too bad."

"Mom…" Chloe looked up at me with tear-filled eyes, as I approached her. "Mom, I'm really worried about Grace, and Rosella and Fenris… and Sophia."

"My dear…" I sat myself beside her and brushed back her sweaty, matted locks of hair. "They will be alright. I'm sure of it."

She shook her head. "I don't think so… You didn't see Olmond… They…" Her lips quivered as she fought back a sob.

"Hush now, you need rest," I whispered gently. "Let me take care of you, okay?"

"Felan?" a quiet voice uttered.

I looked up to see Creg standing in the doorway. "Yes, Creg, dear?"

The tired man rubbed at the back of his head. "Thank you for the water… Are you… Are you alright? And how is Chloe?"

I gave him a sad look. "Oh, I'm okay, but I'm afraid Chloe took a hit. Going to help her with this." I held up the small jar of cream in my palm. "Say, Creg, could you possibly assist me?"

Creg came over, and awkwardly glanced over Chloe and me. "Um… What can I do?"

"Just hold her arms down." I looked to Chloe. "Lift them up."

Chloe worried at her bottom lip as she hesitantly raised her arms above her head, but kept them flat to the bed.

Creg's eyes darted from me, to Chloe, and then back to me again.

A stern expression crossed my face. "Creg. Please."

Although uncomfortable, the detective approached, and gingerly grasped Chloe's wrists. "L-Like this?"

"Make your grip a little firmer." I set the jar down at Chloe's side, and twisted the lid off. "Hmm..." I got up and shuffled back over to the drawer I got the cream from.

"What are you doing?" Creg asked.

I pulled out a thick piece of fabric. "We don't want to alert anyone else." I returned to Chloe's side. "I'm sorry to do this to you, sweetie."

Chloe shook her head and opened her mouth.

Carefully, I tied the fabric around the lower half of her face. "Okay... Not too tight I hope."

She nodded tiredly.

"Alright." I locked eyes with Creg. "I need you to hold her very still..."

Chloe squeezed her eyes shut as she braced herself, her stomach sucking in on instinct. I told her to be brave as I scooped out some of the medicinal cream, and then cautiously stroked over her wound. Immediately, Chloe screamed, and thrashed upon the bed, but Creg held her still without trouble.

My heart sank at the tears that quickly flooded Chloe's face. "Just hang in there," I called over her agonizing cries. "It'll be over shortly."

"What the hell is this stuff made of!?" Creg demanded.

"It's a combination of snodaful powder and silver nitrate," I explained. "The silver nitrate cauterizes the wound, while the snodaful powder repairs the damage. They work quite well together."

The detective's eyes bulged out of his head. "How..." He fell silent at my narrowed gaze.

"None of your business," I snapped. "I may be willing to share the forest, but I refuse to disclose my medical methods to anyone outside the family." My eyes flickered back to Chloe, and my gaze softened. Her screams of misery had dwindled to mere whimpers now. "As helpful as this concoction is, it's unforgiving to the flesh. The first time I had to use it, it was frightening, because I thought it was doing more harm than good. She was only a child then, no more than five, when she got a cut on her finger. Closed the wound right up." I pulled the gag free from her mouth. "Feel better?"

Chloe's chest rose and fell with each heaving breath that brushed her dried lips, as she managed a meek nod. "Y-Yeah..." she whispered. "B-Better..."

"Good..." I continued rubbing the cream into her wound. "Creg, would you mind getting her some water? There are glasses in one of the cabinets, but I can't recall which."

"Sure." He spared an apologetic look to Chloe, turned on his heel, and hurried out the door.

"I'm sorry, Chloe," I whispered. "My goodness, you're sweaty."

"That's... okay..." Chloe's clammy head lulled to the side. "Mom... I'm so tired..."

Chains of sadness locked around my aching heart. "Chloe..."

"I got the water." Creg slipped back into the room with a glass of water.

"Good. You get her to sip from that, while I fetch her some spare clothes."

"It's okay, Mom, I can get them myself," Chloe rasped.

I put my hands on my hips. "I need to get you a bandage anyway, and you're far too weak to move. Just stay put, and let him tend to you."

I wandered off to the adjacent bathroom, where I went searching for my medical kit. I couldn't recall when I'd used it last, and if I remembered to put it back in the cabinet. To my chagrin, I had not, and so while muttering curses under my breath, I exited the bathroom, and went shuffling across the bedroom to the living room.

Frank was slouched on the couch upon my entry, his eyes closed. I figured he was sleeping, so I crept past him as quietly as I could. My slippers creaked very quietly along the floorboards, an annoyance I hoped he wouldn't hear, during my trek to the kitchen.

"Damn thing, where is it?" My weary eyes scanned the kitchen. "Should be here somewhere..." I approached the cabinets beneath the sink and opened them. "Oh good lord." I snatched the medical kit, and shook my head. "Felan, you old git. What will you do next? Store the cream cheese in the toilet? Or maybe leave your cellphone in the freezer?"

I hurried down the hall to the living room, but paused outside the doorway of my bedroom. I caught wind of Creg and Chloe talking amongst themselves, and though I never enjoyed eavesdropping, I had to admit that their conversation was rather intriguing.

"Ivy is missing, and you haven't told Frank?" Chloe asked.

"No... I didn't want him to worry." Creg sighed. "Monique, my wife, was distraught when she called me earlier today, and said that Aaron told her that he'd found a note... Something about needing to go to the forest. Ivy wrote that she wasn't coming back, though."

"Just like Rosella..."

The pain in Chloe's voice made a whimper bubble in my throat. But as my eyes watered, I stayed silent, and continued to listen.

"I won't ever see her again, Creg. Never."

"I know how you feel Chloe, it pains me too. But we have to let them go. It's for the best."

"I know... but it's hard."

I clapped a hand over my eyes, and soaked my palm in tears. This had been so hard for Chloe, and me too. It wasn't fair. All this time, she wanted a child of her own, I a grandchild, to nurture and help grow. But like how Chloe had been torn from Adrienne's arms, now Rosella had been torn from Chloe's...

My daughter would've loved Chloe, had she survived her birth, but Hollow's magic couldn't stop Ashen's curse. Adrienne begged me to take care of Chloe, before she died, and I did so out of pity, loneliness, and grief. I couldn't bear to see the child growing up without at least a mother, and over the years, we became so close that I now considered her my second daughter. Deep in my heart, even if she wasn't related to me at all, I loved Chloe all the same, because I raised her.

"Felan, are you okay?"

I paused mid-sob and looked up to see Frank approaching me. "O-Oh, I'm fine. Just a little tired is all."

He cocked his head. "You're crying..."

I nodded slowly. "Yes, yes I am... because I'm sad."

Frank gently laid a hand atop my shoulder. "Why don't you sit down for a bit? I'll help Creg take care of Chloe."

My eyes widened in surprise. "Oh, no, it's alright, really."

"Please, I insist."

I bowed my head in defeat. "Oh, alright... I suppose I could rest a spell."

Frank kindly guided me across the room to the couch, and sat me down. He gave a respectful nod as he took the medical kit before departing, leaving me to reflect on tonight's events. After all that had happened, I couldn't help but feel guilty for not doing more to prevent this outcome. Yes, everyone made it out alive, but Chloe had gotten hurt, and...

I closed my eyes, and leaned back into the couch. No, not everyone made it out. The bodies littering the ground outside my home were only the remains of once thriving lives within these woods. Though, technically, they were already dead...

"I can't leave them that way," I told myself. "Perhaps the boys can help me lay their bodies to rest." I gave a huff, and slapped my hands against the cushions. "No more time to wallow in self-pity. There's too much to be done before the next sunrise. Boys!"

Creg poked his head out of the doorway. "Yes, Miss Felan?"

I gave him a stern eye. "After I take some time to rest, I'm gonna need your help with some digging. We got some bodies to bury."

Creg's eyes widened in surprise.

"The Lurkers," I clarified. "We need to bury their bodies."

He opened his mouth to say something, but closed it again, as his face twisted in confusion.

"Just trust me on this, okay?"

Creg didn't argue, and instead gave a silent nod, before retreating back into the bedroom.

Frank&Creg

"Hey, Felan just told me she's gonna need our help to bury the Lurker bodies." Creg stepped into the room with his arms crossed. "How are you doing, Chloe?"

Chloe propped herself up on her elbows. "I'm doing okay... Ow." She uttered a hiss through her teeth. "Ngh..."

"Sorry," Frank whispered gently. He was busy applying a bandage to Chloe's wound.

"Anyways, she asked Frank and me to help her with that. Not sure why, though. The bodies burn up in the sun. Why not wait until then?"

"Because they can't find peace otherwise," Chloe explained. She grunted, as she threw her head back. "Ah, easy there, Frank."

"God, they really did a number on you, huh?" Frank beckoned me over. "Dude, she's bruised real bad." He lifted the loose bandage to reveal the dark, swollen welt in her stomach. "You think she needs a doctor?"

"No, she should be okay." Creg came over to sit beside her. "Chloe, how is your pain? Can you give a scale of one to ten?"

Chloe shrugged. "It's about a seven I think." She blew air from her lips. "It works fast. Should be better by morning." She rested the back of her hand to her forehead. "God, it was awful. I couldn't comprehend what was happening. I had the Lurker, but then, it threw me down... All of a sudden, I felt this tingling in my arms and legs. I could still kinda move, but I'd lost complete control of my limbs. And then, that Lurker was holding me up by my arms, and that vine struck my gut and..." Her face fell into a deep frown. "It was filling my stomach with something... I was literally drowning."

"Wait, you *lost control* of your limbs?" Frank gawked at her. "What the hell does that mean?"

"It means what it means," Chloe stated firmly. "I couldn't move. I don't know why." Her brow furrowed deeper. "Though, I wonder..."

"What is it?" Creg asked her.

Chloe's hand fell from her head to the bed, her eyes to the ceiling. "The paper lanterns... When they were taken down, I knew right away that the Lurkers couldn't have touched them, but after some quick brainstorming with Mom..."

"You think Grace might've done it, don't you?" Creg guessed.

Chloe nodded silently. "I mean, she took off into the woods, but... She... She is a Husk, after all..." She eyed Frank and Creg. "You two... You couldn't have..."

"Don't even think about it," Frank warned. "Creg and I would never."

"You can't blame her for being suspicious," Creg pointed out. "We were with Grace when Chloe went inside."

"Okay, but still..." Frank gave his partner a pleading look. "We don't know for sure that Grace did this. Maybe the Lurkers somehow found a way to tear them down."

Creg's mouth fell open in shock. *You gotta be kidding me, man! She attacked you! Remember?*

Yes, but that was because of Chloe! Frank glared at her. "She said that Chloe turned her back on her and Sarah."

Chloe kneaded her lips together, a look of frustration on her face.

"We heard everything," Frank went on. "And you still haven't shared with us the whole truth..." His eyes narrowed. "Grace was trapped there for years... She said you left her there."

"Frank." Creg reached a hand over to his partner's shoulder. "Take it easy."

"You only got half of the story," Chloe stated under her breath. "You don't know the other..."

Frank shot up from the bed. "Then tell us!" he exclaimed. "Tell us!"

Chloe and Creg both jumped from the sudden rise of volume in Frank's voice.

"Tell us what happened, Chloe!" Frank demanded again. "I wanna know!" He pointed at himself. "She was our friend, more so mine that Creg's, but still a friend!"

Chloe propped herself up on her elbows with a fiery glare. "It's not my fault! I was a child! Innocent and confused!"

Frank's nostrils flared as his eyes glowed silver, his face red with rage. "How do I know you're telling the truth? Huh?"

"Frank! That's enough!" Creg growled. "Knock it off."

Frank whirled on his partner next. "Oh! Right, I forgot, you two been gettin' cozy these last couple days. Wonder how Monique would feel about that?"

Boiling anger ruptured Creg's mind, but he bit back a regretful response, and opted for a better one instead. "Frank... I think you need to take a chill pill. Go step outside, and calm yourself down."

"Why, so you can continue your cuddle session?"

"God, you never stop!" Chloe snapped. "Ever since you met me, you've done nothing but expect the absolute worst of me!" She sat herself up. "You need more than a chill pill. You need the whole fucking artic to extinguish that fiery temper of yours!"

"Chloe, settle down!" Creg demanded, as he pressed his hands to her shoulders. "You need to rest."

"Ugh... Aaaaaah!" Frank clawed at his head, and stormed out of the room.

Creg watched him go, then turned to Chloe again. "Lie down and rest."

Chloe looked ready to argue, but changed her mind at the sight of Creg's stern silver eyes.

"God..." Creg plopped down on the bed, beside her. "I'm going to fix your bandage here, and then I'm going after fucking Frank," he muttered. "Don't you dare try to move. You are hurt, and need to rest."

Chloe winced against the pain of Creg's palms pressing the bandage down. "Ah, ow."

"Sorry," he mumbled, and lightened the pressure.

"It's okay," she whispered.

Creg muttered a curse under his breath when he was finished. "Okay... Now to go find Frank." He ran back to the living room, where he about bumped into Felan.

"Oh! Creg!" Felan stumbled back a step, eyes wide. "Oh, um, is everything okay? I heard you all yelling."

"Oh yes, everything is fine," he said hurriedly. "I, uh, gotta go. Frank ran off, and I gotta catch him."

He left Felan standing there questioningly, as he swung open the door, and darted out. His shoes pounded the steps, three at a time, and hit the ground running when he reached it. He could see Frank stomping ahead, and raced to catch up with him.

"Frank! Wait!" Creg reached out to grab his partner, who quickly whirled around on him with an angry snarl.

"Look, I get it, you and her are friends. I'm not jealous of that!" Frank jabbed a finger in his partner's face. "But I am not going to sit here, and let that woman badmouth Grace. I know she's not that bad, I know she's not!"

Creg clutched at his shoulders, and stared him square in the face. "Frank, listen to me. After what happened earlier, I really don't think she's trustworthy. As for you, you have *got* to learn to control that *fucking* temper of yours. Flying off the handle like that was inexcusable, and downright childish, and you know it."

Frank curled his lip. "Grace needs our help," he growled through his teeth. "We can't abandon her."

"What other fucking choice do we have?" Creg motioned to the trees around them. "You wanna look for her out here in these fucking woods!? Be my guest! But I'm telling you right now, that damn forest goddess said that we have to trust Chloe, and I do!"

"But Grace was trapped there at that damn hag's place of residence, and she—"

"Grace could've fed us what we wanted to hear!" Creg retaliated.

Frank smeared his hands over his face, then waved them at either side of his head. "You know what? I'm tired, I almost died today. I need to go home and see my wife, and get some fucking sleep."

"Oh, so *now* you listen!" Creg slapped at his sides. "*Now* you take the fucking advice I've been encouraging you to follow for quite some time."

Frank opened his mouth to say something else, but closed it when he felt a vibration in his pocket and retrieved his phone from it.

"Hey, I'm not done talking to you!" Creg snapped.

Frank put up a finger. "It's fucking Martin, shut up!" He put the phone to his ear. "Hello? Yeah, it's me."

Creg impatiently tapped a toe against the ground, his hands planted to his sides.

"Uh-huh... Yeah..." Frank's angry expression fell into a blank stare. "You sure?"

"What is it?" Creg muttered.

"Hang on." Frank put his fingers over the phone's mic and gave Creg a horrified look. "Martin says he was examining Georgia's body... He said her corpse was full of dirt, no organs."

Creg's stomach dropped, and a chill coursed down his spine. "Wh-What do you mean?"

"I'm saying that it happened, just like before..." Through the darkness, Creg witnessed Frank's face pale. "Creg, she underwent the transformation."

CHAPTER 23

I HAD NO CLUE what started the mess of things. All I knew was that Chloe and the detectives had gotten into a fight, and when I went to ask her about it, Chloe went into hysterics that took several minutes to settle. Thus, to soothe my frayed nerves, sipping a piping hot cup of tea was in order.

"Damn it," I muttered under my breath. "Damn it all…"

The Lurker corpses were still lying about the clearing, and now that the detectives were gone, I had no way of burying them. I could only hope that the rotting smell wouldn't knock me out, or that I wouldn't be haunted by their spirits, if they were even still there… Deep down, I knew the latter wouldn't be the case, as they were now free of their pain, but I wouldn't have blamed them if they did.

"Mom?"

My eyes lit up at the sound of Chloe's calm tone, and from my rocking chair, I peered over my shoulder. "Oh, there you are! How was your shower?"

Chloe slipped out onto the deck in a fresh sweater and pants with socks. "I'm good. You?"

"Fine," I told her, and flexed my knuckles. I bit back a curse when I felt them pop. "Just…" I worried at my bottom lip, as the searing pain carried down to my fingertips. "I'm just a little tired, but alright."

Chloe nodded, and looked down at her sweater. "Man, I'm really glad I didn't stop you from storing 'backup clothes'. I know I said that it felt weird, because I'm an adult now, but it's nice to always have a mom who looks out for ya."

I gave her a sly smile. "And now that you've admitted it, I won't ever let you forget it."

With an amused laugh, she shook her head. "Geez…"

My face fell into a frown. "Chloe… You wanna tell me what happened back there, with the two men?"

Chloe's eyes darted to their corners. "It was nothing. Frank got mad because I suspected that Grace may have had something to do with sabotaging the paper lanterns."

"Would you like me to make you some tea?" I offered. "It's helped me calm down."

"No," she mumbled. "Just... Hmm?" Chloe slipped a hand into her pants pocket, and pulled out her phone. "Huh, I got a text from Creg. He said that the body examiner at the station called them." Chloe gave me a stern look. "They looked over Georgia's body."

"Georgia?" I asked, confused.

"Yeah, don't you remember? She died."

"I must've forgotten," I said, and rubbed at my temple. "Oh, it's been a time." I eyed her stomach. "How's your tummy doing?"

"It's bruised, but fine." Chloe gingerly stroked some of her damp hair behind her ear, eyes still averting my gaze.

"Chloe, please don't hide your thoughts from me, okay? I promise you, I'm not going to blow up like that hot-headed detective did."

She sighed. "I... I was just thinking about the Lurkers," she said hurriedly. "The fact that they were elders. Makes me wonder why they'd be tossed out like that, and then there's the whole thing with Grace, and Olmond..." Chloe buried her eyes in her free hand. "Mom... So much happened at once."

"Olmond..." I stroked my chin while pondering this change of subject. "You said that Lurker brought up Maura, Olva, and Cree."

She bowed her head, and I gave a tired sigh.

"If it really was Olmond, then..." I shook my head. "Based upon your reaction, I'm sure you somewhat remember them. They were one of the few that Fenris met, and came to know very well. They had a family. Maura was Olmond's partner, and Olva and Cree were their children. Olmond was the only one of the four who survived, when the curse fell upon this forest..." I frowned. "Tell me, did you see their heart beating?"

Chloe shrugged. "I honestly don't recall, Mom. It all happened so fast, it's a blur."

"I see..."

The fact that at least one of them tried to remain as they were, *if* their heart was still beating, indicating that they were still alive... But why at that moment? None of the others acted that way, so why would one reveal themself now? Were they hiding from Ashen? Was their spirit strong enough to stay intact?

Chloe looked down at her phone again, and muttered a curse under her breath.

"What is it?" I asked.

Chloe silently shoved the phone in my face, and I squinted from the blinding light.

"Chloe, please!" I leaned back in my rocking chair. "Just tell me what the man said."

She lowered the phone, and sucked in a shaky breath. "C-Creg said... He said..." A terrified expression surfaced to her face. "He said that Georgia's corpse... was full of dirt..."

My eyes widened. "Wh-What?"

Chloe inhaled deeply, then calmly exhaled. "You heard me... Her corpse had *no organs* in it." She shuddered, and turned her back to me. "I have to get back home... I'll call you as soon as I get any more updates."

"Chloe, wait!" I pleaded. "Hang on now!"

"Hey! You guys still here?" Creg's voice suddenly resounded throughout the cabin. "Chloe? Felan?"

"We're here!" I shouted. "Just hang on!"

Chloe

My throbbing stomach was flipping about like a fish out of water. I wanted to run to the bathroom and throw up, but I knew nothing would come of it, so I was stuck struggling with the torturous nausea, as Mom and I greeted the detectives in the living room. As soon as Frank and I locked eyes, I immediately cowered behind her.

"I'm so sorry," Creg said, "but it's important we talk."

"No, no! It's fine!" Mom waved a carefree hand. "Chloe said that you'd texted her."

"Yeah, I did." Creg rubbed at the back of his head. "Ugh, it's about Georgia…"

"Her corpse was… chock full of earth," I uttered timidly.

"Yeah, it was…" Creg shot Frank a dirty look. "Before we continue, though, I think Frank owes you an apology."

Frank bowed his head. "I'm sorry," he muttered.

I winced at the cutting edge to his voice, as it sliced through my anxiety like a knife to flesh.

"Creg, why don't we let these two talk things out in the kitchen?" Mom piped up. She glanced over at me, and my face paled.

"You know, that's a great idea," Creg said.

Frank gave him the nastiest glare that, if possible, would've killed his partner on the spot.

"Chloe?" Mom's amber eyes bore deep into my conscience as she stared me down.

Accepting my dreaded fate, since I was smart enough not to engage in a losing argument with her, I motioned to the hall behind me. "F-Frank," I stammered, "shall we?"

Frank stiffly nodded, and with clear discontent, squared his shoulders as he strode forward.

I felt his brooding stare scorching my back the entire way, and I waited for flames to ignite. Since they never came, I figured that Husks didn't have that power. Nonetheless, I was set on edge, due to the power I knew he was capable of wielding. Plus, he had a gun…

"I'm not gonna shoot you, if that's what you're worried about," Frank sneered, as if he secretly could read my mind.

My eyes darted to the right, as he came around me. "Still, I want you to put it on the counter, away from us."

"Fine." Frank begrudgingly removed his weapon from its holster, and went over to the counter, where he slammed it down. "Better?"

"Yes," I said quietly, and stiffly seated myself.

Frank followed suit across from me. "Well, I'm not gonna beat around the bush. Georgia underwent the transformation."

"Transformation?"

Frank crossed his arms over his chest. "We're called Husks for a reason. Remember when we told you that Husks needed water to survive on? Though we can suffer starvation, we won't die of it."

That fuzzy feeling in my brain had returned again, and my brow furrowed. "She... She is..."

"I take it you're having trouble understanding that she's a Husk. It's understandable, why that is. In fact, Creg and I were actually curious to know whether you were aware or not, and as it turns out, you weren't." Frank crossed his arms over his chest. "She can easily manipulate people, as that's her main power, which is why the town hasn't done jack-shit about her or her niece."

My eyes widened at the mention of Caroline. "Wait... Caroline..."

"Yeah, I told you, she's a Husk, and so is Georgia."

Right then, at his words, the mental fog in my mind had cleared just enough, and the missing puzzle pieces finally came together. All this time, I had a gut feeling that something wasn't right about Caroline, but Georgia was harder to figure out. Now that I knew, for sure, it all made sense.

"I'm well aware that she forged those photos of supposed 'cult happenings'," Frank went on. "I don't know if you've heard, but she also pulled the same trick on a billionaire she'd killed. He found out she was stealin' cash from him, because he was immune to her magic, so she made his death look like a suicide."

"I remember that story," I said, as my face paled. "That poor man was found hanging outside of his hotel window, the curtain wound tight around his neck..."

"You don't seem like you're completely immune, but you are enough," Frank observed. "And since I've told you, your resistance is growing stronger, because I am a fellow Husk whose word you trust." He raised a suspecting brow. "At least, I hope that is still the case."

"Y-Yeah..." I gave a slow nod. "So then... If she really is... one of you, then...?" I cocked my head. "What exactly happened to her? If she didn't actually die?"

Frank kneaded his fingers into his temples, and he sighed. "Well, you already know that we need water to survive. But we also need to eat, like normal humans, so we have energy. See, we... Hah, god... We have a weird system in our bodies. To put it bluntly, we're walking sacks of fertilizer."

I tried to picture one of those anatomical models medical experts used in my head, but in place of the plastic organs, there were vines and dirt. It was a strange image.

"What I mean by that is, we don't have human organs in our bodies. At least, not anymore. The food we eat, it's absorbed into our systems, much like water is into our hearts."

"Okay, I follow you so far."

"Well, that being said, food plays into the most important part of being a Husk," Frank explained. "It's the magic part. Food gives us energy to use our powers, which we're supposed to channel, and help grow, so that the transformation phase is a success."

"And since you're..." My brow furrowed. "... walking fertilizer sacks... I'm guessing that's why you're so thirsty?"

"Yes." His eyes wandered to the ceiling. "Creg and I, we witnessed our first transformation many years ago. It'd been a couple weeks since Grace had vanished with that little girl, and we couldn't stop thinking about what she'd told us, how they were doing things in there..." His eyes flickered to the table, and his stone-hard glare softened some. "That's why I got so up in arms about Grace, because she told us, that night she escaped, that she was trapped there for years."

Guilt seeped into my heart, and I had to fight back tears. "Frank, I..."

"I wanted to investigate, and since Creg didn't want me going alone, we decided to infiltrate the shelter together."

I nervously shuffled in my seat. "How did you get in so easily?"

Instead of answering my question, he gave a different response. "While under their control, Ashen could easily enter our thoughts, with or without our knowledge, as well as track each and every one of us, the same way we could track each other."

"And that's how you knew Grace was there?" I guessed.

His steely gaze softened further. "Yes... You see, Grace was a dear friend, more so to me since Creg kept his distance, though there were times when all three of us were together. And Sarah... was kinda like a second mother to us." He lowered his head. "Ya know, I sometimes wished she was my mother…"

I held back a sob at those words. *She was like a second mother to me, too.*

Frank cocked a curious brow. "You knew her well, right?"

"When she first met me, it was a little cold outside," I murmured. "She gave me her sweater, so I'd stay warm… As a 'thank you', Mom crafted a little pouch that I gave to her a few days later, when I returned the sweater…"

The memory of when Sarah and I first met played fresh in my mind, like it had happened yesterday. It was in the midst of autumn, and I'd wandered out with no shoes on. The cold nipped at my toes, but it wasn't so bad. It actually felt kind of nice.

Mom had warned me to stay away from the border of the trees, but I wanted to know where that beautiful singing came from. She had a gentle voice, soft like silk. And when she spotted me, instead of running away, I'd told her how pretty her singing was.

Oh, you poor dear! You have no shoes on, or a jacket! And you're out here in the cold! Here, you can have this!

I didn't get to talk with her long, as Fenris had come looking for me. But she was so nice, and so was her sweater. It was pink, with a pattern of little white flowers. And underneath her sleeves were thin silver bracelets around her wrists, a beautiful heart-shaped locket around her neck.

If I recall correctly, it was green, with a golden trim. I closed my eyes. "She always wore that locket. I mean, she had other necklaces, but she always wore that one. Sometimes, she'd be wearing a ring or two."

Frank gave a strained chuckle. "She was like a princess with her necklaces and rings, and she always wore those pretty little earrings. You could barely see them, because they were small, but when the sun hit them, they sparkled."

I opened my eyes to the detective again. "A kindhearted princess… When I was growing up, I read stories about them, though most times they required rescuing."

He snorted. "Mmm, I'm sorry for straying off topic.."

I shook my head. "It's okay, go on... About the shelter..." As much as I wanted to reminisce about Sarah, it was far too painful, and I had to know more about this "transformation" business, as it involved Georgia.

"Right. Getting back to where we were, Creg and I were curious to see what was going on in the shelter," Frank continued, "so we snuck out at night. It took us some time, when we got there, but we managed to find an unlocked door at the back of the building. Again, Ashen had to have known we were coming..."

I gave a meek nod.

"Anyway, so there we were, traversing the dark halls. It was deathly silent. You could hear a pin drop. That is, until we rounded one corner, and heard it." His face went blank. "The scream was so loud that it would've made our ears bleed, had we still been normal humans, like you. Anyways, once we recovered from the shock, we continued on, until we found another door cracked open. We crept over to it, curious as to what was going on." His expression fell back into a hard frown, and he pressed a knuckle against his mouth.

"Frank?" I leaned forward in my seat, concerned.

He lowered his head, as his fist fell to the table, his expression unchanged. "The sight was frightening. There was a man there, a Husk... He was covered in what looked like welts, maybe blisters or boils... And, he just..." Frank's stern eyes met mine. "He was screaming so loud. Creg and I jumped when we heard him hit the concrete, but we dared not move. And then..." His hands began to shiver upon the table. "The nasty bumps on his body burst open, and dirt seeped out of them. Black tendrils tore through his torso and stomach. It was like something out of a horror movie, and it scared the shit outta both me and my partner."

I shivered. "I-I can imagine."

"You don't want to," Frank warned. "It was a god awful sight."

"Did you know this man?"

"I did not, and neither did Creg. We always kept to ourselves, as Ashen only ever told us to confide in each other anytime we felt lonely or bored, and that was fine, because we liked being together." His face paled. "That night, when we watched that man go through his transformation, I mean to tell you, we were screaming at each other's minds to move.

But it was like we couldn't hear anything. We were both paralyzed with fear."

My heart pounded in my chest, as my mind conjured a makeshift image of what they saw, and my stomach twisted in knots.

"We didn't quite understand what was happening, until another being crawled out of him. His skin was a light silver, but his short dark hair had remained unchanged. However, when he peered over his shoulder, we saw his empty black eyes, and that crooked grin..." Frank's quivering hands pressed to his face.

"Frank?" I whispered to him. "Frank."

He dropped his hands in his lap. "It was like the devil my bible-thumpin' parents feared was looking straight into our souls, and I am not kidding when I say that we ran outta there like bats outta hell." He stifled a shaky breath. "It was horrifying..."

I sat back in my chair, my arms hanging at my sides. *That shelter is the root of evil, and it's claimed the forest.* I bit my lip. *How are we going to stop it?*

"Creg and I vowed never to go anywhere near there again," Frank went on. "And for years, we feared either that man, or Ashen, would come for us, and soon after, our families as well..."

Silence drifted between us for the next couple minutes, so I processed everything he'd said during this time. Once I was finished, I gave an understanding nod, before continuing our conversation.

"So, to recap, you spent most, if not all, of your time with each other, whether together or apart. Grace was there for a short time when you were kids, but then she disappeared for several years. When she came back, she'd had Sophia with her, and the following morning, they both vanished. You were still curious about where she'd come from, so you ventured to the shelter, and that's when you discovered what you both truly were."

"That is all correct," he murmured.

"And for years after, you feared for your lives, because you weren't sure if the same fate awaited you." I cocked my head. "Because you were under Ashen's control, I'm guessing that you joined the force because it was the best way to keep up your roles as Ashen's personal spies?"

"Ashen seemed pleased with us when we enrolled," Frank said. "If it meant keeping us alive, then we'd do so." His shoulders relaxed a little, and his smile faintly returned. "Creg and I did manage to find some solace though. I met Cathy, and he'd found Monique. They're humans, and very kind ones... For instance, my wife, Cathy. She taught me things Creg couldn't, the biggest lesson being how to trust others. Creg had always been the one to stand by me, to be the one I could go to when I was scared, but I'd trusted him all my life. Since Cathy was an outsider, I had a better time learning."

"Reminds me of Benjamin," I said. "I always trusted Felan, since she raised me as her own, but Ben always proved to be a good listener when she wasn't around. He handled my heart with great care."

"That's how I feel with Cathy, ya know. She just makes my day brighter, and I don't want to lose that..." Frank snorted. "Hell, even the forest goddess is someone I've learned to trust. When she first came to us, she told us that we'd be okay. Turns out she was right."

"You know, it doesn't hurt to trust others." I glowered at him. "It also doesn't hurt to *not* jump down someone's throat the moment they look at you the wrong way."

"Creg's told me that, many times." Frank sighed. "Well, to conclude this long haul of a story, we got more involved with the forest when a case was presented to us a few months ago. A woman, residing at the shelter, had taken a random boy hostage." He blew air from his lips, as he pinched the bridge of his nose. "Unfortunately, I had to shoot her, because if I didn't, then the boy would've died. And at the same time this went down, a younger girl went fleeing into the trees."

"Who?"

"Alicia Morgan."

I felt a chill rattle my spine. "Alicia... Morgan?"

"Yeah, Alicia Morgan," Frank said again, suspicion taking hold of his face once more. "You know her?"

"Yeah..." I squirmed in my seat, as nausea settled in the pit of my stomach. "She's a Vessel."

Frank's eyes widened. "She is?"

"Y-Yes," I whispered.

"How did she wind up there?" Frank shot up from his seat, his palms pressed to the table. "Does Miss Sally know she's a Vessel? And if so, what about Rosella?"

My eyes darted to their corners. "I'm sure she does. Why else would she be keeping Rosella there?"

"Then, how come you willingly went there?"

My shoulders went stiff, and I felt hairs rise on the back of my neck.

"Chloe..."

"What went down with the body examiner?" I asked, dodging his question.

"Creg and I had to silence our shock," Frank answered, "so as not to alert the body examiner to our knowledge."

I dared a glance back in his direction. "And... that's it?"

His eyes narrowed. "Chloe, I know you're scared, but you promised..."

Frank

The entire time I'd sat there with Chloe, she listened to everything I had to say, and I held my temper. I even began to feel horrible for lashing out at her earlier on, but in my defense, things were tense. We'd just fought off a bunch of those damn tree monsters, and my fucking back was killing me at that time. I was fine now, since we recover quickly, but...

We sat there in strained silence, and I was gradually losing my patience once again. Creg had told me not to push her, but I needed to know. We held up our end of the bargain, so it was time she held up hers.

"Look, you asked us to trust you, and we are." I crossed my arms over my chest. "If you can't be honest with us, then..." I fell silent when she uttered a sob.

"I don't... I don't want..."

My brow furrowed deeper. *What doesn't she want? To be honest?*

"I was so stupid. I just wanted to help her." Tears spilled out of her empty brown eyes as she inhaled a quivering gust of air with trembling lips. "B-Ben... He... Oh god." She grabbed at a tuft of hair at either side of her head as she began to rock in her seat. "I-It's my fault... It's my fault. It's all my fault."

"Chloe... Chloe, listen to me." I grabbed her shoulders. "Hey."

"I couldn't save her," she whispered. "I couldn't save her."

"Chloe."

"Oh god!"

I jolted in surprise when she abruptly clutched at my arms, and I staggered back a step, as Chloe slid out of her chair and sunk to the floor. I knelt down with her, as she buried her face in my chest.

"Oh god... Ali..." She whimpered into my shirt. "I'm... sorry..."

"H-Hey." Overwhelmed, I began to panic. *Shit! The hell did I do!?*

Chloe released a pained sob. "I'm so sorry! I'm so sorry! I'm so sorry!"

Regret weighed me down just as much as this woman wallowing in my arms. Fuck, why wasn't Creg with me? Usually, I wasn't that big of a moron with him around. Now, I'd really fucked up, and I had no clue to fix my mistake.

"Chloe, Chloe!" I attempted to gently pull her off of me, but that only made her burrow deeper into my torso. "Shit... Chloe." I tried again, this time with a firmer grip on her arms, and with much force, managed to rip her off of me.

Chloe sat upon her knees, a sobbing mess of sweat and tears, like a helpless child being scolded for drawing on the walls.

"Chloe... I'm sorry," I told her. "I'm so sorry."

She continued to cry, as she buried the heels of her palms in her red-rimmed eyes.

"Hey, take a minute to calm down. Come on..." I slipped a hand behind her back, and rubbed soft circles into it. "Come on now... Ssssshh... It's okay."

Under the comfort of my gentle tone, her relentless sobbing gradually dwindled to pitiful whimpers, then went completely silent.

"Chloe... I..." Defeated, I gave a sigh. "Why don't you get some rest, okay?"

Chloe didn't acknowledge me.

"Get some rest, don't worry about anything else for the time being."

"Hey, Frank."

My blood ran cold as Creg strode up behind me. "Y-Yeah?"

"Let's get her home. After that, we need to talk."

The sharp tone in his voice struck me like my father's belt to my back, but I didn't argue.

Felan didn't say a word as the three of us exited the kitchen together. As we passed her by, I noticed the worried expression she shared with Creg and Chloe, but when she looked at me, it hardened into a disappointed frown. I couldn't blame the old woman for thinking so badly of me, so I didn't.

"You all get home safe," Felan called, albeit begrudgingly toward me. "Call me when you can."

Creg

"How's Chloe doing?" Frank sheepishly asked.

"She's fine," I muttered, as I stepped out onto the back porch with him. "Got her settled in the living room. She says she needs a minute before she heads to bed." I gave him a threatening scowl. "The fuck is wrong with you, man? We sent you in there to work things out with her, not tear her further down."

"I wasn't trying to," Frank explained. "I was actually on the right track, but then—"

"'But' nothing! Frank, I've had it up to here!" I emphasized my words with my palm facing the ground, as I held it near my neck. "Seriously! You have got to stop."

"I know! I know..." Frank put his hands up in surrender. "I fucked up, I get it. I'm sorry."

"You fucked up more times than I care to count," I snapped. "I can't keep this up." My grey eyes softened. "Look... I understand that you got some personal issues to work out, but you've gone too far with this shit. I get that you're worried about Grace, and those other girls, but you have *got* to learn to work with others!" I motioned toward the trees beyond the backyard. "The fucking shit we saw tonight!? That should've proved to you that we need to work together. So you got a choice to make here. You either drop this vengeful pissing on Chloe and put yourself in check, or you can just go home and let me take care of this shit by myself."

"You and me make the team!" Frank argued. "Remember?"

"Are we still a team?"

"Yes. We are..."

I hung my head, arms limp at my sides. "God... I'm so fucking tired." And that certainly was the truth. I was so fucking tired that I considered saying to Frank, "Nighty night," and just dropping right there.

"Look, I know that my temper gets the best of me sometimes," Frank proceeded slowly. "And I'm really sorry about that. I don't want to lose this case, and I certainly don't want to lose you."

I looked up, and through the tears clouding his blue eyes, I found that frightened little boy curled up tight against the tree all those years ago.

"Please... Don't leave me."

My heart broke at those words, those same words he spoke to me that day, when my mother had called me home for dinner, a plea of protection from the ferocious beasts he called parents. They were the proclamation that firmly attached him to me ever since.

And I'm not leaving you for that reason, I told him with a silent, but stern gaze. *I would never do that to you. Just... Go home and get some rest, come back tomorrow with a cool head, and help me figure this out.*

Frank gave a stiff nod. "I understand," he whispered. "I do..."

"Then go for it." With a turn of my heel, I proceeded toward the back door of the house. "I told Chloe that I'd stay with her a bit longer." I rested my hand on the handle of the door, and peered over my shoulder. "I'll see you in the..." My words trailed off, my focus now on the dark figure that suddenly shot out from the side of the house.

Frank whirled around when he heard the grass crunching behind him. "The hell is... Hey!"

The figure stopped at Frank's call, their back to us.

"Hey, you!" Frank ran after the stranger, while I hung back.

The figure slowly turned around, once Frank was within close range, and to both our shock...

"Marcus Thompson?" I breathed.

Sure enough, it was the boy whom we'd talked to that day in the school library. I recognized his sandy blonde hair and olive-green eyes.

"Hey!" Frank called. "You wanna—Aaaah!"

Before he could react, Marcus had grabbed Frank, and then his teeth were sinking deep into his arm.

Frank thrashed about in the boy's grip, and he whipped his head over his shoulder. "Help me!"

I shot from the back porch after him. "Shit!"

Marcus suddenly shoved Frank backwards, sending him pummeling into me. We both tumbled to the ground, spitting curses.

"Guys!?" Chloe's voice rang out behind us. "Oh my god!" She came running over to help us, as Marcus made a beeline for the trees.

"Ah... God..." I scrambled to my feet, my body racked with pain. "That kid... He..." I watched his fleeing form disappear into the darkness of the woods. "Holy shit..." I wiped the beads of sweat from my forehead, then looked to Frank, who was now cradling his injured arm with the other. "You alright!?"

Frank gritted his teeth and screwed his eyes shut. "Ngh... Guh..."

"Let's get him inside!" Chloe slipped her arms under Frank's, and lifted him to his feet. "Come on, it's okay!"

"Ah... I'll be... alright," he grunted. "I just need to... Ah... F-Fuck... Little bastard sunk his teeth so far in... like a fucking vampire."

Chloe and Frank proceeded back to the house together, while I lingered in the backyard. My eyes darted in all directions, as I sought out any other signs of suspicious activity, my vision enhanced through magic. The world drained of color around me, my arsenal of attacks at the ready, should anything pop out at me.

The hell was that? I thought to myself. *Damn kid came at him like a maniac.*

Still on edge, my nerves crawling with anticipation, I braced myself for the next several minutes. I jumped at every brush of air against my neck, the slightest crunch of grass. But there was no one else around. It was just me, and the gentle chirping of crickets, or grasshoppers, or something.

"Creg!"

I turned around to face Chloe, who came rushing out to me.

"Frank's okay. Are you alright?" She scanned me over. "You don't look hurt." Her gaze locked with mine, and then a frightened look sprung to her face.

"It's okay," I told her calmly, as my vision regained color. "I just wanted to make sure I was prepared."

Chloe nodded hesitantly, and looked back to the house. "Frank... Frank said that it was okay, that he could heal on his own. He won't let me help him. He said... He said that..." Her words were brittle with sadness. "He said that he didn't deserve my help."

Fucking Frank... I groaned. "Just... Just... Ugh." I stormed around her. "I'll go check on him, see if he actually needs help. Come on."

Chloe followed me up to the house, but then paused at the back porch. I peered over my shoulder, beckoning her to follow me, but she shook her head. Too tired to argue, I went back in by myself, and found Frank seated at the kitchen table with his head bowed.

"Dude, let her look at your arm," I muttered. "I'm sure it's fine."

"I couldn't ask her to do that, not after the way I've treated her," Frank mumbled. "It's fine, it's not bad." He showed me his injury. Truth be told, it was a small bite, but instead of blood seeping out, it was soil. "Besides, I don't think she's mentally prepared for any more surprises."

"God, Frank..." I plopped into the seat across from him. "We sure are a group, aren't we?"

"Yeah we are." His head raised upon Chloe's cautious entry. "Hey."

Chloe's fingers were wiggling nervously at either side of her, tension gripping her shoulders tight.

"Are you alright?" Frank asked calmly. "You're not hurt, are you?"

"N-No, I'm not," Chloe mumbled.

"Thank god." Frank threw his head back. "Man..."

I kneaded my fingertips into my forehead, my elbows propped upon the table. "Okay, so what now? We can't just go running in there. It's too dangerous, but if we don't, then that kid could get himself killed."

"I don't think we should go after him."

My eyes darted in Frank's direction. "Why not?"

A troubled frown settled on his face. "I just don't think it's a good idea. Something was really off with him."

"You mean, besides the fact that he *bit* you?" Chloe chimed in.

He nodded to her. "Besides that. I mean, I sensed something about him." Frank's gaze fell to the floor. "I don't understand what it was... It just... felt strange."

Chloe cocked a brow. "Strange..."

"Yeah... It was like something had a hold of him, but no one was there." He stroked his chin. "I can't figure it out."

Chloe turned around, her back now to us. "God, Rosella..."

I shuddered. *Her child is out there, just like mine, and like Chloe, I won't ever get to see my girl again. Because Ivy is a Vessel...*

I was terrified for Ivy. Knowing she was out there, with those things, and whatever else existed, it rattled me with fear. And knowing that I'd never see her again, it only made the pain worse. However, I wasn't alone, since Chloe was in the same corner as me.

Not that I ever felt alone to begin with, because I've always had Frank. We make the team, and that's—

"Chloe." Frank disrupted my thoughts, as well as grabbed Chloe's attention. "I know we got off on the wrong foot, and that's my fault." He gave her an apologetic look. "I'm truly sorry, really... I'm sure you got a lot on your plate, so until you're ready to tell us everything, I'll patiently wait for it." He then glanced my way. "He and I always say we are the only ones needed to make the team..."

My eyebrows rose with curiosity. *Where you goin' with this, man?*

He sighed. "When Grace and I first met, I quickly became attached to her, because she was like us. I felt I could trust her. And like you, Sarah meant a lot to me, so much so that I felt a maternal attachment to her. But then, Sarah and Grace both vanished from my life, and Creg was all I had left, for many years to come." His eyes flickered back to Chloe, who was listening intently. "I really want to help Grace, to regain a piece of what I've lost, and protect her. True horrors lie within that place, just like that forest."

Chloe stepped around me, and with a gentle outreach, she laid her hands atop Frank's shoulders. "I get it. Really, I do."

Frank gazed up at her. "Grace and Sarah meant the world to me, because they were vulnerable... They needed me... And though they're gone, that doesn't mean I should abandon the girls at the shelter. They need me. But they also need you and Creg."

"So what are you saying?" Chloe asked.

"Creg and me make the team... but that's not all we need..."

I did a quick sift through Frank's thoughts, suspicious of his words.

I mean what I said. He returned his gaze to me. *We can't do this without her.*

"If you really mean that..." Chloe bent over, so she was eye-level with Frank. "Then you need to promise me that."

He gave a solemn nod. "I promise."

I had to admit, I was proud of Frank for trying to ease the tension between the two of them. I could tell that Chloe was still wary of him, and he of her. But there was considerably less stress weighed upon their shoulders with this awkward truce now in place, and I took that as a win.

"We three make the team, right?" I dared ask.

Chloe and Frank looked at each other, and nodded.

"Alright." I got up from my seat, and confidently thumped my fist against my chest. "Tomorrow we start fresh. No more fighting, and no more grudges."

CHAPTER 24

F ENRIS WAS SOUND ASLEEP when I awoke sometime during the night. Despite his tail burying his muzzle, that *didn't* contain his extremely loud snoring. I tried wrapping the pillow around my head, burying myself in the sheets, even sticking my fingers in my ears. Nothing worked, so the only other option I had was to chop them off with Dad's knife, and I *definitely* wasn't doin' that.

Disgruntled, I slid out of bed. "Well, I got a nap in at least, and Fenris' finally gettin' some shut-eye himself." I tiptoed over to him, my hands on my hips. "Ya know, you're a loud snorer."

Fenris snuffed a wisp of air, but didn't stir.

"Geez." I knelt down to stroke over his twitching snout. "I'm sure you feel safer here than out there..."

"Ngh... Sa..." the snoozing wolf mumbled sleepily. "N... Pl... Sto..."

"Hey, it's okay." I patted his head. "You're alright."

"Ro... Rosella... Can't... Please..." His furry brow wrinkled, and his face scrunched with discomfort. "No... Not.... you..."

I shushed him. "Rest now, Fenris."

His face relaxed at the sound of my voice, and he returned to his relentless, god awful snoring.

Satisfied, I returned to the bed, and silently resumed my restless toss-and-turn. I writhed and twisted my limbs and back, my body contorted in different ways. In the end, nothing proved comfortable, and I caved with a curse under my breath, as I laid there stiff as a board.

It felt like an eternity, but over time Fenris' obnoxious snoring started to fade, and soon after my body relaxed...

I found myself in the empty field yet again, and like the last time, my father was missing. Though the sky had returned, the sun high in position, I expected either the ground to cave or myself to fall through it, but nothing happened, as I stepped forward.

"Rosella."

My heart skipped a beat when I heard the voice behind me, but I didn't dare turn around. What if it was a trick of my mind?

"Hey... Ro-Ro."

No one called me that except for... "D-Dad?" I peered over my shoulder, and then completely turned myself around to face him. "D-Daddy?"

Indeed, it was him, and this time he was smiling.

"Daddy!" I shot into his arms the moment he raised them, and I buried my tear-stained face into his chest. "Dad! I miss you! So much..." I paused. *This is all a dream. Any moment now, I'll wake up, and he'll be gone.* I pulled away from him, my head hung low. This was just a dream. He wasn't really here. He was gone.

"Ro-Ro?"

I didn't respond, and instead turned on my heel. But when I went to take the first step, a hand latched tightly to my wrist.

"Rosella." His voice was firm, but not aggressive. "Turn around and face me, please."

"I can't," I whispered. "You're not..." A single tear streaked the side of my face, my aching heart clenched in a painful vice of turmoil and doubt. "You're not really here. This is all just a dream. I want to wake up now."

"Rosella... Rosella, it's me. Your father."

I shook my head. "No, you're not."

"Rosella." He gave a slight tug on my arm. "Rosella, please..."

I glanced over my shoulder, and to my surprise...

"Oh, Ro-Ro." A film of tears traced the rims of his blue eyes, his mouth curved in a pained frown. "Ro-Ro."

"D-Daddy..." No, I'd never seen him cry before. Ever. He... He never cried in front of me. Sure, I'd seen him a little upset sometimes, but he'd never...

"Rosella, I'm so sorry," he uttered. "I'm so sorry, baby."

Another tear sprang to my eye.. "D-Dad."

He let go of my wrist, and again held out his arms to me. "Ro-Ro. It's me. Please... Please see that." There was a glint of urgency in his eyes, like he really was trying to convince me that this was real, that he was here, with me...

I hesitantly stepped into his embrace, my body stiff, as his arms wrapped tight around me. This... This was unbelievable. It wasn't like a phantom hugging my body. This was... a real, genuine hug.

"It's okay, honey..." He rubbed small circles into my back. "It's alright, Ro-Ro. I'm still here." His fingers, they were really there. I could feel the pressure of them against my spine. But this couldn't be real.

"No you're not..." I whimpered. "You're... You're not really here. You're just in my head..." *He can't really be here. He's dead.*

"No, Ro-Ro." He cradled my face in his hands, and gently tilted my head up, so I was facing him. "Sweetheart, it's really me." A fiery spark of determination flashed in his eyes. "It's really me."

As I stared him down, I quickly sought out any sort of trickery. But there was none. The look on his face, the tone of his voice, the glint in his eyes... "D-Dad." A sob bubbled up my throat. "D-Daddy..."

And there it was again, that comforting smile I'd longed to see just one more time, every day I woke up. "Ro-Ro."

"D... Dad!" I buried my tear-stained face into his chest "Dad! It is you! It really is! I-I don't know how, but I don't care!" My fingers hooked into his forearms. *"D-Daaaaaaaaad!!!!!"*

My father held me in his arms, in silence, and allowed me to weep in peace. He was... He was really here. And as he shushed me, and whispered soothing words of comfort, I felt blessed by his presence. My only wish now, was that Mom could be here with us...

"Ro-Ro," he cooed.

"D-Dad... I'm... I..." I couldn't think of what to say. I was still in so much shock.

"Ro-Ro, there isn't much time." He ran his fingers through my hair, a troubled expression on his face. "Listen carefully to me, okay? The voice inside your head... You need to trust it."

I frowned. How did he...?

"Trust me, honey. And I promise, you'll be alright." He cupped the side of my face, as another smile broke across his face. "I miss you so much. But I know you'll be okay. Just don't give up. And help them where you can."

"B-But... How...?" My words trailed off as he shook his head.

"Remember to stay strong, and blossom into the strongest bloom you can be." He nuzzled his forehead against mine. "I love you, Rosella."

"Daddy…" I reached up to grasp his hand, only to find it gone. I blinked, and found I was alone again. "Dad!" Panic-stricken, I sought out my father. "D-Dad!"

I didn't want him to go yet. It'd been so, so long! I wanted to sit with him. I wanted to tell him about some of the good things that'd happened, about how I'd gotten back into art, about how Fenris had come back into my life. I wanted to tell him about my experience in school, how Sophia and I had become close. I…

I didn't want him to leave me… ever again.

Rosella…

"Dad!" I raised a foot to take a step, but paused. My eyes… They were getting heavy. "N-No! No… Not… Not… yet…" I dropped to my knees against my will, and fell flat on my face, as my eyes quickly drifted shut.

Rosella… Rosella… "Rosella! Wake up!"

I shot upright with a frantic gasp, my eyes wide open. "D-Dad!"

"Rosella… Rosella? Can you hear me?"

"Dad??" I looked around me. "Look, I… Huh? Wh-Where am I now?"

"It's okay… Don't be afraid."

"Hey!" Confused anger roiled in my mind. "What the hell is this!? Huh!? Who are you, and where am I!?" My eyes darted every which way in hopes of finding either my father or Fenris. "Where am I!? What the hell is this!?"

"Goodness, such fiery temper compared to before." A voice, one that sounded oddly familiar, echoed within my surroundings. "I didn't expect this development!"

"I'm serious!" I pointed at the air. "Show yourself!"

"I can't," the unknown voice mumbled. "However, you can… Just look down."

"What?"

"You heard me."

I cocked a suspecting brow. "Look… Look down…" I did as instructed, and a look of surprise sprung to my face. "No… No way…" Eyes glued to my mirrored self, I stared into my reflection on the floor. It rippled like water, every time I maneuvered around. But what really threw me was the fact that it changed into a completely different person.

"Do you see?"

The reflection was a blur, but I saw her pink eyes, and long, pitch black hair. "What...?" *No way, I must be dreaming still... Right?* I blinked, and suddenly another girl was staring up at me, this one with long blonde hair, and dark blue eyes.

"You can see her, right?" the voice urged.

"Uh..." Dumbfounded, I stared down, still as a statue. Several moments of silence passed, as the reflection wavered, and shortly after, I was staring back at myself. "What... What was that?"

"You don't recall, do you?"

I didn't answer.

"I understand," the voice replied. "At least you're the strongest Vessel."

Vessel? What's a... Vessel?

"A wandering spirit searching for her way home," the voice proclaimed. "The blonde girl you saw is still lost, like you once were. Now that you've been found, we're one step closer to reuniting. You seem ready."

I glowered at the air with further confusion. "Show yourself to me! Who are you? Sarah maybe?"

"You're so much closer now than you ever were," the voice carried on. "Please, Rosella... don't stray from the path now. Keep going forward, and remain strong."

The dreaded weight of drowsiness settled upon my eyelids once again. "Wait... Wait, I still..."

I didn't get the chance to finish my sentence. My feet stumbled, and I fell backwards, but instead of slamming against the floor, I fell through it into a never-ending darkness. The spark of warmth I'd once experienced reignited, and I cradled my lukewarm chest, as I descended further into the darkness.

Fenris

I awakened to the birth of a new day, a blending palette of blue and green painting the sky. I glanced over at Rosella, who was sound asleep in the bed, then peered out the window to the trees.

We're so close now... too close. I stifled a whimper. "I can't let it happen again... I can't..."

At first, I thought that my nose had been warped by the stench of this dreaded house. But there was a distinct difference, between the stink of Lurker and this place. Their lair was close by, which meant that we were near the end of the forest. At least, as far as I knew, we were.

What lies beyond the end? Is it more trees in a separate area? Perhaps another town? I shook my head. *No need to be concerned about that now.*

Certain they were intimidated by our presence, I deduced that the Lurkers were waiting for the opportunity to present itself, when Rosella was alone, and I shuddered at the thought of my Little Rose held captive. I'd watched her grow so much over the years, and I cherished every ounce of the thriving connection I felt with her.

Even here.

Picking up on the scent of this house was torture. All I could think about what what happened all those years ago. But Rosella needed a safe place to hide, and exploring it with her wasn't as troubling as I'd thought, as her presence made me feel a little better.

I buried my watering eyes in my paws, and curled my tail around myself. *But I hate it here. I don't want to be here.* This house... I couldn't stop thinking about it.

Something's wrong... What is it?

I forcefully digested the remorse I felt for the traumatic events that occurred within that room.

Fenris... Your pain will only manifest into the same darkness I sense within her friend now.

"I can't... I don't..."

But you do, and denial will only make it hurt worse.

"Fenris?"

My ears perked a little at the gentle aroma of rose and clary sage grabbing my attention, and I looked up. "Little Rose..." I cleared my throat, and settled my tone. "I am sorry, did I wake you?"

"I'm alright." Rosella sat up, a questioning look to her face. "Fenris...why are you crying?"

Tragedy has cursed this place, I wanted to say.

"Fenris?"

"I'm sorry, you must be mistaken," I said instead.

Rosella shook her head. "No. I don't think I am. I sensed you were crying."

My eyes widened a little. I was astonished by her response.

"Tell me what's wrong," she urged. "Please, you can trust me."

Say something, Fenris... Please.

"It's okay, I can handle it." Rosella crawled out of the bed, and knelt to my level. "Remember, we're in this together."

I felt her comforting hand stroke my fur, and leaned into her heavenly touch.

You're not alone... I'm here...

"Fenris..." Rosella pressed her entire body into mine. "Talk to me."

My jawline wavered.

"Fenris."

Go ahead. It's okay.

Overwhelmed with pressure, my emotional turmoil overflowed. If I didn't come clean at this moment, I'd drown in it. "Rosella, Chloe and I found this place after something happened," I began, as a gut-wrenching knot tormented my stomach.

Rosella cocked her head. "What do you mean?"

I avoided her gaze. "Chloe snuck out one night, when Felan had fallen asleep, Adrienne's dagger in hand."

"Adrienne? You mean my grandmother?"

It'd been so long, yet the memory permanently scarred my mind. "Yes." I shivered. "It was a weapon she crafted, before her death. It saved Chloe's life that night…" I choked on a sob. "… Th-that night Chloe set out to free Sarah of her role as the Lurker Queen."

Rosella didn't speak a word, and patiently waited for me to continue.

"I recall picking up Chloe's scent, and then the Lurkers', but I wasn't close enough to hear anything." I paused with a shaking breath, as an image of a young girl, with long chestnut locks, trekking through the woods came to mind. "I didn't know where exactly she was going, but when I spotted her and the dagger in her hand, I knew it meant danger. Chloe traveled for a few hours, before she fell from exhaustion…" I eyed Rosella. "And that was when I made my presence known to her, for the first time."

I could easily quote the entirety of our short conversation as if it'd just happened. Chloe was absolutely terrified, pleading for her life, as I appeared before her. At the time, she didn't know much about the dangers of the forest, especially a damn pond that she once almost fell into as a toddler.

"She was a frightened child begging not to be eaten, but I reassured her. And then, the Lurkers appeared, and those nightmarish fiends scared Chloe out of her wits. So, I took them out, before they could harm her, but she ran from me." I glowered at the ceiling. "Following her lingering honeydew scent, I tried my hardest to convince her it was out of good intentions, and that was what led me into a clearing. There, Chloe had stopped dead in her tracks, because ahead of her was…" My glare softened with sorrow, as my heart sunk to the floor.

Unsurprisingly, Rosella whispered her name. "Sarah…"

"She stood before Chloe," I went on, my voice low, "but it was not the girl whom Chloe had sought after. This was a different person, a shadow of who she once was, like the Lurkers." A muffled whine curdled in my throat. "I didn't know what else to do. She was going to attack Chloe, so I…" The fur atop my back arched. "I struck the girl down when she thrust herself at Chloe. The Lurkers prepared an attack in response, but I was thankfully faster. I fled with both girls, in a blind panic, through the darkness…"

"And?" Rosella pressed gently.

"I took my chances, when I picked up this house's scent. Though the Lurkers had lost sight of us, I didn't think it was safe to just sit out in the open, and Sarah was..." Guilt pulled my head to the floor, as my mind replayed the traumatic scene. "Th-That room..."

I'd never forget Chloe's pleas, how hard she fought for this girl. And the dread-inducing bloodbath that spilled upon that bed, in *that room*... Like the dried petals of red on the sheets, my mind was permanently stained with the gut-wrenching memory.

I longed to put it all behind me. And for a time, I felt I had. Chloe and Benjamin met, and Ben turned out to be a great guy. They got married, had Rosella, and I became locked in the thought that they could all live happily together in the forest. They came to see Felan and me as much as possible, even after Rosella was born.

Until she was nine, I had to stay hidden from her, yet they still made time for me. But then, I started seeing less and less of them, because the curse had infiltrated Ben's mind and body. I wanted to leave the trees, to stand by Benjamin's side, as he wilted away inside his home, but I couldn't. Imprisoned by my duties, the trees formed a cage that I could easily slip out of, though doing so could cost me my life. But I accepted that, because I was still far from...

"This house... Being inside it is suffocating," I admitted. "I want to run from this place, and never look back. But I can't, as I'm committed to keeping you safe, as your noble wolf, and this is currently the safest place to be. No matter what, I will protect you from the evil rot that's claimed these trees, and face my past, just as bravely as you have thrown yourself out here."

"Fenris... I..."

"I couldn't protect Benjamin, my dear friend, from the curse," I murmured, "the same way I couldn't protect Sarah. When he fell ill, I wanted to be beside him. But I couldn't, and I was forced to accept that..." I glanced up at the ceiling again. "My heart, it aches within these walls, because they remind me of the pain, but I promise I can bear it."

Concern was sculpted into Rosella's face, her vibrant blue eyes wide with worry. "What... What happened to Sarah? Can you tell me?"

"Right..." I nodded slowly. "Sh-She thanked me for saving her, for relieving her of her pain. And Chloe..." I trembled, as the memory again plagued my mind. "Chloe came over, hugged me, and..." An onslaught of tears pricked the edges of my eyes. "She told me she hated herself for not being able to save her, and that she deserved to die..."

"What happened after that?" Rosella asked gently.

I exhaled a quivering breath. "I brought Chloe back to Felan the following day. Poor dear was hysterical, but thankful Chloe was alive."

Rosella hugged my neck. "Fenris... I'm so sorry... I can't imagine the pain you must've suffered."

"I suffered no pain... But Sarah and Chloe did."

"Fenris..."

Rosella

The urge to bombard Fenris with questions regarding my peculiar dream had long since dissipated, as I held him close, the bridge of his muzzle pressed to my torso. And as his silent tears dampened my shirt for several minutes, I stayed for every second. He harbored personal demons of his own, with no one to disclose them with, unlike me, as I had Sophia. However, she wasn't here with me right now. And as much as it pained me to focus on someone else, the wolf's broken heart lay shattered upon the floor, and needed someone to help piece them back together. And I wanted to be that someone, because he was important to me too.

"Fenris... You told me you'd be there for me..." I nuzzled my head to his. "But it's my turn to be there for you."

"Rosella..." He blinked away the remaining tears glistening like little stars in his moonlit eyes. "I... I don't want you, or your friend, to wind up like Sarah. I want to protect you, but I'm afraid. What if I'm not there, and you are backed into a corner?"

I rested my head against his. "You will be there, always, because you promised you would. As my noble wolf, I know you would never break that promise. But I don't want to depend on you all the time. I need to be able to stand up for myself." At those words, I reminded myself of my personal turmoil from earlier, and sighed. "While you were out hunting yesterday, I thought about Mom, and Great Granny Felan, and Sophia, and told myself how I'd never changed... Well, I understand now."

"Understand?"

"Yes." I got to my feet. "Fenris, take some time to clean yourself up, okay? I'm going to use the bathroom."

I did as I told Fenris I would. Though, when I was finished, I strode over to the second door at the left of the hall. It creaked open as I pushed on it, and I peeked through the gap to find the bloodstained bed.

This room... I pushed the door completely open, and stepped inside. *It's... sad.* This room, those stains... *It reeks of death.* I crept toward the bed, and reached for the curtains that shielded the horrific sight from view.

A disturbing image festered in my mind. A young girl with the likeness of my mother was at one side of the bed, Fenris at the other. A second, slightly older girl, Sarah, lay upon it, with nasty wounds. She looked like a broken doll with frail limbs spread, her ebony hair splayed out upon the pillow. I imagined that her small chest rose and fell with short, quick breaths, as she fought for her life.

"Fenris, I'm sure you don't want to be here," I whispered, "but I'm grateful you put everything aside, just to accommodate my needs." I put a hand to my chest. "Thank you."

Rosella! Rosella, can you hear me?

I cocked a brow, and my eyes grew wide. *The voice? From in the void?*

Good, you can.

"You again..." My smile fell into a frown. "Seriously, who are you?"

"Uh, last I checked, my name is Fenris. Have you forgotten?"

My cheeks grew hot at the wolf's sudden appearance beside me. "Oh, uh... Sorry."

"I am confused..." Fenris murmured. "You didn't return right away, so I..." He shrank back a little. "I, uh, wanted to know if everything was alright."

I fiddled with a lock of hair draped over my shoulder. "Fenris, remember when I mentioned hearing a voice in my head, back when we found the trail leading to this house?"

"Oh, yes, I remember."

"Okay, well... It's still happening, only now it's more frequent, and I have no clue what's going on... I tried asking if it was Sarah, but apparently it's not. Or, maybe it is, and I'm not supposed to know."

Look in the box.

My brow furrowed. "And... this same voice also appeared in a dream I had last night— Hey!"

Fenris had suddenly dashed out of the room, leaving me in utter confusion.

"Fenris!" I called.

"Rosella, in here!"

I sped down the hall, and found the wolf looming over a cardboard box, in the first room on the right. "Hey." I curiously approached him. "Why'd you take off like that?"

"This. Open it."

Go on.

Suspicious, I eyed the wolf. "Fenris..."

He nodded, without taking his eyes off of the box. "Go on, open it."

I cautiously leaned down, and traced the frayed edges of the box's flaps while pondering this sudden turn of events. Fenris seemed confused, when I first told him about the voice, back when we found the marked tree. But now, it was like they were synced.

"Rosella?" He was watching me intently.

I eyed him inquisitively. "Fenris, what brought this on? Just a minute ago, I was talking with you about that voice in my head."

"Yes, you told me about it."

"How come you're suddenly telling me to open this box, then?" I challenged. "When the voice also told me to?"

Fenris' forehead crinkled, concern rippling his furry brow. *"Did* the voice tell you to check this box?"

"Indeed it did." I set my face in a stern expression. "So, I want to know what brought this on. Can you hear it or not?"

Fenris opened his mouth to speak.

Don't interrogate him.

"What do you mean?" I asked aloud.

Trust me, Rosella. For now, just follow my instructions, okay?

"Rosella? What's happening?" Fenris asked nervously.

I searched his alluring eyes for any sense of trickery.

Have you still not learned to trust in others? Don't tell me you're suddenly questioning his loyalty to you.

"No, of course not…" I shuddered from the lash of guilt to my conscience. "I'm sorry Fenris, I'll look in this box now." I pulled the flaps of the box apart. Inside was a small black pen.

Remove the back of it.

The back… Following the strange voice's instructions, I twisted off the back end of the pen. My eyes widened, as I spotted a thin piece of rolled up paper sticking out.

"What's that?" Fenris asked.

I pinched it between my fingers, and pulled on it. "Looks like… some kind of note." I squinted at the tiny, scrabbled lettering. "'Open the door of secret hidden in the room of sorrow, and you will find the key to happiness.'" I nodded. "Fenris, wait here for a moment."

"Why?"

I sprung back up. "I need to go back to the room Sarah died in. Just give me a second." I proceeded there, and looked around. "Secret… Secret…" My eyes landed on the wardrobe. I ran over, threw the doors open, and felt around the back for any sort of secret piece that I could tear off or something.

Not there.

"Okay, then where?" I asked. "Help me."

"Rosella?" Fenris poked his head into the doorway. "Everything alright?"

"I'm trying to figure out the meaning on that piece of paper. It said something about a secret door, so I thought I'd check the wardrobe." I shrugged. "Based on a movie I once saw, sometimes wardrobes have secret doors."

Fenris shuffled his paws upon the floor, a troubled look on his face. "Hmm…"

"Fenris, you don't have to be in here," I told him gently. "Please don't trouble yourself."

"Hang on, I got something." His nose ran along the floorboards, and he followed it to the bed. "If my nose is correct..." He perked his ears. "Rosella, check that stuffed toy there."

I approached the bed, and my eyes locked onto the stuffed bunny perched against the pillow. "I wonder..." I grabbed it, and looked it over. "Ah! There's a tear in its back."

I slipped a hand into the stuffed bunny's torn back, and wiggled my fingers around in its fluffy insides until they grazed along something cold and hard. As I grabbed hold and pulled, the bunny's head sank inward, though it bounced back to its original shape upon my successful retrieval.

"It's a rusty key," I said.

"Hmm, it seems to be important," Fenris observed. "Why else would it be hidden?"

A mental lightbulb suddenly went off in my head. "I think that I might know where this goes." I walked out of the room, and went down the hall towards the second door on the right. Rusty key in hand, I tried it, and nearly jumped for joy when I heard the clicking sound.

"Wonderful, now we can see what's inside!" Fenris urged.

"Yep." I turned the knob, and pushed. "I wonder if it's some kind of safe room, or..." I stopped in mid-sentence. "... Oh... my... god..."

I couldn't believe what I was seeing. This room was completely out of place from the rest of the house. The sun's rays cast a sheen of glitter over the golden walls, the soft carpet a sea of vibrant blue, with a single round glass table in the middle. Atop the table, there rested a small white chest lined with a golden trim, and a hefty heart-shaped padlock sealing whatever contents may be inside.

"Look at this place!" I gawked at the beauty of the room, as I stepped inside. "It's... wow."

"Indeed..." Fenris carefully inched halfway through the doorway. "I don't recall ever setting foot into this room, so I cannot say if it's always been this way."

I cocked my head. "That's real weird, though. Why would a room like this exist in a house that probably existed in the early to mid 1900's?"

"Rosella, take a look at this chest."

"Huh?"

"This chest here." He tapped his nose to the small white chest. "Its padlock is shaped like a heart..."

"Yeah, I know... Oh!." Connecting the dots, I approached the chest, and slipped a hand into my pocket. When I found the heart-shaped key, I inserted it into the padlock. I heard a click, and slowly lifted the top of the chest. "Oooooh, wow..."

My eyes stared in awe at the large, light pink jewel resting upon a cushion within the chest. From appearance, it was of extremely high value. I gently cupped my hands under it. To my surprise, it was heavier than expected. I was no expert at math, but this beautiful jewel, projecting arrays of color that illuminated the walls with the sun's absorbed light, felt like it weighed around twenty pounds.

"Fenris, look at this thing. Ugh, it's heavy!" My wrists strained against the pressure of the weight in my hands. "Gah!"

"Has to be around ten kilograms or so, based upon size and quality," Fenris said.

"How do you know that?" I asked.

"Felan taught me a little about measurements."

"Oh." I looked down at the jewel with discomfort. "Feels kinda like I'm holding my cat Pooter."

"There's something inside. Do you see it?"

"Huh?" I attempted to lift the jewel to my face. "Oh yeah." I squinted my eyes a bit, so as to get a better look. "It's super tiny, but looks like yet another key."

Fenris' face fell with disappointment. "As lovely as this jewel is, we'll have break it."

"Yeah, guess so." Without warning, I let slip the jewel from my hands, then threw them to my face as a loud shatter disrupted the peaceful air and pink shards went flying.

Fenris yipped with surprise. "Rosella!"

"Sorry..." I ducked down to pick up the key. "I don't usually think of material things as important, and didn't think it'd be that bad." Attaching myself to material things was a rarity, since they couldn't breathe nor feel pain. *Like my sketchbook,* I thought to myself. *But that's actually important to me.*

Fenris shook his body about. "Oi... Oh, Rosella."

"Hmm?"

Fenris started sniffing around the table. "Ah..." He tore through the carpeting with an eager claw. "Aha! Here!"

"What is it?" I asked.

The wolf pointed with his nose. "Here, this little door."

"Oh, I see! Here, lemme try this key." I slipped the key in with ease, and seconds after, I heard a click. "Okay, it's unlocked. But we gotta move this table."

I got up and carefully gripped the table. My arms ached a bit from the force I imposed on them, but the table proved otherwise easy to move. Once it was maneuvered far enough over, I dropped back to the floor.

"Alright... Got it." The trap door now open, I reached Inside for an envelope. "What's in here?" I tore into it, and something dropped into my hands. "Huh... It's a locket that's got some initials on it: 'S. N. M.'"

"Sarah Nicole Mitchell," Fenris stated. "That is her full name."

I raised a curious brow. "How do you know?"

"Chloe once told me."

"Oh." I stared down at the locket, a beautiful green piece, with golden trimming around the edge. "So this belonged to Sarah..." That awful story Fenris told me a bit ago pierced back into my heart like a knife, as I held the locket close. *This could be a memento she left behind.*

"I am unsure how, but my guess is she lost it?" Fenris questioned.

I shrugged. "Maybe... I wonder if anything's inside." I grazed my thumb along the small button at the side and pushed on it. "Oh my god!"

"What is it?"

"It's... It's water!" Though my hands shook from excitement, the liquid never left the locket. "Ah, it's like it's glued inside of it or something!"

Fenris lightly sniffed the tiny piece of jewelry in my hands, and his ears drooped. "I sense her sadness within that locket."

I gave him a confused frown. "What do you mean?"

"It has her scent. And since it's a liquid..."

I winced at the pang of understanding. "I get it. The little girl's room, the one Sarah died in, isn't the 'room of sorrow'. It's this one, and the door of secret was the trapdoor. As for the liquid in this locket, it's Sarah's tears." I looked over the glistening walls of gold around me. "Ya know, this reminds me of a story Mom once told me, about a young girl who was part of a family that didn't understand her."

Fenris sat down with a curious look. "Is that so?"

"Yeah... She didn't tell me where she heard it, but there was this girl who spoke an entirely different language from the rest." I looked to the wolf with a thoughtful expression. "They showered her with gifts, since they were very rich. She had a beautiful room made of gold and silver, kinda like this one, with the prettiest of gowns and everything. However, she was unable to tell them that she wanted love, instead of material things. Since they couldn't understand her, they thought that she just wanted more gifts.

The girl was extremely saddened by this, so she cried, every day and night. She would just sit in her room of treasures, and cry, all because she couldn't tell them that she just wanted to be loved, not spoiled. Then, one night, she was feeling so lonely, that she actually wept herself to death." I looked down at the locket. "Like Sarah, this lonely girl had a locket, but she kept a picture of her family in hers. After her death, when her mother found and opened it, instead of the photo, she discovered her daughter's tears. The mother was horrified of this, and decided to hide the locket underneath a rug in the girl's room."

"And?"

"Another young girl found that locket many years later." I continued. "Somehow, she found out the lonely girl's story, and decided to bury the locket, thinking it a way of putting the deceased to rest. That's when a beautiful Weeping Willow tree grew, and the spirit of the lonely girl emerged from it. She thanked the one who'd set her free, and promised to shower her with all the luck in the world." I locked eyes with Fenris. "I don't know about Sarah's past, but maybe something happened before then..." I shook my head, and wiped a hand across my dampened brow. "Fenris, can we take a break? I haven't eaten anything yet, and holding that jewel made me tired."

"Certainly." He rose up from his haunches. "I'm going to hunt, as I too need to recharge. As always, I won't be far away."

"Alright."

He trotted to the door. "Hey, Rosella." He peered over his shoulder. "Ya know, if you'd like, perhaps I could... maybe..."

"What is it?"

"Well..." He curled his front half around, his solemn gaze drawing me closer to him. "I was wondering if I could teach you how to fight."

"F-Fight? What do you mean?" *Me? Fight? I couldn't even take on Caroline! But... But I don't...*

"I understand if it's uncomfortable for you. I merely ask because I am concerned for your safety." The wolf pressed his forehead to mine. "I just want you to be safe, Little Rose... That's all I'm asking."

"Fenris, I..." *I'm tired of having to depend on others... But I've never seen myself as something more than just timid little Rosella...* I shook my head.

"I see." Fenris pulled away with a look of silent discontent. "I'll be quick, and—"

"No, I want to learn how to fight."

Mystical eyes aglow with newfound hope, his tail flailed with excitement at the prospect. "Rosella, are you truly open to the opportunity?"

Like a raging fire battling the cold of winter, the freezing fear of failure melted off of me, as the familiar presence of courageous heat flared in my chest. "I want to become stronger, since the chance is being gifted to me," I told him. "I'm absolutely terrified of failing to rescue Sophia... So I have to try. My father told me that he wanted me to blossom into the strongest Bloom I could. And, in order for me to do that, I have to brave myself for it. Sophia needs me, the same way I'd need her."

A fond chuckle emitted from Fenris' curved maw. "I'm glad to hear you still feel this way, Rosella. And like I told you, I will be there to protect you. I will keep you safe."

I nodded, more surely than ever, with a grin of my own. "Thanks Fenris, that means a lot."

CHAPTER 25

F ENRIS AND I WERE greeted with a fresh breeze as I threw the front door open, and we stepped out into the crisp, clear air. Compared to the stuffy, musty stench of the house, it was certainly a pleasant change.

"Ah, so much nicer out here!" I skipped across the porch and down the rickety steps. "Much more open."

"We should make haste," Fenris told me. "The sun won't last forever."

"Right." I took my position several feet from the house, and reached into the side pocket of my pants for my father's knife. *Dad... I hope you've been watching me. I've learned so much...* My face fell into a frown. *I never wanted to learn how to fight because, to me, I never felt I stood a chance. Fighting also brings war, doesn't it?* I shuddered. *War... That's what I'm prepping myself for.*

"Now, hold out your blade with a firm grasp on the hilt."

Returning my focus to Fenris, I did as I was told.

"Very good," Fenris said. "Now, try taking a position."

I slowly slid my left foot back, while my right firmly planted itself to the ground. My right hand held my Dad's knife, my arm outstretched, as my left was bent at an angle beside me. "Like this?"

"That's good, you're a natural!" he praised.

I rubbed at the back of my head. "Well, now... I wouldn't go that far."

Fenris chuckled at that. "You are stronger than you think. Now, let's first try a simple jab. Pretend that something is front of you, and you're sparring with it."

"Okay," I said, and started furiously jabbing the knife into the air.

"Good, "Fenris said. "Try tightening your wrist a bit."

I flexed the hand of my outstretched arm, wrist taut. "How's this?"

"Better. Now, try swinging the knife around some. There you go, just like that." Fenris wagged his tail with his excitement, and gave a praised howl as I did a twirl, my right arm extending outward.

I swiftly dropped to one knee. "Not bad?"

"You're really getting the hang of it, just like your mother," Fenris added. "However, you'll need to be quicker. The Lurkers are swift and quite strong, so you'll have to be light on your feet."

I straightened up, confused. "How am I supposed to do that?"

"Adrenaline is your companion in a fight," he explained, "but do not be greedy. Too much to drink, and you lose sight of what's in front of you."

"I don't... I don't get it."

"You will." He trotted in the direction of the trees. "Say, I have a good idea that may help you... Follow me."

"Where are we going?" I asked, trailing after him. "Isn't that back the way we came?"

The wolf glanced over his shoulder. "We'll use one of the trees as target practice. My master will not mind, and neither will this tree."

I nodded in understanding. "I see."

Out of the cluster of trees, we found one that was distanced nicely from some of the others, and in view of the trail. Fenris silently bowed to the tree, then scratched a sharp mark across it. He then turned to me with a nod, and I clenched the knife's hilt with confidence.

I'm doing this for Sophia... I'm doing this for me... I'm probably doing this to save the world. My eyes connected with the initials etched into the blade, as I held it close to my face. *Dad... This blossom will bloom and stand tall.*

"Envision this tree as a target," Fenris instructed. "Strike it with passion."

Passion... I swiped the tree with the tip of the knife in hesitancy. Barely even a scratch was left, and I lowered my head in shame. "Sorry..."

"That's alright, just try again."

"I..." My hand trembled a bit. "I'm sorry, I guess I'm just..." A heavy weight of uncertainty sunk into my chest, momentarily constricting my lungs.

"It's alright," Fenris ushered. "Just take a deep breath, ease your mind, and deliver it to your blade."

"Deep breath..." I filled my lungs with an adequate dose of oxygen, and held it there. *Ease your mind...* My eyes fell shut. *... and deliver it to your blade.* Heat rekindled once more within my chest, and trailed down my arm to my grip, where I harnessed it within my blade.

"Envision yourself as a gentle breeze brushing over these trees. It's your duty to make their voices heard. You have to stir their leaves, excite them into chatter."

"A gentle breeze... over the trees." Through sealed eyes, I envisioned a view of the tree in my mind, and again raised my father's knife.

"Start out slow, build up your strength."

"Slow... Build up my strength."

"Comb the bark with your air... and charge it into a whip of wind."

My arm slow to start, it tightened with each breath of air I claimed. The tip of the knife grazed the bark in front of me the first five times, like the uplifting breeze to my arm. A faint tap turned into a light scratch, then the sixth hit, and the light scratch was a hair deeper. Seventh, eighth, ninth and tenth, I felt the tip chip away a speck of bark. A rustling of leaves sounded around me, as if manipulated by my swinging arm.

My forearm pulled taut, my knuckles ached with the strain, though I wouldn't relent. I increased speed, with sharp lashes to the crackling wood, and the knife penetrated centimeters deeper every time. Flecks of sawdust pricked my eyes, though the gust of mental wind never left my conscience, and my ignorance blew them back like they were nothing.

The tree before me never screamed once in pain, despite its inflictions, and instead joined in the frenzied whispering of the others urging me on. It promised forgiveness, knowing its purpose was to assist me in my training.

My knife abruptly latched into the bark, this time rendered immobile. Brought back to my senses, I opened my eyes. "Holy..." My shocked gaze locked to the knife lodged inches into the tree, as I dropped my hand from the hilt. "Did I... Did I do that?"

"Indeed you did..." Fenris positioned himself next to me. "And you are on your way, but remember not to indulge too deeply in adrenaline. Sweet as nectar in your veins, an overdose will prove consequential."

I clutched tightly at the hilt of the knife, and with a burst of strength, I freed it from the tree. My shoulder jerked in retaliation, so I spent a minute massaging the pain away.

"You possess far more a will to survive than you are aware," the wolf said. "And with patience, you will come to understand it." A solemn expression settled on Fenris' face. "Control, however, is not so easy to come by."

"Like Sophia..." I turned my gloved hand over, and stared at my wrist. "She was furious with Caroline for her actions, but not once did she physically act on her anger, because she kept in control. Or, she at least tried against Caroline. But when she was trying to help me get to the nurse's office, and that guy, Dale, came at her, she lashed out. Kicked him hard between the legs if I recall correctly."

"Sophia knows how to fend for herself," Fenris said. "However, losing her temper through words does not make a difference."

I bowed my head. "Yeah, I guess not, huh?" I thought back to the incident at the mall. It seemed so long ago now... "She apologized to me when she exploded, went on about how she should've held her tongue and that she'd do better..." My mind then drifted to that dreadful night, when she was kidnapped. "She didn't know how to defend herself against the Lurkers. When I saw her in my backyard, she looked so lost. I expected her to start throwing curses and tell it off, but she was silent. Maybe she thought that provoking it was a bad idea." I screwed my eyes shut in an attempt to stop the fresh wave of tears. "The one time she held her tongue..."

"And if you remember, she was screaming for you."

"I didn't know how to fight back!" I whipped around to face him, offended by the sting of his words. "I was scared, and so was she because, for once, she was up against something she couldn't take down."

A determined glow entered his eyes. "But you granted yourself a chance by throwing yourself out here, a chance to learn how to defend yourself, to become strong. And once you absorb this newfound knowledge, you will prove to her that she was right to call your name."

Warm tears stained my vision. "Sophia..." I whispered in a wavered breath. "I won't give up on you... You can depend on me... I'll save you..."

"Rosella, do you need another minute to recover?" Fenris asked.

With a shake of my head, the tears vanished, and I refocused. "No, let's keep going. I'm doing this for her. I can't stop." *I can't let my emotions get the best of me anymore.*

"Alright then. Let's try some work without the knife. Punching and kicking is essential, when you lack a weapon. We'll continue to use this tree for as long as possible. Your gloves should protect your hands."

I slipped the knife back into the right side pocket of my cargo pants. "Alright... How long do you think this may take?"

"A simple stab into the tree is definitely not enough, but it is a start." The wolf got up and walked a few feet away from me. "As for this next exercise, it is more so for emergency, as handling a weapon proves much more effective in defeating the Lurkers." He gave me a determined look. "Shall we?"

I nodded confidently. "Got it."

At first, punching the tree was frightening, as I was sure I'd hurt myself. My fist would fly upon launch, but abruptly slow to a snail's pace inches away, and gently bump the wood. Fenris assured me that it would be fine though, so after the first few cowardly punches, I threw one for real. To my relief, it didn't hurt much at all.

"Using this tree will educate you on focus," Fenris stated. "I don't condone hitting anything that angers you, but it's good to have a physical object to vent on. It also feels more adequate than a fist to the air."

"Yeah, I think I get what you mean." I winced upon my next fist to the tree. My knuckles cracked, and the fear of breaking them robbed me of my confidence.

"Don't be afraid, or impose too greatly," Fenris said. "Find a nice balance that will leave an impact, and your hand still usable."

I nodded, and again hurled a balled fist at the tree, albeit with a smidgen less force. My knuckles didn't crack that time.

"Try kicking now."

I raised a leg, and tapped my heel against the bark.

He chuckled. "Good, but... Try using more force."

I nodded shyly. "Right, right..."

Just like with the punches, I hesitated at first with kicks. But over time, my confidence meter went up. In the while that I'd trained with this tree, I'd managed to strike some decent kicks good enough to at least leave a slight dent in something. My arms and legs grumbled from the tension, though I knew it was for good reason, so I didn't complain.

"You've gotten the hang of the bare basics," Fenris declared. "Perhaps you should learn how to back-flip next."

I gawked at him. "Back-flip?"

"Your mother used it as a rebounding technique," he explained. "Flawless act, many times."

"Yes, but she's thin and fit," I chided.

"It may come in handy someday." The wolf shook his head. "For now, we'll look past it. Do you know how to roll? Somersault?"

"I do."

"Alright then." He lowered upon his haunches. "Try sparring with me now."

My nervous heart pounded in my chest as I held my tongue. *Sparring... with Fenris... I...*

"You seem troubled," Fenris uttered, and cocked his head. "Something wrong?"

"Well, it's just that..." I squeezed my forearms. "I don't want to hurt you on accident, and, well, you're a totally different being from me. How would that work?"

His brow furrowed. "I will be careful of where to strike, Little Rose. I trust my claws not to harm those important to me."

Seems like a stretch there, wolf.

"You've trusted me thus far, yes?"

I nodded slowly. "I have."

His alluring gaze drew me in, and a glint of promise shimmered in them. "Then trust me now."

I sighed. "Alright."

I was a bit heavy on my feet, during the first few sparring rounds. Fenris would come at me with a careful bite or swipe of the claw, and almost every time, I was close to injury, though no blood was drawn. He would always miss, no matter what angle I was at. I figured that he was missing on purpose, like he knew exactly what coordinates I'd be positioned in, as those close calls couldn't have been avoided miraculously.

"You must quicken your reaction time, Rosella!" Fenris lunged at me yet again. "Pay closer attention to your surroundings!"

"Fenris, quick question." I ducked beneath another swing of the claws. "You're not going easy on me, are you?"

"If I were going easy on you, you would learn nothing," he proclaimed. "You must learn to fight with raw truth."

"That's a blunt way to put it," I noted, "but I know it's out of respect, so I'm cool with it."

Fenris nodded. "I don't wish to harm you. I also promised I wouldn't. I would never lie to you, not anymore."

I came to a halt beside the wolf. "Fenris…" I sternly stared him square in the face. "You never lied to me. Sure, you were hiding your pain, but you never lied to me… You told me that you were afraid to tell me what was wrong because you didn't want to be a burden. That is not a lie. That is your way of trying to be strong for someone else."

He gazed back with a somber grin. "I suppose so…"

I gently bumped a fist to his side. "I trust you, so you don't have to worry about hiding from me. Not anymore."

Continuing on, without letting my mind wander too far, I imagined Fenris as a noble warrior giving me the chance to follow in his footsteps. As we sparred, he and I were like two separate forces dancing in an ethereal space, and I worked to mirror his movements. In a short time, I stopped stumbling around with two left feet, having swapped out one for a right.

To my amazement, my reaction time had quickened, and soon, it looked like Fenris' claws were purposefully trying to perform the opposite of his promise. He let the reins loosen, as I learned how to duck and dodge at the right time, and together we engaged in official battle, undeterred by fear of harming each other.

Trust was the link that bonded our hearts. No matter how hard the tug, it never broke, not even as I slid and dodged another attempted swipe, and landed my first blow, a knee to his chest.

Panic washed over me, though, as he sunk to the ground coughing, and I rushed to his aid. "Are you okay?"

He gave a raspy chuckle. "G-Good job, Rosella. You're getting it."

Relieved, I let out a concerned chuckle. "Oh, good. I was worried that maybe I, uh, damaged something." I looked up. "Oh…" Above, a thick cluster of dark clouds had gathered overhead, blocking out the sun completely. "Looks like it might rain soon."

Fenris mirrored my solemn expression. "Yes, we should head inside now." His legs wobbled like gelatin, as he stumbled to his paws. "Goodness, you might've actually dealt a bit of damage. Luckily, I recover easily."

I patted his head. "Sorry."

"It's alright. Come, let us return."

The walk back to the house was extremely short, which was a very good thing, because as soon as we hit the steps, the sound of thunder roared overhead, and I silently prayed that the house could withstand the impending thunderstorm.

"Say, um... I was wondering if, maybe, we could..." My eyes darted Fenris at my right. "I'm sure you're tired, but maybe we could look..."

He seemed to understand my unfinished question. "I picked up on a familiar scent that may be Lurker." Fenris stared ahead with a glare. "Don't get your hopes up yet, but they could be closer than we think."

If that's true, that means Sophia is close! I hope she's okay... I nervously twiddled my fingers. "Well, we'll see."

"Indeed," Fenris said. "I just don't want you soaring with false hope, then crash into the ground of despair, should it not work out..." Head bowed, he trotted ahead of me.

"I will make sure that doesn't happen," I assured, while following after him. "As for the time being, what would you like to do?"

"I am unsure," the wolf answered. "Perhaps, after the rain that's to fall, we could explore a bit more..."

"Sure." I brushed a lock of hair behind my ear. "Let's take this time to rest, then."

We opted to cozying together in the library with the book of fairy tales, as it seemed comfiest. The soft pitter-patter of raindrops tapped against the windows, as Fenris laid in front of the empty fireplace with me snuggled into his side, his tail a furry blanket over my lap.

"Can you see the pictures okay?" I asked him, as I held the book in front of me.

"Kind of, but that's alright."

I giggled at the affectionate lick to my cheek. "Hey!"

Fenris chuckled fondly, and settled his head next to me.

"Geez…" I looked over the picture of Rapunzel sitting at the top of her tower, gazing idly at the sky, as she pondered the world beyond her prison. "You know, I actually have a drawing of you that I made at home. It's in my sketchbook."

"Oh, so you are still drawing?"

My hand stroked over the page. "Uh-huh. I've even considered going to an art college after high school."

"What is this 'college'?" he asked.

Amused by his question, I gave a light chuckle. "It's a school that comes after high school. You basically relearn everything you should already know from normal school, but take more specific courses that build up to your career. After you pass, you get a piece of paper called a degree. Basically like high school, except it's for something more specific."

Fenris nodded with an understanding look, but then frowned. "How come you need a piece of paper?"

"Well, it's to show your level of knowledge, so people can confirm." *That sounds kinda silly, but it's basically the truth…*

"I see." Fenris flicked an ear, a pondering look to his face. "I guess there are many?"

"Yeah," I said, "but I've been told that art is a difficult field to navigate, unless you make your 'big break', or basically find success, usually by miracle." My face fell. "It's a little scary to think about, because I really like to draw. Even if I get a degree in art, that won't help me much, except with maybe a teaching job. But I don't want to teach. I want to make unique illustrations for art books and stuff."

"And you need a degree for that?" the wolf asked, confused. "That seems useless."

I scrambled for a response. "Well… I want to spend my time in college figuring it out. Perhaps I could go into animation, or learn to make comics. I could even get involved with art galleries. There are many possibilities."

His eyes widened. "Sounds like a broad career field."

I nodded. "Think of it this way. There are several different trails hidden in the forest, and each serves as a type of art job. The trail you follow is the path you've chosen, but in order to find the right trail, you have to work your way through the trees. Once you find yourself being surrounded by certain ones, and they disperse around a clear trail, that's how you know you've found what you want to do."

Fenris' eyes glimmered with amazement. "I see! An interesting way to explain it, but surely understandable."

A weary smile ghosted my lips. "Thanks... Sophia's the one who showed me the way. Always my biggest cheerleader, she's adamant that I claim art as a profession..." A tear crept at the corner of my eye, as my nose burned.

"My dear Little Rose..." I felt a poke to the back from what I assumed was Fenris' nose. "Rosella... It's okay."

"Sophia gave me a lot, despite being one person," I mumbled. "She was the only one who welcomed my presence outside of the house..." I set the fairy tale book aside, and leaned forward for my backpack. "In here... In here is..." I unzipped it, and stuffed my hand inside. "... this" From my backpack, I pulled the Moonpaw hoodie. "I know I said I don't usually get attached to material things. But like my sketchbook, and the bracelet Dad gave me, this is a material thing that I am attached to. She bought this for me as a little gift, out of kindness."

A playful spark glimmered in Fenris' eyes. "Interesting design."

A soft chuckle left my lips. "I know, coincidental huh?" I buried my face in it. *Ah... It's so warm... and it feels like her...* I nuzzled my cheek against the fabric. "I brought this with me, so as to remember what I was fighting for... See, like I told you already, I didn't know what I was doing, and what you said about drinking in too much adrenaline during our sparring match... I guess I drank too much, back at the start. My desire to be like her drove me to do something drastic, and I was worried that, maybe, I would suddenly chicken out. Keeping this hoodie with me kinda helped me stay strong. But I know what I did was abrupt, and stupid."

"Rosella..."

I leaned into his side. "Fenris, I miss her so, so much." Hugging the hoodie to my chest, the stray tear shed from my eye.

"I wish I could take your pain away," the wolf whispered, "and if I could, I would."

I grimaced through the hoodie at his words. "You shouldn't say that. You've suffered enough for anyone."

"If it means relieving someone of pain, I am willing to carry the burden, no matter the cost."

I dropped the hoodie, my eyes wide. "F-Fenris..."

He stared me down with nobility and truth, his words carried with bold confidence. "Rosella, I was created to protect what's important. This forest is important to my master, so I must protect it. Sophia is important to you, so I must protect her. You are important to Felan and Chloe and Ben, so I must protect you... And you all are important to me, so I must, and want, to protect all of you."

"F-Fenris..."

"Do you remember how I kept going on about how this place looked? How I brought up Felan a few times?"

I chuckled. "Yes, I remember. And you told me it was because you missed her."

He looked up with a somber face. "This place is full of death and sorrow. But Felan can make it better... And I still miss her Rosella, the same way I miss Ben... I just couldn't stand not seeing him there, and I didn't want you, or Chloe to see. So, I confided in Felan. She listened to me, and comforted me through my troubles. She's near and dear to me." A fiery blaze of passion burned bright in the wolf's eyes, as he stared back down at me. "She won't be there forever, I know. But I won't ever forget everything she's done for me."

A feeling of sadness, mixed with understanding, seeped into my heart. "Fenris..."

"My precious Little Rose... No matter what happens, I will always be there to keep you safe, to protect your fragile petals from wilting in the dark. I promised my master, Chloe and Ben, even myself, because you are equally important."

Lips pressed tight, I tucked my arms around his thick neck, and planted a blessed kiss to his head. "Geez. I don't know what else to say, besides 'thank you'."

"That is alright with me."

"Heh..." I gave him a gentle squeeze. "In that case, thank you." I released him from my grip. "So..."

Fenris looked over to the window. "It seems it might rain for some time. It's picking up a bit."

"Yeah." I glanced at the Moonpaw hoodie, and my face fell slightly. "Rosella."

I found Fenris' eyes boring into mine when I looked back up, and like the many times before, I lost myself in them. However, I was able to blink out of the trance this time. "Yes?"

"Perhaps tomorrow, we can start making our move. But we'll have to go slow, else we'll trip over our shortcomings. This battle must be won through patience and careful planning."

I nodded. "Yeah, you're right." I rubbed at an arm. "Um... I... I think I'm gonna go spruce up a bit. I still have plenty of wipes left. Also kinda hungry again."

"Yes," Fenris said. "I plan to hunt again, once the rain lets up."

"Alright," I said. "While you prepare to hunt, I'm gonna go clean up and find something to snack on."

"Very well." Fenris' tail released me as he got up, and he trotted back through the library, rather than leave through the closer exit.

Once the wolf was gone, I examined myself. It'd been a few days since I'd last showered, and it was finally starting to show. From what I could see without a mirror, my hair was matted at the ends, and my armpits were drenched in sweat, though that wasn't nearly as bad as... My face grew hot at the thought of my "personal space".

I wonder... I did a quick search of my backpack's pockets. I hadn't thought to pack it... "Thank you, Great Granny Felan!" I victoriously pumped my fist in the air, when I found a razor with a sticky note attached that said, "Just in case :) Be careful~" concealed in a pocket within the main compartment of the backpack. "Okay... Time to spruce myself up a bit."

CHAPTER 26

T HE RAIN WAS LOCKED in a steady downpour for some time, so when it finally let up, I was pleased to find a wandering doe during my quick search for food. I had to chase her a ways through the trees, thus putting some distance between me and the house, but I reassured myself several times that Rosella was fine.

I bit at the doe's legs when I caught up, prompting her to collapse, and ended her life with a swift chomp to her neck. Her body flailed for a few seconds before going still, and once I felt the poor creature's life had truly vanished, I feasted upon her carcass with gratitude that Rosella would probably have misread.

I banished the bothersome image of her fearful eyes on me from my mind, and focused on replenishing my strength, as Rosella would need someone powerful to back her up. *And what of Sophia?* I tore into the doe's intestines with more aggression than intended, my frustration over having not recovered her gnawing at my conscience as aggressively as I was into this doe. *Her scent is strong, but I can't help this sinking feeling I have about her, that she's deceitful... She is a Husk, after all.* I recalled that moment when I stepped out that night, and we locked eyes. She knew what I was, and she knew that I knew what she was. *It wasn't the Lurker she was afraid of... It was me...*

I silenced my troubled mind, and gobbled the liver up whole, a particularly tasty part of the carcass, before digging my head into the belly of the doe and scavenging for other organs. My teeth ravaged the doe's tendrils, like she was my last meal, and though my stomach appreciated the filling, it nervously waned on the edge of upset.

I spent way longer than I'd liked to lick the bones clean, because I wanted to make sure I truly had my fill before making the trip back. I wasn't sure when I'd be able to find something again, what with being so close to the Lurkers' lair, and so I anticipated a long, grueling fight ahead.

I wormed the tip of my tongue into the crevices of my teeth and along my gums, then sleeked it all the way across my maw. "Hopefully I got everything…" I stared down at the remains of the doe, a meager pile of bones in the dirt, and sighed. "Thank you for giving your life to me. I'm sorry for taking you from your family, if you had one."

As I'd done with captured prey in the past, I dug a large hole to bury the remains in. It was my way of showing respect, besides being typical wolf behavior. They were innocent animals who fought hard to survive, like me, so I wanted to make sure their return to the earth was properly handled.

I did the same thing upon finding random corpses out in the open, left behind by their predators to rot. Their tattered remains exposed to the elements, empty eyes staring up at nothing, it was a heartbreaking sight I could not bear. Without a bed of dirt to absorb them in peace, their sacred passage into the afterlife was insulted. It was supposed to be a private transition between the deceased and earth only.

"There you go," I whispered, upon scuffing the last bit of dirt over the doe's bones. "May you find peace, and your spirit wander freely among the trees." I looked to the dark canopy of leaves above. "I hope your journey is an easy one." A hint of blood suddenly pricked my nose. *Rosella!?*

I prepared to launch myself into a sprint back, then paused. It was just a pinch, nothing strong. Maybe she'd pricked her finger on something. With an amused chuckle, I shook my head, and continued on with a casual walk. But what if… I stiffened. What if they could smell it?

No no, she's fine. The sun is still setting, and you're not far away. I jumped at the sound of something rustling behind me. It was awfully loud… My tail swayed in anticipation. *No, stop it. Stop it, she's fine.*

I trotted back as calmly as possible, albeit with a spring in my step. The house came into view after several agonizing minutes, and as I rounded the corner, I began my trek up to the porch. The scent of Rosella's blood strengthened, and a horrid thought of the Lurkers again tormented my mind, like an annoying itch I just couldn't scratch. They were close by… Way too close.

I plastered my nose to the surface, and sucked in. Dust lingering between the floorboards drifted up my nostrils in consequence, and with an irritated snort, I whipped my head about as my sense of smell became murky, and dust particles crawled along my nostril walls. I stumbled to the side, my paws carrying me toward the edge of the deck, though I quickly regained balance, and walked back into the house.

More nervous now than before, I proceeded through the living room, down the hall, and up the staircase, at a feverish pace. The door to the second floor bathroom slightly ajar, I padded toward it, the faint scent of blood grazing the inside of my nose.

"Rosella! Are you in there?" I called.

"Fenris?" she asked.

Oh, good. She's safe... With a small nod, I turned around. "Thank goodness..."

"Ah!"

Immediately, without a second thought, I whirled around at the sound of Rosella's cry, and shoved the door open with my head. "Rosella!"

There was a loud slam, and Rosella shrieked in response.

"Rosella! Are you okay!?" My fur standing at attention, my ruffled tail thrust itself between my legs. "I heard you cry out!" I found myself peering down at a pair of bared quivering legs, where I saw a trickle of blood running down the calf of the right. "Oh no! You're hurt!" I started toward her, so as to examine her wound.

"Fenris!"

I looked up, and my eyes connected with Rosella's frightened expression.

"Why did you do that!?" she demanded. "You scared the hell out of me!"

"Your leg! It's bleeding!" I retorted.

"Yes! Because I cut myself." She turned to the side, and nodded at the sink. "See, I was shaving."

I dumbly cocked my head. "Huh?"

Rosella walked over to the sink, and picked up a strange tool. "It's called a razor," she uttered with slight irritation. "I was using it to shave."

My eyes widened with curiosity. "Oh... A razor... I... Huh."

I gazed again at her legs. There was only the trickle of blood oozing down to her ankle. Scanning her further, I found no tears in her cloak, no bloodstains on the floor or the walls or on her, no bruises to her face and bare arms. She was just holding the cloak very tightly, one hand clasped to the lower half of her body, the other at her chest, almost as if she were trying to cover up...

A loud yip of surprise escaped my maw upon realization, and I stumbled back with a baffled look. "I... Oh my!" A hot blush burned my furry cheeks. "R-Rosella, I-I-I am sorry!" I knocked my head into the door, and winced at the ache piercing my rattled skull.

"Fenris! Are you okay?"

"I-I-I'm fine." I turned my dizzy head. "I-I-I j-just— Oof!" My elongated snout smacked right into the doorframe, sending another wave of pain coursing through my skull. I clumsily slipped out of the bathroom, the floor like ice, as my paws flew out beneath me. My rear slumped to the floor, as my head tucked into the crook of my neck.

"Oh no!" Rosella ran toward me, her hands fighting to keep the cloak clasped around her. "Fenris!"

"P-P-Please, forgive me! I-I did not realize y-y-y-you were u-u-unclothed!" My fur bristled when I felt her hug my head. "R-R-R-Rosella!" My furry cheeks flared, as she pressed against me, my eyes tightly shut. My muzzle burrowed into her chest, I cringed at the soft muscles, and tried very hard to remove myself with a shake of my head.

"It's okay," she told me calmly. "Geez... Guess your sense of smell is better than I thought."

"N-N-No! P-P-P-Please!" I managed to wriggle out of her arms. "O-Oh goodness, e-e-excuse me!"

"Fenris!"

Face beet red, I scurried to the adjacent master bedroom, despite Rosella's frantic call, and cowered in the corner by the window, my tail still tucked between my legs. My face burrowed into my paws with great shame, my ears flattened to my skull.

Shame on you, Fenris! What were you thinking, intruding upon her like that!? I ushered a low whine. *Goodness... My fear for her safety, it's blinding me from my actions! I shouldn't have acted so irrationally!* The thought made my scorching blush burn harder, as I curled into myself. *Shame on you... Absolute shame.*

I stayed hunkered down, my nose rooted into my corner of shame, without moving a single inch for some time. Eventually, I heard the quiet sound of small feet padding along the floor, and one ear sprung up. I shivered when I registered her approach, but did my best to keep calm.

"Fenris, come on now," Rosella urged. "We've already been through this routine, remember?"

Rosella, please. You should be ashamed of me for barging in like that.

"Hey."

You should be enraged at my actions! And I shouldn't have become alarmed so easily! I... She effectively silenced my frantic thoughts with a simple hand to my back.

"I'm really sorry if I frightened you," she murmured. "And don't worry, I'm actually quite glad you barged in. It means you care, right?" Smooth, gentle strokes eased the tension between my shoulders. She sounded calm, kind, understanding.

I whimpered with a sheepish frown. "Y-Yes, but I shouldn't have done that."

"Oh, don't worry about it."

I dared peer over my shoulder. To my relief, she was clothed in her shirt and cargo pants, with her cloak slung over her shoulder.

"Fenris..." Her warm smile complimented those beautiful rosy dimples. "I'm glad you came to check on me."

"Y-You sure?" I mumbled shyly.

"Yes." Rosella dropped to her knees, and threw her arms over me. "Fenris, forgive me for sounding weird, but you're such a good boy."

My tail wagged at her comment. "I... I try."

"Heh." She gave a yawn, and rubbed at a tired eye. "Oh, sorry! Guess I'm... a little tired."

Both ears perked this time, I sat up a little. "Perhaps, it's time to settle down for the night?"

"Yeah." Rosella got up and walked over to the bed. "I'm gonna lay here for a bit. I don't feel quite ready for bed yet, but I'm too tired to really do anything else."

I rose upon my haunches, and trotted over. "I'll rest next to you, just in case." *And this time, I won't feel so anxious.*

Rosella hopped into the bed, while I lay on my side, right next to her. My head rested nicely upon the floor, my eyes glued to the door. They were close, and now that the sun had set once again, I was on high alert. So I'd hold out as long as possible, just like before.

"Fenris?"

My eyes crept to their corners. "Yes?"

"I can't get comfortable. Could I maybe lay with you for a bit?"

My heart welled with joy, and I eagerly nodded. "Oh, sure! Come on down." I rolled onto my stomach.

"Thanks," she whispered, and climbed down to nuzzle into my side.

I curled my tail over her legs, serving it as a blanket. "There now, is this alright?"

She nodded sleepily. "Yeah..."

A fond chuckle left my maw, as I watched her knead a fist into her tired eye. "I thought you weren't ready for bed yet."

"Well, I was lying there for a bit, and... I was okay." Rosella sunk deeper into my side, her eyes falling shut. "But this feels nice."

"I'm glad."

"Yeah..."

I observed her small hands' tender grasping of my tail, and I wished I could hold them, just once, to experience how it felt. I wanted to squeeze them, to let my adoration for her seep into her palms. I wanted to hold her in my arms, to comb my claws through her hair, and listen to her talk about her day. I wanted to watch her draw, to see her demonstrate herself as an artist.

Though she was only a fragment of this forest, I accepted her as so much more. She was a timid child, fighting for what she cared about, and as her trusted protector, I promised to assist her in her quest. She breathed like a human, talked like a human, felt emotion like a human, and I'd come to know her as a dear friend. But what would happen to her when all of that fell apart, when she—

"Hey, Fenris?"

Pulled free from my troubles, I glanced at her. "Yes?"

Rosella cracked a sleepy eye open. "If you need to move, feel free to. I won't be bothered."

"I think I'll be okay," I assured her gently. "You get some rest now."

She could barely nod, she was so tired. Adorable.

"Rest well," I whispered, "Little Rose."

I exhaled a satisfied sigh as she settled further into my fur, her arms cuddling my quietly excited tail close. I was happy to have gained her trust, to be there for her. An innocent child wrapped in the safety of her noble wolf's embrace, it was a pleasant thought.

Hold your heart close, but keep your distance and do not let it break.

I sighed. *I haven't forgotten, Hollow... But until the time comes that we must part ways, I will protect my Vessel, and shower her with the love and adoration she lacks from her father, because that's what he asked of me.*

I laid my head down, and closed my eyes. Now would be a good time to gather, as I knew not what tomorrow would bring, and I would still feel Rosella right next to me. So, when the floor beneath gave way, I did not panic, and calmly embraced my descent into the abysmal darkness below. While Rosella slept beside my physical body, deep in my mind, I was dropping into the Central Void.

The Central Void was the safest place for one to be. The core of both a Vessel and Guardian's mind, access was a difficult lesson only possible to learn through patience. Since Rosella was sleeping, she could not follow me, but this didn't trouble me. She was safe by my side. If needed, I'd return to her in a heartbeat.

My paws found the reflecting floor, the familiar empty grey space soothing to see. "Are you here? My friends?" I began to wander, my paws manipulating the reflecting floor with each step. "Anyone?"

"Yes, we're here," one voice called. "Can you hear us?"

I nodded. "I bear some news, Seraph. Are the others here?"

"Oi, that's some good news, eh?" another voice chimed in.

"Yes, Rumi," I said.

"Fenris, what of the Vessel?" Seraph asked. "How is she coping? Is she well?"

"She is," I confirmed. "In fact, she's resting peacefully right next to me."

"Good for her..." a third voice grumbled.

I snorted. "You could at least *pretend* to be interested."

Rumi laughed. "Just ignore Checkers, mate. He's always been a downer."

"She told us to be brave," a fourth voice added, "but I don't know if I can do this anymore... My Vessel is suffering."

"Your Vessel's fine, Nana!" Rumi said. "She just needs a little perkin' upper!"

"Tell that to my Vessel," Checkers muttered. "Ugh, she's a mental wreck."

"Everyone, please!" Seraph called. "We've already discussed our situations, and now it is his turn. Fenris, you have the floor again."

I shook my head, with a tired sigh. "My friends, I am worried. My Vessel and I are not far from the Lurkers' lair, and today she learned the basics of combat. I fear that tomorrow may bring about bloodshed, so I wanted to make sure she was prepared."

"Yikes!" Rumi exclaimed. "That's not good."

"Oh no! This is terrible news!" Nana squeaked.

"Has anything happened yet?" Seraph urged.

"No, nothing yet," I assured him. "But tomorrow..." I screwed my eyes shut. "I... I am worried. What if I cannot protect her?"

"Noble wolf, remember what she told us," Seraph reminded me. "Hold your heart close, but keep your distance and don't ever let it break."

"If ya need anythin', we'll be there in a jiffy!" Rumi declared.

"Agreed," Nana chimed in. "We will help where we can."

"Uh-huh..." Checkers uttered.

A tear grazed my eye. "I appreciate that, very much so."

"Say, friendo, what took ya so long to get here anyhow?" Rumi questioned.

"Well, like I said, we were learning combat," I told them, "and also exploring the old house. We still have yet to find her best friend. She... She is nervous, but confident that we'll get back home safe."

"Wait! Is she not aware!?" Nana cried.

"Well, what do you think?" Checkers snapped. "He would've told us if she was."

"Checkers, please," Seraph scolded, "pin that rudeness to your tongue, and leave it there. Do not let it slip again."

I put up a paw. "Be easy on him, Seraph. As a Guardian, a lot of stress is weighed upon his shoulders."

"Fenris is right!" Rumi said. "We shouldn't be angry with each other."

Seraph sighed. "I understand, but sometimes he must be put in his place."

"Look," Checkers jumped in, "I can't help being tired."

Rumi groaned. "Let's get back on topic, eh?"

"Of course," Seraph said. "Now then... About your Vessel, Fenris. How is she doing? Has she become *any* sort of aware yet?"

"Not yet," I went on, "but Hollow has broken through."

Nana gasped. "That means she is close then."

"I know..." I sighed. "She's a sweet child. I wish you could meet her."

"Perhaps soon," Seraph said, "but not now my loyal friend." There was a pause, and then he continued. "My Vessel is quite stubborn herself, though she too is a sweet child. Anyway, how is the forest looking for everyone? I haven't picked up on any disturbances, though I am currently wandering it."

"Nothing of note here," Checkers said. "Though, as you all know, I'm underground, and it's already fucked up."

"I-I haven't seen anything!" Nana shrieked. "Should I look?"

"Nah," Rumi said. "I'm sure you're fine where you are."

"How do you know!?" Nana argued.

"They don't," Checkers muttered. "They're just trying to play your mind."

"Hey, calm down," I said. "Everything will be fine. We're doing exactly what we should be, and that's guarding our Vessels."

"But what if something is happening right now," Nana challenged, "and we're not paying attention!?"

"Believe me, I'm just as concerned about everything," I said. "My Vessel is the closest to the source of the curse, and it terrifies me." As I straightened up, my confident smile returned. "But I can't let fear deter me, and neither should you."

"Fenris is right," Seraph declared. "We all must be on our guard, no matter what."

A sudden frown surfaced upon my face, and the fur atop my back became rigid.

"Fenris?" Seraph asked. "Is something wrong?"

"My friends... I must be off," I uttered. "I sense danger."

"We understand. Be safe, Fenris, and may your Vessel prevail."

My head dipped forward, and my body splashed into the rippling floor beneath me. The burning courage within my chest guided me through the darkness, as I raced toward the light. I could hear the frantic tone in Rosella's voice. Definitely a bad sign...

"...mething's... side! Fenris!"

My eyes popped open as I bolted upright, and I shuffled to my paws, a darkened ridge of silver riveting down my spine. That smell... It almost made me gag. It was like the house had been filled with rotting corpses.

"Rosella." I quickly sought her out. "What's going on?"

Rosella was scrambling to slip on her boots, her head nodding to the window. "Out there!"

I followed her gesture, and my pupils dilated. "Oh no."

"Fenris, something's— Hey! Wait!"

I was already up and out the door, my paws thundering against the floorboards. I careened across the hall, and practically flew down the winding stairs a few at a time. I leaped from the sixth to last step when the bottom floor came within reach, and hurried down the hall to the living room, the aging floorboards creaking loudly beneath my weight.

Behind, Rosella called out to me from the middle of the staircase, and I strained an ear to listen for her.

"F-Fenris? Rosella stammered, as she struggled to catch up with me. "P-Please talk to me."

I skidded to a stop. "Rosella," I breathed, "I sense danger outside." A low growl erupted from within my throat, my teeth bared from my crinkled muzzle, as I stalked toward the front door.

Rosella hesitantly stepped forward. "M-Maybe, we should check it out."

"I don't know if that's a good idea," I warned.

"But if we don't, we won't know." She crept further toward the door and peered over her shoulder, her cautious gaze locked with mine. "I-I'm not afraid, Fenris. I have you by my side. I trust you to protect me from harm. And I will do the same for you if I can."

She trusts me to keep her safe. That's good. I let a small sigh slip my lips. "Rosella, stay close to me, and if anything happens, you do exactly as I say, without question. Alright?"

"Alright."

I nodded.

"Okay... Let's see what's going on out there..." She tiptoed forth and curled her small fingers around the doorknob, and with a timid yank, the door flew wide open.

CHAPTER 27

I WAS SLEEPING PEACEFULLY next to Fenris, safe and warm in his fur. But then, something strange had wafted up my nose. At first it was sour, and then it was burning, and then it was utterly *nauseating*. I awoke with my stomach in knots, a hefty lump ready to launch from my throat to the floor. Then the *god awful* itching set in once again, like maggots burrowing into my skin, and I couldn't get them out, no matter how deep I scratched.

The uncomfortable sting of my marred skin stirred me from my slumber, and when I opened my eyes, I saw the bright ray of light casting the entire room a sinister shade of maroon. In a panic, I called out to Fenris, and he awoke right as I shoved my boots on.

Now, here we were, taken aback by the putrid blast of rot and charred deadwood, upon my abrupt yanking of the front door. The unbearable stench that stormed my nostrils made my stomach churn, and I stumbled back into Fenris' head. He steadied me on my feet with the bridge of his muzzle, then waited until I moved out onto the porch so he could follow.

Through the disturbing atmosphere, I spotted the thick, dark clouds dispelling a light spritzing of rain over the trees, while a thick blanket of bloody red fog lay over the ground, making it difficult to find the bottom of the steps.

My eyes locked on the fog below. *God... I hope there's nothing hiding in there.*

Fenris slunk ahead and descended. Beyond the bottom step, the fog swallowed his paws, as he crept out into the open area. "I think it's alright," he said. "I don't sense any other forms of life. However, there is definitely something amiss."

"Obviously." I hurried down to join him. "What do you think is going on?"

"I'm not sure, so I feel we should tread with immense caution."

I clutched at my chest with a nervous hand. "Fenris... That horrid smell... I didn't know what to think. I was just drifting into a deep sleep when it appeared out of nowhere, and I..." I scratched at my sore sides and flinched. My skin burned raw from irritation, as if I was covered in infected mosquito bites.

Fenris craned his neck to the right. "Rosella, be on your guard."

"R-Right." I fumbled for Dad's knife in my pants' pocket. "Ah... A-Ah, I got it." Relief washed over me, when my hand found the hilt.

"The presence of the Lurkers is strong, yet none are around." Fenris turned around to face me. "Let's take a look. But remember to stay close."

"Fenris, I—!" A stimulating ember flourished within my chest, as a tidal wave of pain flooded my skull, interrupting my response.

"Rosella?"

I put my other hand to my head, as a hiss grazed my teeth. Overwhelmed, my knees hit the ground, and my eyes screwed shut.

... must hurry! Now!

... promised you... ... what you wish... follow through with it.

Please... now more than ever.

... you find your way back?

.... taken into account the risks bearing this forest, and whether it will survive... our home...

But the curse...

Those voices... I faintly recognized them.

... promise you... face to face.

... know it's you?

"Rosella!" Fenris' panicked voice rang clear through my conscience, startling me. "Are you okay?"

"Ah... I'm fine..." The unexpected headache reduced to a numbing sting, as the heat within my chest extinguished. Though disoriented, I found balance upon my feet once more, and with the crack of an eye, I could just make out a large, blurry form.

"Rosella..."

My vision cleared, and I was grateful to find the relieving presence of Fenris. "It's okay, I just... had a moment." I ignored the shudder dancing across my shoulders. *This place... There's definitely something bad brewing, but I'm not scared.*

"Maybe you should wait inside?" Fenris offered.

My eyes widened, as my heart skipped a beat. "No!" I snatched Fenris by the sides of his face. "I don't want you getting hurt!"

A look of shock flashed across the wolf's face, but faded as quickly as it'd come. "A-Alright, just... remember to..."

"Stay close." I gave a curt nod. "I know."

The trees were still, not even the slightest breeze to give a breath of life, and the fog at our feet served as our sense of guidance upon the moon's absence. We found through physical contact, the moment I put my hand to his fur, and it was like a single drop into a rippling pond. A sense of security, it was an escape from our cell of anxiety.

It's okay. We can do this, I thought to myself. *As long as we stay together, we'll make it.*

"Rosella..." Fenris glanced my way. "Are you well?"

"I am," I assured, "for the most part."

Despite the trauma inflicted upon this forest, I pondered over how calm I was. A normal human being would be utterly terrified, walking through a spooky red fog that either didn't exist in the real world, or maybe always did, and no one ever knew. As timid as I typically was, having never experienced such a thing, fear should've overcome me right away. And yet it hadn't.

And those weird thoughts that occurred a moment ago... I heard that term again... "Vessel"... It means something. But what? I caught Fenris peering my way with a worried glance again. "Sorry, just thinking about stuff."

"Yes, you were," he murmured.

Those eyes... They enthralled, astounded, and confused me all at once, like looking into a two-way mirror, but I could see only on the side that reflected back at me.

His eyes view only the truth, Rosella. No one can lie to them. Even when blinded, they see well enough.

"Fenris..." I tightened my grasp around his fur, and bowed my head. "I... I'm thinking about what happened just now. I had this strange headache all of a sudden, and I heard voices. And what's weirder, is that one of the voices..." I hesitantly loosened contact with him, my eyes darting to the right at a peculiar sound. "Fenris! Listen."

The wolf came to a stop with a strained ear. "I hear it..."

Amongst themselves, the trees were engaged in a hushed whisper, and out of the corner of my eye, I spotted something. I silently pointed toward it, and Fenris nodded. With grave caution, we crept through the red fog now misting up our ankles. I squinted in attempts to better examine the form in question, and a chill coursed down my spine.

First, an elongated, bony finger. Next, small legs, possibly feet, devoured by the bloody fog. Hmm, looked kind of tall, a bit lanky. Another bony finger, and then another. There were five of them, attached to something. A long stick? No, it was an arm. Why couldn't I see its face, though? Were the leaves covering it?

O-Oh god... Oh no. Not again. The agonizing itch resurfaced upon my skin, and the hairs at the nape of my neck stood on end. *Please, get out. Get out.* I clawed at my quivering throat with feverish hands, my burning fingers bearing faint tips of red. *It hurts. Why? Why is it so painful!?* Needles were jabbing at my neck, down my shoulders. So, so itchy! *Make it stop! Stop it stop it stop it!* My nails tore into something soft, though my eyes refused to acknowledge it. They were locked to the figure sleeking through the fog with us. *Who are you? Are you doing this to me?*

Suddenly, the figure looked at me, a cast of red light capturing its frightening display. Empty eyes, a vine tightly grasping their crooked neck, reaching out a decrepit hand—

"Rosella!"

The wind was knocked right out of me, as something heavy collided with my body and pummeled me to the ground. In an instant, the painful itching dissipated, and when I looked toward the trees, I saw that the sinister figure was gone.

Fenris loomed over me, his fur bristled, moonlit eyes wide with horror. "I'm sorry, Little Rose! You were hurting yourself. I had to stop you."

I slipped out from under him, and stumbled back to my feet, a nervous air about me. "Eh?" Upon noticing a tear through my sleeve, I examined it further. A scratch...

"They're on your neck as well," Fenris went on. "You wouldn't stop, so I pushed you."

My fingers feathered over the thin, rough streaks to my throat. *How hard had I scratched?*

"They don't look deep. Just... be careful. And, to be safe..." The wolf offered his side once more. "I want you to permanently stick to me. I want to feel your hand practically digging into my flesh, and under no circumstances are you to let go."

His steely gaze set on me, I did as I was told.

"Good. Now, let's be off."

Silence again drove us apart, though my hand remained connected to his side. Every once in a bit, he'd look to me, and those comforting eyes would cure me of the swirling anxiety clouding my mind. When they left me, however, I was lost again in my wandering thoughts of fear and...

Realization hit me upon recognizing the voices I'd heard, and I halted in my tracks.

Fenris came to a stop right next to me. "Rosella?"

"You were talking to someone," I uttered, my eyes staring blankly ahead of me, "and it kinda sounded like the voice that appeared in my head. They were talking to you."

"Don't be afraid of it," Fenris stated firmly, but calmly. "You've changed far more than you know, and it's finally starting to surface."

I looked to him with a confused frown. "I... I don't follow."

The light of the red fog illuminated his face. "Trust me, you'll know when the time comes."

Trust me... You'll know... guarding this Vessel... when the time comes.

"!" My heart fluttered upon the returning heat, and I rested my palm against my chest. It burned, yet there was no pain.

"Rosella?" Fenris leaned into the hand still clasping his fur. "If you need to sit again, you can."

"It's... It's fine." I closed my eyes, and relaxed my wavering head. "I'm okay."

... must hurry! Now!

Hollow, I promised you that I'd do what you wish, but I don't know if I can follow through with it.

Please, Fenris. I need you now more than ever.

But how will you find your way back?

I have taken into account the risks bearing this forest, and whether it will survive... Unfortunately, this is all I can think of. I promise, I will fight to save our home.

But the curse... What if you're playing right into Ashen's evil clutches? What if you...

Fenris, you can rest assured, you will hear my voice again.

How will I know it's you?

You will, because Ashen's curse will not claim me.

And, what of the others? Will they do their part?

I've already spoken with them. You have been given the most difficult to handle, as she will be closer to the curse than all the others. Don't forget that.

I promise... I won't.

My heart thundered in my chest. *Mom and Dad... They welcomed me into theirs when I lost mine...*

I will return to you, when the time comes... And when we meet again, it will be face to face. I promise you that...

I understand. I'll go, then. I... I hope you know what you're doing.

It will hurt you both greatly, I know. But Chloe will come to understand, and one day, Rosella will too.

"Rosella." Fenris' voice broke through the mental fog in my head, and I found him staring out into the distance. "Rosella, I sense something. Do not let go of me."

"Wh-What is it?" I whispered.

His eyes narrowed through a fierce glare. "Someone is watching us."

I winced at the tiny tap to my cheek. It felt like a raindrop, though when I put a finger to it, I could tell it wasn't water. "This isn't blood either," I whispered, while observing the liquid staining my finger. It was dark, and a little thick, kind of like mud.

"What is it?" Fenris asked.

I extended an arm around my chest. "This."

Fenris' nose brushed the tip of my offered finger, and his snout wrinkled in disgust. "You're right. It smells of ash and rot, but the substance is more like wet soil." A second drop landed atop the center of his muzzle, and he looked up. "This is an omen, and not a good one."

"Aren't all omens bad?" I pondered.

"Not all. There are such things as good omens. But they are not in our sights today, nor tomorrow."

Troubled by his words, I asked him the daring question. "How do you know?"

The wolf didn't appear to want to answer, his maw sealed tight in a tense frown.

More drops of whatever it was fell from the sky, wetting my hair. "Fenris, we should get moving."

He gave a curt nod. "Let us be off."

Fenris and I meandered about our dreary surroundings, unsure of where we were going. The red fog had grown stronger, by this time covering our knees. I peered over my shoulder, in hopes of finding the abandoned house in our sights, and to my relief, it was still there. The faint structure was clouded by the fog, but I could still make out the shape.

"Fenris, I think we should head back soon," I warned. "We might lose sight of the house."

"You are right, Little Rose." Fenris came to a stop alongside me. "Why don't we backtrack just a bit?" He wrinkled his muzzle, his face suddenly morphing into a strange look.

"Is something wrong?" I asked.

Fenris shook his head. "I... I'm losing the scent of the house." A rigid line of fur rose atop his back. "I don't understand. We couldn't have gone that far already."

"I just saw it myself..." I turned around, my one hand falling away from the wolf so the other could take its place. But when I went to grab for him... "Fenris?" I swatted the air. "Fenris!" I whipped my head to my right, where I thought he was standing. I didn't see him, so I looked to the left. "Oh no... Fenris. Fenris!" My heart started to throb, my breathing hitched. "F-Fenris! Where are you!?"

"Rosella!?" I heard him call out.

"Fenris!"

"Rosella!" he cried. "I-I can hear you! I just can't see you!"

My chest clenched with the thundering panic of my heart. "Fenris! Where are you!?"

"My dear, calm down!" he yelled. "It will be alright. I will try to seek you out, just hold on."

"Please hurry." I hugged my sides. "I don't... I don't want to be alone." *Loneliness... I don't like that. I need someone with me.*

"Psst, Rosella..."

I jumped at the brush of air against my ear, and whirled around.

"Over here... Over here, Rosella~! Follow me."

Follow who? I looked around me. "Hello?"

"Yes. Over here."

Something sleeked over my shoulder, and my hand was quick to slap at it. However, I felt nothing there.

"Rosella, I want to show you something~! It's really cool. Won't you follow me?"

I gasped at the pinch to my side and looked down. Nothing but red fog, red fog, more red fog.

"It's over here."

"S-Stop it." Something pulled my hair. "Ouch. Stop it!" I threw my hands out in front of me, and they disappeared into the fog.

"Hehe~! Oh, isn't this fun?"

A chill coursed down my spine. I couldn't... I couldn't feel my hands. I couldn't move them. "F-Fenris?" I attempted to take a step forward, but my left foot wouldn't move.

"Rosella."

"Fenris!" I called again. "Fenris! Help!" Something cold wrapped around my right ankle, and I trembled with fear. "F-Fenris... Fenris, please."

"He can't help you, silly! But I can~! Just follow me."

"No! I don't want this! Let go!" I struggled to pull my hands free of the fog, but something, whatever it was, held me tight. "Please! Let go! Fenris! Fenris, help!"

"Poor, timid little Rosella... All alone, with no one around~!"

"Fenris!"

"And now it's too late!"

"Wh-What?"

"Sweet, little blonde Red, without her Guardian for protection..."

My captured hands were suddenly pulled above my head.

"Pink and plump, good enough to eat, but not so for us~! We have much... much... bigger plans... for you."

A numbing seal crept along my trembling lips, effectively cutting off a frightened sob pleading for escape, as my head abruptly locked in place. Unable to move a muscle, I could utter only a muffled whimper, as something sharp began its icy stroke across my abdomen.

"Warm, plush insides to spill, your blood will drench the earth. We'll bury your remains in a prison of soil far underground, though your spirit will remain locked in the cage of your mind. Without your body, you will feel disconnected."

"Rosella!" I heard Fenris calling out to me. "Rosella, can you hear me!? Rosella!"

My heart sank deeper into despair, my tearful eyes screwing shut. *I hear you... But my voice can't tell you.*

"Rosella! Rosella, don't lose your light! You must hang on!"

I want to hang on... The fog was so thick... *But I'm losing my grip.* I couldn't see a thing.

"Rosella! Rosel..."

The fog devoured Fenris' frantic cries, and then there was nothing.

"Wilt in the darkness, and rot beneath the earth."

The invisible force released me, and my chin slammed into the ground as I fell forward, resulting in a searing pain to my jaw as it craaaaaaaaaaaaaaaaaaaaaaaaaaaaaaaaaaaaaaaaaaaaaaaaaaaa aaaaaaaaaaaaaaaaaaaaaaaaaaaaaaaaaaaaaaaaaaa aaaaa aaa a   a   aa aa a a   a—

To care and t o   p r o t e c   t   R   O   S   E   L L A

When you're found, you will f i   n   d   home home HOME HOOOOOME home.

Y o u are our l o   Ving

da u g

htEr,

S we et

r   o   S

E

L a

An abrupt gasp tore from my lips, and I scrambled with ferocity upon the ground. My hands tore blades of empty-toned grass as I shot to my feet, and I ran blindly through the bloody fog, soil smeared against my boots. A boiling fire breached my chest, melting away the freezing blanket of air from my body.

My nerves screamed, though not of pain. They craved satiation for their hunger of the heat. It coiled around my limbs, singing the tips of my fingers and toes in response, as a quivering exhale relinquished my lips.

"WILT IN THE DARKNESS, AND ROT IN THE EARTH!!!! YOU ARE TOO LATE!!! YOU ARE OURS!!!!"

I dropped to my knees, hands clasped to my head. "NO no No nO NOOOOOOOOOOOOOOOOOOOOOOOOOOOOOOOOOOOOOOO!!!!"

Whispering, chattering, scratching in my ears, itching, so itchy! Nails clawing at flesh, relieve the itch, remove the festering maggots! The heat is turning cold, don't go! Return to me, please give me back my heat! I'm shivering! Please come back! I need it need need need it need it need it need it need it NEED IT! Screaming, crying, I'm going under, the soil is choking me. It's freezing!

ROSELLA!!!!!!

My pain released in one shrill cry, and I bolted with blind direction.

Don't give in, Rosella! Bloom in the light! They're coming! Quick! NOW!

Powerful heat radiated within me, as a blinding aura of red set my surroundings ablaze. The creeping tendrils that licked my ankles burst into a fit of flames, then crumbled to ash, the grass unscathed by the heroic embers. I whirled around to face the commotion, my vision a crimson glow, and I stared in awe at the unfolding scene.

Pinned to the ground with their suffering, the roots of darkness mindlessly squirmed with fear. Perilous squawking permeated the air, drowning out the crackling waves of the fire. Smoke drifted high, while the smell of charred wood lingered near the ground.

They've got a hold of you, Rosella! Don't give in! Fight it!

I looked down and gasped at the stray root coiled around my ankle like a serpent. Terror gripped my heart, as it pierced deep into my flesh and bone, and the target spot quickly festered into rotting ash. Hot, searing pain bubbled from the tips of my toes to my upper thigh.

Their infection is coursing in your veins! Don't let them take you!

I don't understand what's happening! I screamed in my mind. *What is this!? Why am I... Why am I...*

My leg felt like it was weighted with lead, unable to move, and through the various tears in my pants, I saw that the infection had discolored my veins, and turned my flesh a pasty white. The darkness was devouring the light inside of me, a freezing chill vanquishing my comforting heat.

"You're a foolish weed," a sinister voice purred, "*with an empty shell and no willpower.*"

I shook my head. *That's not true. I'm... I'm not...*

"*Don't you realize what's happening here? You broke everything. Your mother set you up, gave you happiness, and you broke it.*"

No, I didn't... I didn't mean to...

"*Sophia never loved you. She only loved what she couldn't have.*"

No! That's a lie! Tears spilled from my burning eyes. *Sophia loved me very much!*

"*You know what you are, so why not just give in? You don't have anything else to do, as you have no home to go back to.*"

I do! Because... Because...

"*HA! You are hiding from the truth! Why, even that wolf has pushed you right into the abyss. Wrapping you in a filthy rag of lies and deceit, he only longs to see his master, and through you, he can!*"

"NO! I REFUSE TO LISTEN TO YOU!!!" I roared.

"*WILT IN THE DARKNESS, YOU PUNY WEED! NEVER AGAIN WILL YOU EMBRACE THE LIGHT.*"

The world around me started spinning around and around and around and around and around and around and around and around and around around and around and around and around and around and around and around and around and around and around and around around and around and around and around and around and around and arou—

Voices... Red... Memories... Roses, flowers... Mother... Mother! Mother! MOTHER! Make the pain stop, oh god it hurts please make it stop.

Mercy

Mercy...

BLOOD

My chest frantically jutted in and out, in a bout of hyperventilation. I could hear voices, voices, whispering, hisses around me.

Drip drip drip... Oh, how the blood drips so softly to the floor... It pools all around... Her conscious... The swollen blister inside her... It's growing...

OHGODITHURTS... PLEASE... Makeitstopohgodplease... Pleading, hurting, dying, suffering, crying, laughing... IthurtsithurtsITHURTSITHURTS...

ROSELLA... ROSE... Ro...

Blood, crying, screaming, hurting, dying, suffering, burning, pain, blood, laughing, laughter, so much laughter! HahahahahahahahahahahaHAHAHAHAHAHAHAHAHAHAHAHAHA!!!!!!!

I shrieked and clasped my hands over my ears to drown out the noise, but IT JUST WOULDN'T STOP.

"The lovely red fog and how it makes her heart just feel so warm and fuzzy! Oh, how its glow makes her just want to dance in the bloody rain that falls all around her! She is dancing, her mouth wide open with laughter. Her feet are prancing about in the pools of blood that are quickly flooding her senses."

As the devious voice foretold, Mom was there, bathing in the bloody shower, a newborn babe in her arms.

"See the hopeless mother swaddling her Vessel child, her blood-stained Vessel child, in her battered arms~! She is laughing and crying at the same time, her bloody tears rolling relentlessly down her face. She is laughing hysterically as she peels away at her face, her fingers digging deep into her cheeks, into muscle and bone. She is laughing! Ha ha! Ha ha ha ha ha! "HaAaHhahAahaHaHAhahahAAHAAahA!!!!!"

Mom! Stop! Stop it! The scene unfolding before me, I couldn't unsee it.

"Her haunting, nightmarish face, her bloody eyes wet with red. Blood gushes from her mouth, choking her fractured laughter, but her maniacal cackles remain undeterred."

I didn't want to see, I didn't want to see... That wasn't her. Make it stop!

Flashes... Flashes...

Rosella!

RosellablondeoneRoSELLaBlonDEOneRosBLondEOnE

Rosella!

I closed my eyes, and began to rock myself. "Stop it," I whispered. "Stop it... Get out of my head, get out of my head." But it burrowed deep, into my mind, against my pleas.

"She is fading away. She can't help you now! She hates you! She hates your guts! Cut yourself open! Let your insides spill out! Let the world see what lies within! The hot viscera is slapping at your sides as it hangs out of your torn belly! You're helpless, but you don't care! Hahahahaha!!!! Keep laughing! Laughing! Hurting! Crying! Pain! Pain! Burning! Crying! YesyesyesYES!YESSS!!!!!"

"Stop it..."

Mother dearest please make it stopNO! Please make it stopNO!

I wanted it to stop. It hurt. It—

NONONONononononONo!   OHGodIthuRTS!!!!!!!!!!!!!!! It'scrawlinginsideinsidetheretherethere! Thesweetmoon is rising... Rising... high... High! Blood, guts... BloodbloodBLOOD! Must have it! Must! Must! Must!

FOOLFOOLFOOL FOOL FOOLFOOLFOOL FOO L F OOL F O OL FOOLFOO LF OO L FOOL

FOOL FOOL FOOL WILT IN THE DARK

FOOL

FOOL FOO—

A crack snapped the air like it was a twig, and I dropped to the ground.

CHAPTER 28

MY STAGGERING MIND WAS dry of ideas, much like my mouth and throat. I was beyond parched, and my head was pounding. As I punched my balled fists into the ground, and cried frustrated tears, my fingers throbbed in protest. They were sore as hell from tearing through the dead earth caked deep under my nails. Even worse, sweat mixed with tiny grains of dirt scorched the nicks in my dry, scaly skin, each sting like the ferocious bite of a fire ant.

I peered down at my filthy palms. They were black as soot, and… Ugh. I scrunched my nose. They smelled like rot, much like the rest of myself. *God I feel gross… Why can't they let me bathe somewhere?* I whimpered at the thought of water. *And I'm so thirsty…* A low growl escaped my stomach. *And hungry…*

It had to have been days, at least a week? Perhaps longer? Frustrated, I ran a hand through coarse strands of hair that hung stiff, like straw, around my face. Having abandoned my hair tie, the freedom made my scalp itch more, and as tempting as it was to relieve the irritation, I'd already clawed it raw. Any more could result in bleeding.

God… Why the hell was I was like this? I was deteriorating faster than Caroline, and she'd been here for about the same time as me. What the hell was going on?

"So, you're finally giving up?"

God, I hate you. I hate you, I hate you, I HATE you.

"Huh, guess you lack glory more than guts."

I glared up at Caroline as she approached me. "What the hell do you want?" My voice, unlike hers, was raspy from my sore throat, and each word I uttered felt like I'd swallowed hot shards of glass. *How is she not going through this?* I looked over her matted hair. It wasn't coarse like mine. I gawked at her complexion. Her skin looked smooth and healthy. She was practically *glowing* compared to me.

Caroline crossed her arms over her chest. "It's interesting watchin' you lose your mind." A smirk formed across her lips. Those perfect, ruby lips, unlike the cracked flaps that lined my mouth.

I ran the back of my dirtied hand across my sore eyes, to conceal the burning tears, and wound up smearing them into the faint dusting of dirt at my cheeks.

"Aw, what's the matter?" Caroline leaned forward, with a mocking pout. "Did I hurt your feelings?"

I opened my mouth to retaliate, but was interrupted by the sudden appearance of a Lurker.

"Leader order us to give food," the towering creature grumbled, and dropped something between us. *"Eat."*

I rested a hand to my biting gut. The thought of food alone was a pleasant taste in my mouth, but without water, I knew I couldn't bear it. Still, I laid eyes on the pile of meat strips atop that crinkled leaf, and for a moment, I forgot about the situation I was in. There were several pieces, enough to split between me and Caroline.

My stomach grumbled at the thought of sharing, and I clamped my mouth shut, in order to keep what little saliva I had from spilling.

The Lurker blankly stared down at us, waiting.

Meanwhile, Caroline scoffed at the meal presented to her. "Ew! I'm not touching anything you weirdos handle. How do I know it wasn't poisoned or some shit!?"

Ignoring Caroline, I plucked a thick, flimsy strip of the meat, and examined it. It was a nice, brown color, though the texture was a bit dry. Dry... My sandy tongue grazed the cracked roof of my mouth.

At least it's cooked... And I am hungry... Hesitantly, my tongue snatched the strip from my hand and pushed it to the back of my mouth.

My stomach willed me to continue stuffing my face, but the salty strip set my entire mouth ablaze, and I had to cough it back out. Blood spattered onto the ground, as I coughed and wheezed, and I helplessly clutched at my burning throat.

Caroline scowled at me. "Gross."

"Why won't Red Head eat?" the Lurker questioned dumbly. *"Red Head not hungry?"*

"I told you, I'm not touching anything you freaks handle." She rolled her eyes in my direction. "Unlike someone..."

I ignored Caroline, and instead gave the Lurker a pleading look.

It cocked its head, questioningly, at my attempt to beg it for water, the idiot. *"What matter?"*

Caroline snorted. "She needs water, you moron."

I gave another harsh cough, and with it, a crackled moan. "P-Please..." Oh god, it hurt so much to talk, I could barely get the words out.

"You gonna get her some water, or sit there and let her suffer?" Caroline questioned. "Not that I care. I'm just curious."

I scowled at her. *I hate you. I FUCKING hate you.*

Caroline laughed. "God, look at you!" She came closer, and knelt down in front of me, her eyes locked with mine. Her lips spread apart, revealing her pearly white teeth. "You're... finished..."

I raised a fist, and it connected with her jaw. Her head jerked to the side, as she stumbled back, but instead of screaming curses with a hand clutching the side of her face, I was the one cowering in immense pain, cradling my tender wrist. It was like I'd punched concrete, my knuckles throbbed so badly. And as I doubled over, Caroline cackled at my misery.

I wanted to scream in her face how much I hated her, that she deserved to die a thousand deaths, but I couldn't even do that. That salty meat strip had done in what little bit of my throat was left.

"We rise in the dark, while she wilts in it..."

"Huh?" Caroline turned to her right, where a lone Lurker clawing at its face loitered about, seemingly without harm.

"She feeds off of the light... We crave the dark..."

"The hell you goin' on about?"

The Lurker's neck snapped our way. *"Light is against us... She uses it against us... We cannot thrive off of it. We bloom in the dark, and wilt in the light."*

"Right... Whoa, what the fuck?" Caroline had looked away from the Lurker, her eyes now on something else.

I stumbled to my feet, and followed her line of sight. My mouth dropped open, my eyes wide with fear.

Encircling the enormous raging ball of dancing embers, the Lurkers held their decaying arms high into the air, accompanied with a choir of disorienting caws, and the one that lingered near me and Caroline went to join its brethren, whilst stomping its stocky legs. All were absorbed in their excited routine, their leader guiding them with a foreign incantation.

"Ah, onwa she tah merbuk!" the leader declared.

"Woh sha nee may!" their people responded.

Despite my sickly condition, my vision was still in perfect working order, and it assisted me in spotting the streaks of lavender slithering through the exhaled smoke of the embers. The black gem embedded in the leader Lurker's excited heart began to glow a bright purple, just like it did before, and I grimaced against the throbbing pain of my annoying blisters.

"Nwa yo tah me doh!" the leader exclaimed. *"Shaaaaaaaaaa!!"* Claws wriggling with excitement, they stomped a foot several times, and threw their head to the ground.

I stared in astonishment at the neurotic flames as they engulfed their bed of wood, and lapped at the air. The lavender wisps of light coiled around the embers, prompting their crackling limbs to writhe, as if with erotic tension. The tighter the constriction, the more they wriggled.

The ground began to quiver beneath everyone's feet, and I was quick to kneel alongside Caroline, though the Lurkers remained unaffected. The lead Lurker's decrepit hand clutched tightly to their illuminated chest, and to my continued confusion, they relinquished something from within their beating muscle.

The frightened seam, threading from the spool of fear, tightened within my frantic heart, when I registered the beautiful red rose in the leader's grasp. *Please... No...*

With a reaper's leer, the monster craned their head in my direction.

I forced a blank stare, a meager attempt to mask my fright.

"Reach inside, and pluck her petals, one by one, as she struggles," the leader whispered. *"Drag her deep into the darkness, drain her of light, and she shall wilt..."* With a delicate pluck, one by one, each frail petal was torn from the base of the innocent rose resting within their palm, each one carried away into the flames. The creature then pointed in my direction, and uttered a single word. *"Mootah."*

Four Lurkers began a threatening trek toward me and Caroline, and I looked to her with a terrified gaze.

Caroline stumbled back several steps. "Why the fuck are they pointing at us!?" She backed further away from me. "T-Take her! She's the one you want, right?"

My lip curled in a snarl. *Why do you always think for yourself!? You selfish bitch!* Fear streamed through the tears in my eyes, as I looked toward the monstrosities inches from us, and then back at her.

" *H a h a h a h a h a h a h a* ... *HAHAHAHAHAHAHAHAHAHAHAHAHAHAHAHAHA!!!!!!!!!!*" A sinister smile, dripping with venomous intent, cracked the leader's shriveled face, as it pointed my way. *"Nye... Shimah ah teek."*

I gasped as I was abruptly yanked back, my hands thrust behind me.

Caroline gawked at my situation, then looked to the Lurkers. They were now focused on her, and she shook her head. "N-No... No... No!"

Quaked with fear, Caroline bolted for the trees, but her escape was swiftly intercepted with a sprouting black root that sprung from the ground. It aggressively twisted her ankle, and with a sickening crack, she collapsed, her unbearable agony expressed through her blood-curdling scream.

Terror gripped me far more tightly than my restraints, as I watched Caroline get pulled back.

"Now... Commence!"

Squiggling roots writhed from beneath the soil, quickly trapping my legs, and pulled me down.

"Seize her!" the leading Lurker commanded.

"NO! STOP!!!" I pleaded, my screech tearing through my raw throat. *"NO!!!!"*

"Hold it!"

The Lurkers went still all at once, as if they'd suddenly become statues, except for the leader, who craned their head toward the edge of the clearing. Caroline and I followed their line of sight, where a silver foot slunk out from beyond the rustling trees, and both our jaws dropped at the appearance of a beautiful, silver-skinned woman. Clad in a thin black dress that draped a few feet out behind her, she waltzed into view without a care in the world, and flicked a lock of her long crimson hair behind her.

She pursed her black lips, her porcelain eyes set on us. "Hello, girls. I've been meaning to speak with the both of you."

Caroline's eyes welled with tears. "A... Au..." She struggled to get the words out, but I knew what she was trying to say.

"Before we proceed, allow me to explain." The woman stepped forward, and lifted her sleek, silver arm to the air. A cloud of purple dust flicked from her fingertips, and then two bodies had formed in front of her. "Recognize these two?"

I thought my eyes were deceiving me. *No... It can't be...*

"N-No way!" Caroline's head whipped in my direction, then her aunt, eyes wide with shock. "That's... That's Marcus! And the nurse lady!"

A ways from us, Patricia and Marcus stood with blank stares, as clear as day, their arms planted at their sides. Neither one moved or spoke.

Caroline's nose crinkled. "Ew! What the hell is that on Marcus' face!?"

I too took notice of the dirt crusting the corner of Marcus' mouth, and cringed.

"Oh, just that pesky, hot-headed detective." Georgia waved at the air with a lazy hand. "He got nosy, so he got bit."

Frank Stormer... I closed my eyes, and tried my best to picture him in my mind. *That's right, he was working on a case, and questioned us.* My eyes reopened, and wandered to Marcus. *Why is he here, then? And Patricia... Were they captured?*

"Caroline, my dear." Georgia strolled around both Marcus and Patricia, her arms behind her. "Remember when I told you that Ashen chose your auntie as their second in-command? Well, I'm here to tell you that you are about to achieve what I sadly cannot~! Ashen believes that you are far more superior, and believe me when I say, you will be ecstatic to know why~!" She gave a giddy squeal, and clapped her hands together. "Oh, my sweet little niece, you have so much ahead of you!"

I struggled in my restraints, prompting Georgia to turn her snake-like eyes on me.

"Oh, of course, how could I forget you." She glided toward me, her dress dragging the ground with each majestic step. "I've been waiting to see you again. Why, you've grown so prettily."

"Ge... Get away..." I rasped.

A sinister cackle slipped her tenacious grin, as her fingers curled around my tethered throat like a vise. "Still defiant as usual. Ashen was right to get rid of you."

The faint wheeze that grazed my cracked lips was so quiet, that even the drop of a pin needle could drown out my broken voice.

She cocked her head. "How was your meal, by the way? Hopefully not too salty." The corner of her mouth twitched as she caught my flinch.

Still, I ignored the stinging pain of her nails hooked into my skin, and struck her with the sharpest glare I could muster.

"Ah, if it's one thing I enjoy more than power, it's watching the weak struggle for their next breath..." She flitted a free hand at her face. "Tell me, how would you rather die, by my hand, or your parched tongue?"

How's about you choke on your pride? I wanted to say, but her dominating hand around my throat effectively silenced me with a squeeze.

"I'll bet you're wondering why it is we're doing this, right?" Georgia nodded to Marcus and Patricia standing a ways behind her. "Like these two, everyone is a puppet to me. As their master, I enjoy controlling their actions. My niece easily came to understand that joy, so I don't have to worry about putting her in her place, unlike *you*."

I clenched my jaw. *I'm not giving you anything. You won't break me.*

Georgia sighed. "You are tough, aren't you? No matter, I have more... *drastic* measures up my sleeve." She raised her hand to the air, and gracefully flipped her wrist. "Vanish! You are no longer needed!"

Dirt spilled from Marcus and Patricia's eyes and mouths, as their arms and legs went limp, their necks cocked at odd angles, and they sunk to the ground, before vanishing in a cloud of purple mist.

Fresh, scorching tears sprung to my eyes at the sight, my mouth agape.

"Ah, yes... Isn't that something?" Georgia turned back to me with sinister glee. "Needed something to throw you off the trail. You always were a little more observant, just like those detectives, and that stupid bitch..." Her eyes narrowed, a malicious glint to both. "But you? You are that little piece of resistance that must be crushed first."

Patricia's words suddenly returned to mind, and my blood ran cold.

Sophia, I may have only known you for a month or so but, out of everyone here... You are the most honest of them all. You are that little piece of resistance that defies this town's regimen, whatever that is.

Georgia raised an eyebrow. "You really are a foolish girl, though I can't blame you. Your mother's the one who taught you your stupidity. Did you know that she's out here, right now, looking for you?"

My stomach dropped to the earthy floor. Mom... She was looking for me?

"That's right," Georgia purred, as her mouth spread a little wider. "Sadly, though, she can't track you here, nor can you track her. See, there's a border of magic lining this clearing. That's why you couldn't leave, you know. Boy, that was a fun sight! Ha!" She brought her face closer to mine, until our foreheads were touching. "How does it feel, no longer being in control?"

Don't give in to her mind games... Be strong.

"I don't understand why you're putting up such a fight," Georgia said. "Just give up already. You're finished."

"N-No," I choked out. "Y-You're... wrong..." God, each syllable was like a shard of glass cutting into my throat.

Georgia laughed. "Oh, don't worry dear! You won't be forgotten! You're just being put in storage." She peered over at her niece. "Caroline, you're going to need to trust Auntie now. I promise, after the pain, you will feel wonderful!"

Caroline stared back with a look of confusion "What are you saying, Auntie?"

"Trust me, dear." Georgia looked back to me. "As for you... Why don't you sit back and relax?"

Her hand unlatched from my throat, and a squeak crawled its way out, as I was yanked to the ground upon my rear.

"Now then..." Georgia nodded to the Lurkers. "Please, continue."

I gawked at the sight of the Lurkers crowding around Caroline like a pack of wild beasts, in silent horror. What the fuck were they planning to do?

"*Rejoice, Brunette!*" the Lurker leader called. "*Rejoice in your desire to see this flesh-bearing maggot suffer.*"

"Auntie!" Caroline screamed, as the Lurkers overwhelmed her. "STOP IT!!!! NO!!!!! *IT HURTS!!!!!*"

I stared in utter shock, my mouth hung open in a silent scream, as the lead Lurker crept into view of me.

"Our preparations complete, all we need now is a Queen." They prowled forward, and Georgia stepped aside, so they could take her place in front of me.

My nose crinkled at the nauseating stench intruding my nostrils, and I gave them the most ferocious scowl. "Get the... *fuck* outta my face, Ashen," I hissed. "Your puppet's breath... smells like *rotten shit!*"

Their expression faltered. *"Foul-mouthed Brunette... You annoy me with your stubbornness..."* They aggressively clutched at my waist, and growled. *"We break her treasure, we break her... Break her stem... and she wilts... You... You are her stem... so it's time... we break you."*

I grunted against the constricting pressure. and coughed up a spat of blood.

"Easy now, my master, not too hard," Georgia scolded. "She must be kept in one piece."

I glowered at the both of them. "You... won't... get away..."

Georgia scoffed at me. "Oh, my dear. We already have."

Caroline

With a rush of air to her lungs, Caroline gasped, and shot to her feet without a second thought. What had happened? And... where the hell was this? Just a moment ago, those freakish things had captured her and Sophia, and then her auntie... Auntie Georgia!

"Auntie!?" Caroline whipped her fiery head about her. "Hey! Where are you!?"

All around her were empty trees, their branches poised like threatening hands, waiting to grab her. They swam in a pooling red fog, troubling her vision. She took a hesitant step forward, as she lacked shoes, and then another. She'd recalled Sophia being yanked to the ground, and then Caroline herself being *dogpiled* by those things upon her own auntie's request. It was like being attacked by a frenzy of piranha. And, why would Auntie Georgia do that to her!?

"God, what the hell is this?" Caroline asked herself, in a frightened whisper. She scrubbed at her arms. "Fuck, Auntie."

"Caroline?"

The red head stiffened. *That voice...*

"Caroline? Is that you?"

A glare capable of murder worked its way onto Caroline's face, as she spotted the familiar figure come waltzing into view, her small hands clasped behind her back. "Bloom!" Nostrils flared, Caroline stormed toward her target. "You fat, pig bitch! You did this! You got me into this mess! You freak!"

Rosella silently stared back, a blank expression on her face.

"You're gonna pay!" Caroline shoved a finger at the opposite girl's chest. "Oh, I'm gonna get you *so hard!* I..." Her voice went silent at Rosella's abrupt giggle. "What the hell is so funny, you fucking freak!?"

Rosella didn't respond to her question. She just kept giggling, then uttered a strong chuckle that grew into explosive laughter, then maniacal cackling. A tainted sea of twisted joy swirling in those abysmal blue eyes, as her mouth spread wider, and wider, until the corners spread to her ears, her cheeks stretched like elastic.

Caroline backed away from her. This was clearly *not* the Rosella Bloom she was used to.

"Caroline?" Rosella's neck abruptly snapped to the side, her malevolent expression unchanged. "What's the matter? You look uncomfortable."

Caroline winced as the blonde's head curved far over her shoulder. How Rosella's neck wasn't broken was beyond her.

"Hey... Wanna paint these trees with me? I could show you how. I am an artist after all."

Caroline felt her stomach drop as Rosella brandished a knife. "What's that for?"

"Oh? This?" Rosella's disturbing grin disappeared, as her crooked neck yanked back to normal position, her head still unnaturally angled. "This here is my paintbrush. I use it to paint the trees."

"Th-That's not—"

"Wanna know where I get the paint?" She raised the knife. "I can show you..." Rosella scooted a bit to the left. "Here."

A faint whimper grazed Caroline's ear, and her mouth dropped.

Suspending from a tree by her ankles, her hands bound below her head, Sophia squirmed about the air. A thick root was coiled around her mouth, blocking her screams.

Caroline couldn't believe what she was seeing. "What... You... What the fuck?"

Rosella approached her best friend, and traced the knife from the middle of her hips, down to her chest. "Don't worry, Sophia. I promise to be gentle."

A frantic cry exploded from behind Sophia's gag, her tears raining the ground below.

"The hell's going on here?" Caroline asked. "I thought she was your friend?"

Rosella ignored her as she brought the knife back to the middle of her best friend's hips, and tore a neat slit down the lower half of her shirt.

Sophia thrashed about like a helpless doe about to be gutted, her eyes wide with fear.

"Seriously!" Caroline shrieked. "What the hell's goin' on here!?"

An evil smirk graced Rosella's lips. "Aw, listen to that, Sophia! I think she feels sorry for you! Isn't that just sweet?"

The tip of the knife circled Sophia's quivering navel, and she shuddered with a trembling whimper.

"Oh please, I could care less." Caroline crossed her arms over her shoulders, and shrugged. "You wanna kill her, go right ahead."

Rosella suddenly whirled on Caroline with feral, bloodshot eyes. "OF COURSE YOU WOULD SAY THAT!" she roared in a distorted bout. "YOU DON'T CARE ABOUT ANYONE BUT YOURSELF! YOU JUST WANNA MAKE US SUFFER!"

Caroline stumbled back, shocked by Rosella's aggressive behavior.

"Hey Caroline, remember me?"

She peered over her shoulder. "Wh-Wha!?"

Another blonde, with long straight locks, and pale rings tracing the edges of her dark blue eyes, strode toward her. "Remember me, Caroline? All I wanted was a friend, and you dangled that in front of my face before taking it away... And now look at me. I'm nothing... Nothing!" Pills spilled from the lacerations she tore into her throat, her fingers stained red.

"Oh god, it's you," Caroline whispered, her eyes wide. "I... I thought you were..."

"How about me!? Huh, Caroline!?" Yet another girl, with a red bob cut, appeared in front of her. "Huh!? I just wanted to make a difference for the school! And look what happened to me!" The girl yanked the collar of her top down, revealing two large rats tearing through her breasts. They snapped their frothing jaws, as she stomped toward Caroline with a furious scowl. "LOOK AT ME!!!! LOOK WHAT YOU DID TO ME!!!!!"

Caroline let out a blood-curdling scream, as she fell to the ground and scrambled away from the horrific scene splayed before her. "GET AWAY FROM ME!!! LEAVE ME ALONE!!!!" She gasped as she bumped into something, and looked up to that menacing, psychotic grin looming above her.

"So, want to help me?" Rosella cooed. "All it takes is a little cut..."

Caroline shot from her spot, and ran blindly into the bloody fog. As her feet slipped several paces ahead, and she fell face-first into the fog, roots reeking of soot and decay pierced through the ground, and made quick work of binding her limbs.

"NO!!!! LET ME GO!!!!!" Her matted locks slapped at her face, as she thrashed her head from side to side. "LET ME G—!!!!!"

Something thin, cold, and hard suddenly pierced her chest, and Caroline's mouth dropped open, as tears of blood pricked her eyes. Fingers curled stiff like talons, as her limbs contorted into unnatural position, she snapped her head back, and a faint wheeze grazed her throat.

Hot pain ruptured her gut, and sent her panicked nerves scampering for relief, but there was none. It felt like a rabid animal was tearing through her insides, and she could do nothing but flail like a fish out of water.

Please! Make it stop! It hurts! Auntie!

A wet tear split the air, and then everything went dark. The pain vanished as Caroline went still.

CHAPTER 29

M Y VISION BECAME SHROUDED in darkness, the moment the racket started. I could hear everything going on around me, but I couldn't move to stop the horrific bellows that ripped from Caroline's throat, or what I assumed were the Lurkers chanting in their mysterious language.

The quaking ground violently rattled me about, as if I were a jar of coins, and my pinned limbs trembled within their bindings. My chattering teeth unintentionally chewed through the left side of my mouth, the taste of copper and spit mixed in an unpleasant taste, upon my parched tongue.

"Rise, now! Rejoice, our Queen has arrived!!"

All around me, the Lurkers howled and whooped, like the annoying jocks that catcalled me back at school. God, I'd give anything just to be there, *right now,* instead of here. I'd put up with those penis-minded idiots any day of the week, compared to this. This... This was a nightmare, from which I feared there was no waking.

Caroline's agonizing wails pierced my skull once more, and tore a permanent mental lesion into my brain. *God, please... Please make it stop! Please! PLEASE!*

As if my silent pleading had been answered by a higher power, the world around me suddenly came to a halt. The ground went still, the screaming stopped, and the white noise buzzing in my pulsing ears gradually faded.

I gasped as my bindings vanished from my arms and legs, and suddenly the view of the world had returned to me. Heart hammering in my chest, I shot up, and frantically looked around.

"C-Caro... Caroline!" I squeaked. Against the crippling pain that ruptured my neck and stomach, I scrambled to my feet. "Ah..."

My eyes glanced over the thick, ashy circle, then around the rest of the clearing. The other Lurkers... Where were they? The leader lingered some ways off, still as a statue, with only Georgia beside them. But the others were gone. And Caroline...

Before my very eyes, her naked flesh was stripped from her limbs, as if by an invisible peeler, exposing muscle that quickly morphed into wood, while the front of her torso and down to her lower abdomen discolored a pale ivory. Dark purple veins crept up the sides of the blister that sprouted and grew to bulbous size in the center of her chest, as five glowing circles of unique lettering rotated at various speeds, from the center of her bare stomach down into her navel. The markings glowed a luminous purple aura that gradually faded, as they became small carvings etched into her skin.

Her matted, mahogany locks fell away in clumps, as her scalp sprouted several deadwood branches, each adorned with clusters of mini orange poppy flowers. As her porcelain eyes fluttered open, black veins dripped like ink down her smooth doll-like face, and to the corners of her ebony lips.

"Carol... ine..." I whispered, as she was lifted from the ground, and placed upon her feet.

Her wooden neck cracked, as her head whipped in my direction, her empty stare coursing a chill down my spine.

"Rejoice, Brunette. Our Queen has arrived."

Though the Lurker leader's sudden presence from behind startled me, I whirled around to face them with blossoming fury in my heart, my tear failing to douse the fiery anger in my eyes.

"You squeamish little Husk... You appear strong, but your muscles are weak. You feel tough, but your heart is soft. You long for forgiveness, as you're full of regret..." They spread arms wide, a crooked sneer sculpted in their distorted face. *"You wanted her to suffer, but here she stands, stronger than before."*

"I..." I glanced over my shoulder at Caroline, and shook my head. *No, this can't be...*

"Power is what she craves, and thanks to you, she now has it."

"Auntie?" The newly-transformed redhead looked down at her hands, with utter curiosity. "What happened to me?"

"Why, look at you!" Georgia strode over, and threw her silver arms around her niece. "Oh! You look amazing, even prettier than me!"

Caroline looked up at her aunt. "What happened? Auntie, it hurt so much! I didn't…" She looked over at me, and her eyes widened in surprise. "Oh, Mitchell… You're okay."

I pressed a hand over my mouth. *What have they done to you?*

Georgia cocked a devious smirk in my direction. "Well, now, what do you think? Isn't she pretty?"

My hand fell away. "Why…? How could you…? She…" I clamped my mouth shut.

"Can't even get the words out, can you?" Georgia threw her head back and laughed, then looked to her niece, and caressed her cheek. "Paying mind to more important matters, my dear Caroline, you don't have to worry anymore about manipulating those worthless fleshbags with your charm. You have a new destiny now."

Caroline scoffed at her. "What!? But what about the money? And shoes? And…" Her cheeks flushed a bright pink. "I mean, some of the boys were actually kinda cute, and they could… well… yeah."

Georgia sighed. "Oh, so much to learn." She placed one hand on her hip, the other on Caroline's shoulder. "You don't need them anymore. Now, you have these…"

Georgia raised the hand atop Caroline's shoulder, and with a flick of her wrist, a purple cloud of dust sparkled behind her niece. A group of tall monstrous beings, made of rotting wood and vines, appeared within the cloud as it dissipated, each one at attention, like a trained soldier.

"These, my dear, will be your servants now," Georgia purred. "They will protect you, while I teach you how to control the trees, and summon your own subordinates, like these."

Dread wormed into the pit of my stomach, as a sinister smirk spread across Caroline's face. "Really? That sounds exciting."

"Indeed it is." Georgia's eyes flickered to me. "But first, we have some… unfinished business to attend to."

Behind me, the Lurker leader cackled. *"It's your turn now, Brunette, to embrace the poisoned soil… and welcome home your darkness."*

I flinched. There was tiny movement in my stomach. I didn't like it. I wanted it to stop. *No… I… I don't want… Not like this.*

"It's too late now. Look at what you've achieved for yourself."

I connected eyes with the Lurker leader, the dying flames of my courageous anger sizzling out, as my fearful tears abruptly drowned them.

With frightening confirmation, their cold porcelain stare haunted my soul. *"Welcome home your darkness, my poison, Brunette, and embrace the poisoned soil. You claimed your paradise with Blonde One out of greed, thinking you could run from regret, but fate has finally come to claim you. You cannot hide anymore."*

I eyed the bordering trees just beyond. *Have to... Have to run. I have to get back to her. Have to warn Ro!*

Fear as my adrenaline rush, my sneakers hit the dirt like lightning, and thundered the ground with aggression. I slunk past the Lurker leader, far too easily, without fail. Doom weighed heavily in the pit of my stomach, but I banished it, out of fear it'd slow me down. I could get out of here. I could find freedom, find the sun again, see Rosella again... and be happy.

You turned your back on your destiny. You betrayed us all.

As soon as I shot through the trees, I was horrified to discover the bloody fog that had settled. I stumbled forward, and went sinking into the blinding bed of red from another harsh jab of pain. The grind of the soil against my flesh-covered bone was rock against steel, yet feasible, in comparison to the unbearable throbbing in my abdomen.

Fear clamped its firm jaws into my mind, as my quivering fingertips curled into my shirt and pulled. Oh... O-Oh dear god... It was moving... It was *moving*. Something... Something was trying to *get out.*

Get out. Get out. Nails grazing the surface, I could feel it. *Have to... get it out.* Get it out, get it out, get it out get it out get it out GET. IT. OUT. If I get it out, it'll go away. I'll be fine.

"You are lost to Ashen's darkness, Sophia!" Georgia's voice resounded within the trees. "Embrace it!"

Scratching harder, the edge of my nails worked at the rough exterior. A swelling drop of warm, black fluid squeezed from the distended bulb, staining my fingertips. The sides became malformed, like the crumbling shell of a boiled egg, a cluster of flakes gathering under my nails. Peeling away the thin crust, a rubber mass of red beneath remained, a thin white seam encircling the edge that attached it to my skin.

"Get out," I whispered. "Get out... Get out... Please. Get out." My shaking hands hovered over the bulge, my wrists stiff with hesitancy. "Get out... Please... Please, get out. H-Have... Have to get it out." A sob bubbled up my throat. "G-G-Ge-et... out..." *Have to get it out. Have to get rid of it. Do it. Just get rid of it. I don't want this anymore I don't want to be a Husk anymore.*

I was in control, not Ashen. I was my own person. Stubborn as a bull, that's how I'd roll, by my own terms. I wasn't going to let them keep Rosella and me apart. I would fight alongside her.

My eyes honed in. "H-Have to get it... get it out. Ha-Have t—" I was promptly silenced, as my vision turned black. All I could comprehend now were sheer, mounting levels of ungodly pain, and the malicious coo of Caroline's voice beside my ear.

"Guess I came out on top after all, huh, Mitchell?"

I compelled my body to move, but found I had no control.

"Foolish girls you are for thinking you could live happy, human lives together. You drowned each other in your pipe dreams." She gave a curt laugh. "Her days of freedom are numbered, but yours are over. You as her stem, now that we've broken you, we can break her. As for you... Embrace Ashen's darkness, and wilt within it, alongside her."

"Ngh, no... no..." I felt myself being pulled to my feet. "S-Stop... Stop it!"

Trapped in what I assumed were Caroline's arms, I could barely utter a squeak, as I was pulled back toward my prison grounds. I tried to blink the darkness away, but it did no good. It was like someone had pushed me into a pitch dark room.

"Why don't we wait for her~?" Caroline suggested. "With these newly-acquired powers, I'm actually picking up on her presence now..." She nipped at my ear, and I flinched. "Oh... What a sweet reunion this will be..."

"St-Stop," I rasped. "P-Please... They're... using you!"

"You don't know me!" Caroline's harsh hand clutched at my jaw. "You refused to welcome your true self," she growled. "So Ashen made me your replacement, and now you're scared, because *I* have power over *you.*"

My hair was abruptly yanked from my sore scalp, and I cried out.

"And now..."

I whimpered at the claws drumming against the blister on my neck.

Caroline flicked her tongue at my ear, but before she could say anything more, another voice, the one I longed to hear again, called from a distance.

I wanted to scream, to beg her to run, but Caroline's hand was quick to silence me.

"She's close~!" Georgia cooed.

"Looks like it won't be long now," Caroline whispered, her hot breath wisping my ear. "I can hardly wait..."

I quivered in place, unable to move, and a tear grazed my cheek. *Rosella... I'm sorry...*

Felan

I was uncertain when I'd fallen asleep, but when I awoke to the alarming sight before me, I knew it was serious. At first, I thought my bedroom walls were bleeding, and though I was glad to see they weren't, the bright red light did not ease my mind.

My aged feet hit the soft fluffy slippers awaiting them at the floor, and I shuffled over to my nightstand in a frantic pace. As I grabbed a hair tie from the drawer and threw my messy hair into a bun, several strands fell loose and teased my face. But I ignored them. There were far more important things to worry about.

Despite the arthritis that claimed my knees as I lowered myself down, I reached under my bed. Ugh, it felt like I was kneeling on rocks, for those several seconds my fingers fiddled with the loose floorboard. Thankfully, it came loose after a short time, and I relished for a moment in my victory with a hearty laugh, before spending the next minute trying to get back up again.

"Oh... Oh my aching back!" I pressed my hand to it, as I stumbled forward. "Wonder how many others have said that?" I lifted the object of interest to my face. "Okay, let's see now..." Clasped in the palm of my hand was the emergency item I'd been entrusted with. I was very much against using it, because of the circumstances, but rebelling was not the smart thing to do right now.

My trip down the front steps of the cabin wasn't easy. The fog covered nearly every step in front of me, and my feet slipped a couple of times trying to find them. I had only one free hand to grab hold of the railing, as the other held a watering can, filled halfway with water, I'd thankfully had sitting around. However, even that and the railing were hard to see, let alone focus on. There was nothing but bright red all around me, and the foul smell torturing my nostrils made my stomach flop like a freshly-caught carp.

The bottom of the steps took an eternity to greet me, though I was grateful all the same for it. I stepped off onto the ground, then begrudgingly fell to my knees again. It didn't matter where I planted it, though not every square foot was easy to dig into with my bare hands.

"Ah, here's a good spot," I told myself, and retrieved from the pocket of my nightgown a large white seed. "Alright, now I need to... do this." Pinching it between my thumb and forefinger, I scraped at the dirt with my free hand. To my surprise, it was actually harder than I initially thought. "Well now, good thinking on their part..." I scowled. "But not good enough to outwit me."

Sacrificing my knees for the sake of the world, I worked the seed into the earth, for several seconds. To my relief, my throbbing knuckles possessed just enough strength to succeed. Once I was finished, I splayed my exhausted hands beneath me, and wobbled my way back up to my feet.

My knees burned from the sore printing left by the soil. Overwhelmed by lack of use, they threatened to buckle like a house of cards, as I reigned them in with desperate control. Reaching for the watering can, my lower back was stiff from the strained posture, thus proving it quite difficult to stand straight.

"Th-There we go. Alright then." Proud of myself for completing my task, I wiped the faint layer of sweat from my brow. "Now, it's time to take shelter, and pray that things play out in our favor. I have fulfilled my role... Need to call Chloe, and deliver the news..."

The trek back up the agonizing trail of steps was a slow and tedious process, and with each inch forward, I felt the last ounce of power gradually shedding from my legs. Still, my hands clung to the stair railing with fervency, and urged me on. Tiresome minutes that felt like hours ticked by, but I knew I couldn't relax yet.

When I finally made it to the top of the stairs, I meandered into the cabin with exhausted legs. They were so tired. They needed to stop, and as I snatched my phone, they announced their limit. With seconds to spare, I tumbled straight into my bed, and landed upon the soft mattress against my back.

Heaving in strong gulps of air, I gave myself time to settle, before finding it in me to pull up Chloe's number, and dial the buttons. Clammy with sweat, my lips tasted like salt.

A breath grazed the phone as my daughter answered it. "Chloe... Chloe, listen to me..." I rasped. "There's not much time... I... I had to... plant the seed... The barrier... should be... up soon..." My eyes began to roll, and the phone slipped my hand. "I don't know what's going on... Just... I'll be fine... I just need... to rest..."

Amidst Chloe's distant cries through the phone, I felt myself drifting away. I wouldn't give in, not yet. *I will be fine... Just need to rest the eyes a bit. I won't leave until I see this through, to the end...*

Chloe

"Mom..." I strained to listen for any signs of life. I could barely hear it, but she was still breathing on the other end. "Damn it..."

I hung up, and looked out into the backyard. Everything appeared fine here. The moon was beginning its descent, though it'd still be a few hours before the sun would rise again. But within those trees...

I clutched a hand to my chest. "My beloved, please watch over them for me." I felt my phone buzz, and checked it for a message.

"I'm here," the text message read.

I ran back inside, slammed the back door shut, and ran through the kitchen to the living room. "Creg! Hey!"

The tired man slouched against the counter in his pajamas, eyes sagging with sleep. "Ugh, what's goin' on? I was just startin' to fall asleep when you called, and since it's 3am, I'm here for either an emergency or a sleepover. Take your pick."

I spared one more glance over my shoulder, then sighed, and turned back to Creg. "I... I..." I sucked in a sharp breath, then slowly exhaled. "Something's happened in the forest."

My past would have to wait just a little longer to be told. Right now, I had more important matters to attend to. Mom couldn't tell me exactly what was going on, but the fact she had to plant the Barrier Seed, that told me impending doom awaited us.

Rosella... I let the tears fall for my beloved daughter one last time. *I'll never forget you. And hopefully, you won't ever forget me either.*

CHAPTER 30

Fenris

I WAS NO FOOL. The scorching scent of charred, decaying wood that bled into Rosella's sweet fragrance was a clear sign. Following it, I aimlessly scoured the clouded forest with what little I had to go on. Where had she been taken?

"Rosella!" I called yet again. "Rosella! Where are you?"

Fenris!

My ears up on high alert, I whipped my head around. "Yes! I'm here! Who is that?"

It's me, my friend! Seraph! What's happening to the forest?

"Seraph… It's bad. I am surrounded by a red fog, and this unbearable scent is preventing me from finding Rosella."

I am so sorry. Would you like me to come to your aid?

"No, stay where you are. Your Vessel needs you now more than ever. Just…" A tear pricked at my eye, and I lowered my head. "Please, stay in contact with me, won't you?" I tucked my tail between my legs. "I am afraid."

Noble wolf, do not cower in fear, Seraph implored. *She needs you, the same as my Vessel needs me.*

I stamped the ground with a paw. "If only I could pick up on just a bit more, then I could help her!"

Just calm down. Try and think with your head for once, not your nose.

"Easier said than done," I grumbled. Scent is my strongest feature."

And so is your mind. Use that.

I plopped onto my rear. "Mind…" My mind, how could I? It was running rampant, like a decapitated chicken.

"Help! Help me!"

"!" My head shot up, my tail at attention. "Seraph! I heard a voice!"

Was it your Vessel's!?

"I am afraid not, but…" I strained an ear to listen closer.

"Please! Help me!"

That voice! Dread uncoiled within the pit of my stomach. Blood… Lots and lots of it…

"Help!"

My paws left the soil, and in my mad sprint, a sheath of dust gathered into a mist, and inflamed my nostrils with the stench of smoke and deadwood. Knowing an empty sky of nothing resided beyond the fog, I couldn't rely on the comforting light of the moon.

Another bad omen... Shrugging off the discomfort, I drove my nose into the charred soil, where each sniff was dusted with ash. *My weak sense of smell will hopefully direct me to your location.* My nostrils sought out the stranger's fragrance. *Even just a hint would suffice, a speck of her being to lead me to her. And maybe, just maybe, Rosella too...*

My eyes darted every which way, in hopes of spotting Rosella surface alive. I prayed that the fog was lying to me, that her corpse was not awaiting my discovery, and reveled in the pit of despair, the noose of reality looped around my neck. It tightened with every step, each breath held one second longer than the last.

She's here, I know she is. Somewhere, they've hidden her away. But where? I choked on the ashen grain that scalded my nasal passages, and a puff of sooty dust spat into my eyes. I squeezed them shut, worsening the irritation. *They can blind me if they wish. But they won't destroy my nose.*

I carried on, with firmly-sealed eyes, my dependence completely on my nose. I risked an inhale, and instantly regretted it, as I hacked and wheezed through the torturous burn flaring hot like fire.

This reeks of rot, I thought to myself, then froze. Could it be? Like the thinnest thread through a needle... the sweet, comforting aroma of rose and clary sage... It was faint, but it was there. *She is here... But that voice. It wasn't hers. But her scent!*

My paws sifting the fog, hope flooded the gates to my heart, where it vigorously pumped into my bloodstream, my determined legs driving me forward. Puffs of ash clouded around me, smearing my silvery coat with a dusting of black.

A contrasting onslaught of clary sage and death seared the walls of my nasal passages, sparking the sting of tears to my luminous eyes, but they graciously washed away the grains of soot that assaulted my vision.

Fenris! Fenris, can you hear me?

Alerted, my ears rose at attention, and I leaped for joy. "My dear master! Is that you?" I wagged my tail with excitement. "Please, tell me it's you."

Fenris, I'm so sorry. I'm sorry!

My tail went still. "Please! Do not apologize! Tell me, where are you? What's going on with Rosella?"

They've attempted to claim her soul, but I am doing what I can to help her. You just keep going! Don't stop!

"Where is she now? I-I'm trying to find my way out, and I think I heard another person's voice!"

Fenris, you have to get her out before it's too late. Don't let her wind up like Sarah.

Chains of fear latched around my heart. "Wait! What are you saying!?"

With the way I've planned this, a great burden has been placed on all of you, but fear not. Your efforts will be rewarded.

"What are you saying!?" I exclaimed again.

I know you crave rest, but you cannot yet. There is still much to do. Fenris... Thank you.

"Wait!" I begged. "Please!"

But she was already gone. Her presence had faded.

"Damn it all... Damn it all to hell!" I brushed the fog with a frustrated claw. "Why? Why did this have to happen?" I craned an ear to the air again, and waited in silence. *Come on, I know you're out there. Say something! So I can find you!*

"Help me!" the voice from before called out again. "Please! Someone!"

"Yes! I hear you!" I cried. "Tell me where you are!"

"Ben... Benjamin!? Is that you!? No, no! Frank?"

I padded in a circle, my helpless nose to the air. "I cannot see you, so I will follow your voice! Tell me if I'm close!" Focusing only on sound, I was determined to seek the stranger out.

"Who are you!? What is this!?"

She is close... But how close? I padded forward in what I felt was the right direction.

"Tell me what's going on! Please!"

Keep talking. Don't stop, so I can find you.

"I just want my daughter back! Please!"

I squinted. A tall, slender figure was drifting into view.

"Sophia! If you can hear me, I'm here!" the voice called. "I won't let Ashen hurt you, baby! I'll bring you home, and we'll live happily together as mother and daughter, just like always! I promise you that Chloe's betrayal will be for naught!"

Chloe's betrayal? I was a few feet away now.

"Please... Please, give me back my baby! And I'll personally deliver Chloe to you! Just, please, don't take Sophia from me too! I already lost my sister! Please don't turn her into the Queen!"

My eyes widened. That long ebony hair, and that blue ribbon... It couldn't be... "Sarah?"

There, a woman of Sarah's likeness, whirled around, and gasped.

I was left with no time to react. She came at me with something sharp, and then the vision in my right eye went dark. I stumbled back from the throbbing pain that erupted within my skull. Warm liquid oozed down the side of my face, and the tip of my tongue tasted copper.

"No! Stay away from me!" The woman sped off into the fog.

"W-Wait!" Still recuperating from the shock, I stumbled after her. "Wait! P-Please!"

A dragging paw slipped beneath me, and I went down with a heavy thud. I grunted with discomfort, my neck flat against the ground as I attempted to lift my right eyelid, only to discover sticky strands of red barred my distorted view, and a powerful sting forced it shut again.

"Ah, damn it... No... Not like this..." Racked with overwhelming pain, my legs wobbled like unstable stilts, during their struggle to stand me up once more. "Can't... give up yet. Have to keep fighting." *Have to protect Rosella, save her friend, and find that stranger. She said... Sophia was her daughter, so that means...* As I struggled, more of Felan's wise words echoed in my mind.

It's always good to keep your distance, you know? You can be close with someone, but remember this: No matter how close we are, we must part ways when the journey ends... Mine... is almost over, but yours is still ongoing. So even after I'm gone, you keep running. Show Rosella how to be strong. Help her make Ben proud while you can, because your time with her won't last.

I sighed. "Felan... I promised Benjamin that I would protect her." My heart sank at the thought of him. *You were just as stubborn as your wife, perhaps more so than Felan, or even me. You gave every drop of fight you had, and rained on Ashen's dreary parade, drowned them in your willpower, until you couldn't anymore.* I paused the burning flow of tears from my damaged eye. *Like I promised, I will protect Rosella in your place, because she was your daughter, and I shall do the same for Chloe. I miss you...*

Benjamin was always one for discovery. He told me himself that his dream was to take both Chloe and Rosella on a trip around the world, to explore every foot of the ground, swim in every body of water with them, and even though I claimed it to be impossible, he denied it.

Fenris, I've accomplished so much in my travels, and one day I want to share that experience with my girls. If the forest exists the way that it does, then anything is possible.

"Perhaps you're right..." *But possibility is limited, while impossibility lasts forever.*

You're right about that. But that doesn't make possibility any less existent. There is still a chance, Fenris, a chance for us to fight. A chance for us to discover how to beat Ashen... and we won't know until we find it. And when we do, I will laugh in their face, and show my girls that bravery is all it takes.

I regained sturdy footing before continuing blindly through the fog, and like Benjamin, I concealed my pain with unwavering pride. I knew Ashen was watching, waiting for me to fall to pieces, so they could pounce.

I won't give them the satisfaction. I'll find Rosella, and we'll get out of here together. Somehow... I just have to be brave, like him.

With a heavy sigh, my thoughts fell silent... And then I sensed it. Something knocked at my paws. Lip curled back in a snarl, my fur spiked, and I leered at the ground, waiting for something to grab at me. But it didn't happen. Instead, there was another knock, then a hard pounding, and then a spark of heat pricking my chest.

My eyes widened. *Could it be...?* "Rosella!? Is that you!?"

The peculiar smacking stopped.

"Rosella! Rosella! It's me! Fenris! Please, tell me if it's you!" I wagged my tail when a harmless wave of heat scorched my heart. "Rosella!"

The pounding started up again, stronger this time.

"Oh my god!" I shuffled with utter anticipation. "Rosella! Just hang on! I... I, uh..." *What do I do!?*

Try and think with your head for once, not your nose.

"Right... Think. Think." I feverishly paced the ground. "Come on... Think... Think...!" An idea sprung to mind, and I hoped she'd understand. "Rosella! Head to the Central Void! I'll meet you there!" I ducked my head, and screwed my eyes shut. *Please be there. Please be there.*

The haunting, bloody fog cleared around me, as the ground fell away, and I descended into the darkness once more. I came to stand upon the reflecting floor moments later, my nose still tainted from the stink of the fog, as I sped onward.

The Central Void provided a path between minds, and mine was on the edge of breaking, unless I located my precious Little Rose. Without the assurance of her scent, how could I be sure she was really—

I scrambled to a screeching halt, my paws sliding against the rippling floor. My lone, working eye had caught sight of her through the reflection below, and I looked ahead with a beaming smile. "Rosella!"

Rosella

What happened? The last thing I remembered was my leg being under attack by that black vine, and then everything going dark. And that voice I'd heard... Was it a Lurker? Or perhaps something else? It told me that I would "wilt in the dark." What did that mean?

My leg felt numb, nonexistent. What did that thing do to me? I couldn't move it, but at least it didn't hurt anymore. Wait, what about my other leg? Nope, couldn't move that one either. Hell, I had no clue if they were even intact, but if they weren't, then it should've hurt. What was going on here?

"Rosella! Rosella, are you alright!?"

That voice...

"It's okay, I got you."

It was...

"Oh, Rosella..."

I felt something gently wrap around me. What was that?

"You're okay now. I've got you. I managed to get you out in time. Please, don't be afraid."

There was a light stroke across my... head? Back? Or could it be my arm?

"I know you're questioning what exactly has happened to you. Please, spare me a moment, will you?"

That flaring heat that radiated like an undying fire in my chest... Where was my chest? It didn't feel like it was there. The heat, though! It was so hot, but didn't hurt.

"There now. You should be able to see."

She was right. I could see her. Her? Yes, her. Someone was looking right at me, and it was her...

"You poor thing... I am so sorry this happened. I am a terrible person for letting it get this far. I promise I'll get you back to your body. It's just... gonna take a few minutes. I... I'm going to let you go now..."

The support cradling me fell away, but I was fine. I couldn't look down, nor up, only straight ahead, but I was fine.

"Rosella, there is not much time, so I have to be quick."

What do you mean? I don't understa... Ah, my thoughts! I could hear them again!

She gave a weak chuckle. "I... I can sense your excitement."

Yes, but..."

"Rosella, for a long time, you've come to know Chloe and Benjamin Bloom as your parents. You grew up with them, lived a happy life with them, though sometimes it was rough, since you were stuck with my timidness. Truth be told, helplessness is all I've ever known. I didn't know how to make the world better. And now, my people have been dragged into my mess. The Guardians I created... They were my meek excuse at assisting my people... But all I've done is force my responsibilities onto them, and now everything is falling apart."

Wait… Please, don't cry. It's okay.

"I am so sorry, Rosella. I am so sorry for everything! I don't know how to fight, I don't know how to protect! I had no business bringing lives into the world, knowing full well they couldn't count on me! I was selfish! And my people… You've seen them, right? The elders are being tossed out due to their frailness. And the rest…" A prolonged sob rang out through the darkness. "They never wanted this, nor deserved this. And now, they're suffering, and it's all my fault!"

No, I didn't want her to cry. She didn't mean for this to happen…

"What was I thinking? Running away like the coward I am?"

Stop it, that's not true. If anyone's guilty of cowardice, it's me.

"It's all my fault!"

"Please don't cry! It is not your fault!"

She gawked at me with teary eyes. "But it is! I let this happen! This forest was our home, but it was *my* responsibility to protect it!"

"Everyone makes mistakes!" I shouted. *"You and I both know that if Fenris was here right now, he'd vouch for me. He'd agree that it wasn't your fault, and not just because he's loyal to those he trusts. He would help you fix your mistakes, instead of holding them against you."*

"But what of the others?" she asked. "What if they…" She hid her face in her hands. "Oh Rosella… I'm so sorry."

It was like looking in a mirror. Just like me, she was timid and small, blaming herself for everything. She was a coward, fearful of the outside world with no knowledge as navigation.

Just like me. Because she was me, and I was her.

"T-Tell me how I was born," I pleaded. *"Please, I have a right to know…"* Something familiar lingered at the back of my mind, just out of reach…

"Chloe was otherwise infertile, but a good friend, so I gave her empty womb what Benjamin could not, and in return she would protect us… But again, it was my cowardice, and selfishness, that put us all here. I just wanted to get away so I could think. But that was clearly stupid."

I said nothing, so as not to interrupt.

"There are more of you, five in total," she went on, "and I reside in each and every one of you. But you, Rosella, are the closest connection I have. Being so close to home, you never lost touch with it. And over these last few days, I was finally able to reach you, to actually talk with you. You, out of all of them, are the only one that I can currently communicate with, because you are..."

She fell silent, as the realization hit me, and swallowed me up in a tidal wave of memories. They flashed by in a blink, like the history of the universe was being played in the span of ten seconds, leaving me no time to ponder specific moments. Many I recognized in an instant, despite not being there, not as myself, as Rosella Bloom. Except... That's not all I was anymore.

An out-of-body experience, but a familiar one all the same, I came to realize that I was one of Hollow's Vessels, a form of escape from Ashen's curse, because they invaded my home, hungry for my power. Except, it wasn't *my* power, or *my* home. Or, perhaps it was ours? I was her, and she was me, just different individuals...

"You are currently but a light in my hands, hence why your body is nonexistent. However, in another minute or so, it should return."

Drawn out of my messy thoughts, I returned focus to my current situation. *"What happened to me before?"* I asked. *"How did I get like this?"*

Her eyes narrowed. "Ashen. They managed to open the door to your mind."

"You mean, like my third eye or something?"

"Kind of? I never really understood the whole 'third eye' stuff." She shook her head. "Anyway, when you regain yourself, you must go to the Central Void, the place where you and I first really talked."

"The blank space, right?"

She nodded.

"But why? Shouldn't I find Fenris?"

"You will, in time. But for now, the Central Void is the safest place for you to be." She clasped her hands at her chest, as if to pray. "Neither Ashen, or the Lurkers, can track you there."

I bit back a sob at her mention of the Lurkers, as another painful memory forced its way into my mind, despite my desperation to ignore it. I saw flashes of helpless tree creatures helplessly abandoning their homes, tripping over each other as they ran for their lives, only to be consumed by the dark mist hunting them down...

Even though *I* wasn't there, I *was* there. And I couldn't save them, because I chose to... No, I couldn't think like that. It wasn't my fault.

Ashen's existence was out of my control... Her control? Ours? Either way, it happened. There was no undoing the damage that had been done, and that hurt worse than being skinned alive. They were innocent creatures who had their lives taken from them. And now, only their walking corpses remained, with remnants of their souls trapped inside.

"Rosella..."

Hollow's voice drew me out of my grief, and I would've shook my head if I could. *"Wh-What is it?"*

Sadness graced her face. "It is time for us to part. But fear not, I will still be by your side." Her expression went blank. "And remember this. Words mean something, but actions mean everything, and impossibility... lasts forever."

"Wait!"

She vanished into thin air, despite my protest, as a powerful wave of heat consumed me from the inside. My view started blinking, things were wiggling, and something began pumping. A hand was lifted in front of my face. My burning fingers, they were dancing with experimentation. Yes, they were there, and so were my hands, and my legs and feet.

Something draped over my shoulders. I pulled it closer to me. It felt warm, and smelled like home. Home... They gave me theirs when I lost mine, and raised me as their own, a gift to defy the impossible...

"But impossibility lasts forever." A tear grazed my eye. "Mom... That's why you hid Fenris from me for so long, why you wanted to move, because... because then I wouldn't have found out what I really am, and the Lurkers..." I gasped. "The Lurkers. Oh god... I... I have to get back!" I whipped my head around. "Shoot! How?" Surrounded by darkness, I had no clue what to do. "How do I get out of here? Hey, you still there? Hello...?" My shoulders sagged. "Great..."

I threw my hands to the air, and hit something solid. Frowning, I did it again. There was indeed something there, like a ceiling. I smacked my palms hard against it, in hopes that maybe I could push it up like a lid on a box. It didn't work.

"No! I can't... I can't get out!" I rapped at it with my knuckles. "Hey! If anyone can hear me, I'm here! Someone! Anyone!"

"Rosella!? Is that you!?"

I paused in my panicked state, my heart stirring with hesitant hope. *No way! Is that...!?*

"*Rosella! Rosella! It's me! Fenris! Please, tell me if it's you!*"

My chest flourished with intense heat. "Fenris! It's me! It's me!"

"*Rosella!*"

Tears sprang to my eyes, as my fists thundered against the barrier above me. "Fenris! It's me, it's me!"

"*Oh my god! Rosella! Just hang on! I... I, uh...*"

A few agonizing seconds of silence passed. "Fenris! Fenris, are you there!?" *NO! Tell me they didn't get him!*

"*Rosella! Head to the Central Void! I'll meet you there!*"

"The Central Void! Of course!" I waved my hands in front of me. "Okay, okay... Uh... Shoot... Crap!" Panicking once more, my chest tightened with anxiety. *How do I do it!? I... I don't know how.*

Rosella, focus on your mind!

"Hollow?" My heart did a leap in my chest. "Hollow! That is you, isn't it?"

Yes! Just focus on your mind! It's in your mind!

"In my mind?" What the hell did that mean?

The Central Void is in your mind, your conscience.

"My conscience..." I gave a slow nod, somewhat understanding. "Okay, I... I'll try... Okay..." I settled myself with a long, drawn out breath. "Right, inside my mind... It's the safest place to be... the safest place... to be..."

Following Hollow's words, I thought back to that strange place, that empty grey space of nothing. I pictured it clearly in my head, and channeled my desire into confirmation. I wanted to go there, in order to find Fenris. I wanted to see him again. I needed to see him again.

A faint mist festered at my ankles, and thickened into a fog, as it spread out around me. But I knew not to be afraid, and instead, willingly bathed in the calming body of light enveloping me. Unmoving, an unknown surface emerged beneath my boots, and when I peered down, I found my rippling reflection staring back up at me.

Rosella, look up.

I did as instructed, and squinted. The fog was so thick, it was hard to see through. So I waited for it to clear a bit.

"Rosella!"

The thick midnight fog clouding my conscience evaporated at the sound of his voice, and I found his mesmerizing moonlit eyes in the everlasting void. Lured toward his ethereal embrace, my legs carried me with a burst of speed. I buried myself in the warmth of his silver fur upon reaching him, a stream of tears spilling around my relieved grin.

"Fenris!" I wailed. *"Fenris!"*

"Rosella! I finally found you! Thank goodness you're safe!"

"God..." I choked on a laugh. "Ah... F-Fenris... Oh god..."

"It's alright now, I'm here."

I nuzzled my face into his neck with a sob, and held him tight. "D-Don't ever leave my side again, okay? Please..."

"It's okay, Little Rose. It's okay."

I relaxed against him, my fingertips kneading into his soft, silky fur. "Fenris..." My heart sank. I wanted this moment to last a little longer, but... "Fenris, I remember."

He frowned in confusion, as he pulled away from me. "Remember? Remember what?"

I pressed my forehead against his, and our eyes locked. "It's Rosella, but it's also me..."

For a moment, the wolf remained puzzled. But then, a flicker of understanding flashed in his eyes, and his maw dropped slightly open.

"My friend... I'm so sorry." The blinding tears continued to fall from my eyes, and I squeezed them. "I'm so sorry..."

"Hol..." He cleared his throat, and corrected himself. "Rosella."

"I'm so sorry, Fenris... for putting... all this... on you..."

It felt so strange. Even though I was her, I was still me, Rosella Bloom. So, was I apologizing myself, or on her behalf? It was all so confusing, like wandering a house of mirrors, only every reflection was hers instead of mine. And she was weeping upon her knees, because I broke my promise...

"All this time, I was worried about putting my trust in others, but in the end, it's *you* who should be afraid of trusting *me*."

Fenris frowned. "What do you mean?"

"You know what I mean," I said. "For one, I was so scared of entering this place, and didn't know if I was going to survive. I told you from the start that I didn't think I was ready to take the leap! And two, I..." My mouth fell shut as Fenris raised a paw.

"I asked you if you trusted yourself to take on the Lurkers and rescue Sophia," he uttered calmly, "and even though you said no, you are here. It was never about me trusting you or you trusting me. It was about you trusting yourself."

My eyes widened a little as I pointed at myself. "Me... Me trusting myself..."

"Yes, you, trusting yourself to take on a brave task."

I gave a slow nod. "Trust in myself... Y-Yeah." I blinked the remains of tears away to clear my vision. "Right... I guess... Oh! Oh my god!" Heart racing, my hands clasped at Fenris' head. "F-Fenris! Your eye!" During my self-pity party, I failed to notice the ugly red slash incapacitating his right eye, thus making me feel even worse about myself.

"It's fine, I'm sure it'll heal," he assured me. "It's just... difficult to see out of."

"Oh, Fenris." I cradled his face in my hands, and closely examined the wound. "It's a deep cut, but maybe Great Granny Felan can help. How did you get this?"

"Someone, a woman I think, was looking for her daughter. She was calling out to the Lurkers I presume, begging for her return. I thought she mentioned Sophia..." His ears fell to his head. "I was trying to help her, only to startle and prompt her into attacking me."

A new level of fear coiled around my heart. "No, no no no." I shook my head. "No no no." *Please tell me she didn't...*

"Rosella?"

I wrapped my arms around my sides. "G-Grace... Grace Mitchell... She's... Sophia's mother. She was distraught, upon finding out Sophia's kidnapping."

"The stranger... The stranger I encountered..." If the wolf's face could pale, it was expressed through his grave expression of fear.

I gave him a nervous look. "F-Fenris?"

"Rosella, I..." His lone bulging eye averted my frightened gaze. "When I heard her calling out for Sophia, she mentioned something about wanting her back... and Chloe's betrayal..."

"Fenris, where was she!?" I pleaded. "Is she okay!?"

The wolf's legs quivered as his ears fell against his head. "Rosella... She..." Tail tucked between his legs, he faced me with his cowardice. "Rosella, she said something about Chloe's betrayal, and begged them not to turn Sophia into the Lurker Queen."

I clasped my hands at my quivering chest. "Oh my god..."

"You told Felan that Chloe left you two alone," Fenris went on. "Did she do it on purpose?"

I shook my head. "No, no, she didn't. She wouldn't." I stepped toward the wolf. "What about Sophia becoming the Queen? What exactly did Grace say?"

His gaze drifted to the floor. "Grace said that she would bring Chloe to them I think, in exchange for Sophia, and she wanted to return home, and live a happy life with her daughter." His head rose, and his working eye flickered to me. "Rosella, I am fearing the worst for your best friend. If she really is the Queen Lurker, then... that means..."

If Sophia really was transformed, then that means only one thing. I stifled a low whimper. "I'll have to kill her, won't I?"

He didn't answer. He didn't need to.

I screwed my eyes shut, and the weight of dread clamped down hard on my shoulders. *Sophia...*

Rosella... Hollow's voice echoed in my head. *There's still a chance... Don't give up hope yet.*

"Little Rose, do you...?"

I shook my head, and blinked away the wall of tears blurring my vision. "If she is the Queen Lurker, I'll do what I have to in order to save her. She's my best friend, and I am not turning my back on her. Not now, not ever."

Fenris shuffled his paws, and the floor rippled beneath. "Even though... Even though she's...?

"She's what?" I asked.

Rosella, Sophia is one of them.

"One of... Oh... Oh god." Another bout of unwanted realization reared its ugly head, and I blankly stared into my shocked reflection in the floor. I'd never heard the term per se, but I knew it. "She's a... Husk, isn't she?"

Fenris' eye widened, as a look of surprise sprung to his face. "I-I didn't... want to consider an enemy..."

I shook my head. *Oh god... Sophia...*

She's not, Rosella. She's been fighting Ashen's curse for years, Rosella, ever since she was born. But because of her actions, she has no magic to fight with, and so she's suffering...

"Suffering..." Swallowing the awaiting cries bubbling in my throat, I balled my hands into fists at my sides. "All the more reason to help her, no matter what. She may be a..." I stumbled upon the uncomfortable term. "... H-Husk, but she's still a person, like me, and she's my best friend... So, I have to do something." I raised my head, and locked eyes with Fenris. "Let's go find her, and if we can, bring her home."

CHAPTER 31

Frank

"FRANK, HEY. ARE YOU alright?"

I looked up from my laptop, and found Cathy in yet another nice ensemble, this time a pale yellow sundress with fancy white gloves. Draped atop her shoulders was her blue knit blouse her mother sent her for her birthday last year.

"Oh, hey hon. You headin' out to another tea party?"

"Yes, but I wanted to know how you were doing. You look more tired than usual today, yet you've been off for some time." Cathy's eyes drifted away from me. "Frank, I... I think there's something wrong. I can't really put my finger on it, and I know you don't like... well..."

"It's alright, sweetie. Don't be afraid to share your thoughts with me. Really, it's okay."

"If you say so..." Cathy took in a deep breath, and gently exhaled through those light rose lips. "Frank, I... I'm a little worried about you. You've been more distant lately, and it makes me wonder if I did something wrong."

I got up from the kitchen table, and came around to her. "I'm sorry Cathy, I don't mean to make you feel bad." On the outside, I looked calm. But on the inside, I was falling to pieces. It broke my heart to see Cathy hurt, because she meant a lot to me.

"Maybe it's nothing." She bowed her head, and fiddled with the buttons of her blouse. "I should leave you be. You have lots of work to do yet I'm sure, and I've got..."

Cathy's eyes went wide, as my lips suddenly crashed against hers in a passionate kiss. I cradled her soft, gentle face in my hands, and relished in the moment of bliss. At first, I wasn't sure what brought this on, and while we stood there, locked in our romantic embrace, I tried to think of what to say once we were finished.

I pulled away a few moments later, and a smile crept across my face. "Ah, takes me back to our first date every time." *I wish we could go back to peacefully siting under that walnut tree, just you and me, wrapped in each other's arms...*

She pinched the silver cross resting against her collarbone, a wondrous glint to her eyes. "My, what's this all of a sudden?"

"I just wanted you to know that I love you," I told her. "I really do." *I miss this.* I caressed her free hand in mine. *I miss just spending time with you.*

It'd been some time since Cathy and I last spent quality time alone together. During those golden days, I'd come home from a hard day at work, and help her with dinner. Afterward, we'd enjoy our meal at the table, then snuggle on the couch together. I'd listen to her tell me about her day, and she'd be so happy about it. But lately, things were different, because of my involvement in the shelter case. With each passing day, I feared the wedge forming in our relationship would completely pry us apart, and even though we'd tell each other it was fine, we both knew it was becoming more and more irritating to bear.

Time with Cathy was one of the few things I depended on most, a comfort I cherished with all my heart. And like I confessed to Chloe last night, I was terrified of losing people I cared about. But I had to realize that I wasn't the only one facing this fear head-on. She was going through this too, and so was Creg.

He never told me Ivy left... And I know why he kept it from me. It was because he knew I wouldn't understand in the same way Chloe would. My brow knitted into a frown. *But it still hurts, because he's my partner.*

"Darling?"

"I'm sorry I've been so distant, and uncomfortable to be around lately," I continued, returning my focus to Cathy. "Something serious has come up regarding Chloe Bloom..." I kneaded my mouth shut before I could spill the beans. The last thing I wanted was to drag Cathy into all this. *I can't, I won't...*

"Whatever it is, it must be serious." Cathy's eyes drifted to the floor. "You know, I worry about whether her mother really is what they say she is..."

"I can't say for sure whether or not angels and demons exist," I uttered without hesitation. "I also can't confirm the existence of God and Satan, or Lucifer, even though I feel like I can. However, I can assure you that Felan is not what the town says she is, because I have met her."

Cathy gawked at me. "You have?"

My heart sank as I recalled the last time I saw her, how frustrated she was with me, and I wrung my clammy hands together behind my back. "Y-Yes, and she's a wonderful woman. In fact, sometime I'd like you to meet her. She loves to bake, and sew, and she's very talented at gardening." I planted another soft smooch to Cathy's forehead, and stroked her cheek with my knuckle. "I've gotta go for now, but have a good time today, okay? And say hi to everyone for me. If possible, ask them if they'd like to have dinner with us soon. It's been a while since we've had guests."

A fresh, beaming grin lit her face, as her eyes sparkled. "Oh, Frank! You really mean it? That is so nice to hear!"

"Absolutely." I nuzzled her head against mine. "I think it'd be good for both of us. And like I told you, I love you Cathy, with all my heart."

"Well, I love you more." She threw her arms around my neck, and a wisp of her expensive perfume teased my nostrils.

"*Cerasus Flores* by Lá Bamelle?" I wondered aloud.

Cathy nodded eagerly. "Yes! It's my favorite anniversary present from you."

"Ah yes, of course." I stroked my fingers down her forearms, past her elbows, and with gentle hands, I straddled her sides. "Maybe later tonight, we can cuddle together on the couch, watch a movie." I nestled my face into the crook of her neck, and inhaled the intoxicating fragrance. *I might fall asleep, if I stay like this any longer.*

"Frank, this is so nice," Cathy whispered. Her breath brushed my ear, sending a tingle down my spine. "I wish we could just stand here, forever, like this."

I kneaded my thumbs into the dip of her ribs. "So do I..." My shoulders stiffened as I forced myself to pull away, my face set in a solemn expression. "But we've both got someplace to be."

"Well, that's okay!" She beamed at me. "I'll see you this evening! Just like always."

"Yeah..." Though the lustrous fire in my heart had dimmed a little, I kept my strong posture. "Tonight will be nice."

"Yes." Cathy rested her head against my chest, and sighed. "Frank, do be careful, won't you?"

I hugged her close, my face buried in her hair. "Yeah." I kissed her head one more time, but my arms refused to let her go. I wasn't ready for this moment to end yet.

"Darling…"

I looked down to see her staring up at me with a worried expression.

"Be safe, okay?"

I reflected her concern. "You as well. You know how paranoid I can be, beings I work for the police."

"I'll call you when I get there," Cathy assured.

"Alright."

Cathy's arms reluctantly fell from my sides, and I allowed her to slip out of my grasp. As she turned to leave, the temptation to pull her retreating form back into my arms weighed heavy upon my heart, but I reigned myself in, and silently saw Cathy out.

Once the door shut behind her, I called up Chloe. "Hey, it's me." I strode down the hall to the closet, and threw the door open. "I should be there soon."

"That's okay, take your time."

I sighed. She sounded distant, like she wanted to be as far from me as possible. I couldn't blame her.

"I guess I'll see you when you get here."

Before I could say another word, there was a click on the other end of the line, and I hit the "end call" button on my phone. "Dammit…" I reached up to the top shelf for the small box containing my gun and holster. Cathy preferred them to be out of sight, not that I minded. The less reminders about work, the better it was for me.

I found my car keys on the coffee table in the living room, then headed out the door to my car, and drove the way through town in strained silence, my complicated thoughts on Chloe the entire way. Perhaps it was best I made myself scarce, as last night was pretty intense. No, that might give her the wrong idea.

I gave a frustrated sigh, as I closed in on the parted trees around the lone road to the Bloom house, and pulled the car to a stop. *I'll figure out what to do once I get there,* I thought. *I'm sure it'll be…*

Out of nowhere, my heart skipped three beats at a time, my breathing hitched, and I broke out in a heavy sweat. My clammy hands were shaking, and my stomach flopped. The inside of the car had suddenly become stuffy, as if it'd been turned into a sauna with the steam level cranked incredibly high. Alarmed, I fumbled for the button at my door that controlled my window, and with only seconds to spare, it dropped just enough for the cool rush of air to seep in and settle the nausea bubbling up my throat. My head fell back against the headrest of my seat as I worked to calm my frazzled nerves with several slow, deep breaths. In, and out, and in, and out...

"Frank?"

"Gah!" I threw my hands up, as my frantic heart about burst out of my chest.

"Frank! Shit, sorry." Creg grabbed hold of the door from the top. "Are you alright?"

I eyed him with a furious scowl. "You motherfucker! You scared the hell out of me!"

"I'm sorry. Chloe said you were coming, so I thought I'd meet you here. My car's just up ahead."

"God..." I wiped my sweaty forehead with the back of one hand, and slapped at my calves. "Hah... Well, I spoke with Cathy just a bit ago. She's having another tea day, should be out until evening. I promised her we'd have some time together when I got home tonight, and I'll be damned if some freaky tree monsters keep that from happening."

"Speaking of those..."

My scowl deepened. "No, stop."

"Can't. She says it's bad, real bad. Even proved it."

"What do you mean?"

Creg sighed. "That forest beyond the backyard? You're not gonna believe this. It's closed."

I cocked my brow in confusion. "What do you mean?"

"I mean, it's locked up like Fort Knox. No one's getting in or out. It's just a wall of trees."

"... Lemme see for myself."

Creg patted the top of my car. "Sure thing, bud."

I followed Creg's car the rest of the way, where Chloe awaited us at her porch. I slipped out and greeted her first. She seemed uneasy, just like

I thought, though something told me it was for a different reason. She nodded toward the side of the house, and so I went around to the back.

As I jogged alongside the backyard fence, I thought that my eyes were deceiving me, but it was just as Creg had told me. The trees were pressed so close together that no gap could be seen, and the entrance was now gone. This worried me as I thought of Felan. Would she be able to protect herself? And what about that boy, Marcus Thompson? He'd taken off like a fuckin' bullet last night. And of course, there were Sophia and Caroline, and...

"Rosella." I nervously pulled at the collar of my button-down shirt. "Damn, Grace too..."

"Frank."

I peered over my shoulder with a frightened face. "Yeah?"

Behind me, Chloe held a stoic expression, her hands to her chest. "Thank you for coming. There's a lot to do. I hope I can count on you."

My gaze softened into a look of concern. "Can I?"

She nodded hesitantly. "Y-Yeah..."

I observed her for several second, then gave a silent nod, and proceeded back to the house with her. *Even if she doesn't come clean to us now, I'm sure she will later. I have to trust her.*

You promise?

I nodded to my partner, as I spotted him waiting on the back porch. *Yeah...*

Rosella

"The forest should be closed off by now, which means that no one is getting in or out." Fenris looked to his left, and then his right. "I think the coast is clear."

"Yeah, speaking of clear..." I looked around me. "You think that Hollow did away with that fog?"

"Either that, or it's because you broke the spell yourself. Still, I'm glad it's gone."

The bloody fog had long since dissipated. Though a welcoming sight, it was still quite dark. I could barely see a thing as we resumed our trek through the trees, and though Fenris seemed to have no trouble with sight despite his injured eye, his lack of smell was what put him on edge. Not even my promise to stay close could ease his troubles, and I was sitting atop his back, as we trekked through the trees.

"That spell was meant to separate us," he went on. "I'm certain it was also to tamper with my senses. Without my nose, it'll be much harder to track things."

"Don't worry, once we find Sophia we can head back," I assured. "I'm sure Great Granny Felan can conjure up something for your eye, too." My mind wandered to that of the Barrier Seed. "That seed you told me about... How does it work?"

"Once planted, it sprouts roots that grow into full-fledged trees overnight. But there's one difference between the trees around us, and the seed's trees. They're tough as stone. Not even Ashen's curse can break them down."

"I see. Are they real trees, though? Or, are they really made of stone?"

"They're made up of Hollow's magic, like the rest of this forest. And I said, nothing can destroy. However, that doesn't make the forest itself invincible..."

It didn't take a rocket scientist for me to figure out where he was headed with those words, and I shuddered at his grave tone. This place was my lifeline. If it died, then I was certain I would too... And I couldn't let that happen to me, let alone to the others out there, but especially him. He was my noble wolf...

"Rosella?" Can I be honest with you about something else?"

The wolf's soothing voice freed me of my troubled thoughts, and I gave a nod. "Always."

He bowed his head slightly. "Benjamin... Remember when he fell ill years ago?"

"Yes, of course," I said. "Why do you ask?"

"Well, he was inflicted with Ashen's curse."

My eyebrows raised in surprise. "R-Really?"

"Yes, and the way it happened..." He sighed. "It was a long time ago, six years since that Sunday has passed."

My jaw dropped open, then quickly closed again.

"You were exhausted from the excitement of the day's events, so your parents put you to bed as soon as you'd all returned home."

That's right, I thought. *Fenris and I had finally met, and it was the best day of my life. Somehow, he answered the hundreds of questions I threw at him without fail. He wasn't the least bit irked either.*

"I believe your mother had gone to bed shortly after you did," Fenris went on. "But your father chose to stay up late, because he wanted to get some work done, and you know how he was about his writing."

I smiled at that. "The fiery passion my father had for his work never dwindled."

"Well, he said that he went to check on you sometime after eleven, but you weren't in bed. So he started looking around the house. There was no sign of you, and he began to panic, until he spotted you in the backyard from the back door of the kitchen."

As the wolf paused, a familiar statement, from the cashier at Clover Alley, sprung to my mind, and my stomach twisted in knots.

Why, that night she wandered into the forest by herself, and her late father had to run in after her.

"Confused, he ran out to get you... You'd never slept-walked before, so he thought that maybe you wanted to venture out and see me again. But as he called out to you, he knew something was wrong." Fenris' ears drooped at either side of his head. "Because someone else was calling beyond the forest. And it wasn't me or Felan."

"It was Ashen, wasn't it?" I guessed.

He uttered a low growl. "Benjamin couldn't reach you in time. When he reached the backyard you were out of sight, so he was forced to chase after you. Luckily, he didn't have to go far..."

I gulped down the nervous lump that sprang up my throat. "He wasn't... hurt, was he?"

"He said he'd never seen anything like them before, but that wasn't important. All he cared about was you, and so like the courageous father he was, he threw himself in front of you, right as Ashen attacked. He suffered a swift hit to the heart, but that didn't sway him in the slightest." The wolf glanced over his shoulder. "He laid his life on the line, for you."

My father... I always knew he was brave, and strong, and would do everything in his power to protect me. But I never thought he would actually stand up to something far beyond our world, or whatever the hell Ashen was.

My heart grew heavy with the weight of guilt. He would still be alive, if I hadn't wandered out that night. He wouldn't have gotten sick, and Mom wouldn't have worried about my safety, or even thought about moving, or—

Rosella, you did nothing wrong.

I sucked in a sharp, quivering breath, as a tear sprung to my eye. *But I... I am the reason, aren't I?*

You had no control over your actions. I know, because I tried to help you, but my magic wasn't strong enough... So you can't blame yourself.

"Little Rose? Are you alright?"

My gaze wandered back to Fenris, though the sight of him was blurred by a wall of tears.

"I am sorry, I didn't mean to upset you," he said.

"I-It's okay..." I choked out, and wiped at my wet eyes. "Tell me... Wh-What happened next?"

"I showed up, effectively scaring Ashen away. But the worst was yet to come..." His words laced with sadness, a low whimper slipped Fenris' maw. "Benjamin was too weak in the knees to walk back, so I had to carry him while he held you in his arms. It was risky, being exposed, but even the short distance between the backyard and the house was a challenge for him."

"Then how did he get me back inside? You couldn't have fit."

"He said he managed," Fenris answered, albeit begrudgingly. "He wouldn't take my offer of asking Felan if you both could stay with her. Couldn't blame him though, what with the events that had just transpired. But anyways, he awoke the following morning, seemingly fresh as a daisy, but there was something slightly off. At first, he couldn't put his finger on it, but as he went about his day, he noticed the dizzy spells, and his struggle to hold things."

"Dad played off his struggles well," I whispered with a pained breath. "Once, he tripped down the back steps of Great Granny Felan's cabin, and she joked that they were a pair of stumbling fools." I gave a sad chuckle. "He got a real kick out of that, and from then on, he kept a little notepad to keep track..."

"They certainly were a pair..." Fenris stared forward again, and sighed. "She's still fighting it herself."

My face paled. "Y-You mean... She's..." I hung my head in defeat, and screwed my eyes shut, so as to block further tears from falling. "Why? Why did this happen? Hollow told me this was her... my... our fault... that this happened."

"Hollow didn't tell you the whole story, did she?"

I didn't respond.

"Rosella?"

"I... I saw them, Fenris... While I was speaking to her, I saw them..." Yet another tear sprung to my eye, but I aggressively rubbed it away with a knuckle. "The Woodlocks..."

Fenris sighed. "Or, as you know them as, the Lurkers..."

"Y-Yeah."

A low whine slipped the wolf's maw. "Olmond, and Maura, and their children... They were some of my dearest friends..." He glanced over his shoulder, this time with his damaged eye. "Tell me, did she say how Ashen came into existence?"

I shook my head. "No, I'm sorry, she didn't..." My brow furrowed. "Fenris, tell me about... who they were... the Woodlocks, before they turned undead..."

He gave a shallow nod. "They were a peaceful race that could grow anything, much like Felan. They could also reproduce asexually at high speed, and because they practically live forever, it was nearly impossible for them to ever go extinct. Ashen must've caught wind of this, as they are now the Lurkers." He bowed his head again, as he came to a stop. "And I only sense Ashen within their minds now, which is why I am so quick to tear them down."

"But they're still there, Fenris."

"How can you tell?"

"Because I can."

The wolf uttered a threatening growl. "Hollow…" He cleared his throat. "Sorry, *Rosella*, I—"

I pulled my hood over my head and silently grieved over all this. Dad, Fenris, Sophia, Great Granny Felan, Mom, the Woodlocks… Because of this curse, and the fact that she… I… ran from it, the people we loved had been subjected to undeserved pain and suffering, and it wasn't fair. We were all living peacefully amongst the trees, but Ashen…

My blood began to boil with rage, as I glanced around my grim surroundings with tear-filled eyes. Ashen turned this place, our home, upside down, and gutted it alive, like a bound, helpless creature… I wanted to seek them out, get in their face, if they had one, and demand that they remove their curse, and find their place to haunt. They couldn't have my power, no matter how much they craved it.

"Rosella, there is one more thing I feel I should tell you."

Fenris' voice again pulled me out of my troubled thoughts, and I found him glancing up at me yet again. "A-Another info dump?"

"I apologize," Fenris mumbled shamefully.

"It's okay, go on."

"Though Hollow ignores the card of immortality in her deck, she can easily manipulate any life that falls into her hand. Immortality, to her, is a life without rest, a curse more so than a blessing…" He scoffed at the air. "Why would someone want to be alive longer than anyone, without the possibly of death?"

"Because all life has an end," I added. "But if you're immortal, then you have no end to either your life or the suffering ahead." I nodded with understanding. "Makes sense."

"We cannot speak for anyone but ourselves. At least, that's how Hollow and I see it." He flicked an ear, as he looked to the trees. "Anyways, Felan is one of Hollow's dearest friends, and has been entrusted with what power Hollow can give, even though Felan is merely a human… But my master was unsure of who else viewed things the same way as her."

As Fenris picked up cautious pace again, we both resigned ourselves to the silence. This gave us both time to absorb the entirety of our prolonged conversation, but the process was exhausting for me. So much had been exchanged in so little time, it felt like I was back in math class, and my scrambled brain was fighting to undo the knots in the messy threads of equations. I found myself almost dozing, while trying to work it all out, but the abrupt crunching of leaves beneath Fenris' paws brought me back every time.

Fenris... What was he thinking right now? Was he thinking? Or was he struggling to stay focused, like me? For the most part, he kept a leveled head on his shoulders, even when engaged in battle.

"I think that adds to the list of fears," I uttered aloud, without thinking, "not knowing what someone thinks."

The wolf peered up at me. "I'm curious to know what you mean."

"Say someone is happy to live forever, and don't say why. How do you know they wouldn't love to see the world burn, and watch others suffer while they enjoy themselves?"

A look of discomfort sprang to Fenris' face.

"Exactly."

Fenris' ears perked, as a frown broke across his maw, and his head jerked forward. "Rosella! We're close."

My heart did a frantic leap in my chest. "H-How c-close?" I stammered.

"Very." A menacing growl thundered deep in his throat. "Do you smell anything?"

My fingers hooked tighter into Fenris' neck fur. "No... I mean, I smell the trees. It's pine and cedar, but no stink." Anxiety swarmed my mind, as I eyed the columns of trees at either side of us.

"We're almost there," Fenris whispered. He stopped, and peered over his shoulder to me, with his good eye, once more. "Are you ready?"

I stared down the hall of deadwood trees ahead of us. She was there... My best friend... *Sophia...*

The comforting heat of Hollow's magic graced my chest once again, as memories of the past few days flashed across my mind. It all seemed like forever ago, when I was walking through the school with my head down, hoping to god everyone would ignore me. Sophia was by my side, either chatting up a storm about something, or mocking the cat-calling jocks. But it was okay, because I was used to that life. We only had to put up with them for eight hours, and then we were free.

But not here. Here, I was a different person, faced with different obstacles. Two different worlds, and this was the one I wanted most to be in. Among the trees, living a peaceful life...

I still can... right? Because this place is my home, always has been. A stern frown settled on my face. *Ashen stole it from me, but I'm here to get it back.*

"Rosella?"

I shut down the raging current of thoughts racing through my mind, and nodded to Fenris. "Let's go."

Same as the day I first rode Fenris, the world sped by in a blur, as the wind carried my flailing red cloak. Only steps remained between us and Sophia now, and my heart welled with hope at our reunion. What would I say when I found her? "Sorry I took so long?" No, that wouldn't be good.

It doesn't matter, I thought to myself. *Because we're here.* My eyes spied a speck of light ahead, and then another. There, beyond the leaves...

Fenris skidded to a stop a couple of feet before the entrance, and I slid off of him.

This is it! We're here! My heart thundered in my chest, as my legs shook with excitement. My wriggling fingers were itching to tear through those trees, knowing full well Sophia was on the other side of them.

"She is here," Fenris said.

"Sophia!" I cried. "Sophia! Can you hear me? It's me, Rosella!" I couldn't contain myself. I shot ahead of the wolf.

"Little Rose, be careful!"

"Come on!" I ravaged the trees in front of me. "Sophia!" Branches slapped at my face, as I stumbled through the opening. "Sophia! I'm here!"

A large clearing, with a dying bonfire in the center, awaited me. All around, twigs and leaves were scattered about, with a circle of ash off to the side. My eyes scanned over every inch of the place, hoping and praying that I'd find Sophia safe and sound, not—

"Well, look what we have here..."

My stomach dropped to the ground, and my eyes went wide.

"Took you long enough, didn't it?"

No... No, there's no way...

"Rosella? Any luck?" Fenris appeared behind me, whilst shaking himself out. "Where is Sophia?"

I didn't respond. My eyes were locked on the figure sleeking around the dying bonfire, my battered best friend writhing helplessly in her constricted grasp.

"Hey, Gloomy Bloomy~!" Her purring voice was like a shot of ice water in my veins. "It's been a while, hasn't it?"

The crown of orange mini poppy blossoms brushed against one another with each sway of the branches jutting from her head. Deadwood framed her ivory, doll-like face, her eerie porcelain eyes wide, as she pursed her ebony lips. She tapped a smooth, barky toe to the ground, a clawed hand clasped tightly over Sophia's mouth.

I feared that Sophia would've been the one to have been turned, and that her blood would've stained my hands. But that nightmarish thought, it was nothing compared to the bone-chilling sight before me.

My breathing hitched, as a lump caught in my throat. "C... Car..." I couldn't utter her name, I was in so much shock.

"Look, Sophia! It's Rosella! She came to save you!"

"Mmph! Ngh!" Tears flew from her blacked-out eyes, as she whipped her head from side to side.

"Rosella!" Fenris rushed to my side, his ears laid back, as his tail swung from side to side. His maw curled into a vicious snarl, his narrowed gaze set hard on Caroline.

"F-Fenris..." My head mechanically swiveled in the wolf's direction. "That's..."

Sophia cried through the hand over her mouth, snapping us both back at attention.

Fenris uttered a low growl, as he dropped to the ground, and a dark silver ridge rose atop his back. "Release her. Now." His words laced with malice, he prepared to launch from his spot.

"Aw, she brought a puppy~! How cute!" Another voice, one I wasn't quite as familiar with, resounded at my left. "This should be fun!"

I dared to glance over, and found a slender woman, clothed in a black dress, sleeking toward us. Contrasting her silver skin, her hair was a vibrant crimson.

"Rosella!"

My head snapped back to Sophia's hoarse cry. "Sophia!"

"You have to run!" she protested, as she struggled in Caroline's wicked claws. "Get the hell out of here!" Her words were raspy and weak, like she'd scarfed down hot coals.

I shook my head. "No! I'm not leaving you!"

"How sweet..." Caroline rested her branching head atop Sophia's shoulder, as she stroked a threatening claw across her quivering neck. "Too bad this won't last long."

Angry tears welled in my eyes, as I scuffed a boot in the dirt. "Let her go, Caroline!"

"Why~?" Caroline sang.

I snarled at her. "Caroline!" I stormed a few steps forward, but then stopped, as she squeezed Sophia's throat.

"One more step!" Caroline warned. "And that's it!"

This fucking bitch... Temper boiling, I clenched my free hand into a fist, as I bore a dagger-sharp glare into Caroline's form. *I don't know how or why she's here, but I have to stop her.*

"P-Please Ro," Sophia breathed. Her face had paled, her eyes bulging from the lack of oxygen, as sweat beaded her forehead. "G-Go."

"Oh?" Caroline cocked a brow. "I thought you wanted her to help you." She slightly loosened her grip on Sophia's throat. "Are you really going to give up that easily, Mitchell? Come on, I know you better than that." She nodded to me. "Go on, cry for her. Do it."

I held back the tears pricking at my eyes, as Sophia squared her jaw in defiance. Even when it came to life or death, she was still stubborn as a bull.

"Come on now..." Caroline moved her hand to Sophia's shoulder. "Just one little cry."

Sophia still didn't say anything.

"Here, let me help you!" Caroline suddenly burrowed her claws into Sophia's shoulder, and a crackled, blood-curdling scream tore through the air.

"That's better!" Caroline called over Sophia's agonizing wails. "Now! Call for her, you pathetic wench!"

"Rosella!" Sophia screeched. "Please! Help!"

"Louder!" Caroline's gripped tightened, and Sophia screamed harder.

"ROSELLA!!! PLEASE HELP ME!!!! PLEASE!!!!!"

"I DON'T THINK SHE CAN HEAR YOU!!!!!" Caroline dug her other set of claws into Sophia's torso, and Sophia threw her head back with yet another gut-wrenching scream.

"Stop it! Let her go!" I screamed, and sprang forward a few steps, my father's knife raised.

"AUGH!"

I whirled around at the sharp yip behind me. "F-Fenris!"

The wolf was a crumpled heap upon the ground, while the strange woman towered proudly over him with both hands on her hips.

"Go on, sweetie!" she called. "Finish that girl off!"

A malicious, bone-chilling grin spread wide across Caroline's face, as I looked back over my shoulder, and she gave a menacing cackle. "Time to paint the trees red!" She ripped her claw from Sophia's shoulder, and clutched at her gut. "Wilt in the darkness, *FOREVER!!*"

I turned on the ball of my foot, and shot forward with a scream, but tripped over myself, an arm outstretched. Sophia's eyes locked with mine as our lives together flashed between the two of us: our hangouts after school, pulling late-night study sessions through phone calls... And all of it splashed to the ground in a pile of soil, as Caroline gutted Sophia alive.

A black claw shot out amidst the horrific flood, and came at my face with a ferocious slap. My spine slammed against the hard ground, and my body was racked with pain. I grunted, and with a quivering hand, I found my burning cheek. Something warm and sticky was stuck to it. I examined my gloved palm, and was shocked to find it stained black.

"Wilt in Ashen's darkness!" Caroline roared. "That's where you belong!"

I sat up just in time to see Sophia being tossed to the ground like a useless piece of garbage. "*SOPHIA!!!!*" Her name ruptured my throat in a violent screech, but before I could charge after her, the thin black arm came at me again. I sliced through it with ease, and watched it crumble to ash and soil at my feet.

"Let us go," the woman stated. "Come, Caroline!"

"Right behind you!" Caroline called.

Horrified, I looked over to Sophia. She was lying there, unmoving, without a sound. *Sophia...* My eyes then drifted to Caroline, who was happily skipping toward the woman. *You...*

Like a volcano preparing for eruption, steaming hot anger boiled inside of me. I raised my father's knife without thinking and prepared to strike as she drew closer. This... This... *fucking* monster *hurt* my best friend, someone who mattered most to me. She had to pay...

"Ro... Rosella..."

The hoarse call of my name startled me out of my furious state, and mid-swing, my knife flew from my grasp, right past Caroline's back. It clattered several feet away from me.

"Rosella!" Fenris' cry resounded beside me, but he wasn't the one who'd first caught my attention.

"Ro... sella..." From where she lay, Sophia raised her trembling hand to me, her dull emerald eyes barely alight with life. "Ro..."

"Sophia!" I ran to her, and sunk to my knees. "Oh god! Sophia!" Gently, I turned her onto her back, and gasped at the soil spilling out of her torn stomach.

"Ro..." A weak smile trickling with dirt water spread across her sweaty, ghostly white face, her voice barely a whisper. "Y-You came..."

"Oh god, Sophia..." I pressed the back of my hand to my mouth, as I fought back tears.

"Rosella!"

I whipped my head over my shoulder. "Fenris! It's bad! She's hurt! Bad!"

The wolf wobbled to his paws, his breathing hitched. "Li... Little Rose... They are gone... They have left."

I looked around. Indeed, Caroline was nowhere in sight, nor the woman with her. "Fuck!" I peered back down at Sophia. "Look, it's going to be okay. We'll get you some help..."

She shook her head. "Ro..." A weak hand rose from her side, but it fell back against her chest.

"Sophia!"

"Ro..." Empty, tear-filled eyes stared up at me. "I'm sorry... I couldn't protect you..." Her face went blank. "Keep... going... for me..." Her head lulled to the side, as a gentle sigh grazed her lips.

"S-Sophia? Sophia?" I gave her a gentle shake. "Sophia. C-Come on."
There was no response.

"N-No... No... No, no no no." I shook my head. "No... No..."

"Little Rose..." Fenris limped over to me. "Did she...?"

"No... No no no no no. Sophia. Come on." I lifted her up, and pressed my forehead to hers. "Come on, please. Don't do this to me. Please, don't do this."

Fenris dropped on his rear beside me. "Little Rose, I don't think she's..."

"No! She's fine!" I cried. "She's fine!" Unable to hold them back any longer, my eyes released the onslaught of blurring tears. "S-Sophia... P-Please... Please, don't go... I-I'm sorry... I'm sorry for not getting here sooner. P-Please, give me another chance! Please!"

I pressed two fingers to her neck in frantic search of a pulse, and my heart sank further into the depths of reality. I let her fall from my grasp, my hands clapped over my gaping mouth. I choked on a muffled sob, and doubled over.

"No... No no no no... No... No."

My best friend, who'd saved me from everything...

"No, Sophia..."

All I had to do was save her from one thing... but I failed.

"Ngh... Ngh..."

Sophia, my best friend, who stood by me through thick and thin, had just died in my arms.

Fenris

I felt helpless, watching my Little Rose succumb to her grief. She came all this way...

Rosella's tearful eyes continued to rain down her face, as she sucked in a sharp breath, and pressed her friend's head into her chest. "N... Nnnn... Nnnnnnnn... Nnnnnnn... *NNNAAAAAAAAAAAAAAAAAAAGH!!!!!!!!!!!!!!!!!!!!!!!!*"

Rosella's agonizing wail reverberated throughout the entire clearing, and all I could do was sit there and listen, watch her go through this emotional turmoil. It was a fate far worse than death. She came all this way...

It tore me to pieces hearing Rosella scream her name many times, as she rocked back and forth, and continued to bellow at the trees, until she was blue in the face. But she didn't stop. She just kept screaming, pleading for a god, Hollow, anyone, to give her friend back to her.

My heart sank into a pool of despair at the sight of that lifeless girl in my Little Rose's arms. I was right there. I could've easily torn the Queen down, and freed Sophia from her grasp. But I couldn't, because that woman... She did something to my mind, clouded it with useless thoughts.

It was meant as a distraction... A pained hiss grazed my teeth. *And now, it's too late...*

Defeated, I pitifully slumped back onto my rear, my head hung low, and waited patiently for Rosella to completely expel her grief. I couldn't bring myself to face her until I heard her cries begin to dwindle, and I looked up to see the exhaustion etched into her tired face. I was quick to catch her, as she lulled upon her knees. I winced against the sharp wave of pain, as she collapsed into my side, but I stayed put for several grueling minutes more, before finally daring to speak.

"Rosella," I whispered, "are you alright?"

Amidst the heaving gulps of air she inhaled, she gave a tired nod.

"I am so sorry for what has happened," I continued. "I wish I could fix it."

She didn't respond.

"We can't leave her like this, my dear."

She still didn't say anything.

"We can't really move her anywhere... so it'll have to be here." I looked about the ground. "Hatred and pain linger about this place, but I'm certain her spirit is strong enough to free itself of it." I nudged the top of Rosella's head with my nose. "Do you wish to help me?"

She managed to look up at me, and my heart shattered into many pieces. Her blue eyes were dull from lack of their usual light, both rimmed red from the nonstop flow of tears. "S-Sure..." Her voice was so quiet, I almost didn't hear her.

Still, I managed a slow nod. "Okay..."

Rosella held Sophia's hand tight, and watched as I dug into the ground. The soil was extremely dry, making it difficult, but nothing my claws couldn't handle. Every now and again, I'd glance over to them, and every time, I was greeted with the painful sight of Rosella mourning over her friend's corpse.

I didn't stop until I was completely immersed in the dirt, and I poked my head out of the gaping hole I'd dug. "Okay, Rosella... I've made it fairly deep, should be enough."

"Oh god..." Rosella stroked a hand over her friend's face, and gently closed her eyes. "Sophia..."

My ears flattened to my head. *She just looks like a haunting of her former self, like Chloe when Sarah died.* I sighed. "Little Rose, I am so sorry." I climbed out of the hole, and toward Rosella. The throbbing of my side had long since faded, so it was no trouble getting around.

"Fenris..." Rosella looked over to me, with an exhausted face. "I..." Her head bowed. "I'm sorry... I feel... I feel a little tired."

I nodded. "Don't worry, this will be quick."

Rosella looked down at her friend, one last time, and a sorrowful smile broke across her face. "Sophia... I—"

"Sophia!"

Blood drained from Rosella's face, her eyes wide.

"Sophia! Baby! I'm here!" A hopeful woman came barreling through the trees, her emerald eyes scanning her surroundings. "Sophia, honey! Mommy came to save you! Don't worry, everything's going to be fine!"

CHAPTER 32

P ANIC-STRICKEN, MY MOUTH DROPPED open in a silent scream, as I hugged Sophia to my chest. As if things couldn't get *any* worse, out of all the damn people in the world who *had* to spontaneously show up...

Behind me, I heard a gasp. "Rosella! Oh my god..."

I screwed my eyes shut. *Please... Grace, don't come over. Please, god, DON'T.*

"Who... is that?" Her shoes quietly crunched across the dirt. "You're one of the Guardians, aren't you?"

Fenris was quick to shield both me and Sophia's body, as Grace approached. "Yes, my name is Fenris. I recognize you. You were the one who attacked me in the fog."

"Ah, I... Oh my god, I'm sorry." Grace stopped before the wolf. "Are you okay?"

"I am fine," he said calmly. "But you shouldn't be here."

"Actually, I should, because my daughter's here." Grace tried to sidestep him, and he blocked her path with his paw.

I drew a knuckle to my mouth, and bit down on it. *Please, please don't look.*

"She is not here," Fenris said. "We just checked."

"That can't be true!" Grace protested. "I sensed her presence here! You can't keep her from me!"

My arm tightened around Sophia, my chest pounding against hers.

"You... You sensed her?"

"Yes!"

I cracked open one eye, as my teeth gnawed through my glove, into my knuckle.

"She was here," Grace said. "Normally, Husks can't seek each other out in the forest, but..." She again tried to step around the wolf, and again, he prevented her from doing so.

"I'm afraid I cannot let you pass," Fenris stated. "I am worried about your safety."

"Please, I can take care of myself. Rosella, are you over there?"

My eyes darted to their corners. "Y-Yeah... I'm here."

"Is everything alright? This wolf won't let me go around him."

I sucked in a heavy breath. "E-Everything's fine. Sophia is not here."

"No! Wait!" Fenris shot from the ground. "Please!"

I heard Grace's shoes pounding dirt, and lowered my head as she slipped in front of me. Through my bangs, I saw Grace's knees quiver to the ground, her arms at her sides. As I bit my bottom lip, I carefully allowed Sophia to drift out of my arms, and into Grace's.

Grace stared down, horrified, at the sight before her. "M-My baby..." Her mouth dropped open, and she uttered a soft whimper.

I didn't say anything. What could I have told her? Sorry?

Grace's fingers traced her daughter's cold face. "Sophia... Y-You... You were always so stubborn..."

"G-Grace... I'm so sorry. I..." I winced at the burning of my nostrils, and blinked away the fresh wave of burning tears. "I am sorry... I was trying to rescue her. I didn't do anything when she was captured. I am so sorry." A whimper bubbled up my throat, and slipped my quivering lips. "I'm sorry! I wanted to help her! She was my best friend, and I let her die!"

Grace raised her head to me, a look of shock on her face.

"I am so sorry!" I wailed. "I never meant to get her killed! I am so sorry!" I dropped my head to the ground, and wept before her. "I'm sorry..."

A gentle hand came to rest atop my head, and Grace gave a sigh. "Oh, Rosella... You sweet, innocent child..."

My chin grazed the ground, as I looked up at her, and I frowned in confusion.

Grace was smiling, warmly, like nothing was wrong. "Rosella, it's okay. Really."

Okay!? I sprung up on my palms. "O-Okay!?"

"My dear, it's alright." Grace's hand slid down the side of my head, her palm resting against my cheek. "I... I'm happy to hear you were honest with me..."

I gawked at her. "Wh-What...?"

"Rosella... Sophia looked up to you..." The hand holding her daughter's head slipped out from under it, and cradled my other cheek. "Rosella, you really cared about her, didn't you?"

I gave a slight, hesitant nod.

"I see..." The corner's of Grace's mouth widened a little. "And, you wish you could be with her, right?"

"M-Mo... More th-than anything," I stammered. "I-I want her back." And that was the truth. I wished for this all to be a dream, that any moment I'd wake up back home. But this wasn't a dream. This was a nightmare, and I was awake.

A blank expression crossed Grace's face. "I see. Then, I won't feel bad for doing this to you."

The moment passed by so quickly. We were staring into each other's eyes, and then the vision in my left went dark. Then there was a painful eruption of nerves. And then, I was screaming, as I fell back clutching at my face.

Fenris sprung into action, right as I hit the ground, and I heard a bout of growls and animalistic shrieks. The pain, and the noise, it didn't last long. As quick as my infliction had come, I succumbed to the intense level of pain, and fell into darkness...

Rosella, it's okay! Hollow's voice rang out in my conscience, as clear as a bell. *Fenris will get you someplace safe! Just hang on!*

I couldn't respond. I'd drifted into an unexpected sleep.

Felan

The fog was gone when I opened my eyes to midday, and I shot up in alarm. I peered out my window, and to my relief, my old eyes weren't deceiving me. However, one thing still nagged at my mind: planting the seed had now trapped everyone here.

I sighed. "Oh, better to keep the bad guys in I suppose."

I meandered out of bed, and slipped my aching feet into my slippers, but then paused. The Barrier Seed had been planted, which meant that no one could get in or out... The realization of it hit me hard, and I worried at my bottom lip. What if it was a mistake to do that? What if not everyone was here?

"Ooooooh... Fudge!" I rapped a fist against my bed. "I need some fresh air!"

I whipped me up a nice cup of coffee, after my five minute travel from the bedroom to the kitchen, then proceeded out onto the back of the wraparound deck. It felt nice, being able to enjoy nature again, even if just for a short bit. I was sure Hollow wouldn't mind.

I sipped from the hot beverage with caution, and hummed at the warm tingling of my lips. This was relaxing, just what I...

"Dear lord!" I slammed my cup against the table, and sprung from my seat like it'd been lit ablaze. "Fenris!" I hurried down the back steps of the deck. "My god! What happened!?"

Battered, but alive, Fenris came limping up, Rosella sprawled over his back. "It's Rosella! She's hurt!"

"I can see that!" I surveyed the situation presented to me, then rested a hand against my frantic heart. "And so are you!"

"Please, help her first!" Fenris breathed. "She's in worse shape than I am."

"I am capable of caring for both of you at the same time!" I stated. "Lemme get my medical things ready."

I scurried back up the steps, and flew from the kitchen to the bedroom in seconds. I went rummaging through my closet for my medical kit, as that was where I last left it. I had plenty of that snodaful cream left over, plus a hefty stock of bandages. I also grabbed some towels, and a pillow for Rosella to lay her head on.

I met the wolf out on the back of the deck, then laid out a couple towels and the pillow. I instructed Fenris to carefully lay Rosella down, and he did just that by lowering upon his haunches, and shimmying her off. Once she was situated on her back, I told him to sit, and he did, like a good doggy.

"Alright, let's see now." I glanced over his bloody maw. "My dear, did you get something to eat before your return?"

Fenris' head dropped with shame, as his ears fell flat.

"Fenris?"

He refused to look at me. "That woman attacked Rosella. She was a Husk, like Sophia... If I'm not mistaken, she was Sarah's sister."

My heart sank at his words. "So... she found you?"

"I don't know how, or why, she was there. But she arrived after Rosella and I reached Sophia, when the girl died in Rosella's arms..."

I tearfully looked down at my great-granddaughter. "Oh, Rosella..."

"She knew the Queen by name, Felan. She said her name was Caroline."

I nodded. "She was Rosella's bully. And her aunt, from what I understand, has changed forms. She shed her Husk shell in favor of a new body."

"She must've been the woman we encountered there," Fenris said. "She and the Lurker Queen seemed to get along well."

"Fenris, I am sorry for both of you, and Sophia..." I worried at my bottom lip, hesitant to ask about her.

"After I struck down Sarah's sister, I gave Sophia a fast, but proper burial. It wasn't easy, but I managed to keep her together. After that, I made quick work of securing Rosella, and hightailed it out of there."

"You did good, Fenris." I slowly lowered myself to my knees. "Oh, this is foolish of me to do, but you won't fit in my house, and I want you present before my eyes. You've been gone so long, I started forgetting what you looked like."

Fenris gave a soft chuckle. "Oh, you haven't changed a bit since we've been gone."

"No, indeed."

My poor great-granddaughter's eye had been completely gouged out. All that was left was a meager scrap of muscle, that which I handled with great care. Using some of the cream, I gently smeared a dollop over the injury, then set to work on properly bandaging the eye. The cream would do most of the work, and heal the wound by the following day

"Just like your neck, Fenris." I glanced over my shoulder to him. "Rosella had told me that you'd suffered a great deal during that Lurker attack in the backyard. Good thing I gave some to Chloe to take home. She said that it wasn't a big deal, but I told her that it was better to be safe than sorry."

"I'm surprised to hear that from you," Fenris said. "She's always been anxious of the forest, so I figured she'd want that protection."

I shrugged. "I don't know, perhaps she was trying to ease up a bit on herself and Rosella." I gave a sigh. "I have to ask you... Did you kill Grace?"

Fenris' eyes averted my gaze. "No... And I don't know how she'll fair out there, injured as she is."

I shook my head, as I finished patching up Rosella's eye. "Grace just wanted to give that child a happy life. She was always afraid of Ashen, much like the lot of them..."

Fenris raised his head, ears perked. "Felan, Sophia's spirit... Do you think this forest will welcome her within it?"

"Oh, I'm sure. Hollow wouldn't have allowed Rosella to be close to her if she didn't like the girl." I gave a nod of approval to my handiwork. "Alright then, time to look you over, wolfy."

"As you wish."

I frowned at him. "Whether it's a wish or not, I am taking care of you."

He gave an exhausted chuckle. "Of course."

CHAPTER 33

T HE WIND COMBED THE blades of grass crunching under my boots, as I traversed the empty field. My eyes locked ahead of me, I marched toward my father, and stopped a few feet away. Several seconds passed, before he turned around.

"Ro-Ro..." Dad's brow was curled into a concerned frown. "Baby..."

I didn't bother holding back the tears. I couldn't.

Dad extended his arms to me. "C'mere."

I ran into his warm embrace, and wept into his chest.

"It's okay... There, there now..."

Dad's hand rubbed gentle circles into my back, as he held me close. I felt like I didn't deserve it. I'd failed to carry out my quest, to bring Sophia back home alive. And yet, he kept telling me that it was okay. It wasn't my fault. I did what I could.

"But I didn't!" I cried. "I stood there, like an idiot, watching Caroline torture her!" My knees buckled beneath me, and my fingers hooked into Dad's torso, as I fell forward with a sob.

Dad lowered himself to the ground, taking me with him, and pulled me into his lap. "Rosella, it's okay..." He maneuvered my head into the crook of his neck, and with tender fingers, he brushed aside the hair in my tear-stained face.

"I should've done something," I croaked. "I should've..." I curled into a ball, and covered my face with my hands. "Oh god..."

"Ro-Ro, listen to me... Hey." His gentle hand stroked a tear from my cheek. "Sweetheart, you are the bravest person I know. You went all the way out there, despite the risks... You knew that you were putting your life on the line, but you did it for her. Because she needed you."

I gave a meek nod.

"Sophia held out hope that you'd come for her, and even though things have played out the way they have, she could never hold a grudge against you, ever."

A hiss grazed my teeth, as my hands fell from my face, and I glowered at my father. "How can she?" I whispered. "She's dead..."

A smile graced Dad's face. "Because she's here, Ro-Ro. And she's rooting for you, just like me."

I gawked at his words, but before I could say anything more, I found myself staring up at a wooden ceiling, with only one working eye, under the warmth of thick blankets upon a bed. Moonlight poured in from the window beside me, Fenris nowhere around, and the lingering memory of Grace coming at me with a knife suddenly came flooding back.

On instinct, my fingers explored the left side of my face, whereupon I discovered the thick patch blocking my view, though I hesitated on removing it. There was a reason it was there, and if I recalled correctly, I'd felt immense pain.

"Rosella?"

I craned my head to the right, and my heart leaped in my chest. That voice... "G-Great... Granny..."

"Oh, honey..." Great Granny Felan slipped into view from the darkness that shielded the left half of my vision. "Sweetheart..."

A single tear welled in my right eye, but my wavering mouth refused to utter more syllables, as I sat up to face her.

"Don't try to speak, dear." She hurried over, and planted herself on the bed. "Just relax, everything's going to be fine." Her cool hands reached over, and took hold of mine. "Oh Rosella..."

I kneaded my fingers into her soft palms, and bowed my head. A sob had worked its way up my throat, but only a strained squeak slipped out.

"Rosella..."

Great Granny Felan's hands slipped out of mine, as she wrapped her arms tightly around me, and I buried my face into her shoulder. She kneaded her fingers into the back of my head, as she gently rocked me back and forth, and whispered comforting thoughts into my ear.

Tears streamed from my right eye, though none formed at the left. I contemplated on whether to ask what was wrong, but once my brain began to process what had happened, it didn't take me long to figure out.

"F-Fe..." My voice was hoarse despite my throat being fine, and I struggled to get the words out. "Fen... He... Where is... he?"

"He's out on a hunt, but he'll be back shortly," she told me. "Oh, Rosella, I am so glad you're alright. My sweet little Rosella..." Great

Granny Felan pulled away, revealing her tear-stained face. "I was so scared that I wasn't going to see either of you again. My god."

I shook my head. "N-No... We were..." I cleared my throat. "We were there, and we found her. We found Sophia."

"Fenris told me everything," Great Granny Felan said. "He told me what happened..." Her head lowered. "Oh Rosella, I am so sorry. Truly, I am."

I bit back another sob, and nodded. "It's okay... It's okay." I turned to face the moonlit window. "Can I... go out there?"

Great Granny Felan kneaded her lips into a thin line. "Oh, honey, I don't know. You're really out of it."

"Please..." I gave her a pleading look. "I need to see him."

"Oh... Oh, I guess it's alright..." Hesitantly, Great Granny Felan got up from the bed, and her hand fell from mine. "Just... be careful, and please don't take off."

"I won't..." I tossed the covers over me to the side, and found that I was clothed in a comfortable t-shirt, with some shorts and warm socks.

"Your other clothes were dingy," Great Granny Felan explained. "Surprised they lasted that long. I didn't bother trying to bathe you, though. Figured that might be crossing too much over the line."

I gave a slight chuckle. "It's okay, I wouldn't have minded."

She shrugged. "Well, better safe than sorry."

Great Granny Felan wrapped a gentle arm around me, and I slowly proceeded out of bed. My legs were like jelly when my feet hit the floor, and I would've toppled over, had she not been there to assist me. Great Granny Felan patiently guided me across the room, as I worked to regain feeling in my legs. I felt safe on my own when we reached the door, and gave her a confirming nod.

"I'll go check out front first," I told her.

"Be careful," she warned.

I gave a nod of understanding. "I know."

I didn't see Fenris upon stepping out, so I went along the wraparound deck to the back. There, just beyond the trees, I spotted *both* of his glowing blue eyes, and he rushed out into the open once noticing me. I waited for him at the top of the steps, then threw my arms around his neck.

"Little Rose!" he exclaimed, his tail wagging wildly. "Thank goodness you're awake!"

"Fenris..." I croaked. I nuzzled my face into his. "I'm so glad to see you." My fingers kneaded into his fur. God, I was beyond relieved to see he was okay.

"I am so sorry," he whispered. "I'm so sorry..."

"I-It's okay... Really..."

He gave me a sad look. "No, it's not. We failed... I failed to help you save your best friend."

I pulled away from him. "But you tried your best... and that's all that matters." My father's words sprang to mind. "A-And so did I..."

Both of his ears flattened against his head, the corners of the wolf's maw pulled into a frown. "Rosella, you should be furious with me. You should be unforgiving of me. You should disown me. I failed you..." He bowed his head with shame. "I must accept that punishment."

I gently cupped either side of his face, and raised it so he was looking at me again. "Fenris." I stared him straight in the eyes. "It is not your fault Sophia died, and you did what you could to help me save her. You stayed by my side the entire time, like the noble wolf you are, and always will be."

The wolf's moonlit eyes widened, and gleaming tears rimmed their edges. "Rosella..."

I pressed my lips to his head, and gave him a gentle kiss. "Thank you... for everything you've done for me..."

We embraced each other once more, and stayed that way for a long while. It felt comforting, snuggling him like this. After everything we'd been through together, we needed this time...

"Rosella, there are things you aren't aware of yet," Fenris uttered after some time. "It's about Grace, and Sophia..."

I didn't say anything, as I didn't want to interrupt him.

"I've been thinking about what happened back there, when that red fog appeared, and I bumped into Grace... When I called out to her, she never once asked me what was going on, or why the fog was there. In fact, she never acknowledged it."

"Maybe her fear had gotten the best of her," I suggested.

He nodded slowly. "Exactly my point. She was calling out to Sophia, and also said something about Chloe, how she wanted to trade her for Sophia."

"Yes, but I think you told me that," I said.

"Well, Felan said that Grace tried to attack Chloe back here at the cabin hours before the fog hit, and ran into the trees..." Dread crossed the wolf's face. "I don't know if you've noticed, but the paper lanterns are no longer working because Grace destroyed them."

"Wait... What?" I warily looked around me, and my jaw dropped.

"Based upon your reaction, I guess not."

"Y-Yeah... Which means the Lurkers..." I frowned. *No, they're gone. At least, I think they are. They were nowhere to be found, when we entered the clearing.*

"Do you want to hear my thoughts?" Great Granny Felan came shuffling up behind me. "If you don't mind..."

Fenris and I both turned to her for guidance.

"I've spent some time thinking this over since your return," she began, "and after gathering what I could, I feel like I've figured things out." She wrung her aged hands together. "Grace had been acting quite strangely since Sophia's kidnapping. Chloe had said that, in the beginning, she was distraught. But then, she got quiet, kept mostly to herself. She wouldn't even confide in the detectives, both of whom she knew for a time when she was little."

"The detectives..." A mental lightbulb went off, as I recalled their names. "Stormer and Kenneth!"

"That's right, dear. They are Husks too."

My lone eye widened. "Th-They are? H-Hollow never..."

A look of concern flashed across Great Granny Felan's face. "So then, you really are aware of... what you are."

I nodded slowly. "I am."

"Understood then." She put her hands on her hips, and a stern frown hardened her expression. "Well, at any rate, I feel as though Grace had been plotting something, that all this was her doing, though she didn't expect Sophia to be killed."

"Are you saying that Grace might've caused that red fog to appear?" Fenris asked.

"You said you found her there, Fenris, and she didn't question it once."

"No, I know. I just wasn't sure if you were thinking that. But, can Husks do that? I thought they were typically given only one special ability?"

"Grace might be a special case, though I can't confirm," Great Granny Felan concluded. "I am merely grasping at straws here."

I pondered everything that was being said, then thought of a response. "Well... If that's the case, then does that mean she wanted me dead?"

Great Granny Felan shrugged. "I don't know, dear... But I do know that she has it out for your mother."

My heart galloped in my chest at the horrid thought of finding my mother's dead body at Grace's feet. "B-But, if that's the case..."

"No one can leave, and no one can enter, now that the Barrier Seed has been planted," Great Granny Felan assured. "You should know what that is, because Fenris told me so."

Another mental lightbulb went off in my head, and I gave a curt nod. "Y-Yeah... It's an emergency measure, but it's only supposed to be used once all six Vessels have been brought back here." I locked eyes with her. "If Grace really did cause that fog to appear, then she must've used it as a scare tactic..."

Great Granny Felan mirrored my sense of fear, and she clutched at her chest. "My god... What have I done..."

"I must speak with the other Guardians," Fenris piped up. "I will go find out if their Vessels are here within the forest." The wolf slipped around me, and padded over to the other side of the deck. "I'll be gone just a minute."

"Don't rush," I told him. "Take your time. Great Granny Felan and I will keep watch." I peered over the wooden railing. "Hmm... I wonder..."

"Rosella?" Great Granny Felan came over to me. "What is it?"

"Hang on... Just need to focus..." I closed my eyes. "I wonder..." Hollow and I were one in the same, so surely... "Yes... That's it..." I embraced the warmth, and urged it to become stronger. "Come to me... Help me fix what's broken."

A faint red aura began to glow within my chest, and as it blossomed into a bright red rose of light, glowing emerald vines sprouted around it, and spread out all across the cabin. They coiled all along the wooden railing of the wraparound deck, continued over the trim of the roof, and down the stilts of the cabin, leaving in their wake a beautiful array of vibrant, colorful flowers that expelled a shimmering, sweet-smelling powder. The vines vanished, once their work was complete.

Great Granny stared in awe at the sight of her newly-decorated home, her jaw hung wide.

"This should do it," I said, and tapped a finger against the petal of a light blue flower, prompting it to spit a dusting of powder. "With these, you won't have to worry about protection anymore. These blooms are indestructible, and produce a repellent that should keep all of Ashen's influence away."

"What do you mean by that?" she asked me.

"It'll mask your scent, as well as anyone else's within this clearing, and act as a poison toward Ashen or any of their associates." I gave her a solemn look. "Unfortunately, this includes Grace, as well as Sophia, if she were still alive."

"Wh-Why?" Great Granny Felan's arms hung at her sides, her eyes wide with shock. "Why would you...?"

"Because you need protection, and I want to do what I can to stop Ashen," I said. "It was a tough decision to make, but I had to..." My eyes wandered to Fenris, who gave me an apologetic look. "I will find a way to end this war peacefully, but I must also accept that defense is a necessity, even if it proves harmful..." I returned my gaze to Great Granny Felan. "I don't want you getting hurt... I love you so much, and I'll be damned if I lose you too."

"Oh... Rosella!" Great Granny Felan lunged for me, and threw her arms tightly around my neck. "Oh, Rosella..."

As she wept into my shoulder, I firmly hugged her back. "I love you, Great Granny Felan... And I promise, I won't let anything happen to you. You've done so much for me, and now it's time for me to do something for you, and everyone else."

Fenris

My trip back to the Central Void was a pleasant one, though I had no pleasant news to share with my comrades.

"Friends! I'm here!" I called out. "Please... Come to me, won't you? I must speak with you right away."

"Sorry mate, can't stay long!" Rumi shouted. "Currently busy with stuff, what's up?"

"Is everything okay?" Nana asked nervously.

"Fenris, what news of your Vessel?" Seraph questioned.

"Sounds like something happened," Checkers said.

"I need to know if your Vessels are all here!" I explained. "Please, tell me they are here within these woods." My heart was racing within my chest. If even one Vessel was missing, this would all be for naught.

"You know mine is present," Seraph said.

"I-I am sad to say mine is unfortunately here too," Nana admitted. "I-I-I am terrified for her, but she's here because she knows she has to be."

"Mine's been here for about the same time as Fenris'," Checkers muttered. "But... we've made progress."

"Ah yeh, mine's here as well!" Rumi exclaimed. "She's real upset, though! Can't seem to figure out what happened."

I gave a major sigh of relief. "Thank goodness... I ask, because Felan has planted the Barrier Seed, which means that now everyone here is stuck."

"She planted the Barrier Seed!?" Nana shrieked. "NOOOOO!!"

My ears flattened to my head at the fearful tone in her voice. "C-Calm down, Nana. It will be alright."

"NONONONONONONO NOOOOOOO!!!!!" she wailed. "IVY CAN'T GO THROUGH THIS! NO!!!!"

"Nana," Seraph urged, "please calm yourself!"

"Nanners, listen! It'll be alright," Rumi chimed in. "Just breathe. Remember what we all talked about. We knew this day would come."

"B-B-But..." Nana's voice crumbled into pitiful sobbing.

"I am sorry it had to be this way," I explained. "But it had to be done. That red fog appeared, and we were tricked into assuming it was Ashen's takeover."

"You saw it too, huh?" Rumi asked. "Mari was wondering about it."

"If it wasn't Ashen, then who was it?" Checkers added. "Not that Alicia and I saw it. But I am curious."

"It was her, wasn't it, Fenris?" Seraph's tone had taken on an edge of uneasiness. "Please... Tell us."

I gave a troubled sigh. "Yes... I believe so. Grace may be the culprit behind the red fog, but we can't say for sure."

"I never trusted that one," Rumi grumbled. "She was always a bit of an oddball."

"Nonetheless," Seraph proclaimed, "we must protect our Vessels. It is our duty."

Nana cleared her throat of lingering whimpers. "Y-Yeah... You're right about that... B-But, I'm still worried. My poor little Ivy... Her family is hurt, because they know they won't ever see her again."

"It's okay," I told her gently. "I'm sure we can find a way around this somehow... Let's have a little hope, huh?"

"We should hurry back to our Vessels," Rumi said quietly. "I sense danger ahead."

"Yes, let us return to our positions," Seraph declared. "We will meet again very soon."

I bowed my head. "Understood."

I allowed myself to fall into the clear, rippling floor beneath my paws, and when I came to, I found Rosella kneeling in front of me. She had a worried look on her face, but I reassured her with a silent nod.

"We are all on edge," I said, "but we are still willing to fight."

Rosella nodded back. "Yeah... I'm glad." She reached over, and pressed her palm against my head.

"Little Rose…" I leaned into her comforting touch. "No matter what… I will protect you, I will keep you safe."

"I know you will, Fenris…"

"Rosella, how does your injury feel?" Felan asked, as she came up behind her.

"It feels better than before," Rosella said. "I mean, it didn't really hurt much at all, when I woke up. It was just the feeling of not having an eye there that shocked me."

I blinked a couple times. "Mine is already fully healed, which is a good thing. Not trying to brag, by the way."

Rosella giggled. "You're fine, Fenris. It's good that at least one of us has two eyes."

The corners of my maw curved upward. "Rosella, you really are the light to my darkness…"

She reflected my expression. "And I promise to keep it that way…"

MOONPAW
EPILOGUE

GREAT GRANNY FELAN SAYS *that Grace has been through a lot. First, she watched her sister Sarah die, and then she was captured, and turned into a Husk. Then, years later, she broke out of the prison she was confined within, and raised Sophia as her own, after Sophia lost her biological parents. Both had lost their families, but then found each other, and that's all Grace wanted.* "A family to call her own..." I sighed and rubbed at my sleeved arms. "She was lonely, and heartbroken, lost... Makes me wonder if Sophia ever felt the same way."

A month had passed since Sophia's death. Great Granny Felan didn't mind me sitting around moping all day, said that it was my way of grieving, though I didn't do it for long. It would've been a disservice to Sophia, this forest, and everyone else still within it.

So, I stepped out, after ten lonely days, embraced nature's breeze, and began my proper adaption into life within these woods. Despite now having a place of my own, I spent most of my time outdoors. I didn't feel confined when I was outside, and could use this time to practice with Fenris, or on the trees.

"Great Granny Felan told me my new cloak should be about ready," I said, and gracefully threw my father's knife in a random direction. It hit the target tree dead-center. "I'll keep it handy for when it's cold."

"Very nice shot!" Fenris praised.

I gave a soft laugh, and went over to retrieve the knife. "Thanks." I grabbed hold of the hilt, and with a firm tug, it came free. "Thank you for finding this and bringing it back to me, by the way."

"I can't take all the credit. I had a friend help me."

I nodded. "Right... One of the other guardians... Seraph, right?"

"That is correct. I ran into him on my way there."

I peered over my shoulder, and my face fell at the wolf's pained expression as he stared at the ground. "Hey..."

He raised his head, ears perked.

"It's okay." A faint smirk crossed my face. "And next time you see him, tell him I said thanks."

His tail thumped quietly behind him. "I will."

My ponytail wavered behind me as I looked to the trees above, and my smirk spread into a grin. Their leaves were swaying gently in the breeze, whispering amongst themselves, like the town I never called home. Home... This forest was my home now, the one I'd always wanted. And unlike the town, the trees told no lies.

"Rosella! Rosella, dear!" Great Granny Felan appeared from around one of the trees. "The bread is done!"

"Great Granny Felan, you should be more careful out here!" I shuffled through the sea of leaves at my feet. "See all this? You could trip!"

She batted a hand. "Oh, nevermind that! I'll be fine, you just come on over, and enjoy some of my sweet banana bread I made from the bananas I grew in the garden!"

"You keep feeding me sweets, and I'm going to gain fifty pounds or more. I'm already wide enough!"

"When you stop giving me things I want, I'll stop feeding you sweets!" Great Granny Felan pouted at me. "And besides, you've lost quite a bit of weight these last few weeks. You need more to build up muscle!"

I looked down at myself. My hips were still pretty wide, but not as much as before, since my diet had changed, and I was exercising more frequently. "I haven't lost that much, just enough. And don't worry, not all of this is going away."

Great Granny Felan nodded with approval. "Good! You need some meat on you."

I snickered. "Come on, Fenris, let's head back."

The wolf happily followed after me and Great Granny Felan, and together we all proceeded toward the enormous tree house I conjured up for myself. It had two sets of stairs, one at the front and one at the back, with a wraparound deck, just like the one at Great Granny Felan's cabin.

I made sure the space was large enough that even Fenris could fit inside, as well as some comfortable furniture crafted from the trees. Great Granny Felan had plenty of material to make pillows and blankets with, as well as cushions for the couch and chairs.

"How's that stove working out?" I asked. "It's made of rock, so it should be sturdy."

"I like it a lot!" Great Granny Felan said. "I think it's a nice touch to the 'earthy' feel of your home."

I proudly put my hands on my hips. "I'm glad to hear that. I worked really hard on it."

Great Granny Felan started up the steps. "You really outdid yourself, dear! Feels like a hotel compared to my meek little cabin!"

"Feel free to move in if you'd like," I offered.

"Oh no, I am quite content with my little bit of space." She smiled down at me. "Rosella, I have longed for this time with you. I know it's hard that your mother isn't here, but you'll see her again. I'm sure of it."

"Maybe..." As he slipped by, I gave the wolf a pat on the side, and he gave a contented growl.

"Alright, let's get some bread!" Great Granny Felan cheerfully sang aloud a tune I wasn't familiar with, as she continued up the steps. I followed after her, Fenris by my side.

"How are you doing?" he asked me quietly, so that Great Granny Felan hopefully wouldn't hear.

"I am okay," I told him. "I still miss her, but I will be strong. She would want it that way, and it needs to be that way." I ran a hand along the smooth oak railing, my eyes to the sky. "Sophia, I won't let you down, not again. Same to you too, Dad. I'll become the strongest Bloom I can be, and stand tall." My head lowered, as I pulled up the sleeve of my Moonpaw hoodie, my eyes locked to the rubber bracelet. "I promise."

Hollow

Ties to Rosella had become stronger than they'd ever been. Not once labeling her a puppet at my disposal, I treasured her as a dear friend, the Vessel I've surely grown closest to. But what of the others? Curious,

I sifted through the many visions. The only one I could clearly see was Rosella's.

Her heart, a comforting warmth in my hands, glowed a vibrant red hue. The darkness of the curse hadn't consumed it, unlike… I glanced over at the floating wisp of light beside me. Her blue essence was dim, a swirling cloud of black having sprouted within. When I placed my palm against it, it felt cold to the touch, a signal that I should be worried.

"You need to help her," I said. "You've always been a bull-headed scruffball, ever since you were born. You didn't ask for me to create you, and I'm sorry for putting such a burden on you. But please, don't punish Alicia for it. She is afraid, and needs you by her side. I need you there, so I can reach out to her." I bowed my head. "Please, Checkers. Don't turn your back on us."

Master, I have news to bear.

I shook my head. "Please, do not call me that by name. You know I see myself as your equal."

I am sorry. Force of habit.

"It's alright. What news do you bring?"

I've been forced to move Blankette to a safer, more secluded location, due to the Lurkers' exit.

"She is aware, though. Right, Seraph?"

Indeed.

"Please, keep her safe" I urged. "Both her and Rosella have escaped Ashen's evil clutches, but Alicia is still trapped."

Would you like me to try engaging with Checkers? Seraph asked.

"No, I feel that will only make things worse. Just keep your attention to Blankette. As for Alicia, I will keep trying to reach her."

Understood…

I cocked a brow at his hesitancy. "There is more you have to say, isn't there?"

Hollow… My master… Seraph murmured. *I… I found that girl… the one Rosella… adores so much… but she…*

I clasped my hands against my heart. "Is she… alright?"

He didn't answer.

"Seraph, I am sure Fenris will forgive you for moving her."

I crafted her a beautiful grave, he admitted. *Her body is surrounded by a bed of red roses, though this is not enough. Her soul...*

"I understand," I said. "At least this way, it's still possible to save her, Sarah too."

I am on the lookout for Sophia's location, he went on. *The moment I find anything, you will be the first to know.*

"I appreciate that, and I know both Fenris and Rosella would as well."

Thank you, Hollow. I must be off now, for Blankette is waiting for me to brush her hair after her bath.

"Alright. Please let her know that I haven't forgotten her. I just need her to stay put."

Very well.

Seraph retreated, ending our conversation, and I returned my attention to the small glowing red light in my hands. In due time, Rosella and I would return to each other, and we would fight side by side.

"And, if it all works out, the rest will join me. My Vessels, I know I am putting you through a lot. But I promise, you will find solace in this wretched world. My Guardians, please do your best to protect them. They are people, just like you... I'm counting on you." I set my brow into a stern frown. "And Ashen... I am coming for you. Just you wait. My people and I will regain our home..."

In due time, my Vessels would come together, and once that happened, I would regain my full form. But until then, I would wait...

"And I won't run away. Not anymore."

NEXT IN THIS SERIES

A trip down the well, she's fallen straight into hell! What will become of her? Poor thing! Wallow in agony, or embrace the Madness!
The story continues in Hollow's Vessels Book Two: Little Rabbit
coming soon...

BONUS ARTWORK

MOONPAW

ACKNOWLEDGEMENTS

There are a lot of people who helped me put this together, and I want to take a moment to thank each and every one of you. (I will have everyone's Twitter @'s so you can find them if you'd like to learn more about them.)

First, I'd like to take a moment to acknowledge my team of beta readers:

Thank you, Sara R. Cleveland (@shcleveland), for giving me ideas on how to make Frank Stormer and Creg Kenneth deeper characters than just two detectives on a case.

Thank you, Midori Anzai (@MidoriAnzai), for teaching me how to grow thick skin, and for being a wonderful friend. Thank you.

Thank you, Andy (@bookishly_me_), for correcting me on where exactly hair follicles are on the head (seriously, thank you so much for that lol).

Thank you, John Walker (his Twitter is currently inactive to my knowledge), for inspiring me to make Fenris the noble wolf he now is, and for teaching me some interesting facts about wolves. You are an honorable advocate for these beautiful animals, and I hope you continue to spread the word about how important they are to the world.

Thank you, Mimi (@MimiBunny6), for helping me just a bit, and for putting up with my nonsense. We bump heads at times, but I hope you're doing well.

Thank you, Jen (@Valerie_Storm), for jumping on last minute (girl, you are a trooper!), and helping me pull this thing to the finish line. I wasn't quite sure it was ready, and I'm sure as hell glad I got you. Thank you SO SO SO much for volunteering.

And finally... Thank you, Amanda N. Newman (@Amanda_N_Newman). Special thanks go out to you, Amanda, for showering me with all your support. From putting together an entire website for me, to formatting this entire book, from cover to cover, and for beta-reading (and also for being extremely inspiring), I don't know how I could ever repay you for everything you've done for me. You're working so hard on your own things, yet somehow made time for me, and I couldn't ask for anything more. I don't know where I'd be without a friend like you. Thank you, my friend, for being the light to my darkness, and helping me stand tall as the strongest bloom I can be in a world littered with weeds of doubt. I hope our friendship lasts for years to come.

I also give a special thank you to Mirai Amell (@AmellMirai), for reaching out and for also being such an awesome friend, and for letting me read your entire book before it came out. I also hope our friendship lasts for years to come.

There are two other people I'd like to give special thanks to... First, Pat Luther (@plutheus), for granting me the best opportunity ever to help a friend out, and giving me an opportunity to grow as an artist (and also to pay bills). You were a lifesaver.

And finally, Hero (@HeroMakes), for being so understanding, and a good friend too. Hopefully, we'll get to talk more by the time this book gets out, haha.

Thank you, all of you, for your help. I couldn't have done all this without any of you.

ABOUT THE AUTHOR

Hi! My name is Samantha Eno, a twenty-eight-year-old working hard to share her stories with the world! I currently reside in Missouri as a co-cat mom with a family member, and practice art on the side. Sometimes, life gets me down. But no matter how many lemons it deals me, I swallow them whole and demand more.

If you enjoy bold, unique stories of many kinds, some of which bite back, you've probably found the right person to follow! Keep in mind, my stories are not for everyone, and I'm imperfect like everyone else.